Also by S.Y. Thompson:

The Under Series

Under Devil's Snare
Under The Midnight Cloak

Other Titles

Destination Alara
Now You See Me
Fractured Futures

Woeful Pines

S.Y. Thompson

Mystic Books
by Regal Crest

Texas

ISBN 978-1-61929-220-8

First Printing 2015

9 8 7 6 5 4 3 2 1

Cover design by AcornGraphics

Published by:

Regal Crest Enterprises, LLC
229 Sheridan Loop
Belton, Texas 76513

Find us on the World Wide Web at
http://www.regalcrest.biz

Published in the United States of America

Acknowledgments

I'd like to acknowledge and thank the readers, my friends and family as well as the other fiction authors who inspire me. Heartfelt gratitude always to Linda North, who is available anytime I need help brainstorming. No one is a better friend or beta. Heather Flournoy who is the best editor ever, I learn so much from you each time we run through the process. Thanks also to Mary Hettel and Brenda Adcock, part of the wonder team that help me improve as a writer.

Dedication

For the ones who never fail to go along with my crazy habit of writing for hours on end; my fur-children. Bruce, Sassy, Xander, Jazz, Grayson, Bella and Cletus.

"And yet to every bad, there is a worse."
~Thomas Hardy

Chapter One

DRIVING HAD BECOME unsafe. The interstate wound through the mountains, rolling on like the drive to infinity. There weren't any lights along the shoulders of the road in this segment of the Kentucky blacktop. Heavy rainclouds as dark as charcoal inside a grill obscured any sign of a moon, full or otherwise. Wipers failed to sweep the relentless downpour from the windshield, forcing Emily Bannon onto an access lane just a short distance from the main roadway. Warning lights from construction barricades flashed some distance ahead, illuminating a battered sign that announced her arrival into the weather-beaten burg of Woeful Pines.

A chill of foreboding corkscrewed down her spine and Emily attempted to shake it off by speaking aloud. "Cheerful name. Why didn't you call it Devil's Backbone or Hell's Half Acre? I wonder if that explains the welcoming committee."

There wasn't a soul in sight, though she could hardly blame them. The weather wasn't even fit for ducks, much less two-legged, featherless, furless humans. The reduced speed went a long way toward improving visibility but that wasn't really saying much. As quickly as the wipers cleared the rain, the glass fogged. Tall trees scattered the monotonous strobe from the barricades. Overall, the scene was far from cheerful but it was enough to reveal a paint-bare sign, the name all but obscured: Danny's Garage.

"What do you know? A real live service station."

Emily's dry sarcasm was a familiar habit she adopted when unsure of a situation and she fell back on it now. The Chevy's tank was half full but fuel wasn't her priority. The garage would provide an overhang and brief respite from the deluge. Maybe if she was lucky, Emily could find an all night café and get something decent to eat. The closed Dairy Queen a few miles back at Lebanon Junction was the only restaurant of any type she'd seen. Emily was hoping for a Denny's or IHOP to come her way. She could definitely go for a stack of blueberry pancakes smothered in butter and syrup.

She had spent the last week at Pine Mountain Park enjoying her favorite past time, hiking. Emily planned to spend the rest of her somewhat forced vacation at a rustic cabin in the Kentucky hills. The Bureau owned it, but so far she wasn't having the best of luck locating it. The cabin should have only been a few hours' drive from the park, but the storm had started almost as soon as she climbed behind the wheel. Now darkness was pressing in and with the force of the rain, she had to concede to a night spent sleeping in the car.

Finally, Emily located the ramshackle station. The concrete pad it rested on was cracked and weeds had pushed their way up through the openings. She steered the Tahoe into the parking lot next to the defunct pumps and out of the storm. With the rain no longer pounding directly on the roof, the weather didn't seem quite as bad and she looked around curiously. Boarded-up windows masked the interior of the service center. Now that she studied the scene more closely, the whole town seemed deserted. No lights shone from any of the buildings she could see and there weren't any street lamps. Emily recalled the sign announcing her arrival into Woeful Pines was also rather worn and battered. Had she somehow stumbled into a deserted mining town?

It was possible, but not likely. Emily figured the residents had probably all gone home when the lightning started. No doubt, the owner of this particular non-functional business was just another victim of the economy. She wasn't concerned. As a backpacking enthusiast, Emily was familiar with small, backwoods towns that time had all but forgotten. In the morning, the sun would be shining and barefoot kids wearing coveralls would be running all over the place. As long as the temperature didn't drop too drastically, she'd be fine. It was warm enough now, even with the storm, and one more night of roughing it wasn't going to kill her.

Emily shut off the car, unbuckled the seatbelt, and pushed the unruly dark curls away from her face. She slid out from behind the wheel and climbed over the seats into the back. She was in the mountains and it would probably get cool with the engine off. There was no sense in letting the warm air out just to walk around to the back of the car and slide in again.

Lithe and muscular, her physique was a testament to the high conditioning required for her job. She was grateful for that now as she opened the cooler and pulled out a plastic soda bottle. The ice had melted but things inside were still cold, drifting in a sea of frigid water. After a meal of corn chips, a turkey sandwich, and Pepsi, she settled into the sleeping bag. Quarters were tight but she was exhausted from the week's activities and drifted toward sleep. Emily relaxed into the quilted down. While never completely unaware of her surroundings or the dangers presented from sleeping in a parked car, she could still manage a few hours of restful slumber.

THE TWO HIDING behind the old blacksmith's station utilized the cover provided by the huge trees. They did nothing to draw attention to themselves, a deliberate and often used tactic to avoid detection. As they watched in silence, they saw the vehicle pull into Danny's and heard the engine shut off. With a glance of mutual understanding, they agreed to wait to see if the occupant stayed the night. This was a familiar routine enacted so many times the need to speak was rare. The identity of the driver didn't matter, man or woman. The only concern was that the targets were healthy and unimpaired by physical disabilities. By watching how their intended victim moved through the Chevy to climb into the sleeping bag, both requirements were satisfied. It was just a matter of patience now. They would eliminate the target if for any reason their prey somehow failed to measure up to their criteria. The vehicle was a newer model and that was in itself worth the effort of acquiring.

Almost an hour later, the heavy rain came to a grudging halt. It continued to sprinkle for another twenty minutes, but finally the two decided it was time to move. One man, older and more seasoned, led the way. Mike Kurth considered himself the risk taker. He was the one who was always confident and sure of their right to do exactly what they wanted. He felt blessed with a lean and athletic body, and easily avoided the worst of the puddles to stay on firm ground. The slightest noise could wake their target and the game might end before it got a good start.

He saw his brother Joey smile at him and then his eyes fixed on the Chevy. Their movements were silent and well coordinated. Mike moved around behind the car while Joey moved directly to the rear driver-side door. When they were both in position Mike looked down and found the doors locked, but he'd come prepared. He carried a Slim Jim lockout tool. If he had to he'd smash the window, but if he did, speed would be required to subdue their victim and things could get ugly very quickly. On the other side of the vehicle, his brother knelt down near one of the rear wheels.

The crunch of tires on gravel alerted them seconds before a brown Jeep Patriot maneuvered through the trees. ***Bullitt County Sheriff's Department*** was clearly emblazoned on the door. As a precaution, the pair crouched and scuttled back over to the blacksmith's building. Mike expected that the vehicle would drive out of sight and they would be free to continue unimpeded. The storm had started up again and rivulets of rainwater cascaded down his face and soaked into his clothing.

Instead of driving on, the law enforcement vehicle pulled in next to the white SUV. Mike heard the vehicle come to a stop, simultaneously watching his younger brother's expression turn to one with which he was all too familiar. He called it Joey's "whiney face." He raised a hand, motioned for Joey to be quiet, and watched to see what would happen next.

Chapter Two

SHERIFF JENNA YANG frowned at the white Chevy Tahoe, wondering who in the world could be way out here. The vehicle was dark and quiet. She had the feeling it had been sitting for some time. There weren't any motels in the immediate area so whoever owned the vehicle was surely asleep inside. Jenna wasn't afraid of the driver, per se, but in an age where it wasn't uncommon for your next-door neighbor to be a serial killer, a little common sense was in order. She reached for the radio mic and squeezed the button to talk to the night dispatcher.

"Robbie, are you there?"

"No, stepped out to get a burger, Sheriff. What can I do for you?"

Jenna smiled at the young man's good humor. "Hey, run an Ohio plate for wants and warrants, will you?"

"Sure. Is something wrong?"

"Probably not." Jenna gave him the Chevy's plate number and waited for a moment while Robert Landry keyed the information into the computer.

"It comes back to one Emily Denise Bannon. Thirty-seven, black hair, blue eyes. No wants or warrants. Everything okay there?"

"Just fine, Robbie. It looks like Ms. Bannon decided to wait out the storm at Danny Miller's old garage in Woeful Pines."

"Smart move. That storm's pretty bad, especially if you don't know the roads."

"Right. I'll just check on our guest and be on my way home, Robbie."

"Ten-four, Sheriff."

Jenna clipped the mic back to the radio and jammed the Smokey onto her straight black hair. She pulled the neck of the green rain slicker a little tighter and stepped into the soggy night. Mud splashed over the tops of her black waterproof boots, but Jenna barely noticed as she walked to the overhang and what little protection it could provide from the elements. Her eyes remained fixed on the silent vehicle, checking for any movement that would indicate a threat. There were no sounds to disturb the scene other than the rain, not even the pop and tick of a cooling engine. She couldn't feel any heat when she held her hand over the hood. Her first assessment had been correct; the vehicle had been sitting there for a while.

Jenna pulled a flashlight from her Sam Browne belt and clicked it on, shining it around the exterior of the Tahoe out of habit before she checked out the cab. Even before she directed the light inside, she knew the driver wasn't behind the wheel. After a few seconds, she spotted a quilted lump in the rear. The seats had been let down and someone was snoozing away in a sleeping bag. The occupant was about to receive a rude awakening, but better from her than someone else with malicious intent.

Strange happenings had been going on for the last few months. There were things Jenna couldn't quite put her finger on, but something was definitely off. Grim thoughts swirled in her mind as Jenna used the rim of the flashlight to tap on the side glass. The occupant jerked and immediately sat up. Wide, discerning eyes met hers. Though the occupant didn't seem particularly frightened, Jenna rushed to reassure her.

"Bullitt County Sheriff's Department. My name's Sheriff Yang. Are you all right?" Jenna bit back a smile when a look of irritation washed over the stranger's face. The expression gave her the impression that this woman wasn't easily intimidated.

"Well I was. You just scared ten years off my life."

"Sorry about that." The annoyed look remained and Jenna thought Ms. Bannon doubted her sincerity. "Look, I really didn't mean to scare you, but it's not safe to sleep out here by yourself."

Finally, Emily Bannon leaned over and opened the door a crack so they didn't have to shout through the glass. Jenna grasped the edge of the door and opened it enough that they could communicate, but not enough to soak the interior of the car with the rain that dripped off her hat's brim.

"And just what's so dangerous about this place? It looks pretty deserted to me."

Jenna shrugged. "You hear stories every day about things happening. I'd just rather they didn't happen in my county."

"You've got a point, but I didn't really have much of a choice."

"So I see."

Emily glanced overhead. "Yeah, you really have some rain out this way. I thought I'd pull over and try to wait out the storm."

"Actually, I meant that you must have driven over something when you pulled off the main road. You have a flat."

"What?" Emily clearly didn't believe her.

"See for yourself."

The stranger struggled for a moment to extricate herself from the sleeping bag, pausing to push curly black hair out of her eyes, and then stepped out onto the concrete. Jenna detected a sweet scent that reminded her of cloves and vanilla. She noticed that Emily barely reached her shoulder height, but she wasn't really paying attention to Jenna. Emily's attention was on the rear tire.

"That's great. Now what? This gas station doesn't exactly look like it's been open for business recently."

Jenna was accustomed to helping out stranded motorists. It was part of the job description and not unheard of for a small town area.

"It's no problem. Do you have a spare?"

"Yes, but...You're not suggesting that you change it?"

"It's all right. I don't mind."

For a moment, it occurred to Jenna that this woman was saying she wasn't strong enough and she felt tempted to be offended. Then their eyes met and she forgot about the topic of conversation. She felt like someone had just removed all of the oxygen from the world around her. In that brief instant, it was difficult to draw breath. Immediately annoyed, Jenna clamped down on her unexpected reaction. Emily didn't seem to notice and continued speaking.

"I mind. It's cold out here and the wind is blowing rain under the overhang. If you can recommend a hotel, I'll get the tire fixed in the morning. That is, if there's a working service station around here somewhere." Emily hugged herself and Jenna noticed it had cooled significantly with the thunderstorm.

"Why don't you grab whatever you need and hop in my car? I'll run you over to a hotel in Grays Landing. It's only a couple of miles from here and Danny can bring you back to fix the tire in the morning."

Emily smiled for the first time and Jenna was so stunned she almost missed what she said next. "So Danny is still around?"

"Yeah, he moved the station into Grays Landing a few months ago. The business is better there."

"Go figure. All right, Sheriff. I'll take you up on your offer. Let me grab my stuff."

Jenna waited while Emily pulled on a lightweight jacket and began cramming belongings into a bag. Watching the smaller woman's quick strong hands, she felt a shiver of awareness trail down her spine and wondered what was wrong with her. She had moved out to this part of Kentucky five years ago and felt no desire to be with any woman she'd seen. Now, in less than ten minutes, she couldn't seem to keep her eyes off this beautiful stranger.

Emily turned around unexpectedly and caught her staring. Jenna felt heat crawl up her chest, but didn't look away. Emily's eyes sought the ground and even in the darkness, Jenna could see she had embarrassed her.

For all Jenna's supposed professional decorum, Emily was the first to recover. She raised her eyes shyly and held out a hand. "We haven't been properly introduced. I'm Emily Bannon."

Jenna took the offered hand, absorbing the heat and softness of her skin. "Sheriff Jenna Yang."

"So you said," Emily responded with a cheeky grin. "Are you ready to go?"

"Um, yes."

Jenna felt like a stuttering boob and quickly turned back to her car. She opened the door and Emily leaped easily into the passenger seat. Jenna almost swallowed her tongue. The woman was athletic. After closing the door, she walked around to get in on the driver's side. She took the hat off and remembered to shake off the excess water before she stowed it behind the seat. She heard Emily gasp and looked around quickly.

"What?"

"You have beautiful hair. It's like a raven's wing."

She didn't quite know how to respond to a compliment from a woman she'd just been ogling so she settled for safe. "Thanks."

Jenna grabbed the mic and let Robbie know she was driving into Grays Landing before she went off shift. Then she pulled back onto Preston Highway, headed north. "Uh, it's only a couple of miles."

In the course of her daily responsibilities, Jenna spoke with many people. She just couldn't imagine why she was so nervous around Emily. She was probably just tired after such a long day.

EMILY CONCEALED HER smile in the darkness. She was flattered by how flummoxed the sheriff was. She'd caught Yang staring at her butt when she turned around from retrieving her belongings and couldn't help notice the heat in her gaze. Sheriff Yang was gorgeous and Emily wouldn't mind spending some time with her before she left the next morning. She hadn't any misgivings about having a one-night stand with an intriguing woman. It was just sex and Emily preferred to avoid commitments. There was little chance of that though. It was the middle of the night and Sheriff Yang was about to drop her off at a hotel. A second later, Emily's dilemma resolved itself when her stomach growled quite loudly.

Jenna grinned and glanced at her before turning back to the road. "Sounds like you'd better feed that beast."

"Sorry. I've been hiking at Pine Mountain and haven't had a decent meal in over a week. I'll get something out of the vending machines when we get to the hotel."

"There might be a problem with that."

"How so?"

"Well, the Bayside is more of a motel really. I don't know if they have vending machines, much less if they work."

"Oh." Emily frowned in disappointment. "That's too bad."

Jenna glanced over again. "If you're up for it, there's an all-night café just at the outskirts of town. Frank's has the best apple pie around."

"Thank you, Sheriff, but you don't have to do that. I already have you running around in the middle of the night rescuing a stranded motorist. I'm sure you'd like to go home and get some sleep."

Although Emily had instantly been attracted, Jenna looked tired and she felt concerned for her safety. She didn't want Jenna to fall asleep at the wheel while driving home.

"It's no problem," Jenna repeated her words from earlier and Emily wondered where her bravado came from, but was distracted from the thought when she continued. "I'm used to being up at all hours and I could use something to eat myself."

Emily shivered lightly and pictured the officer indulging in something much more intimate than apple pie.

"You all right, Miss Bannon?"

"Yes. Frank's sounds wonderful, and if we're going to share breakfast at two in the morning, I think you should call me Emily."

Jenna smiled and Emily caught the flash of strong, white teeth. "Then it's Jenna to you."

"By the way, how am I going to get back to my car? There aren't any cabs around here, are there?"

"That would be a no, but I could always pick you up in the morning and give you a lift. Since I like to drive around the county at the start of my shift, I can go right by the old garage easily enough."

The offer didn't strike her as something a normal stranger would do and Emily thought the good sheriff might be flirting a little. She could do that. "Do you always offer such personal service?"

Jenna glanced at her and enunciated very clearly, "No."

Did it just get hotter? Minutes later, they pulled into a large parking lot filled with nothing but semis. It was too early in the morning for many locals.

"This place looks busy."

"It's not as crowded as you'd think." Jenna got out of the truck and slammed the door before walking around to the passenger side. Emily was already standing and closed the door as she approached. "A lot of the truck drivers just pull over to sleep. It's safer than parking on the side of the highway."

Emily raised an eyebrow. "You mean like I was doing?"

"No," Jenna laughed. "You were smart enough to pull into a place where you might expect people to be. Also, you weren't parked on the shoulder where someone could hit you."

They walked inside and Emily inhaled the scents of greasy fries and coffee. They were the familiar smells of any nameless café in any part of America.

Jenna led her to the back and they slid into a red plastic booth. Emily realized Jenna had been right. There were only a few scattered men inside the diner. Most of them sat alone or at the bar with vacant stools between them to mark their limited territory. They leaned over cups of strong, black coffee and stared into the inky darkness.

"Hey Sheriff, how you doing?"

A waitress with blonde hair piled on top of her head and too-red lipstick offered Jenna a more than friendly smile. Emily felt her hackles rise and then realized she was being silly. She barely knew these people.

"I'm doing great, Cheryl. How are the kids?"

Cheryl gave a long-suffering sigh. "Bobby's got another cold. I swear that kid stays sick. What can I get ya?"

Jenna ordered a black coffee and Emily asked for a Pepsi, eternally grateful when Cheryl gave them a few minutes alone to look at the menu. She felt the heat of Jenna's knees brush against hers and suddenly wasn't very hungry.

"You said you recommend the apple pie?"

"That's right."

Apparently, Jenna hadn't caught on to the husky tone in Emily's voice. Maybe the contact below the table's edge was incidental. Emily decided to find out.

"Would that be with ice cream or whipped cream?"

There was just enough innuendo to make Jenna inhale sharply and then their eyes met. Jenna's brown eyes darkened and she answered quietly. "I guess that depends on what you're in the mood for."

"And if I wanted it hot and creamy? Could I get that instead?"

Jenna's eyes widened, but she responded quickly. "Oh yes, definitely that."

"Maybe we should eat something more filling first."

"To keep our strength up?"

"Exactly what I had in mind."

"Good idea."

Emily realized she was coming on to a virtual stranger and it felt wonderful. Jenna's exotic good looks captivated her. What was the harm in having a little fling before she got back to work? This was her vacation, or at least that was what everyone was supposed to think.

Cheryl came back and Emily barely heard Jenna order two super breakfast specials. As soon as they were alone she asked, "Yang? Is that Chinese?"

"Very good. Most people would assume it was Japanese."

"I'm not most people."

Jenna's lingering gaze felt like a caress. "No. You most definitely are not."

Emily wanted to jump on her. She wanted to press Jenna down onto the red seats and feel their bodies mashed together. Conversely, she could picture Jenna on top of her, their skin pressing close and warm. She wanted to come with Jenna's fingers deep inside her.

"How did you wind up in Grays Landing?" Emily asked shakily, focusing on the fact that they were in a public place.

"I inherited my dad's house when he passed away."

Jenna's breathy tone told Emily she felt just as deeply affected by her proximity and she reveled in it. "Somehow I think there's more to the story."

"Later. Right now it's all I can do to complete a sentence."

Emily laughed a little shakily. "I know what you mean, but don't worry. As soon as we get out of here I'll make it up to you."

"Oh, really? What did you have in mind?"

"At the moment all I can think of is having my tongue inside you, licking you until you come all over me."

Jenna's jaw clenched for a moment and she seemed to be holding her breath. Finally, she exhaled loudly. "Jesus, Emily! You keep talking like that and we're not going to make it out of the parking lot."

"Hold on to that idea, sweetheart. Here comes Cheryl with our food."

Chapter Three

JENNA SLID BEHIND the Jeep's wheel and glanced over at Emily next to her. Breakfast had been a blur and she hardly recalled eating, but she did know neither of them had ordered the apple pie. She barely noticed that it was still raining. The fire in Emily's eyes was keeping her mind in a haze, but Jenna clearly understood what each of them wanted next. They were both hot and ready. Jenna took a deep breath and set the ball in motion.

"You might be more comfortable staying with me than at the motel. After all, it is a strange town and I'd hate to think of you all alone, surrounded by people you don't know."

Emily flashed a smile. "Do you use that line on all the unattached women passing through here?"

"No, never used it before. Is it working?"

"Oh yeah. Let's get out of here."

Jenna threw the vehicle into reverse and backed out of the parking space. She pulled up to the blacktop and out from under the café lights. She had just stopped to check for cross traffic when Emily slid over and pressed against her side. Emily slid a hand under Jenna's hair and massaged the back of her head, making Jenna look down at her. The promise in the blue eyes stole her breath and she was unable to resist. She kissed Emily hard, inflamed when she felt Emily's soft lips part and her tongue invade her mouth. Jenna pulled away with a groan when Emily's strong fingers pinched her nipple.

"We'll be there in just a few minutes."

"You'd better hurry or I'm going to go off without you."

Jenna stifled another groan and clenched her jaw so hard it ached. She pulled out onto the roadway and headed back the way they had come before.

"Where are we going?"

"I live out near Woeful Pines."

"Oh."

She didn't say anything more and Jenna didn't think Emily really cared where they were headed as long as it contained privacy and a nice, cozy bed. Jenna stayed keyed up with Emily's hand between her legs. She scratched her nails up the seam of Jenna's trousers and swirled over the liquid heat she found.

"You keep that up and you're going to make me crash."

"I'm not even touching you."

It was a lie because Emily's breasts were against Jenna's arms and the tips of her fingers pressed against a pulsing clit. Jenna twitched and stifled a groan. She was relieved when Emily eased up just a little.

Apparently, she wanted Jenna hot, not sated, by the time they arrived.

"Hurry," Emily encouraged, her voice husky with promise.

A few moments later, they pulled onto a familiar gravel road called Horse Fly Hollow. Relief washed over Jenna. She didn't know how much longer she could hold out. A farmhouse came into view, lit by a single porch light. Jenna was almost lightheaded when she pulled into the driveway and keyed a garage opener. The aluminum door was only halfway up when her radio sputtered to life and Robbie's worried voice intruded through the haze of lust.

"Sheriff Yang, respond."

Jenna choked off a growl of frustration and reached for the mic. She had to lean over Emily's arm to do so and her slacks tightened across her distended flesh.

"Go ahead, Robbie."

"I hate to keep you from going off shift, Sheriff, but Mrs. Freeman just called. She said her nephew was coming down from Canada to visit and was supposed to be there yesterday. He never showed up and she's worried something happened to him."

Jenna closed her eyes and took a deep breath. She already knew what came next and cast an apologetic look toward Emily before she addressed the dispatcher. "So why didn't she call it in yesterday?"

"I don't know, Sheriff. You want I should call her back and ask, or have Deputy Brown swing by?"

Jenna cringed internally. Clayton Brown was a deputy that preferred the night shift, mainly so he wouldn't have to do anything but park on a back road and talk to his girlfriend on the cell phone all night. There weren't many of those roads with decent reception, but she was sure Brown knew all of them. If this had been a large city, he never would have passed any kind of police academy, but they didn't have anything like that out here.

Deputy Brown was worthless, in her opinion, not like any real deputy Jenna had ever known. If something really had happened to Lois Freeman's nephew, Brown wouldn't have any idea what to do. Chances were likely that he'd miss the signs entirely.

"No." Jenna realized she sounded cranky and tried to be a little more professional. "I'll take care of it. Let her know I'm on my way. I'll be there in twenty minutes."

"Understood, Sheriff."

Jenna drove out of the storm and into the lit garage. Her hand trembled slightly as she shut off the engine. She took a calming breath before she glanced over at Emily. She had expected her companion to be frustrated, but found instead a wry grin and dancing blue eyes. As she watched, Emily tucked a lock of dark hair behind her ear.

"Look at it this way: I have time to clean up before you get back."

Unaccountably relieved that Emily wasn't irritated, Jenna smiled. "Sounds like a plan. Let me get you situated before I have to leave."

As she got out of the pickup, Emily hoisted her backpack off the floorboard from between her feet and exited the other side. Jenna was acutely aware of Emily following her into the house through the connecting garage door. Seconds before, she hadn't been able to think beyond her own libido, but now Jenna had other concerns. Was the house clean enough for company? Would Emily notice any lingering traces of breakfast in the air? Jenna thought she detected the greasy, if not altogether unpleasant scent of bacon.

If she did notice, Emily didn't comment.

As she led the way through the house, Jenna kept up a steady, nervous monologue. "Help yourself to anything in the kitchen. Bedrooms are here on the first floor with the guest room at the end of the hall. The bathroom is here on the right, towels in the cupboard on the left. I'm not sure how long I'll be, but I'll try to speed things along."

Jenna stopped at the rear of the hallway and turned to face her guest. Emily watched her quietly, her gaze oddly intent. It was the first serious expression Jenna had seen from her since surprising Emily in the disabled Tahoe.

"Is something wrong?"

Without releasing her gaze, Emily squatted slightly and set her gear on the floor. Then she stood and closed the short distance between them. She reached out slowly, until her fingertips softly grazed Jenna's cheek. Jenna stood riveted, trapped in the intensity of the moment.

"You really are gorgeous."

The kiss followed the words so quickly that Jenna hadn't a chance to respond. Strong hands threaded through her hair and Emily's tongue stroked inside her mouth. For several long moments, Jenna allowed the pleasure and excitement to take over, but eventually she pulled away. Emily's pupils had dilated slightly, her desire evident, but Jenna was sure she found amusement there as well.

"That's a reminder of what'll be waiting for you when you get back. Now go take your report."

Jenna took a breath and stepped back before she cleared her throat. "Right. Well. I'll be back as soon as I can."

Emily smiled again, but didn't answer so Jenna walked away. She felt Emily watching and tried not to stumble or otherwise make a complete fool of herself. As soon as she left Emily's presence, Jenna was able to redirect her focus to the missing persons call. Already, she was planning how to approach the scene and the questions she would need to ask.

The light in the garage had shut off automatically, leaving Jenna to navigate to the driver's door primarily by touch and shadows. She shivered slightly and realized her hair and clothes were still wet from the rain. If she'd been thinking clearly, Jenna would have changed, but it was too late now. She wasn't about to go back into the house, or she'd risk not leaving it again tonight.

"Not going there," she muttered, slipping behind the wheel. She slammed the door, hit the garage opener, and turned the heater on full.

As she reached the main road, Jenna leaned forward to grasp the mic. At the same time, she switched on the defroster and windshield wipers. "Deputy Brown, this is Sheriff Yang."

Her tone was clipped and slightly annoyed. When Brown didn't answer immediately, her ire went up another notch. "Deputy Brown, respond."

A few seconds later, she heard his lazy drawl as well as his irritated sigh. "I'm here, Sheriff. What are you doing out so late?"

"My job, as you should be. Put down the cell phone and meet me at Lois Freeman's place."

Static covered the channel for a moment before his whine filled the airways. "Geez, Sheriff. What's so important it takes both of us? Can't you handle it?"

Anger coursed through her veins and Jenna bit back her instinctive response. "*Deputy Brown*, if you still hope to be employed by the Bullitt County Sheriff's Department when the sun comes up, I suggest you get to the Freeman house before I do. Is that clear enough?"

"All right, all right. No need to get testy. I'm on my way."

Jenna clenched her jaw and hooked the mic onto the radio. The rain began to lessen and as it did, her anger started to fade. Deputy Brown was a lazy screw up, but Jenna was truly annoyed with herself and her behavior toward a woman she had just met.

"Talk about unprofessional. I don't even know her. Great first impression of local law enforcement," Jenna mumbled aloud.

Not that Emily seemed to mind.

Jenna quickly squashed the stray thought. Even if Emily wasn't adverse to a one-night stand with a stranger, Jenna couldn't allow it. She was the sheriff. More than that, she prided herself on not getting involved with anyone on a personal level. As long as her job entailed bringing criminals to justice, she couldn't afford the distraction. A relationship would split her focus and result in putting innocent lives in danger. She had learned that the hard way and for the last five years managed to keep within sight of the bigger picture. Jenna was furious for forgetting the past, even for an instant.

Her headlights illuminated a county road sign, drawing her back to the present. She realized the turnoff to the Freeman residence was just ahead. Jenna flicked on the high beams and made the turn onto the rutted lane. This road didn't have a gravel base, just the natural Kentucky dirt. The storm had turned it into muddy soup and Jenna was grateful for her four-wheel drive. The Jeep bounced through the potholes, throwing dirty brown water up over the wheel wells, onto the hood and windshield.

Storm clouds obscured the moon, but her lights easily cut through the fog and darkness. If it weren't for the lateness of the hour and the slush she'd soon be tromping through, the surroundings might almost be pleasant. Jenna found the woods soothing and took a deep breath in a final effort to let go of her arousal and subsequent anger from the earlier indiscretion with Emily.

Jenna told herself it wasn't that big a deal. They were both adults and she just needed to forget about it.

A patrol vehicle with mud up to the bottom of the windows pulled up just as Jenna shut off her engine. The headlights caused her to wince as they struck her directly in the eyes, but they extinguished almost immediately. The Crown Victoria had definitely seen better days, but then again it was over ten years old. For a vehicle driven by an average citizen that might not be so bad, but police cars were different. Louisville received the new cars. After they were driven hard, poorly maintained and just short of having the suspension worn out, they were then donated to the smaller county substations.

Jenna pulled the wet Smokey back down over her black hair and exited her vehicle with notebook in hand. She heard Deputy Brown's patrol vehicle squeak as it was relieved of his weight and looked at him with ill-concealed disgust. His belly lapped over his belt and the buttons of his shirt strained to remain closed. His shoes were scuffed, his hair looked like he'd just crawled out of bed and he desperately needed a shave.

"We're going to talk later about proper uniform maintenance and the personal use of a cell phone while on duty."

"Sure, Sheriff, whatever you say."

Brown punctuated the statement by spitting tobacco juice in a three-foot arc toward the scrub. At least he had the courtesy to turn his head.

"Spit that crap out. What you do on your own time is one thing, but I expect you to present a professional appearance when dealing with the public."

"There ain't no public out here," he argued.

"There's about to be. Lois Freeman is inside, now do it."

Brown scowled in response and didn't move, but when Jenna raised an eyebrow in warning, he finally relented. He stuck an index finger in his mouth and dug around until he removed a foul-smelling black lump. He casually flicked it into the weeds, spit again, and wiped his fingers on his trousers. The action left a stain behind, but Jenna thought it didn't matter. It matched the bits of food on his shirt.

Clearly, it was time to search for a new deputy.

Jenna shook her head and led the way to the front door. Mrs. Freeman was waiting for them in the middle of the doorway. She wore a thick, terry cloth robe that she nervously clutched at with her left hand. Her hair was tied up in curlers, but she offered them a bright, if somewhat worried, smile.

"Sheriff, I'm so glad you could make it out here yourself."

Mrs. Freeman looked at Deputy Brown and her smile faded slightly, but she was too well mannered to show her dislike of the man openly. She graciously pushed the screen door open and invited them inside.

"I hate disturbing you like this, but I'm just so worried about Charles. Would you like some coffee?"

"No, ma'am, thank you very much." Jenna was still full from the late breakfast and didn't want to put the woman out at this time of the morning.

"Don't mind if I do," Brown responded.

Jenna looked at him in disbelief. He had absolutely no sense of etiquette. Jenna wasn't the type to reprimand her people in public, but she ground her teeth at his poor behavior. It was just one more thing to add to her ever-growing list.

The officers settled into the living room while Lois Freeman ran to fetch Deputy Brown's coffee. Jenna settled for giving him a disgruntled look.

"What?"

She ignored him as their host walked back into the room and set a full china cup on the coffee table in front of the deputy. Then Mrs. Freeman sat down in her worn recliner and gave Jenna her undivided attention.

"First I'll need to get a full description..."

Deputy Brown interrupted Jenna when he took a loud slurp from his cup and then smacked his lips in appreciation. "Ah, that's just what the doctor ordered."

Jenna took a deep breath and reminded herself not to kill him in front of witnesses. Instead, she attempted to focus on the task at hand. "...a full description of your nephew and the vehicle he was driving."

"Well, he's twenty-two and a student at—"

"Excuse me, ma'am," Jenna said, gently interrupting. She directed a baleful gaze at the man who was doing nothing more than taking up sofa space. "Perhaps you should be writing this down, Deputy Brown?"

"Huh? Oh, yeah. Right."

Brown sloshed coffee over the rim as he placed the cup down on the coffee table and reached for his notebook. He didn't attempt to wipe up the mess.

"Okay, shoot."

Jenna resisted the urge to roll her eyes. "Please go ahead."

Mrs. Freeman nodded and Jenna noticed that she focused solely on her even though Brown was supposed to record the information. "His name is Charles Harrison Freeman. He's twenty-two and studies Graphic Communications at the University of Toronto. He's blonde-haired and has these adorable blue eyes. Uh, no beard or mustache, he hates facial hair. He's just like his Uncle Martin that way, God rest his soul."

Mrs. Freeman went on to give them scads of information intermingled with many useless details. Her nephew was five foot ten and weighed a hundred and sixty-five pounds. He attended college on a sports scholarship. Jenna did glean that Charles had a muscled, rugby player build. He wouldn't have been easy prey.

Clayton Brown asked the appropriate questions to document the missing person and Jenna was just starting to think there was hope for the man when he asked, "No chance he met a girl and stopped over at a motel for the night?"

"Heavens no." Lois Freeman looked like he'd just asked her to hold a live snake.

"What about them casinos up there? They might be awfully tempting to a young kid out to blow off steam for a few days."

"My nephew is a proper young man. He would never do something like that, and certainly not without letting me know he was going to be late."

Jenna quickly stepped into the conversation and attempted to soothe any ruffled feathers. "I'm sure you're right, Mrs. Freeman. Could you give us a description of the vehicle he was driving?"

Deputy Brown jotted down the rest of the pertinent information while Jenna looked on. From time to time, she was required to prompt him, but he refrained from any more inappropriate remarks. As soon as they were finished, Jenna ended the interview and quickly hustled the deputy from Mrs. Freeman's home.

"Put out a BOLO on the Honda."

"Right," Brown said, jotting down her orders. "Be...on...the...lookout.... Who'd you want to include on that?"

Jenna took a deep breath before replying in a slightly sarcastic tone. "Well, let me think. Where did she say she last heard from her nephew?"

"Just this side of La Grange."

"Then I recommend you send out alerts to every law enforcement station from here to La Grange."

Deputy Brown looked at her in surprise. "That's a lot of stations." His heavy frown told Jenna he didn't want to bother. Brown probably thought he'd come out here to mollify an old woman by taking a report and that would be the end of it.

"Then I suggest you get busy," Jenna ordered, finally losing patience. "Go back to the station and put the information in the system. I'm going home."

"You know, Sheriff, Chuck is probably just having a little fun somewhere. He didn't let his aunt know what he was doing because he didn't think of it. You know how people are these days. It's all about them."

"As far as Charles Freeman deciding to stop for a little action on the way, it's possible. It could also be true that something has happened.

It's not for you to decide arbitrarily that nothing is wrong. Now do your job."

Jenna returned to her Jeep, leaving Deputy Brown standing in the mud and the rain. As she drove home, she couldn't help but wonder how he managed to acquire such a position of authority in the first place. Perhaps Brown was related to someone who got the job for him. It was just astonishing that he would have earned it for himself.

Her house loomed in the darkness and Jenna's thoughts abruptly turned to a more personal nature. The last thing she felt now was amorous. Fortunately, all of the lights were out so it didn't look like her guest was up. Jenna intended to be very quiet, grab a quick shower, and go straight to bed. If she was lucky, she might be able to sleep for three hours before it was time to get ready for her shift.

What was she thinking anyway, Jenna wondered. Taking a stranger home for casual sex was crazy, even if Emily did have the greatest eyes.

Chapter Four

EMILY STIRRED SLOWLY with sunshine streaming through the window and across the bed. Waking up in strange places wasn't anything new and she took a moment to stretch before looking curiously around the room. A heavy mahogany dresser sat in one corner and at a glance, Emily could see it wasn't one of those presswood jobs. The rich brown matched perfectly with the polished hardwood floors. The queen-sized bed was a four-poster, lacking only a canopy to give her the sensation of a bygone era. Tucked under a thick, hand-sewn quilt and lying on heavy pillows, she felt cradled by comfort.

Sheriff Yang had gone for pale yellows and chocolate as a color scheme. Altogether, the room looked designed to be a sanctuary, a place where one could let go and allow their cares to melt away. Emily smiled, pleased that her powers of observation had revealed something so personal about her host.

Jenna was a closet romantic.

A soft thump came to her ears and she was suddenly aware of a delicious aroma.

"Coffee."

Emily jumped naked out of bed and pulled on the blue jeans, bra and blue and white striped polo shirt she'd put out the night before. Then she opened the door and padded barefoot down the hall and into the kitchen. She spotted Jenna as soon as she rounded the corner and came to a halt to enjoy the sight. Jenna stood at the sink, staring out the window above into the woods. Her medium length black hair was still wet from the shower. It was slicked back over her ears and stopped at the neckline of a plain white t-shirt. The hem of her shirt tucked neatly into a pair of sharply pressed green uniform trousers, accentuating the lithe musculature of her arms and abdomen.

Although Jenna wore a black weave-patterned belt threaded through the loops on her trousers, her gun belt lay behind her on a small, square table. Jenna's expression was pensive, even in the light of a newly born day.

"I could paint you."

Jenna blinked and turned to her, a friendly smile replacing her previous expression. "Good morning. Did you sleep well?"

"Like a baby." Emily stretched again and then gestured at the full coffee mug beside the gun belt. "Got another one of those?"

"Sure." Jenna retrieved a cup from the cupboard and filled it from a pot on the side bar before handing it to Emily. "Cream or sugar?"

"No thanks."

Emily took the hot cup, deliberately stroking Jenna's fingers as she did. The darkening in Jenna's eyes indicated her reaction and Emily quickly raised the mug to hide her smile.

"As soon as you're ready, I'll drive you into town so Danny can help you with that flat."

"That's not necessary, but thanks for the offer." Emily pulled out a chair and sat down, maintaining a discreet distance from Jenna's duty weapon.

"Why not?"

"Because I have a spare and I'm perfectly capable of changing a tire when it's not pouring rain."

Jenna sipped her coffee and then replied. "In that case, I'll help you before I go to the station."

"I've got it. Besides, it wouldn't look good if you showed up for your shift with grease on your clothes."

Jenna assessed her quietly. "You talk like a cop."

"Excuse me?"

"I didn't notice it at the time, but last night you said I should go take my *report*. Now you casually mention my *shift*. You sound like you know law enforcement."

Emily hoped the momentary panic didn't show in her expression. She was going to have to be more careful. Jenna didn't miss much. She shrugged negligently. "A testament to my misspent youth watching too many television crime dramas."

Jenna topped off their mugs without asking if Emily needed a refill, her expression neutral. "So if you're not a cop, what do you do?"

"Freelance travel writer."

"Seriously?"

"Why not? I love the outdoors and seeing places I've never been before." Emily raised her cup and tipped it toward the window to indicate the woods. "Maybe I'll create a fascinating tale about this place and bring tourism pouring into Woeful Pines."

Jenna laughed. "That's not journalism. That's a miracle."

Though she smiled and held up her end of the conversation, Emily could see tiny lines around Jenna's dark eyes.

"You look tired. Rough night?"

Jenna blinked and quirked an eyebrow. "Wow, intelligent, beautiful, and observant."

Emily winced a little at the brittle tone. "I wasn't trying to step on your toes. If you don't want to talk about it, that's up to you."

Jenna set her cup down and rubbed her eyes. "I'm sorry. I didn't mean to bite. It was a long night and I don't want to bore you."

"Bore me, I insist. Better yet, let me buy you a drink tonight and you can tell me all the gory details."

"Uh," Jenna hesitated, her eyes rounding slightly. "I don't think that's a good idea."

She seemed apprehensive and Emily decided Jenna didn't socialize much. Last night must have been unusual for her and now she was backing away, attempting to keep things on a professional level. Emily felt strangely compelled to dissuade Jenna from putting distance between them. After all, Emily loved a challenge.

Emily responded to Jenna's trepidation with her most winning smile. "Come on. I promise to keep my hands to myself and you can give me the history of this area. Maybe I really will write a piece."

"I thought you were supposed to be on vacation. Don't you ever take a break?" When Emily didn't respond, Jenna finally relented. "Fine, but don't say I didn't warn you."

"Great. Louisville's only a half hour from here. Maybe you can show me some of the nightlife. Speaking of which, why were you working so late last night? You can't tell me you routinely work twenty-four hours a day."

"No, there was a high school football game and the kids tend to get pretty amped up after a big win." Jenna turned to rinse her mug out and shut off the pot.

"And you were out patrolling to make sure they weren't doing more than playing mailbox baseball when you spotted my car."

"Exactly. Are you finished? I don't mean to rush you, but I need to get going."

So they were back to professional after all. Emily felt disappointed. "No problem."

Emily drained the cup as she stood. She quickly washed it out and sat it beside the other in the bottom of the sink. Jenna was standing close and Emily had the move planned before Jenna could shift away. Emily turned, rose up on her toes, and pressed a soft kiss to Jenna's full lips. Emily held the contact for a few seconds, reacquainting herself with the softness, before she stepped back.

"Sorry. I couldn't resist. Let me grab my things."

"You are dangerous," Jenna muttered as Emily walked out of the room.

"You're just now figuring that out?"

In the bedroom, Emily pulled the covers up and grabbed her backpack from the floor. She was smiling mischievously as she retrieved her jacket from the chair and walked out into the hall. Jenna stood completely dressed for her day, gun belt slung low on her hips. Emily considered an off-color remark, but let it go before it could fully form. She found Jenna attractive, but chasing her away with juvenile comments wouldn't go far for getting what she wanted.

"I'm ready." Emily put the backpack on the floor to pull on her jacket and was surprised when Jenna picked it up.

"What have you got in here, a dead body?"

"My laptop, but the way it's acting it might as well be a corpse."

"You always carry a laptop around in your backpack?"

"No," Emily replied, taking the pack and pulling it over a shoulder.

"But I couldn't exactly leave it in the car overnight."

"True enough."

Jenna led the way into the garage and hit the button to open the overhead doors. Emily took one look outside and made a quick decision.

"You know I really appreciate the offer of a ride, but I think I'd rather walk. It's such a beautiful day and it's not far, is it?"

"No, about three miles," Jenna replied, clearly surprised. "Follow Horse Fly Hollow to the right until it intersects with Beech Grove Road. Turn right and you'll see Woeful Pines up on the left."

"Thanks. I'll pick you up at six."

Jenna smiled and agreed that she would be ready. Emily waited until Jenna had driven away in the Jeep before she set out on the muddy lane. The air smelled fresh and clean and she took a deep breath, savoring the scents. There was a little chill in the early spring air that would eventually give way to the bright sunshine, but Emily intended to enjoy both. This was such beautiful country it was easy to believe that nothing bad could ever happen here. It was just too bad that she knew differently.

Emily strolled up the dirt road, enjoying the scents of earth and flowers blooming. Birds sang overhead and she didn't see a single car. Considering how far back in the Kentucky hills they were, Emily thought that was probably the norm. It was all a considerable change from Cleveland. The landscape was gorgeous, but if not for extenuating circumstances, Emily would have been bored in a day.

Emily smirked and enjoyed the walk back to the old gas station. Her SUV was right where she'd left it, seeming none the worse for wear though she noticed the deflated tire Sheriff Yang had mentioned right away. She set her backpack on the concrete pad and bent over to inspect the flat more closely, frowning as she did. The cap was gone from the valve stem and there wasn't any noticeable damage to the tire. The piece in question was lying on the ground at the rear of the vehicle and she couldn't imagine any natural forces that would have removed it.

Weird. She'd checked the tires the last time she stopped for gas and felt sure she'd tightly secured all the black caps. Emily inspected the bicycle attached to the rear of her vehicle on a rack next, but found it was completely untouched.

As she considered the possibilities, Emily removed her keys from the pack and unlocked the Chevy. Nothing appeared disturbed. She removed a portable pump from under the driver's seat, plugged it into the power port, and connected the end of it to the valve stem. Emily thumbed the switch and it hummed to life. She watched the tire inflate, periodically checking the pressure and finally shutting the device down. After that, she disconnected everything and replaced the cap. The tire seemed to be holding the air, but she realized there could still be a slow leak. It was something to keep an eye on, but instinct told her there was nothing wrong with the tire. Someone had tampered with it. The obvious questions were, who would do such a thing and why?

Emily puzzled over the small mystery as she started the car and pulled out onto the roadway. She still needed to find the cabin, but let that task go for the moment. She'd worry about reaching her destination after a nice hot cup of coffee at Frank's. Fortunately, she knew the way since she'd enjoyed breakfast with the good sheriff. Thoughts of Jenna caused the mystery of the tire to disappear and a smile graced her lips the rest of the way to the diner.

Though the lot was quite full, Emily was able to find a spot close to the front door. She was still smiling when she walked up to the counter. A woman that Emily guessed to be in her early forties returned the smile.

"What can I get for you, sweetie?"

"Coffee, black. Please."

"That's it?" The server lifted an eyebrow. "Don't you know that breakfast is the most important meal of the day?"

Emily's smile grew in relation to the woman's friendly banter. "Actually, I had breakfast here just a few hours ago. It was really good, but a girl has to watch her figure."

"Ah, then Frank's thanks you for your patronage." In a conspiratorial whisper, the waitress added, "And I don't think you have to worry about your figure."

Emily laughed as the woman poured her coffee. She noticed a nametag that read "Millie."

"Who is this elusive Frank anyway?" Emily looked around expecting a middle aged, overweight man with a buzz cut, three days growth of beard and a cigar hanging out of the side of his mouth.

"I am," Millie said, watching Emily for a reaction.

"What? You're kidding."

"Not at all. My name's Millie Franklin."

"Hence the Frank."

"You guessed it." Frank leaned toward her over the counter, resting on her elbows. "And you must be the stranger who had breakfast with our lady sheriff."

"I see news travels fast around here."

"What do you expect? Nothing much happens in such a small place so gossip moves at the speed of light."

Emily sipped her coffee as she glanced around a bit. Most of the patron's eyes were on her, though they turned away as soon as she noticed them. They didn't want to be caught staring. That would be rude.

"Have you got a name, stranger?"

"Yep, sure do." Emily looked at Frank and feigned surprise. "Oh, you want to know what it is."

Frank laughed, unfazed by the teasing. "Only if you want to tell."

"Emily. Emily Bannon."

"And what brings you to our little burg, Miss Bannon?"

"Call me Emily. I'm on vacation. A friend is letting me use his cabin on Pumpkin Road."

"Really? That creepy old place out by itself?" Frank looked disturbed for the first time, piquing Emily's interest.

"I haven't been out there yet. What's so creepy about it?"

Frank blinked. "I guess it's just that it's usually empty, but once in a while someone will report seeing a light on out there."

"Old ghost stories?" Emily feigned interest but in reality, she knew Bureau employees sometimes used the cabin as a safe house. Those visits were probably the source of the rumors. If Emily hadn't experienced the storm and then the flat, her occupancy would probably have joined the gossip mill.

"Maybe. Oh, listen to me. I'm being silly. It's just an old cabin and we're happy to have you visit."

"Hey Frank!" Someone yelled from the rear of the café. "How about a refill?"

"Coming up."

Frank left to make her rounds and Emily took advantage of her absence to check out the café more closely. By any definition, it was a typical roadside diner, except for the posters hung up on a wall at one end behind the counter. From where she sat, Emily counted seven pictures and all of them held a caption that read "Missing". Men and women alike, they all looked fairly young and in fit condition. Given that there were only eleven hundred people in the Grays Landing area, that number was way off the chart for natural occurrences.

No wonder her supervisors had chosen her for this. Whatever was happening here, it was serious.

Emily hadn't noticed the flyers the last time she'd visited Frank's. That thought disturbed her. She'd focused on nothing more than getting into Jenna's pants to pick up on them. Fortunately, they registered now and she made a mental note to get her head back in the game, regardless of how alluring Emily found the local LEO. When Frank wandered back over and topped off her coffee, Emily asked, "What's up with the flyers?"

Frank followed her gaze and turned back with sympathy and concern in her eyes. "Those people aren't from around here. We just let the families put up pictures of their loved ones, hoping it'll give them some peace."

"Why here?"

"I'm sure it isn't just here. They've probably plastered every café, truck stop, and hotel all along whatever route those kids were driving."

Emily's thoughts were swirling. "The flyers look new. When did you start putting them up?"

"Must have been about six months ago."

"All of them? You must find that odd."

"Not really." Frank shook her head and sighed. "The world just seems to get more violent every day."

Emily sipped her coffee and finally responded. "Yes, I suppose it does."

"Why so many questions?" Frank asked, smiling to lessen the impact of her query. "You some kind of private investigator?"

"Me? No, ma'am. Just curious, but I do have another question. Do you know a Danny?"

"The gas station owner?"

"That's the one. I need to have a tire checked."

Frank gave her directions to the station that, as it happened, was only a mile up the road. Emily thanked her and paid for the coffee, promising to return for lunch. Then she was out the door and on her way.

She needed to be more careful, Emily thought for the second time. A simple café owner had almost seen right through her. Of course, Millie Franklin dealt with people every day and had probably seen a lot over the years. There was no one better at profiling than someone who regularly provided a public service.

A brief stop by the shiny new station with all the latest amenities proved two things. One of those was that there was nothing wrong with the tire and the second was that Danny Gilbert was an old-fashioned southerner who believed a woman couldn't survive without a man. Emily was stewing about it as she drove toward the cabin.

"You're just a little bitty thing. You probably just didn't put the cap on tight and all the air leaked out," she mocked Danny as she drove.

"Yeah, and you're a pinhead," she complained, her fists tightening on the steering wheel. "Even if it was loose, the air doesn't just leak out!"

Someone had let the air out deliberately. That combined with all the missing persons posters served to put her on edge. What the hell was going on around here?

Emily turned off Preston Highway onto Beech Grove Road. She passed the lane Jenna lived on, Horse Fly Hollow, but had more pressing matters and didn't have time to think about her much. Up ahead was another turn in the opposite direction. It was Pumpkin Road. The cabin was supposed to be at the end of this and was reputed to be very secluded. It was just what she needed right now and Emily couldn't wait to settle in. She needed some privacy to set up her equipment and think about what she'd learned so far.

The cabin came into view and Emily didn't see anything strange about it. A single story structure, it looked to be quite solid and constructed of individually hewn logs. The porch across the front was made of pine and boasted a strong railing. The quaint and almost required rocking chair was noticeably absent, as were any fixtures intended to stamp the house with the owner's personality. It was as nondescript as it was sequestered. To complete the picture, the blinds were down in every window. Emily thought it was perfect for her needs.

Emily parked beside the house and carried only her backpack up to the front door. The rest of her gear could wait. She unlocked the door with the keys she'd been given and it swung open easily. Regardless of its appearance, the hinges were well oiled and the house was clean. As soon as she closed the door, her cell phone rang.

"Great timing." Emily dropped her pack and answered the call before her phone could ring a second time. "Baptiste here," she said without hesitation. Only one person had this number.

"Are you alone?" a male voice asked. Emily easily identified Assistant Director Latimer.

"Yes. I've just arrived at the location."

"Any problems?"

Emily hesitated before responding. "A flat tire that shouldn't have been. I stopped last night to wait out a storm and someone let the air out."

Brief silence followed before her caller asked, "Do you think it's related?"

"Possibly, although I haven't seen anyone following me around trying to abduct me."

"Keep your eyes open, Agent Baptiste. Have you learned anything yet?"

"Nothing we didn't already know," she said honestly. "There have been a lot of disappearances up here and I was in the car with the sheriff last night when another missing persons call came in."

"You made contact with local law enforcement?" Latimer didn't sound happy.

"Not in an official capacity, sir." Emily explained the situation, keeping the more personal information to herself. She understood how important the slightest detail could be in undercover work. Her impressions were just as valid as the details since this type of case involved working on her instincts.

"Very well, but you are not to take Sheriff Yang into your confidence. She doesn't exactly have a lot of credence with the Bureau."

"Why is that?" Emily asked curiously.

"Sheriff Yang used to be a Boston homicide detective. She was considered one of the best until about five years ago. There's nothing official in her record, but she just handed in her shield and her piece one day without any explanation. Rumor has it she just couldn't cut it."

"And what's that got to do with asking for her help if I get into a jam?"

"I'll remind you, Agent Baptiste that you are undercover," Latimer snapped in response to her disrespectful tone. "Your orders are not to give yourself away to the local populace, and that includes the sheriff. Do you understand?"

Emily resisted the urge to argue further. She was a senior field agent who could usually choose her assignments. The fact that this one had been forced on her illustrated her mission's importance. On the surface, it was a simple case of disappearances, but Emily had the ability to look beyond the obvious. Now wasn't the time to rock the boat.

"All right, can you at least send me a file on Sheriff Yang? If she is a liability, I'd like to know what I'm up against."

"Way ahead of you. Dossiers on the sheriff, her deputies and other prominent locals were already sent to your account. Now set up your system and contact me on a secured line if you come up with anything. And don't forget, regardless what happens I want you checking in every forty-eight hours."

"Understood, Director."

"Emily," he said, indicating the discussion was about to become personal. "Your father would be proud."

A lump in her throat made it difficult for Emily to speak. It wasn't often that the assistant director of the FBI field office became sentimental, but it always affected her when he did. Latimer's friendship with her father sometimes made it hard for Emily to work with him. He was a constant reminder of her parents' sudden and tragic death five years ago. She hadn't been to the family estate since that day, preferring to keep her mind occupied with work.

Latimer was gone before she could say anything else. Emily pushed the painful thoughts away to focus on the job. She wondered at Assistant Director Latimer's attitude, trying to understand his impressions of Jenna. Jenna seemed quite capable, but it was unusual that she'd turn away from a prominent position to become a local law enforcement officer in such an isolated area. What happened for her to make such a decision?

Unexpectedly, Emily yawned so hard that her eyes watered. She was tired from her late night and early morning. At least the cabin came furnished, courtesy of the agency, and she didn't have to worry about making the bed or stocking the pantry.

Emily hoisted her pack and set it on the small, round kitchen table. Most of her equipment was in the Tahoe, but the important gear she carried with her continually. From the pack, she pulled a police scanner and placed it next to the pack. She tuned it to the local frequency but received only static. Emily didn't really expect otherwise in such a rural area. She rubbed her eyes and decided to shower and take a nap before she looked at the data the Bureau had forwarded.

She left the scanner on the table as she moved over to the cabinets. Emily dug around until she found some coffee and filters. She discovered a coffee maker on the counter and set it up for later. Then she took off her jacket and threw it over a chair before she stripped her t-shirt over her head. A .44 magnum revolver, nicknamed "The Judge", rested in a holster clipped to the front of her waistband. It was her favorite weapon when undercover because merely the sight of it was enough to intimidate anyone. Emily unclipped the holster and started toward the bedroom when the scanner sputtered to life.

"Sheriff Yang, respond." Emily assumed the female voice belonged to the dayshift dispatcher.

"Go ahead, Janet," Jenna answered.

"Sheriff, we just got a report about Charles Freeman's car. Staties found it two miles south of Shepherdsville at mile marker one-eighteen. No sign of the driver, but his cell phone was on the seat and the tank was full. They say it looked like he just vanished into thin air."

Emily snorted. "Ridiculous."

"All right, Janet. I guess I'll have to inform Mrs. Freeman. Ask the Highway Patrol if they can hold off on towing the vehicle until I get a look at it."

"Ten-four, Sheriff. I'll pass it along."

Emily briefly considered the development and then pulled her shirt back on. Shepherdsville was about five or six miles north on Highway 65. She could easily make the trip there and have a look around before Jenna was finished speaking with the distraught aunt, assuming she went there first as she'd just indicated. The only problem would arise if Jenna happened to come along while Emily was still looking. How would she explain her presence?

That would be easy, she decided. She would take the bicycle and say she was out for a ride. Emily was on vacation, after all. Surely, she could convince Jenna that her presence was pure coincidence.

No matter whether Jenna believed her or not, Emily had to investigate. Charles Freeman must have been the one reported missing the night before. He was just another in a long line of disappearances and it was vital she arrive before Jenna picked the scene over.

Twenty-five minutes later, Emily slowed and steered her bicycle from the shoulder into the grass just behind the mile marker post. The car Mr. Freeman had driven was long gone, undoubtedly towed to a police impound lot. The state Highway Patrol had vanished along with the vehicle, but she hoped they had missed a vital piece of evidence. It wasn't as if she could go to the impound lot and ask to see their evidence without blowing her cover. Apparently, the Highway Patrol hadn't listened when Jenna requested they leave the car undisturbed.

It figured. Why was it that not even local law enforcement agencies would cooperate with each other?

Emily stepped off her bike and lowered the kickstand. She pulled the water bottle from its cage and took a long swig of water as she looked up and down the roadway. Preston Highway wasn't as busy as Highway 65 and there weren't any cars nearby for the moment. Emily wandered back and forth on the shoulder, her eyes pinned to the ground. She searched for ten minutes, ignoring the few passing vehicles, but didn't find anything. A peal of thunder made her look up at the gathering clouds.

"Great. Doesn't it do anything but rain around here?"

After pushing the bicycle over to the nearby woods, Emily glanced around for anywhere a human being could enter. The brush was especially thick here for anyone who might think to take a shortcut to a farm or anywhere they would reasonably hope to find help. Likewise, it would be unlikely anyone would attempt to kidnap Freeman and remove him from the site by this route. Besides, who could possibly know he would be at this exact spot at just the right time?

That only left the roadway. Freeman could have walked to town on the shoulder if his car broke down, making him an easier target. If that happened, there wouldn't be a trace of him.

Emily needed more information about the victim. Who was he? Did he have any enemies? From the call she'd intercepted on the police scanner, he might be the first victim with a tie to this area. Was the perpetrator getting bolder or simply desperate?

Finally, Emily decided that investigating the shoulder was pointless. She pushed the kickstand up with her foot and turned the bicycle around. She'd just climbed on and pressed the pedal down on the right when she noticed a cigarette butt lying on the ground, rocking gently in the breeze.

"Hello, what's this?"

As she squatted down, Emily pulled a blue surgical glove out of her shorts pocket and picked up the butt. Logic suggested the cigarette could have been tossed from a passing car or blown up by a strong wind. She didn't think that was the case. The butt couldn't have been here very long because it was relatively dry. The heavy rains the night before would have soaked it. Still, the cigarette might have been deposited this morning after the rain stopped. Either way, it didn't really matter without a suspect to match the DNA on the filter. There might not be any evidence on the cigarette anyway.

"Chesterfields...that's a rare brand. I didn't know they even made these anymore."

Emily tucked the butt into the glove and then shoved it in her pocket just as raindrops began to fall. Though there wasn't anyone to compare to for now, she believed in being thorough. Chances were high that any biological evidence would be worthless but the obscurity of the brand was important in itself.

"That's just terrific," she grumbled, pulling the hood up against the rain.

Emily set off toward Pumpkin Road, thinking about the police report concerning this disappearance. Jenna took the report last night so it should be on file by now. Maybe that would tell her what she needed to know. The rain started in earnest and Emily cast a baleful eye overhead at the storm clouds. It was going to be a long ride back to her temporary residence.

An hour and a half later, she stood warm and snug inside the cabin. Fresh out of the shower, Emily slung a towel around her neck, squatted and flipped back the edge of the braided kitchen rug. Attached to a small trap door, an iron ring embedded into the wood allowed a person access to the well-equipped sublevel. Emily didn't think it was very original, but no one would expect such a thing in a remote hunting cabin. In seconds, she signed on to the FBI's internal database on one of the most elaborate computer systems in the world.

"Elaborate spy network and safe house all rolled into one," she mumbled.

At this point in her career, she was accustomed to how covert the government could be in the most unexpected places. It was just too bad they couldn't tell her anything more than Frank already had. There was nothing here except another missing person. With no evidence to speak of, Emily decided it was time to get to know the locals.

Chapter Five

JENNA STIFLED HER yawn and added a touch of perfume to her wrists and neck. She hadn't managed a lot of sleep in the last few days, but couldn't deny her excitement at seeing Emily again. The sound of an engine driving up outside her home drew a smile from her and Jenna headed for the front door. Emily was already bounding up the steps when Jenna opened it and stepped out.

"Hi." Jenna pulled on a rain slicker and looked out into the storm. "Are you sure you really want to do this? It might be smarter to stay out of the rain and enjoy a nice fire."

Emily grinned and ducked out of the weather onto the porch. "Is that an offer?"

"Uh, no. I just meant a fire is always more enjoyable than the rain. You know?"

"Relax, I'm just kidding. Besides, a little water never hurt anyone. I'm eager for you to show me the local sights."

"How local? I promise you the only excitement in Grays Landing happens at Frank's."

"Louisville, remember? I hear it's not very far and is the next up-and-coming lesbian mecca in the United States."

"Really?" Jenna asked, affecting rapt fascination. "From where do you obtain such interesting information, Miss Bannon?"

Emily shook her head. "That's classified. If I told you that, I'd have to kill you."

"We wouldn't want that. Maybe I could offer to buy you a drink instead."

"Sounds like an offer I can't refuse. Now if we're finished with this battle of clichés, I'll race you to the car."

Jenna nodded and stepped into the rain, headed for the Tahoe. "I thought you weren't afraid of getting wet," she said, opening the door.

"Afraid? No, but that doesn't mean I have to like it."

Emily had left the engine running and the heater on. She put the Tahoe in gear and drove out toward the highway. Jenna noticed Emily was a careful driver, not accelerating too quickly in the mud after two days' worth of rain.

"Which way should I go?"

"Head up 65 North. Locals call it the Kentucky Turnpike, but it's really just a two lane road."

"At least they're an imaginative lot," Emily offered.

Jenna smiled. "And you're very gracious. When I first moved here, I just thought they were all inbred and ignorant. They're actually some of the kindest people I've ever known."

"Where did you move here from?"

"Boston."

"That's quite a move. I know you said you inherited your dad's house, but you could have sold it. Why'd you leave the city?"

Jenna frowned a little and didn't respond immediately. She had the feeling she was being gently interrogated, but couldn't imagine why a stranger would do such a thing. Maybe Emily was simply curious. "Too many people, I suppose. When I came here to put my dad's estate in order, I discovered how peaceful the country could be."

"I can certainly understand that," Emily allowed. "God knows I love hiking and all those other woodsy kind of activities, but I have to admit I enjoy being able to grab a good mocha when I feel like it. I assume you worked law enforcement in the old 'Cradle of Liberty'?"

"Do you always ask so many questions?" Jenna asked, finally starting to feel uncomfortable.

"Sorry," Emily relented. "I get a little carried away, sometimes. The hazards of being a travel writer, I suppose. It's become habit to ask a lot of questions when I'm in a new place."

"What about you?" Jenna asked, half turning to face Emily.

Emily's eyes stayed on the road, but she shrugged. "I'm an open book. What do you want to know?"

They talked for the half hour it took to drive to Louisville. Jenna found Emily to be intelligent, witty, and charming. The weather finally cleared just as they pulled into the parking lot of the most popular lesbian club Jenna knew. Her mood improved with it and suddenly she felt that the night held endless possibilities.

The club was the same as other bars all over the country. It was too loud and the air was thick with the smell of stale beer. An occasional bit of smoke wafted in from the covered patio when a patron opened the door to go outside. Only the company had changed, but it made all the difference. Jenna enjoyed dancing with Emily and seeing people she didn't have to worry about writing tickets or locking up for public intoxication. It felt good just to let go for a while and leave the mantle of responsibility at home.

About an hour later Emily asked, "Am I boring you?"

"No. What makes you ask that?"

Emily smiled and took the drink out of Jenna's hand. She set the glass on the table between them. "You've just yawned for the third time in five minutes."

"I'm sorry." Jenna laughed a little self-consciously. "Too many hours and not enough sleep. It's really nothing against you."

"Come on, let's call it a night. We'll try the date thing again when you've had more rest."

Date? Jenna decided to tackle the issue head on. "Emily, just so that we're perfectly clear, I'm not really available right now. I just can't get involved."

Emily's smile slowly disappeared as she leaned closer. When she was near enough to make Jenna concerned she was about to be kissed Emily said, "Jenna. I'm here for a week, maybe a little longer if I decide to extend my vacation. The point is, I'm not asking you to marry me. I just thought we could have some fun together. If that doesn't extend to the physical, I'm fine with that."

"Really?"

"Really, now let's go. I'm driving. You've been drinking."

"It's your car," Jenna pointed out.

Emily nodded. "That, too."

Emily was acting a little silly, but Jenna felt she was doing it to be funny, not because she was inebriated. Emily had imbibed nothing but mineral water all night. She thought it was really sweet that Emily would try to get Jenna to have a little fun.

"You're kind of weird, you know that?"

Emily chuckled and they drove away from the club. Jenna relaxed into the passenger seat and allowed her eyes to close. It wasn't a long drive back to her house, but closing her eyes for a few minutes wouldn't hurt. She didn't intend to sleep, but the hum of tires against the pavement caused her to nod off.

The Tahoe bounced a little and unexpected sudden brightness caused Jenna to jerk awake. She blinked against the illumination, recognizing a gas station's lights as she sat up. She flashed an apologetic smile to Emily for falling asleep. "Something wrong?"

"Just getting some gas. Go ahead and nap if you want."

"I'm good."

Jenna climbed out of the Chevy and rested her hip against the side of the vehicle, watching Emily move. High cheekbones and a straight nose lent her a classical profile. She was strong and agile, her complexion boasting a bone-deep tan. Emily had the curliest black hair Jenna had ever seen. If someone had asked, Jenna would have speculated Emily's heritage as Greek.

She really was something special, Jenna thought. She wondered why she couldn't just let go and have sex with Emily. She sighed quietly, admitting to herself that she just wasn't over Mandy yet. She wondered if that was even possible.

"Well if it isn't Sheriff Yang."

Emily and Jenna turned toward the voice and Jenna cringed internally. Great, this was just what she needed. The whole town would be speculating about Emily's identity by tomorrow. They'd want to know if the sheriff was becoming romantically involved. In such a rural community, discovering the local sheriff was gay could become a serious problem. The Kurth brothers stood at the pump beside them. If Jenna hadn't been so tired and fixated on Emily, she might have noticed them earlier from the noxious fumes pouring off the diesel tow truck.

"Mike, Joey. What brings you two into Louisville?"

Jenna didn't really care. She was more interested in how Emily suddenly lost all expression. She was watching the two men as if they were a questionable smear on the bottom of her shoe.

"Couple of old geezers broke down out near Shepherdsville. Had to drag their skinny butts all the way here." The younger of the two, Joey, snickered at his brother's response. Mike grinned at him and continued. "Guess they were too good to let Danny take a look at their heap."

Mike punctuated his narrative with a long drag on his cigarette. He'd smoked it almost down to the filter and Jenna wondered that he didn't burn his fingers. Nicotine and lack of hygiene discolored his nails.

Jenna thought both of the men disgusting.

"Don't you know smoking near gasoline is dangerous?" Emily asked slowly.

The question was simple, but Jenna noticed how intently she watched the brothers. Her demeanor suggested tension as well as fascination.

"What are you, the smoking police?"

Mike flicked the still burning butt to the ground near Emily's feet. He smiled, silently daring her to respond to the taunt. Instead, Emily quietly returned the hose to the pump and carefully shut off the handle. She never spoke, but she held Mike's gaze, refusing to react to his attitude.

Finally, Mike glanced toward Jenna. "Nice friend you got there, Sheriff. Sure is a looker."

"Is that the best you can come up with?" Jenna asked, annoyed by his display. "Didn't you get enough of the schoolyard bully thing when you were a kid?"

"Ah, now, don't be like that. I was just being friendly."

Joey whimpered a little and tugged at his brother's shirtsleeve. "Mike, we gotta go."

Anger ghosted across Mike's face, but something else quickly replaced it. It was an expression Jenna wouldn't have expected to see from him. Fear. The emotion evaporated as soon as he realized she was watching. His eyes narrowed as though he was about to say something further, but Joey's whining elevated and Mike finally relented. They climbed back into the tow truck and roared away. Jenna didn't remember seeing them fill up.

"Classy couple of guys," Emily observed. She mashed out the cigarette butt with the toe of her boot, careful to extinguish it completely. Then she bent over to retrieve it, looking at the filter for a moment before standing and throwing it into the trash bin.

"Fortunately, they're not the typical example of people in the area."

"So they just have their own special kind of slimy."

Emily retrieved her receipt from the pump and then climbed back into the Tahoe. They were on the highway driving toward Woeful Pines before Emily spoke again. "I understand Mike, small-minded man who's a legend to no one but himself, but what's up with that other guy?"

"Joey? Younger brother, socially inept, homeschooled. From what I understand, their mom died when Joey was born and their dad died in a hunting accident when they were just kids. Mike was barely old enough to prevent the courts from taking custody of his brother."

Conversation was sporadic from there and Jenna was relieved to see her porch light come into view. It had been a long week, but even as attractive as Emily was, all Jenna wanted was a shower and her bed. She looked at Emily, curious if she was equally as exhausted. From what she'd said, Emily had driven quite a lot lately.

"How far is the cabin where you're staying? You don't have a long drive, I hope."

Emily smiled, stopping in the driveway, and rested her arm along the back of the seat. "Turns out it's not far from here. It's at the end of Pumpkin Road."

With Emily's change in position, the atmosphere suddenly became more intimate. Jenna could feel the heat from her body and tried to think of something to say. "The old cabin? I...I don't think I've ever seen the lights on there."

Emily shifted closer and Jenna gulped.

"Don't I get a good night kiss?" Emily asked softly, her lips a breath away.

Jenna leaned forward, eager for the contact, but turned her head at the last second to place a chaste kiss to Emily's cheek.

"You're dangerous," Jenna whispered when she pulled back.

"You've said that before. Are you brave enough to take me on?"

Jenna was tempted for a long moment, but finally she took a deep breath and opened the door. "Good night."

"Chicken."

Jenna laughed and slammed the door. She waved briefly and then walked to the house. She noticed that Emily waited until she was inside before driving away and felt strangely touched by the gesture.

The evening passed slowly, with the effort to keep her thoughts focused on everyday mundane details. Eventually, she ran out of excuses to sit in the chair and try to keep her mind occupied. She pushed out of the easy chair and readied for bed, but her efforts proved in vain.

Jenna lay between the soft sheets staring at the ceiling. She'd been exhausted all evening, practically falling asleep in her wine. Now all she did was toss, turn, and thump the pillow in an effort to get comfortable. What was wrong with her? She knew it wasn't the company. Emily was hard to resist. That was it, she suddenly realized. Emily was the problem.

The moment the Kurth brothers approached them at the Kwik-Pro station kept playing in Jenna's head. More specifically, Emily's reaction to Mike vexed her. Jenna's instincts as a top-notch homicide investigator were under-utilized, but they hadn't abandoned her altogether and they told her that Emily was hiding something.

First, there was her familiarity with law enforcement jargon, passed off as something gleaned from watching television. By itself, it meant nothing, but Emily's body language added another dimension. She moved like a cop. Emily's eyes were always watching, noticing everything in her vicinity. Then there was her guarded response to Mike. Emily hadn't seemed intimidated or threatened by his thuggish behavior.

"She was sizing him up," Jenna muttered. "And why the potent curiosity about a cigarette butt?"

She tossed back the covers and stood in one fluid motion. Before she really thought about it, she was almost dressed. In minutes, Jenna was out the door and driving toward the department substation. She keyed the cipher lock and entered. No one was around to see her less than professional attire, but Jenna didn't really think a pair of jeans and a Boston Celtics sweatshirt was out of place in the middle of the night.

Jenna thought she was probably way off base but logged on to the computer before she could change her mind. Robbie had run Emily's plates and everything checked out, but she wondered if there wasn't more to the story. If she were wrong, Jenna wouldn't have to tell Emily about her suspicions.

After an hour of digging through computer records, Jenna sat back in her chair and closed her eyes to consider all that she discovered. Visions of Emily's mischievous grin drifted in her mind and Jenna's head bobbed toward her chest. She forced her eyes open. Jenna stood and carried her mug across the bullpen. As she refilled her cup with the last bit of coffee in the pot, Jenna thought about the little she'd gleaned from her impromptu computer search.

It didn't surprise her that Emily had a Bachelors in Wildlife Management. She knew Emily loved the outdoors. However, the military background was unexpected. Four years in the military after college was impressive. Jenna just wondered why Emily chose regular enlistment rather than become an officer. Her college degree was the sole requirement for induction into the officer corps.

Jenna walked back over to her desk and read through the timeline she'd hastily jotted onto a notepad.

"Graduated high school at eighteen, Columbus University graduate at twenty-two and honorable discharge at twenty-eight. Busy girl."

Emily's employment history was a little sporadic after that, but not unusual for a freelance writer. Wait a minute. Why hadn't she seen it before? If Emily joined the Marine Corps for a four-year stint straight out of college, why was there a six-year gap before her discharge? Someone screwed up on the math and Jenna thought the background information reeked of make-believe.

Wide awake with the discovery, Jenna started digging through every official channel she could think of. Forty minutes later, she sat back with a snarl of frustration.

There was nothing else to find, not even a listing for her family anywhere in the Columbus area. Emily's story held up only until someone scratched the surface. Regardless, why was she here? Was Emily looking into all of their missing cases? If so, it was about time as far as Jenna was concerned. She'd only been telling the district office that she needed help since this rash of disappearances started. It still raised the question of why Louisville's Major Crimes Unit sent someone in undercover and didn't tell her. They couldn't possibly think Jenna was involved, but it seemed someone didn't trust her.

Jenna sipped the cold, bitter coffee and shuddered in revulsion. Then she logged off the computer and started for home. She needed some rest for what she was about to do, and more than a little luck. If Emily was from the district headquarters, then someone had ordered her to investigate on her own. That didn't mean Jenna couldn't shadow her and provide assistance if needed. Emily wouldn't even realize she had a tail.

Chapter Six

EMILY SMILED AS she considered how she'd fooled Jenna into thinking she'd tossed the cigarette butt into the trash. She'd really palmed it instead. She had removed it upon arrival at the cabin to compare to the one she found on the roadside.

The FBI had seen fit to include a small but sophisticated lab in the basement area and it had come in handy. Emily rubbed her eyes and then looked at the strips on the autoradiograph again. There wasn't any doubt the DNA swabbed from both cigarette filters belonged to the same individual. She'd suspected that might be the case when she noticed the Chesterfield brand Mike smoked was the same as the butt discovered near the abduction site.

She speculated on the odds of finding Mike Kurth's DNA at the exact spot where someone went missing. Was it just coincidence? Did he just happen to drive by that mile marker and toss his smoke from the car window, or was it proof of his direct involvement? If it was evidence, it was thin at best. Emily would need more than this. When they met Mike and Joey at the station, he'd mentioned being out near Shepherdsville to tow an older couple. Chances were he'd thrown the butt from his truck on the way back. If he'd been directly involved in the kidnapping the night before, the cigarette she'd discovered on scene would have been soaked by the previous night's storm. Still, the fact that both cigarettes contained his DNA was a compelling bit of information.

Emily checked her watch and realized how late it had grown. There was no time like the present to get started and the cover of night would help conceal her surveillance of the Kurth brothers.

Emily chose her attire carefully, keeping the weather, terrain and darkness in mind. She'd already pulled up a local map and printed it off so she knew exactly where to find her quarry. Focused and determined, Emily reminded herself that these men might seem simple, but they were smart enough and strong enough to overpower seven people and drag them off somewhere without leaving evidence to tie them to the scene. She wasn't about to become another victim. With that thought in mind, Emily headed out the door.

Thirty minutes later, she selected the best place to keep an eye on the Kurth brothers and scaled the trunk of a massive tree. She was fortunate to find some low-hanging limbs to assist. Thankful that the weather had turned clear and warm, Emily nestled into the branches of the oak tree and tried to get comfortable. At least her tactical gear blended well with the shadows. If anyone chanced to look her way, she doubted they would see her.

Emily cautioned herself not to get cocky. The Kurths wouldn't need to see her to know she was there if she fell out of the tree.

Once settled, Emily inserted an earpiece and immediately heard movement. The small QT Micro-bug she'd attached to the lower corner of the living room window worked perfectly. It was only a quarter of an inch square and had an extended range. Considering the closest concealment to the house was in a tree fifty yards away, that was a particularly useful feature.

The Kurth homestead was a ten-acre spread in the thickest woods around Woeful Pines. The business end of their property, the towing company, fronted State Highway 1494, but the main house was more isolated. A loose gravel road that was really more of a trail, led back to a clearing where the house was situated. The trees there were deliberately torn out, making an unseen approach to the home unlikely.

Unless someone had special training, Emily thought. Now if they'd just give her something she could use so she could stop playing Queen of the Jungle. Emily would much rather be taking Jenna Yang's clothes off than sitting on two hillbilly brothers. She could feel her IQ dropping by the minute.

Emily heard the sound of a man clearing his throat and tried to peer around the scattered hulks of rusted out vehicles littering the landscape, but that was impossible. The Bushnell night goggles didn't shed any light on the subject either so Emily was limited to listening in on the conversation.

"Do we really gotta do this again?" It was Joey's whimpering voice. Even in the sanctity of his own home, he didn't seem to have any confidence.

"You know how it is, and I'm getting tired of explaining it to you. It's us or them."

"But it just don't seem right."

"I'll tell you what ain't right," Mike snarled. "Us taking their place. Is that what you want?"

"No, but maybe we could tell 'em..."

"What, that there aren't anymore? You think Garran's gonna buy that?"

Joey didn't respond, and Emily instinctively leaned forward trying to hear more. Who was Garran and whose place would Joey take doing what? Whatever it was, there was no denying the trepidation in their voices. These two were scared.

"You need to relax, Joey. Things are going fine just like they are."

"Oh, yeah? Things might be okay with Garran, but what about that woman hanging around with the sheriff?"

"Yeah, I could get into that," Mike said suggestively, causing Emily to shudder.

"Didn't you recognize her? It was the same woman from Danny's old gas station."

"So what if she was? She never saw us so who cares?"

"Louisville ain't the first time they were together. Cheryl said she saw them having breakfast at Frank's. What if she's a Fed?"

Emily couldn't believe how quickly Joey had arrived at the right conclusion. Out of everyone she'd met so far, he was the last one she'd have expected to put things together. Fortunately, Mike's chauvinism prevented him from drawing the same conclusion.

"The Feds don't hire women. That's only on TV. Women are too mushy for jobs like that."

"That's what you said about the county hiring a female sheriff," Joey pointed out smugly.

"Are you sassing me?"

Mike's tone had turned threatening and Joey quickly backed down. "No, of course not. It's just that I'm worried. What if they know something? The regent will kill us."

Joey's voice ended on a high-pitched whine that would have been annoying if Emily hadn't been impressed by his fear.

"Shut up. Nobody knows anything and they're not going to know as long as we keep our mouths shut and do what we're told."

Conversation trailed off after that, leaving Emily with several unanswered questions. The mention of a regent implied someone with authority who might be calling the shots on some type of elaborate operation, but it had to be a self-given title. Regents didn't exist in the United States, and she doubted anyone under a monarchy would be dealing with two low-life individuals in the Kentucky hills.

The more answers she had, the more confusing the situation became. Emily was already sure that the Kurth brothers were involved in the recent disappearances of people traveling through the area, but now she believed they had help. More than that, the Kurths were pawns and appeared to be acting under duress. Were the victims still alive and being used for some nefarious purpose? That had to be the answer. If Mike and Joey acted on their own, they would probably be serial killers out for the sport. Instead, it sounded like someone was giving them orders to kidnap people and take them somewhere for some unknown reason. She briefly considered the possibility of human trafficking.

This case was getting bigger and more involved by the second. For a moment, Emily considered contacting her boss and asking him to put a task force together. Then she realized it was a little premature for that. She was in the perfect position to get more information about where the people were and who was giving the orders. If the FBI closed in too soon, they would have nothing but the Kurths. The ringleader would vanish like smoke in the wind.

More determined than ever, Emily continued listening through the miniature receiver until all the lights in the house went out and silence was her only companion. Nothing else of any consequence had been said and the little Emily did get wasn't specific enough to tie them to any criminal activity. It did point to another person's involvement, however. Slowly, the pieces were dropping into place and she had to school herself to be patient. Eventually she would be able to see the bigger picture and then she could act.

Emily remained in place throughout the night on the off chance that the Kurth brothers were restless sleepers. She hoped something else would happen during the night or another important discussion would occur. It didn't and she was left to sit and try to stay awake. A slight lessening of darkness along the horizon announced dawn's imminent arrival so she slid out of the tree and disappeared into the woods. Emily planned to return the following evening and every night after that until she heard something of substance.

It was a short trip through dense woods to reach her Tahoe and even though it was a white vehicle, Emily could barely make it out in the darkness. She'd pulled the Chevy into the brush and covered it with some loose debris so it wouldn't easily be seen from the road. The average citizen wasn't a concern, but Sheriff Yang wasn't stupid. If she found the vehicle, she would demand to know what Emily was doing and until she had concrete evidence Emily wasn't about to involve local law enforcement. Not only were those her orders, but she preferred to work alone anyway. It was less complicated that way and she was the only one to blame if something went wrong.

Less than ten minutes later, Emily drove up in front of the cabin. She caught the reflection of metal off to her left and grinned. Apparently, Jenna was even smarter than Emily thought. Now she had Sheriff Yang staking out the cabin. Emily wondered what had tipped her off.

Emily wasn't concerned, but she would have to take a few extra precautions. To that end, she drove up beside the cabin on the opposite side from where Jenna watched. The back door to the cabin wasn't visible from Jenna's angle so at least she wouldn't see Emily entering the cabin in black tactical gear, complete with throwing knife and utility belt.

While she slept and recharged, Jenna could sit and yawn in the seat of her Jeep. Emily considered bringing her a cup of coffee, but that was taking things a little far. Instead, Emily stripped, showered, and climbed naked under the covers. In a way, she felt like Jenna was watching over her and she easily fell asleep.

Her slumber was deep and undisturbed by dreams. She awakened at eleven-thirty, refreshed and curious to know if Jenna still maintained her vigil. Emily slipped out of bed and moved the curtains aside enough to peer into the bright day. The Jeep was gone and she smiled as she headed toward the kitchen in search of coffee.

Jenna had spent all night keeping tabs on Emily and now she was off to the daily grind. Emily wondered if her intrepid sheriff felt the effects of too little sleep.

In a way, Emily found it humorous that Jenna considered her some type of risk when it was really the Kurths responsible for the present situation. Then again, what did that say for Jenna's deductive skills? Would Emily really want someone who was so far off the mark to watch her back? Perhaps Latimer was right after all. Emily just hoped she didn't need any assistance once the case started to break.

Once showered, dressed, and fueled for the day, Emily stored everything she thought she might need in a backpack and set off through the woods. Her general direction was the tow company. It was easy enough to figure out they were using the business as a cover. If she wanted to catch them in action, watching the office was her best bet since she couldn't know where they were at every minute of the day.

An hour later, Emily emerged from the woods near State Highway 1494. Had she taken her car, she'd have arrived at Kurth Towing in five minutes, but with Sheriff Yang keeping tabs she had to be stealthier. Emily could have ridden her bicycle, but there was always the possibility that Jenna would drive by her on the road and at this juncture, Emily preferred to stay below the radar. An instinct, something she couldn't explain, told her that she was getting close to something big and she had to avoid any distractions. Jenna Yang was definitely a distraction.

An image of liquid brown eyes came to mind and Emily had to force herself to concentrate. The smallest detail could make or break a case and now was no time for woolgathering.

The tow company appeared deserted. There weren't any cars around, not even the tow truck, and she found the front door locked. Emily didn't know if that was normal. Did the boys drive around all day, looking for stranded motorists instead of waiting for a call inside the office? It was possible. She sighed in frustration and found a place to wait in the shade that was out of sight of the front door to settle down. If no one appeared within the next two hours, she would circle around to the main house and see if anything was happening there.

Time passed and Emily waved a lazy buzzing fly away. She could be patient when it was called for, but Emily had the feeling she was simply wasting her time. She left her place of concealment and spent a few minutes traveling carefully around the house, peering in through windows and checking doors. The place was locked up tight and without exigent circumstances or a warrant, she wasn't about to break in. At last frustrated, she decided to go to the cabin for a change of clothes and some dinner. The Kurths were probably out working and most predators saved their extracurricular activities for dark fall. She'd be back in place in plenty of time.

After a quick meal of canned ravioli, Emily donned her black outfit and carefully fitted a throwing knife to the small of her back. She opted out of the .44 magnum since it was too large and heavy to carry on the formfitting outfit. Instead, she attached an ankle holster and inserted a

.32 Tomcat. The weapon was significantly smaller, but still deadly. In deference to the rain, she slipped on a black slicker. A dark blue muffler completed her wardrobe, but Emily pulled the muffler down around her neck. Unless the temperatures dropped with the oncoming night, she wouldn't really need it. She simply wanted to be prepared. Once dressed, Emily returned to the Kurth property and parked her Tahoe in the usual location. She covered the vehicle with brush just as she had previously and then set off through the woods. This was becoming such a habit that she had to caution herself against complacency.

When she arrived on the Kurth property, Emily came up from the rear of the house. She didn't see any cars, other than the broken down heaps, so she headed for her usual hiding spot. Emily climbed into the branches and once settled she had a better view. She could see a police black and white in addition to the tow truck and another car. Worried that she had missed out on something vital, Emily switched on the remote for the micro-bug and slid the earpiece into her right ear. Silence greeted her. She tried switching the control off and then on again with the same result.

Emily frowned and climbed out of the boughs of her favorite tree. For some reason the micro-bug wasn't working. There wasn't even the static of an open line. It was late afternoon and the sun was beginning to set. Some clouds had started forming, but they didn't currently pose any threat. Neither were they good for creating shadows she could use for concealment. Emily needed to check her equipment, but getting close to the house without someone seeing her was going to prove difficult. She needed to be very careful. People were notorious for being pissed off when they found a stranger sneaking around their property.

She sprinted from car to car and then to a stray burn barrel, closing in on her objective. The living room window on the side nearest the woods was her target. All of her senses were on alert in case someone stepped outside. In seconds, she reached her goal, but the bug wasn't where she'd left it. She thought it must have fallen off.

Emily looked around quickly to ensure she was still alone and then started searching in the weeds. Nothing.

The hair stood up on the back of her neck and Emily froze. She hadn't heard anything, not a sound, but somehow she knew she wasn't alone. Emily closed her eyes and lowered her head for a second before she turned around. Two people stood in front of her. Emily started in surprise. She was losing her edge.

"Uh hi, Deputy. Would you believe that my car broke down and I was looking for a lift? I heard someone out here owns a towing company."

The overweight deputy with the three-day beard growth just stood watching her. His companion, Mike Kurth, also had little to say. He did at least sneer at her.

"No? How about, I was just in the neighborhood?"

Clayton Brown removed the toothpick from his mouth. "Looks like you got a trespasser, Mikey."

"Yep, looks that way. Any ideas what I should do about that, Clay?"

"Well, the law says you have the right to defend yourself."

Mike snorted. "She don't look like much of a threat to me."

"She does if she has a gun. Maybe we should search her to be sure."

The men glanced at each other and Emily got the message. They intended to plant a gun on her, if they didn't find the ankle holster, so they could shoot her. If they did that, the joke would be on them. She'd have them disarmed and restrained before they blinked. All she needed was an opening.

"No, we're not going to do that. I have another idea. A better idea."

Mike reached behind him and pulled out a pistol he had obviously concealed in the small of his back. It wasn't an ordinary handgun, but Emily recognized the type and its purpose. Her heart rate increased as he calmly aimed the weapon in her direction.

"Hey, did you get that out of my car?" Brown asked.

"You don't want to do that," Emily objected. "If I go missing, a whole lot of people are going to show up asking questions."

Kurth bobbed his head as if he was considering her assessment, but then he said, "Actually, I really do want to do that. In fact, you're just in time to pull my butt out of the fire. It's time for another delivery."

"Delivery?" Emily had the feeling this conversation wasn't going her way.

"Good night."

Emily quickly reached for the throwing knife at the small of her back. She wasn't fast enough, unable to compete with the speed generated by a tranq gun. The weapon made a hissing sound when it fired and she felt the sharp prick of the tipped barb embed itself in her shoulder. The tranquilizer flowed into her system and Emily only had time to gasp before the lights went out.

Chapter Seven

"SHERIFF? SHERIFF!"

JENNA jumped slightly and sloshed hot coffee across her hand. She jerked again in reaction and this time some of the scalding beverage landed in her lap.

"Shit!"

She carefully set the cup on her desk, wiping absently at the mess while she looked across the bullpen toward Janet Wise. The dayshift dispatcher was trying not to laugh but amusement danced in her blue eyes.

"What?"

"Sorry," the younger woman apologized somewhat insincerely. "I just asked if you were okay. You were in the same position for so long, I thought you'd fallen asleep."

"I'm fine." Jenna stood and walked over to the kitchenette for a wet paper towel. "At least I was before I scorched the flesh off my crotch."

Janet snickered and went back to her paperwork while Jenna dabbed at the wet spot on her trousers, making the stain even worse.

What was she doing anyway, Jenna wondered. She felt exhausted from chasing Emily around at night because she thought...what? That Emily was some sort of ninja assassin sent by the government to uncover conspiracies in Woeful Pines? Please. She was just some woman on vacation who liked to keep odd hours. The information in the computer files was probably meaningless. So Emily was cute? That was no reason for Jenna to stalk her. Now Jenna was falling asleep at her desk and couldn't even focus on work. She decided that was enough.

"Janet, I'm going home. Call me if Deputy Randall can't handle it."

The dispatcher looked surprised, but had the sense not to question her boss. "Okay, Sheriff Yang."

Jenna had just settled into the Jeep when a huge yawn caused tears to leak from the corners of her eyes. She started the car and pulled out of the lot with visions of her pillow dancing in her head. It felt like days since she'd enjoyed a decent sleep. Two miles down the road, her radio sputtered to life.

"Sheriff Yang, respond."

"You've got to be kidding me," she complained before picking up the mic. "Go ahead, Janet."

"Sheriff, Jake Taylor just called. Says he had a blowout and went off the shoulder near Pike's Bend. He called for the Kurth brothers to pull him out of the ditch, but they didn't answer the phone."

Jenna silently counted to five and then asked, "And where's Deputy Randall?"

"Oh, he's up at Mill Creek. Ben Jeffries was complaining about Old Man Crandall's moonshine still again. He's trying to keep them from killing each other."

Perfect. "Do you still have Jake on the phone?"

"Yeah."

"Tell him I'll be there in a few minutes to haul him out with the winch."

"Right, Sheriff. I'll try not to bother you again."

Jenna didn't bother to respond. She hung up the mic and picked up speed. Five minutes later, she turned left on Clermont Road and spotted Jake standing near the shoulder. At first glance, he looked like a mountain man, bushy beard reaching his chest, black eyes glittering in a dangerous manner. Jenna grinned when she saw him. Jake was a nice man with a PhD in botany.

She eased off the road with the front of the Jeep angled toward his white Honda Civic. The shoulder was steep, at almost a thirty-degree incline. Jake definitely needed help pulling his car out of the ditch. The Jeep was equipped with a winch on the front end, standard equipment for these rural settings. In no time, the vehicle was back on the road and Jenna waited until Jake had changed the flat. At least he had a spare and she wouldn't have to ferry him back and forth for a replacement.

Twenty minutes later, Jake thanked her and drove away. Jenna was free to head for home, but she started wondering where Mike and Joey were. Those two never missed the opportunity to make a few dollars. Janet said they hadn't answered the phone when Jake called for a tow, but Jenna knew they always carried a cell with them.

Jenna rubbed her eyes and tried to ignore the headache she felt coming on. It was nearing five o'clock and she wanted nothing more than to go home and straight to bed. She would just drive by their house first and make sure everything was all right. After that, she was going home and she would not chase after the elusive Ms. Bannon tonight.

The morning had dawned clear and bright, but storm clouds had started moving in again around early afternoon. They obscured the sun now and the day began to have the feel of early evening. Jenna hated the rainy season. When she turned off the main road toward the Kurth homestead, trees pressed in on both sides and long shadows reinforced that impression. Jenna's body responded to the dark, urging her toward sleep. Her head nodded forward and she forced her eyes open, shaking her head to clear the cobwebs.

She almost turned around, but realized she was less than a mile from the house. Jenna nosed the vehicle past a fallen tree and into the clearing. She could see the two-story residence as well as the scattered remnants of vehicles dotting the landscape. Jenna wondered why the Kurths kept the old junkers. Did they really think they were going to fix them up and sell them?

Jenna spotted the tow truck and decided the brothers had knocked off early for the day. Question answered. Satisfied, Jenna navigated a tight three-point turn and headed back down the private road. She happened to glance in her side mirror and slammed on the brakes without thinking about it.

What was Deputy Brown's patrol car doing out here? He wasn't scheduled for duty for another two hours and he knew it was against policy to use the county vehicle for private business.

By themselves, each of the tiny incidents of the day meant nothing. If people wanted to take the day off from work that was no big deal. If a deputy decided to promote public relations, there was nothing wrong with that. However, in the five years she'd lived here, the Kurths never took a day off and Deputy Clayton Brown didn't give a damn about public relations.

Something was going on that she needed to know about. Jenna reached down and flipped the vehicle controls into four-wheel drive. The Jeep bounced as she pulled off the road and into the scrub brush. Jenna drove slowly back toward the house but stopped as soon as she had a clear view of the front door. The weeds were tall enough to conceal the vehicle and any stray glints of metal could easily be overlooked considering how much debris already littered the area.

Jenna reached into the glove compartment and removed a pair of binoculars. She trained her sights on the front door and prepared to watch for as long as it took.

Three hours later, she shifted uncomfortably in her seat. So far, she hadn't seen anyone move inside the house though the lights had come on some time ago. She was reluctant to leave because the patrol car still sat in the yard and Brown was an hour late for his shift. Jenna knew he wasn't the most reliable officer, but she didn't think he would completely ignore his responsibilities without a good reason. She just couldn't imagine what it could be and until she did, Jenna wasn't going anywhere.

Except the bathroom, she thought squirming around some more. It was dark. No one would see her.

Jenna ensured that the dome light was switched off before she opened the car door. A few steps away from the vehicle proved far enough for her purpose. She had barely refastened her trousers when Jenna heard the sound of raised voices. Struggling with her gun belt, she held it with one hand and rushed back into the vehicle. Jenna grabbed the binoculars and looked toward the house. With the onset of darkness, she couldn't see very much. She could just make out Deputy Brown and Cheryl Brenner, the waitress from the diner. They were yelling at each other, but Jenna only caught snatches of what they were saying. Cheryl got into her car and drove away. She would have left tread behind if there had been any pavement available.

What was that about?

The front door opened again before Jenna could speculate further.

Mike and Joey Kurth walked out onto the porch, but they were so close to each other that they seemed off balance. Brown didn't seem inclined to assist as he followed them. The brothers carried something heavy and awkward between them. Whatever it was, the object was rolled up in a rug. Jenna couldn't really tell what it was because of the darkness. She lowered the binoculars and tried to make sense of what she was seeing.

Was that...? No, it was way too cliché, but Jenna could have sworn it looked like a body.

Jenna heard the trunk of Deputy Brown's patrol car thump closed. A few seconds later, the vehicle started and headlights came on. Jenna slumped down in the seat even though there was no way they could see her. The Kurth's tow truck also fired up and followed the cruiser slowly down the lane headed for the highway. Instinct filled in the blanks to her questions. She'd seen a body wrapped in a rug tossed into the trunk of a police car.

Automatically, Jenna wondered if these people could be involved in the other disappearances around the area. The brothers certainly had the means to find stranded motorists and she didn't put it above Deputy Brown to abuse his authority. She had nothing more than speculation as far as that situation was concerned, but she did know they were up to something now. Someone was in trouble.

As soon as the vehicles passed, Jenna started her Jeep. She pulled around to get back onto the lane but kept her lights off. When they merged with other traffic, she would have to switch her lights on or become a hazard. Fortunately, other cars would also provide camouflage.

Jenna followed the battered tow truck and police car down the back roads, forming a crude convoy. She trailed them with her lights off and at a considerable distance, far enough away to avoid detection yet close enough not to lose sight of her target. She was tempted to pull them over and see if it really was a person inside the rug. She had the probable cause for such a stop, but held back for a variety of reasons.

It occurred to her this tied in with the plague of disappearances, but there was more. All of those kidnapped were driving through on their way to somewhere else, and reported some type of car trouble. This scenario didn't fit. Then there was Cheryl and Deputy Brown. Their presence indicated involvement. How many others were mixed up in this? Jenna felt strangely betrayed. She had lived with these people and trusted them. Could they really be responsible for all the recent pain and suffering? If so, she was going to need to reconsider her career. She'd fancied herself a better detective. Jenna remembered Emily's reaction to the brothers. Even she, a newcomer to the area, seemed to notice something off about them.

She recalled how Emily's demeanor changed when they encountered Mike. After that, Emily had become scarce and Jenna was surprised to discover she missed spending time with her. Jenna had started thinking Emily was some type of undercover investigator. Had she figured out what Jenna somehow managed to miss?

Brown eyes widened in shock and concern when it occurred to her who was inside the rug. Suddenly, all thoughts of professionalism flew out the window. She had intended to gather evidence to expose the extent of the kidnapping ring before intervening but timing had just become everything. Her foot pressed down harder on the accelerator in an effort to close the gap to her prey.

Jenna prepared to hit the lights and sirens, but the brothers suddenly pulled onto an old logging trail and stopped. The unanticipated move kept her hand off the switch. They were deep in the woods and backup would take a long time in arriving. Jenna realized she'd never been to this place before, but the hulking mounds of earth visible through the trees told her they were near the local cave systems. The Kentucky hills boasted extensive caverns and many of those were popular tourist attractions. These, however, were well off the beaten path.

She started to exit the SUV when Jenna realized her Sam Browne was still unfastened from her impromptu bathroom break. She hitched the heavy belt up with one hand as she climbed out and carefully closed the door. Jenna pulled her uniform back into place, following quietly as she did. In the time that it took her to close in, Deputy Brown helped the brothers unload their cargo from the cruiser. Then he set off on his own, ostensibly to return to duty. Jenna couldn't follow everyone and if she tried to call for backup, Deputy Brown would intercept the radio transmission. She chose to go after the Kurths and try to rescue their victim.

Mike and Joey grunted and cursed enough to make following them down a game trail fairly easy. The fact that one of them carried a flashlight ensured she wouldn't lose them in the darkness. Jenna carried her own light at her waist, but turning it on would give her presence away. She couldn't take the chance.

In the car, Jenna had been ready to stop the brothers and demand to see what, or who, was inside the rug. Now, she schooled herself to patience, sure she was about to discover the meaning behind all of these shenanigans. Most of all, she wanted to keep Emily safe, but couldn't ignore the chance to find any of the other victims.

Up ahead, the boys ducked inside a substantial opening in the rock face. Jenna waited a second and then followed quietly. Her eyes needed a second to adjust, but she didn't take the time. If there was more than one tunnel inside the cave, she might lose them. Jenna kept one hand on the stone wall and walked toward the bobbing light source. At one point, her toe caught a protruding rock and she almost tripped. Jenna bit off a curse and shuffled forward, hoping the Kurths would stop soon.

"Hurry up, Joey. We're burning daylight."

Joey grunted under the weight he carried. "The sun's already down."

"I know that, you idiot. It's an expression."

"Sit her down, Mike. I gotta rest for a second."

"Suck it up," the elder brother sneered. "I don't want Garran to think we're not coming."

Joey didn't respond, but a little farther in Mike said, "Hold on, I need the transmitter."

Jenna stood less than ten feet away, crouched up against the rock wall at the edge of illumination cast by Mike's flashlight. The rug lay on the dirt floor while Joey stretched his back and caught his breath. Mike searched briefly for something in his pockets. He pulled out a device Jenna couldn't identify in the darkness and aimed it at a column of rock. It was just another pile of stone, the same color and appearance as the rest of the cave. She held her breath in anticipation.

Inconceivably, a small green glow started near the base of stone.

"Let's go," Mike ordered.

He shoved the transmitter back into his coat pocket and bent over to grasp the end of the carpet. Joey hefted the other end and the brothers stepped sideways across the front of the pillar toward the wall. Then they stepped into the surface of the cave and vanished.

Jenna blinked in the sudden darkness and reached for her flashlight. She clicked it on and quickly trained the beam on the spot the Kurths had occupied. They were gone, but the green luminescence remained, standing out clearly against the stone. This just wasn't possible.

Jenna rushed toward the wall, convinced there was an opening concealed in shadows. She worried the brothers would get too far ahead to follow. The stone barrier appeared solid, impenetrable. Jenna raised her hand to explore the surface, expecting cold, solid rock. Maybe there was a trigger to open some kind of hidden access.

Palm out, she reached for the wall, but her hand passed right through the stone. When it did, Jenna felt a strong tingling similar to pins and needles covering the invisible limb. Adrenaline surged in her veins and fear left a sour taste in her mouth. Her heart demanded she take a leap of faith and pursue, but her head insisted she'd become trapped inside the hill and suffocate. From the corner of her eye, she noticed the green light pulse and start to dim. She was running out of time.

Whatever Mike carried destabilized the stone. This probably led to another tunnel, but where did those two get such technology? She couldn't worry about it right now. They were getting away with Emily.

That thought alone was the deciding factor. It was her duty to try to save the helpless woman if there was any way possible. Jenna took a deep breath, closed her eyes, and stepped into the cave wall. Part of her expected to bounce back off solid matter. Instead, the tingling she'd experienced on her hand encompassed her entire body. It felt like insects repeatedly biting her skin, but before she could draw breath to scream, it was over. Jenna fell forward onto her hands and knees, panting and trying to slow her racing heart.

After a few moments, her body began to calm. Jenna looked up and was surprised to discover forest all around. A gust of cold wind whipped down her collar, causing her to shiver. Jenna stood and buttoned her jacket. She retrieved her flashlight from the ground, pointing all around in search of her quarry. There was no sign of them. She didn't know what had just happened, but she had to stop the Kurths. She'd kill them if anything happened to Emily.

Jenna refused to analyze that last thought and looked overhead past the treetops. She realized the sky wasn't as dark and thought the hillside must have been blocking the sun. She could just make out the last bit of blue before night fell. A twig snapping in the distance caused her to focus in on the sound. The noise seemed almost hollow, more of an echo, but recognizable as she struck off quickly in hot pursuit. Within minutes, Jenna had difficulty drawing breath. Her muscles burned and she felt as though she'd run three miles. She considered that the elevation at this locale must be higher than she was accustomed to and the air must be thinner. Or it was a product of passing through the iridescent barrier.

Just then, Jenna realized she was closing in on Mike and Joey. The flashlight beam had stopped moving. She slowed to avoid making noise that would give her presence away and eased up to the edge of a large clearing. Mike and Joey had laid their burden in the center of the field and it concerned Jenna that the occupant still hadn't moved. They seemed to be waiting for something.

Jenna took a deep breath to quiet her aching lungs. The forest smelled different. While the scent of dirt remained the same, the vegetation seemed slightly more pungent. She frowned as she looked around and didn't recognize any of the trees species or shrubs near where she was standing. In the darkness, the colors looked unfamiliar as well. She couldn't be sure, but what she'd assumed to be a green vine against the nearest trunk now looked yellow. It wasn't that far off. She'd seen yellow weeds before.

Still, these minute differences nagged at her and added up to something that she couldn't quite put her finger on. Jenna raised her hand to push aside a small tree branch directly in her path. She yanked it back with a hiss when she felt a sharp stabbing pain. Even in the shadows, she could see blood welling from small punctures in her skin, but the wounds were far from life threatening. They weren't much more than pinpricks. Peering closely at the tree limb, Jenna noticed there were spikes that resembled thorns lining each of the leaves on this particular tree. She'd heard of trees that boasted thorns on the branches and even the trunk, but she'd never seen them on leaves before.

She shook her hand and tried to put the stinging out of her mind. Looking to the stars overhead to get her bearings, Jenna gasped. She blinked and shook her head, but the image didn't change. The moon filled the night sky, so huge that it looked as though it was about to crash into the planet. Unlike the lunar orb Jenna was familiar with, this one was awash in blues, whites, and greens. Beside it was a second, smaller moon.

The breath left her in a rush and Jenna dropped onto the ground with her head between her knees as she tried to make sense of what she'd seen. Dizziness swam in her head and she barely resisted losing consciousness. It was a dream. It had to be.

Even as she railed against the truth, Jenna knew it was useless. The place in the cave must have been some kind of doorway, but to what? This was definitely not Earth unless the planet had just pulled in another orbiting moon. Jenna felt like she'd just stepped into an Isaac Asimov novel.

A whirring sound caught her attention and Jenna looked toward the clearing. Mike and Joey were on their feet, watching for something over the tree line. Seconds later, Jenna had that disconnected feeling again. Two flying machines zipped through the air toward the brothers. Each of the machines had one occupant. Clearly made of metal, the contraptions resembled discs approximately four feet in diameter. A clear canopy covered the top of the disc, protecting the driver. Flanking the discs were four other people, but they weren't inside any machines of their own. These people were flying independently, without helmet, goggles or any equipment Jenna could see.

Jetpacks? Jenna didn't think so. At this point, Jenna was past questions or reasoning. The shock from witnessing such an incredible sight made her feel like throwing up. Fighting off the urge, she could only watch in amazement. The twin moons illuminated every detail.

The discs settled slowly to the ground and the canopies opened. A large man in the leading craft climbed out and sauntered toward the clearing. He was unlike any human Jenna had ever seen and would have been beautiful if not for the malicious smile on his pale features.

Wavy blonde hair parted in the center and swept back on each side. It came to rest just at the nape of his neck. He was clean-shaven and heavily muscled. The man wore a long purple cloak that clasped at his neck and rested negligently over his shoulders, sweeping to the ground just above his ankles.

Mike and Joey fell to their knees and leaned over to press their foreheads against the ground. That in itself was surprising enough without the futuristic transportation or dual lunar spheres. Mike Kurth never bowed down to anyone.

Jenna noticed that the stranger was incredibly pale and that his attention focused on the trio in the clearing. More specifically, he seemed fixated on the rug-wrapped parcel. He stopped within a foot of the small group. Jenna was close enough to see a disapproving frown mar the alluring features.

"What is this?" The voice was clear and high, though distinctly male. Jenna detected an accent, but it wasn't one she could place.

Mike shot a calculating look at Joey, who lay facing the turf, and stood up. "She's our offering, Garran."

"*Lord* Garran," the tall blonde man corrected. "You would do well to remember that."

Garran's eyes glowed red in the darkness. Jenna gasped in surprise and then quickly crouched lower into the dense vegetation when the stranger turned in her direction. She held her breath until he redirected his gaze to the business at hand.

"And this foul smelling contraption?" Garran nudged the carpet with the toe of his boot.

"I had to get her here somehow. If anyone saw us carrying an unconscious woman around, it wouldn't take long before they'd put it together. We'd end up in jail."

"Your species is vermin," Garran pronounced. "You are incapable of solving what is in front of you without a primer. Humans are fit for nothing save filling Erisian bellies."

Mike's scowl deepened as the other man spoke. His jaws clenched, but he held back a response.

"Remove this trash from the slave."

Jenna's eyebrows lifted toward her hairline. She was about to find out if Emily was the latest victim as well as the purpose for the kidnappings. Human trafficking certainly wasn't anything new, but somehow she expected alien life forms to be above such depravity.

What was she thinking? Alien life forms? There was no such thing, at least not in the local galaxy. Jenna glanced at the two moons. It was a trick of light, ions reflecting off the ozone or something. There were no kidnapping, human-eating aliens.

Fortunately, Mike began rolling out the carpet, providing the perfect distraction from her troubling thoughts. He surprised her by how gently he handled the hostage, easing the body from the rug and turning Emily onto her back.

Incongruously garbed in black tactical gear, Emily melded with the darkness. The glint of a buckle here and there dispelled the notion of a disembodied head. Dark curly hair framed olive features, cast in profile from Jenna's vantage point. The sight of a woman so filled with vitality lying quiet as death sent a shudder racing through Jenna. She almost burst from her concealment and would have if Garran hadn't spoken once more.

"Exceptional, for all that she remains a mongrel."

Huh? Okay, he didn't like humans much, but why that description? Somehow, Jenna didn't expect the answer to be forthcoming. Clearly, this individual considered humans inferior, but a mongrel hinted that he believed the pedigree to be lacking in some way. It didn't make sense. None of this did.

He turned to his entourage and commanded one of the women to secure Emily. The one who responded was very young, barely an adult. She hurried toward Emily, her expression eager and features sharpened with obvious need. Jenna guessed her to be in her late teens, but was more concerned by how she acted. She seemed almost desperate to get her hands on Emily. Garran stopped the girl with a sharp hand gesture, scant inches from the defenseless woman on the ground.

"Contain your hunger, Chala. Once the hunt is concluded, your thirst will be assuaged."

Chala mewled in protest, but did as ordered. She slowed and knelt at Garran's feet, easily lifting their latest victim into her arms and carrying her toward the flying craft. A young man assisted in securing Emily behind the seat.

"I saw no marks of savagery upon the body," Garran mentioned in a deceptively calm tone, "yet you lack subtlety. How did you render her so completely helpless?"

It was a good question, one Jenna wouldn't mind knowing the answer to.

"I borrowed my cousin's tranquilizer gun. One shot and she dropped like a rock."

"Drugs?" The big man's voice rose in anger. "Your primitive pharmaceuticals will make her blood unpalatable. What have you done?"

"Relax. It'll wear off in a few hours," Mike said nervously.

"But it will be many cycles before her body is clean again. She will be unfit for exsanguination."

The urge to puke was back, stronger than ever. Jenna didn't know what to do. These creatures intended to bleed Emily. She couldn't allow that to happen, but she couldn't fight this mob with just her sidearm either. There were too many of them and she'd be overwhelmed in seconds. However, there were other things said by Garran that gave Jenna hope death wasn't in Emily's immediate future. He'd spoken of a hunt.

"But you'll still accept her?" Joey's words trembled.

Jenna held her breath, hoping the monster would reject Emily. Instead, Garran fixed the brothers with a malevolent stare. His gaze burned, fiery embers blazing from the center of his pupils. Then he turned on his heel to leave.

"Wait," Mike shouted. "Does this mean we're square? We've brought you nine people so we're done now. Right?"

The tall stranger stopped, his back toward the two. He was silent for long moments and Jenna decided he wasn't going to answer.

"The pair of you aren't worthy of the Ti-gon. Pray I don't add you to Saqqara's extraction stock." Garran spoke softly over his shoulder, but the threat was unmistakable. He marched across the clearing, boots striking the ground with hollow thuds. Garran climbed into the small flying vessel and the canopy slid closed.

"Three more," Mike bargained impotently. "We'll make it an even dozen."

Garran and his troops were already gone. Mike turned toward his brother, his countenance sullen and confused. "What's extraction stock?"

"Their blood supply," Joey answered quietly. "Somehow I don't think he's going to let us out of our deal."

"Some deal. Come on, let's go home. I'm tired."

The Kurths headed back into the woods, their goal obviously the portal back to the hillside caves. Jenna was too furious to notice or care about their despondent expressions. As far as she was concerned, the brothers were as guilty as the people in charge. She rose from behind the shrubbery and stepped toward them. She was a little removed from their path, but thought they'd have to walk right by her. With legs splayed and arms akimbo, she waited for the two to notice her presence.

Unexpectedly, Mike led his brother down a previously unseen trail that would take them away from her location. Jenna took a step forward to pursue, but suddenly swayed on her feet. She raised a hand to her forehead and tried to shake the dizziness away. All she succeeded in doing was making it worse. She sat down hard on the foreign vegetation and waited for the vertigo to recede.

Mike and Joey disappeared into the woods and Jenna was suddenly alone. Now what was she supposed to do? She couldn't leave Emily here alone, wherever here was. Yet she certainly couldn't follow the boys back and just leave the victims to their fate. Jenna didn't know how much time they had or what these other people had in mind for them.

Duty forced her decision, and she concentrated on how to proceed next. Garran had mentioned a place called Saqqara when he threatened Mike. That was where she needed to go. She didn't know how far away it was, but failure wasn't an option, even with her limited supplies.

The only food she had consisted of a single energy bar and her equipment was solely what she was able to carry or could fashion on the run. Jenna could only hope that all the camping she did as a kid would work in her favor. Maybe's she'd be able to find something edible out there that was compatible with the human digestive system. On the other hand, Captain Reynolds would be happy to know his survival training had eventually proved useful.

Jenna hadn't thought about her former instructor in years and now wasn't the time. Emily's unconscious features beckoned her to focus. Determined, Jenna vowed that she would save Emily and the others. She was coming. Now if they could just hang on.

Chapter Eight

EMILY BECAME AWARE of her surroundings slowly. Her head pounded and when she finally opened her eyes, everything was blurry. Darkness crouched at the edges of her vision. The last thing she remembered was Mike Kurth aiming a tranquilizer gun in her direction. Fearing she was still in danger from the brutal narcissist, Emily forced her unwilling body to sit up. Her stomach heaved and it was only by the thinnest of margins that she didn't puke. Her brain felt like it was sloshing around in her head, no longer connected but slamming at random against the sides of her cranium. Her mouth was so dry it was almost painful. For long, agonizing moments, she could do nothing but breathe through the discomfort until it finally began to fade.

The darkness she'd perceived moments before was indeed beyond her immediate vicinity. Where she sat inside the...was it a room...was illuminated enough that she could see everything. It felt good to know that she wasn't brain damaged after all.

Though not a hundred percent, her instincts screamed at her to get moving. She had to assess her situation and seek options. With that in mind, Emily finally took a good look around. She appeared to be in a dirt cell of some type. The chamber was roughly eight feet in circumference and she could stand if she hunched over slightly. The feature that stood out most was that the area appeared to be hexagonal, like something found in a beehive.

She reached out to touch the wall and encountered a moist, spongy substance. Wrinkling her nose in disgust, she pulled her hand back and shuffled over to the single exit. Bars covered the front of the chamber, preventing her escape. Emily glanced down at her waist and was surprised to see she'd somehow retained all of her equipment, including her sidearm.

Why wouldn't they confiscate her weapons and exactly where were they? It didn't make sense, not that she was complaining.

After studying the bars, she reached for the throwing knife she carried at the small of her back. Emily had already yanked it loose before she realized it wouldn't do any good. She scowled and peered more closely at the barricades. They weren't made of metal, but of the same stuff that comprised the walls. On top of that, they looked like they were actually part of the cell. It was all one solid structure. She'd never seen anything like this. Where could Mike and Joey have obtained...whatever this was?

Whatever the answer, Emily knew she couldn't dig her way out with a double-edged blade made more for throwing than for excavation. She tried anyway and gasped in surprise when the substance of the bars reformed around the knife as though it had never been disturbed. She removed the blade from the substance with ease, but each time Emily made another cut, the barrier reformed in seconds.

Her headache pounded even harder with the realization that escape was nearly impossible. She dropped her head into her hands and groaned before she muttered, "Did anyone get the number of the bus that hit me?" The question was rhetorical and she was surprised when a male voice responded.

"Hello? Is someone there?"

The harsh whisper came from the left side of her cell and Emily instinctively pressed closer, lowering her voice to match the other. "Yes, I'm here. Who are you, where are we?"

"Oh, thank God. Someone from home."

Emily scowled, thinking the remark seemed strange. This fellow might not be dealing with a full deck. Yet unbalanced or not, he might have some of the answers she needed so she decided to start with the basics. "What's your name?"

"Charles. Charles Freeman."

The man's identity caught her off guard. Jenna was searching for this same person. Part of Emily celebrated the fact that she'd found him, but that feeling was quickly stifled since she couldn't do anything about it.

"Emily Bannon here," she reciprocated, careful to maintain her undercover identity, although at the moment she wasn't sure exactly why.

She heard a muffled noise and realized the young man was sobbing quietly. Her thoughts weren't really on his reaction, but on information obtained in the course of her investigation that pertained to him. This was the college student who'd gone missing a few days ago. By all accounts, he was a strapping young man with above average intelligence. She wouldn't expect such a person to cry like a baby, regardless of the situation. Emily thought his first reaction should be to reassure her, and start planning a way out. They really didn't make men like they used to, and what was that crack about home?

"Charles, do you know where we are?"

"Wha...what? You mean you don't know?" he sniffed.

"I just woke up. One of the people that took me hit me with a tranquilizer gun."

Silence met her comment and when he finally spoke, Charles sounded like he was trying to recall something that had happened a long time ago. "Oh, you mean those guys with the tow truck?"

"Of course, who else would I be talking about?" she asked impatiently. "Look, Charles, no offense, but you sound kind of out of it. Are they keeping you drugged?"

Emily heard another choked off noise and thought he was crying again, but when he spoke, she heard amusement in his voice. "No, definitely no drugs around here. That might provide some sort of mental freedom. Plus, these creatures don't like their food to taste funny."

She felt like growling in frustration. So far, the only useful information she'd obtained was his name.

"Let's start over. Do you know where they've taken us? If we get out of here, maybe we can get to a phone and call the police."

"We're through the looking glass. There are no phones," he responded vaguely. Charles took a deep breath and said, "I'm sorry. I saw them bring you in, but I didn't realize you've missed the most important part. We're not on Earth anymore."

"What's that supposed to mean?"

"Before you say anything else, let me explain."

"This had better be good. I'm not in the mood for games." He was her only source of information, though clearly delusional. Emily guessed she could play along and attempt to make sense of his ramblings, though her patience was waning.

"You'd better be," he said, suddenly serious. "You're in the middle of one and it's a very serious game. I doubt you'll believe what I tell you, but listen anyway."

"All right, go ahead."

"We're on another planet or possibly another dimension. How we got here, I'm not sure. All I know is that I called for a tow truck when my car broke down and a wrecker showed up. There were two men. One of them was really arrogant, you know the type. The other one was sort of wimpy."

It fit the description of the Kurth brothers, Emily allowed.

"I thought everything was going great. I had just reached down to get my wallet out of the car when one of them hit me from behind. The next thing I knew, they were dragging me through the forest. We met some people in a clearing and the towing guys handed me off to them. At least, I thought they were people. Later I found out they aren't human at all. They're vampires."

Emily swallowed her laughter with difficulty. "Are you sure they didn't hit you in the head harder than you thought?"

"Later I saw a girl. She couldn't have been older than sixteen. She drained another guy while I watched."

"Of his blood?" she asked, clearly disbelieving.

"You said you'd listen."

"Right, sorry. Go on."

"The guy they drained looked human and I got to thinking. I believe they come to Earth looking for food. That would be us."

"Uh huh."

"You'll see. They'll come for us soon and then you'll know that I'm telling you the truth."

Emily glanced down and noticed a glint of something shiny under her left sleeve. She pulled the sweater material back and saw that she'd acquired some jewelry. It was a bracelet, but didn't seem constructed of any kind of metal she recognized. It looked a little like burnished brass, but felt like ceramic.

Distracted by thoughts of what possible purpose the bracelet could serve she said, "You mentioned a game."

"The Ti-gon. It's like some training scenario, I think. Not completely sure, but I've been through it once and it's extreme. The Erisians send their youngsters after us, so I think it's a way to hone their skills or something. They take all the captives out of the cells and let us go. At least that's what I thought until I realized they intended to hunt us down."

"What's an Erisian?"

"The vampires," Charles huffed. "Aren't you listening?"

"Yeah, but I'm more concerned with the new addition to my ensemble."

"Huh?"

"The bracelet."

"Oh that. Everyone has them."

That remark drew her full attention back to the conversation. "What do you mean everyone? How many of us are there?"

"I couldn't give you an exact number, but a lot. I guess they'd need a lot of us to feed their species."

Back to that again. Emily rolled her eyes. "The bracelet?" she prompted.

"A locator of some sort, near as I can tell, but it has a twist. They use it to give us a little shock if we get out of hand."

"Can't have the monkeys rattling the cage?"

"I suppose."

"But why choose a device like this? If someone were desperate enough, they'd cut the thing off, or they could cut off their arm. Why not use a microchip?"

"I don't know, but I doubt they'd care. Shh, someone's coming!" he said in a harsh whisper.

Good, maybe she could get some real answers. Emily thought being confined had scrambled his reasoning center. Some people just couldn't handle a lot of stress, no matter how strong they were physically. She stood up as straight as she could in the small space. The shadows outside her cell began to lessen. As the light grew brighter, footsteps advanced and a small group of five halted directly in front. A woman stood at the head of the assembly. Under normal circumstances, Emily would have found the stranger breathtaking. She was tall with long, blonde hair and possessed a supple way of moving. Well muscled and well endowed, she was impressive. The comparison that came to mind was Nordic or Scandinavian. Her appearance reminded Emily of angelic images she had seen. Maybe this woman would have some compassion.

The newcomer clasped her hands behind her back and regarded Emily with a haughty gaze. "Move him," she ordered snidely. "I do not want them communicating."

Maybe not.

Two of the others immediately moved to do her bidding. Emily heard Charles's protestations, but held her captor's gaze. She'd played hostage more than once during her career, usually in an orchestrated scenario, and Emily knew better than to show weakness. Instead, she studied the stranger she instinctively sensed held their fate in her hands. She could have pulled her weapon out and ordered them to release her from confinement, but had a feeling it wouldn't do any good. If these people were concerned, they would have removed the pistol while she was unconscious.

"I am Regent Ilana. Welcome to Eris." Her eyes narrowed as she waited for Emily to respond. When nothing was forthcoming, she tilted her head back slightly and asked, "You have no questions?"

Emily noticed the tips of blazing white fangs just barely visible beneath her top lip. Ilana was sexy in a twisted kind of way, but why go so far with the charade? What possible purpose could there be for making people believe they'd been taken captive by a bunch of vampires? Emily wondered how much she'd paid a dentist for such work.

"Here, you are nothing. You exist merely for our amusement or for our consumption. Before we decide your future, you will experience the honor of the Ti-gon."

"Already heard about that," Emily muttered, unimpressed. "Pass."

Ilana's eyebrow raised and a smile tugged at the corner of her lips. "Once the ritual is concluded, you will either be kept for the hunt, become a slave, or live out the rest of your days as an unconscious contributor to the nourishment tanks. You might hear them referred to as the *bariba*."

"Thanks for the translation. I might not have been able to contain my curiosity." Feigning boredom, Emily yawned and studied her nails. When she glanced up again she caught the swift surge of anger on Ilana's face. It quickly vanished, masked behind an arrogant demeanor. Emily was happy to know she could get under her skin so easily. A volatile nature might be the key to her escape in the future.

"I only have one question I need answered. Make it two questions. Where's the bathroom and when are you going to tell me what's really going on?"

Ilana's jaw locked in fury. She spun around and walked away without another word.

"Talk about no sense of humor," Emily said to the vampire's back.

It was too bad she didn't have any garlic or a cross. She supposed she'd just have to find the bathroom on her own. The problem was, there wasn't one. The cell boasted an earthen floor and gooey walls.

That was it. There wasn't even any furniture. Emily squinted and looked into the farthest corner of the floor. Something was back there in the darkness. Emily froze when she realized what she saw.

Great, that was just what she wanted; a hole in the ground. Well, it wasn't as though she hadn't done this before.

Many countries used such a latrine, but it wouldn't have been her first choice. The important thing was to have a little privacy. She took a quick glance around and didn't see anyone. Unless an individual walked right in front of the cell, they wouldn't be able to see anything either.

Emily removed her black belt and set it nearby since it contained most of her equipment. Then she quickly unfastened her britches, shoved them down, and squatted. Fortunately, there wasn't any backsplash. The relief she felt made the entire embarrassing episode worth it. Without any paper nearby, she prepared to redress when a sudden low hum filled the air. Emily felt a tingling on her backside and barely managed not to shriek as she lunged away. She turned around and saw a light beam washing back and forth over her privy.

A sanitizer. That would come in handy if she had to do something else though she didn't plan to be here for that long. It was just too bad she couldn't wash up.

Emily sat down in the opposite corner from the latrine and lay out her equipment to verify what she had on hand. She had her throwing knife along with the leather sheath. Emily pulled the .32 semi-automatic from the holster and checked to see that it was still loaded. It was, complete with a round in the chamber ready to fire. In addition to the magazine already inside the pistol, Emily had two extra clips of ammunition, a roll of monofilament cord, a small first aid pouch, a single hand grenade secured in a carry case, and a Bushnell waterproof monocular. Besides what she carried on her belt, Emily had also secreted an extra throwing knife in a boot sheath. Now all she needed was the opportunity.

While waiting for what would happen next, Emily picked up her knife and prodded at the bracelet. She didn't see a clasp and the bracelet seemed to be one continuous band except for a single red stone. She decided the closure was hidden underneath, and set about trying to pry the jewel loose.

Emily heard movement from outside the confined area. She quickly repacked the holsters and knife, and walked over to the front of the cell while buckling the belt around her waist. The other prisoners were starting to talk, a few shouted but she couldn't understand what they said. What was all the commotion about?

One word shouted above the noise explained everything. "Food!" Emily was sure she heard Charles call out the word.

She sat down to wait her turn, pleased that their captors weren't about to starve them. Then again, the vampires wouldn't be very wise if they allowed their own food supply to perish. She rolled her eyes at the thought, not really believing the description was accurate.

Eventually she saw movement just out of her field of vision and decided they were feeding the prisoner next to her. She was eager for the server to reach her own chamber, but not just because she was hungry. This person might be able to tell her how to escape or answer any one of a hundred other questions. When it finally stepped up to the cell, she recoiled in horror. The creature serving her dinner was hunched and carried a lump under his coat in the area of his right shoulder. He reminded Emily of Quasimodo. For all that, the man's appearance repelled her. Emily would have felt sympathy for him if not for the malice in his eyes. When he saw her curiosity, he opened his mouth and hissed at her.

Emily's instinctual reaction was to pull away. For the first time, she took relief from the presence of the bars. Her eyes fixed on the being's yellow-tinged fangs. As repulsive as the sight of his teeth was, it was no comparison to the smell of rot expelled on his breath. In Emily's experience, vampires existed only on film. At one point in Earth's history, societies feared the creatures and killed each other over the mere possibility that they were part of the undead. Nowadays, people romanticized vampires but Emily had never seen the attraction. Vampires were monsters. Theoretically, they existed by preying on the life force of others, like a parasite. This man embodied everything she'd ever pictured about vampires and he was far from seductive. In fact, he was positively revolting.

She still wasn't quite ready to give up on everything she knew to be fact and believe what her eyes were telling her. What if she was really drugged or hooked up to some secret government machine that messed with her brain? If that were so, this might be the best representation of normality her mind was able to conjure in order to cope.

Emily shook her head to drive the far-fetched ideas from her thoughts. She had to stop watching so much science fiction.

The sight of the creature was enough to make her rethink all her preconceived notions about elaborate setups. She had to accept the vampires were real and this actually *was* another planet, as preposterous as she found that possibility. She glanced down and noticed the man's long, pointed and very dirty fingernails. Broken and cracked, Emily would have sworn there was half a pound of filth beneath them.

"Uh, you didn't touch anything, did you?"

The vampire's eyes narrowed and he shoved the tray through a small opening beneath the bars. One of the food morsels rolled toward the edge of the plate but stopped short of falling.

The food didn't impress her. The gray cubes resembled tofu and were just as tasteless. She ate it anyway. Her training kicked in and insisted that she consume any nutrition available under the circumstances. Emily shuddered as she washed it all down with the single cup of water. It was sustenance and keeping her strength up was vital if she hoped to get out of this situation. Once she completed her meal, Emily inspected the food tray. It seemed to be some kind of compressed paper like cardboard and just as useless as a weapon. The tools on her belt and her handgun were going to have to be enough.

The vampire returned and stuck his arms through the opening. Emily realized he wanted the tray, but she was having a bad day and felt like goading the creature a little.

"What, you want a tip? I seem to have left my wallet at home. If you let me out, I'll wash the dishes to repay my bill."

The thing opened his mouth and shrieked so loudly Emily thought her eardrums would burst. "All right," she said, holding one hand over her ear and shoving the tray to the beast with the other. "You win."

After he departed, Emily curled up at the back of her cell away from the area with the latrine. She didn't lean against the wall, afraid the gooey surface would contaminate her skin. Instead, she lay on her side facing the entrance and tried to relax her body. Even if she couldn't sleep, she needed to rest. She intended to be ready when her chance for freedom came. With any luck, she could take the other prisoners with her but depending on how tight security was, she might have to settle for coming back with support troops. The craziness of the situation called for flexibility, but survival and escape were still the goal.

To her surprise, Emily found herself nodding off. She dozed for about an hour before she realized that the lights outside the locked chambers had brightened. Now what?

The sound of many feet stepping in the direction of the cells made her sit upright, fully awake and cognizant of every detail. Ilana was back and her group of lackeys had grown to twice as many as before. Men and women with the same light hair and ivory skin gathered in front of the captives. Each carried a wooden baton, capped by a red crystal similar to the one on Emily's bracelet only much larger. The lights in the cavernous room brightened, but not as much as Emily was accustomed to. Many shadows still lingered and she started to understand these creatures operated in the darkness. Just like a monster.

"It's time," Ilana declared. "Release the animals from their prison. Not that one," she amended, as a tall, heavily muscled male approached Emily's cell. "Her blood is still tainted by the Earth drug."

He nodded once and moved on to the compartment adjacent to Emily's. His grin was reminiscent of a snarl and from her vantage point, Emily noticed that he also possessed fangs. His irises were amber, but the pupils were a reddish pinpoint. She shivered unconsciously.

Seconds later, a multitude of prisoners shuffled toward the center of the large outer chamber. There were so many people that Emily couldn't count them, but she felt sure that the Kurth brothers couldn't have kidnapped them all. Others had provided victims for these vampires. She spotted Charles Freeman standing near a couple. The man and woman huddled close to him. Both seemed slightly hunched, as if waiting to ward off a blow. Each of them looked in their thirties, but lines of exhaustion marred their faces and they were very thin from malnutrition. Of the three, Charles appeared the more robust. Emily knew he'd been taken three days ago and had to wonder how long ago the other two were captured.

One particular female caught her eye, largely in part because the captive was watching her. Tall with a thin musculature, the alien had bright, multifaceted blue eyes that identified her as distinctly not human. Her lips looked soft, full, and curvy. Her hair appeared to be deep sable brown one moment and a shade of purple the next. It fell like a waterfall down her back, resting near her tapered waist. She wore a form-fitting leather-like dark navy unitard as well as knee high black boots. It looked to be a uniform of some type. The garment had a high collar and silver decorations at the throat. With her chin raised and her hands fisted on her hips, the woman radiated a quiet intelligence, confidence, and determination. Whoever she was, Emily felt she was a force to be reckoned with.

Lost in those unbelievably blue eyes, it took a moment for a scuffle to penetrate her awareness. One of the prisoners, a small, thin man with nervous eyes, made a break for freedom. Managing a quick, jerky scamper, he made for the opposite side of the chamber from where the group stood. He seemed injured. Emily wondered if a door was open and the possibility of escape became too tempting for the poor man.

A youngster from Ilana's throng bolted after the individual. It was a teenager, barely more than a child. His wavy blonde hair flew backward from his face and he moved so quickly that Emily had difficulty following him with her eyes. What she did see made her heart beat faster and her palms grow sweaty. His pupils gave off the same crimson light she'd noticed from the other man earlier, but it was much more intense. An angry hiss sounded through his open mouth and in a flash, he was on the desperate smaller being. Emily flinched when he buried his teeth in the man's neck and the victim cried out in terror.

In the meantime, Ilana had also moved. She grasped the boy by the nape of his neck and flung him away from the frightened man. A big Erisian placed a foot on the young vampire's chest and held him in place while Ilana dealt with the captive.

"You will have all the chance you desire to elude us," she said in a slow, mesmerizing voice. "The Ti-gon allows you the opportunity to escape. Rejoin the others."

Emily saw the unfortunate man's head weaving from side to side as though hypnotized. Silently, he turned back toward the congregation and limped across the floor. Blood trickled from a wound on his neck.

"He's hurt," Emily pronounced angrily. "How can you keep me in a cage because I still have a sedative in my blood, but put him through your monstrous game? What kind of a devil are you?"

Aware of an appreciative look from the woman with purple-brown hair, Emily tried to focus on Ilana. She'd spoken without thinking, but her sense of honor demanded it. The vampire leader gazed at her with narrow eyes and when she replied, Emily's blood ran cold.

"Did you hear her, Garran? She insists on being included."

The Erisian who'd approached her cell earlier responded. "It would be a shame to deny her request."

"I agree. Release her to join the others." The malice in Ilana's eyes was clear. "You will regret your decision. That I promise."

Emily suppressed her smile. This was exactly what she wanted, an opportunity to seek freedom. With the weapons in her possession and the cumulative years of combat and defensive training, she had a better than even chance of beating the odds.

Warm brown eyes and a heart-wrenching smile flashed through her mind and Emily felt a tugging sensation in her stomach that she identified as regret. Emily hadn't known Jenna long, but knew she was special. At least she was safe in Grays Landing. Emily didn't think she could do this if she had to worry about Jenna.

Garran touched something outside her cell and the barrier sprang open. From where she stood, Emily couldn't see what it was, but she wasn't waiting around anywhere near where his fangs could dig into her neck. She hopped down from a level even with Garran's chest height and stalked confidently toward the group, trademark swagger firmly in place.

She wanted to give the impression that she considered this a cakewalk, even if she was shaking inside. Emily tried not to react to the sudden and unexpected change in temperature. The cells were quite warm, but out here with the others, there was a definite chill in the air. She noticed the human woman trembling. She wasn't sure if it was the cold or fear, but leaned toward the former.

Emily stalked straight up to the alien with the purplish hair and met the shimmering blue eyes. "Want to team up?"

"Silence!" Ilana commanded.

The alien woman didn't respond, but neither did she look away from Emily. At the vampire regent's nod, Garran and the older-looking Erisians shuffled their prisoners toward the exit. Emily thought the opening resembled the huge, overhead doors of a warehouse, but the darkness made it hard to be certain. She still felt sure this was some type of elaborate hoax.

Up ahead, the woman standing near Charles tripped and scraped her knees on the hard floor. Emily heard her male companion call out, "Laurel" in a thick, English accent. His tone clearly conveyed worry as he tried to rush forward to help her. A female vampire Emily hadn't interacted with struck him and shoved him back toward the group.

Garran hauled Laurel to her feet and Emily lost sight of her.

Once outside, Emily followed as the prisoners made a beeline for the forest. It was only thirty feet from the building. She was surprised that none of the Erisians pursued, but her confusion didn't last long. This was a chase. What sport would it be to go after the quarry right away? Deciding to present a more difficult target, Emily sprinted for cover, noticing that purple-hair was right beside her.

The strong, alien woman pointed at her own chest and said very clearly, "Fallon."

"Nice to meet you, I'm Emily. Let's chat later."

Chapter Nine

"SIX HUNDRED NINETY-seven, six hundred ninety-eight..."

Jenna stumbled once again on the uneven terrain and lost count of her steps. She stopped for a moment and looked around, assessing the situation. All she wanted was to close her eyes and sleep but considering the hostile environment, she didn't think that was such a good idea. Logic dictated that she travel in the direction the flying constructs had gone, but so far she'd found nothing promising.

The beautiful yet alien forest had given way to rock and sand. Little vegetation grew in the depleted soil. Without the trees and bushes to break the wind, it whipped her hair around her face and bit deeply into her body like icy needles. Jagged boulders soared into the air, standing out majestically against the blue-gray sky. Two moons had kept pace with her, constantly on her left while simultaneously continuing on their orbital path. Now, they edged closer to the horizon and Jenna thought they might soon set.

Moisture glistened on her skin, cooling in the night air and making her shiver. She shoved her hands deeper into the coat pockets and searched the sky for any indications of where the sun would rise. So far, there wasn't any sign of the star that would bring warmth and light. She'd refused to use her flashlight; afraid she would drain the battery and not have the device when she really needed it.

Jenna sat on the damp ground to rest, telling herself it was only for a moment and that she would not fall asleep. To ensure she didn't, she concentrated on the overhead exotic lunar orbs. They bore no resemblance to the moon seen from Earth. The largest and nearest of the two was a study in color. Swirls of purple, blue, green, and white covered the face. Was the surface comprised of intergalactic gasses? It was so close Jenna felt she should know the answer.

The second moon was approximately one-third the size of its sister and boasted a single hue, bright white. Jenna wondered if this world gained the majority of its nocturnal light from the smaller satellite. Her stomach rumbled, reminding Jenna that she had other things to worry about, and she forced herself into motion. Hunger gnawed at her like a ravening beast. She'd consumed the ration bar hours ago and there hadn't been any water from the start.

"I should have gone back for supplies," she muttered. "I could have arrested the boys and called for backup. Could have been ready for this. Why was I so careless?"

The answer was simple. Emily. The tanned, smiling face came to her frequently while she walked. Jenna didn't really know Emily, but easily recalled the slightly husky timbre of her voice and the habit of pushing dark curls back from her eyes. Most of all, she remembered Emily's kisses and the feel of her warm, strong body.

The throbbing in her fingers chased away her fantasies. Jenna stopped and pulled her hand out of her pocket. In the low light details were hard to make out, but her fingertips looked swollen. She began to think she had an infection. Perhaps that was why she felt so tired. No, she was tired before arriving in this crazy place. She wondered how long the human body could go without sleep. Maybe she should have paid better attention in that survival class.

Jenna checked her watch, turning the dial so that the light from the moons fell directly across, illuminating the numbers. It showed eight a.m. The sun should have been up, but the moons still dominated the night sky. Without a frame of reference, the timepiece wouldn't tell her anything.

Time was meaningless here. How did she even know if this planet or dimension or whatever it was had a twenty-four hour day or thirty-six...or even more? She would have to start keeping track.

"One, two..."

She started walking again, but immediately stumbled over a half-buried rock and went to her knees. Jenna instinctively put her injured hand out to break her fall and cried out at the pain that shot up to her shoulder. For long seconds she lay there panting. Eventually the agony faded, giving way to the familiar perpetual throb. At least it made her forget about the blisters. Her boots were fine for the uniform on a normal day, but they weren't designed for hiking long distances.

The moons were going down now and the shadows had lengthened. Lying on her back in the cool dirt, Jenna finally noticed a pinpoint of bright yellow light in the distance. It took a second to realize she was looking at the sun. The brief surge of joy at seeing it gave way to devastation as it dawned on her that it was now colder and even darker than before. Twilight had turned to midnight since the planet's star was so far away.

"Oh my God, I was walking in this planet's version of daylight."

Jenna groaned in horrified disbelief and curled into herself, tears leaking from the corners of her eyes. She thought about Emily as she lay there. Jenna felt terrible for letting Emily down, but she just didn't know if she could do this. All she really wanted was to return home.

After a while, she quieted and her body relaxed. Her closed eyes fluttered as she drifted in half-sleep, but her conscience wouldn't let her quit. Jenna jerked awake and heaved herself up from the hard ground, by force of will she concentrated on putting one foot in front of the other. She'd been walking for a long time and Jenna prayed she was closer to her destination now than she was from the portal where she had followed the Kurths.

A few steps later, Jenna felt the ground begin to decline. She studied the terrain around her more carefully and realized she was about to descend into a massive canyon. The path she traversed angled steeply and the footing wasn't very good, shifting underneath with loose gravel. It looked to be half a mile before she would reach the bottom. The trail was little more than a twisting and turning lookout over the top of sheer drops and canyon walls.

Jenna gulped, but stepped bravely forward, thoughts of the victims her lure to keep going. She thought of Lois Freeman missing her nephew and the countless others concerned for their loved ones, but it was the memory of Emily's clean scent and laughing blue eyes that proved her most powerful motivation.

Halfway down the incline, Jenna's slick soles slipped in shale. She gasped and tried to catch herself, but knew she was going over. There was nothing but sharp rocks to grasp or break her fall. Cold air rushed past her face and Jenna thought she should have been frightened. To the contrary, she felt numb and wondered if it was because she was so exhausted. Any second she expected the impact that would end her life. Instead, a light began to grow around her. The brilliance was coming closer and in the illumination, she saw a familiar face.

Mandy.

Slowly the light faded and Jenna saw the framed picture of her life partner on the desk back in her cubical at Boston Homicide. Somehow, she realized the images were from another, more painful episode in her life, but Jenna was powerless to push the memories of that last day away. Her mind insisted she relive every torturous detail.

"No, baby. I wish I could come home, but we're so close to catching this guy I can feel it."

Jenna studied her lover's face in the photo before her. The long blonde hair that framed the rounded features resembled a halo and the smiling blue eyes were as familiar as the gentleness of Mandy's touch. Jenna gripped the phone a little tighter, wanting to hang up and drive to the home they'd shared for the last six years, but her duty wouldn't permit it.

Boston's latest serial killer had started calling the precinct, asking for Jenna by name. He was taunting the homicide detectives with their ineptitude. Jenna noticed Lieutenant Forenza frantically signaling for her to get off the phone. Their murderer was on the other line.

"Honey, I have to go. Yeah, I'll call you later. Bye."

This nutcase wouldn't talk to anyone but Jenna. He kept her on the phone long enough for them to trace the call. He was inside Jenna and Mandy's home. She raced over with backup hot on her heels, sirens wailing and red lights inconsequential, but they were too late. There was so much blood.

Another officer had to separate her physically from her dead lover. The other homicide detectives were saddened by Mandy's death and angry on Jenna's behalf. They were resolute in catching the murderer, more determined than ever. As it turned out, the bastard was so focused on punishing Jenna that he'd made critical mistakes. For her own part, vengeance and guilt drove her. She hadn't told Mandy she loved her during that last phone call and she deeply regretted the oversight. She would never have another opportunity. Mandy was gone and her lover's parents wouldn't even look at Jenna at the funeral.

Three weeks later, she caught the son of a bitch and killed him when he drew a gun. The act was bittersweet, adding to her growing guilt for having taken a life, but balanced by her feelings of redemption for purging society of another evil. His death didn't bring Mandy back, nothing ever could, but at least Jenna had avenged her death.

"No," she muttered in her delirium, forcing the memories away. "No more."

Jenna's eyes snapped open and she rose up on her elbows, amazed that she was still alive. Her eyes darted around as the panic from her subconscious terrors gave way to the present. She realized she wasn't in the mountains any longer and it took a few moments to reason out what was going on. Sweat coated her body, but she wore clean clothes and lay on a small, but soft cot. It was so narrow that it appeared to be something a child slept on.

Where was she?

The last she remembered, Jenna was in the middle of a freefall with the ground zooming up fast. She took a deep breath and a dull pain in her chest made her exhale more slowly. She recalled the throbbing in her left hand from where she'd grabbed a branch full of thorns, and looked at the appendage in surprise. The soreness was gone and all of her fingers looked normal once again. In addition to the new ache in her chest, Jenna became aware that her right leg was elevated and her feet were bare. Her blisters were gone. Had she imagined them? Someone had removed all of her clothing, redressed her, and then covered her with a thin blanket.

Jenna remembered falling and then dreaming about Mandy, but nothing more. Hallucinating was probably more accurate. Jenna must have been feverish from the wound in her hand.

Frowning but curious, she looked around. The room was small with a dirt floor. Rough-hewn wooden walls kept most of the elements out, but she could see gaps where the boards didn't fit flush and there were a number of empty knotholes. Differently sized pieces of cloth hung along the walls and Jenna realized they were clothes. The only thing that looked familiar was a long, low cabinet that took up most of one wall. Over the top of it was a basin with a single spigot. The sight of the sink made her salivate. Water.

The room looked as though it belonged in a shanty, but after what she'd been through she didn't really mind. At least it was shelter. Jenna glanced around quickly and grasped the covers, prepared to throw them back and walk over to the faucet, but a furtive sound made her hesitate. Jenna's head snapped to the right where a curtain over a doorway separated the room from another chamber.

A swift surge of fear went through her, but then Jenna realized it didn't make a lot of sense for someone to help her just to turn around and harm her. Mentally pushing the feelings of trepidation away, she resolved to greet her benefactor with gratitude.

Jenna saw the shadows of two people talking on the other side of the thin material. One of them was very small, probably four feet in height. In contrast, the other person stood close to six feet. The voices were clear, but the words unrecognizable. These two spoke a different language, but one very pleasing to the ear. It possessed a singsong quality with lilting inflections. Jenna found the alien words soothing and was surprised to find herself nodding off again. She became fully alert when the curtain abruptly parted and the shorter of the strangers boldly entered the room.

A broad smile curved Jenna's lips when she realized her visitor was a young boy. He grinned when he saw that she was awake and ran over to her side. The child sported shining brown eyes and his hair stuck up from his skull like miniature spikes. The smile on his face was infectious.

"Sho est co thalia! Mei tanza an Soto! Kestranti tau lu?"

"I'm sorry," Jenna apologized. "I don't understand what you're saying."

The curtain ruffled again and a man entered the room. His appearance was similar to the boy's. Both wore tunic type shirts, leggings, and brown boots. He offered a smile and pointed to the child.

"Soto."

"Oh, that's his name. I'm Jenna Yang." She pointed at herself.

The man nodded and said, "Moye Coalis." His voice was rough and gravelly.

Moye made a motion that indicated eating and Jenna's stomach rumbled. Her host smiled and said something to the boy that she didn't understand. Whatever it was, they both left and she heard clinking noises coming from the other room. Seconds later, Soto returned bearing a tray. Two dishes sat on the platter and the smells from the food made Jenna's mouth water. He sat the salver on her lap and then perched closely beside her on the makeshift bed.

The tray itself was nothing more than a plank of rough wood and the bowls carved straight from a tree trunk. Jenna's stomach growled again on seeing the food, but she couldn't really tell what it was. One container held yellowish cubes with green and red flecks from unknown spices. She thought she identified something that looked like potatoes and leeks. At least it appeared edible.

It wasn't so hard to guess what the second bowl held. Large chunks of well-cooked meat were soaked in brown gravy. Mixed in were some unfamiliar vegetables and everything combined was more than she could eat.

A metallic utensil lay beside the food. Curved in the center, it had three tines on the end and resembled a typical fork. Jenna was so hungry she grabbed it up without a second thought and started shoveling her meal into her mouth. She'd swallowed the first bite and stuffed the second inside before she abruptly stopped chewing. Her eyes widened and she fought the urge to spit it out. Sheer willpower and the desire to keep every bit of nutrition in her body forced Jenna to swallow.

"That's hot!"

She meant spicy, but Soto apparently had no problem understanding her. The young man clamped his hand over his mouth and tried to suppress a giggle. Still chuckling, he jumped off the bed and ran over to the sink. Jenna didn't see how he activated it, but moments later he returned with a leaf full of what she assumed to be water. The leaf was huge, easily the size of both of her hands. It was dried and had a single point on one end.

Soto pointed at the tip and shook his head. "*Nai toka est sila.*"

"Trust me, I already know about the thorns."

Jenna looked into the dried foliage, unsure what she would find. There was liquid all right. It had the consistency of water, but it was deep blue. It didn't matter, she finally decided. Hydrogen and oxygen made water, regardless of the color.

She sipped tentatively at first, thrilled when she discovered the fluid was indeed water. It was cooling to her tongue and she felt it ease the ache in her belly. Jenna tried to conserve what the boy gave her and took only a few small swallows. She didn't want to use up all of their supplies. She sat the rest of it on the tray and consumed the balance of her meal more slowly.

From her surroundings, Jenna guessed Soto and Moye to be very poor. She didn't want to take advantage of their good nature by consuming everything they had. Yet at the same time, she didn't want to insult them by not finishing her meal. Finally, she decided the only choice was to accept what they gave her since it wouldn't make sense for them to give her more than they could afford. After she scraped up every morsel, Jenna finished her water. She emptied the leaf and was tempted to lick the bottom of the dried vegetation. Instead, she sat it on the platter and smiled at Soto. He returned the gesture, grabbed the leaf, and dashed back to the water supply.

"Oh no, that's okay. You don't have to do that."

"There is enough water. Drink your fill."

Surprised, Jenna turned quickly toward the doorway. Moye stood there with a fond look on his face as he watched his son.

"You...you can speak English?"

"No, I do not speak your language." Moye shook his head and held up his right hand. "This ring is a communication device. It translates what each of us says and allows us to understand."

"Okay," Jenna said, taking his explanation at face value for the moment. "I'm going to have more questions about that, but I really need to use the bathroom."

"Bath...room?"

"Uh, you know. I have to go."

Moye shook his head and his eyes squinted in what she guessed was his version of a frown. "Go where?"

Jenna heaved a resigned sigh. So much for tact. "I need to empty my bladder."

"Oh!" His light brown skin darkened in embarrassment. "Come with me. I'll show you where to...go."

"Wonderful." She flung back the covers, relieved when the tunic she wore ended at mid-thigh.

Jenna stood carefully, afraid that she wouldn't be able to stand on her own. She felt a stinging sensation in her right leg and sagged slightly.

"Oww."

"Are you still damaged?"

Jenna grimaced, but tried to ignore the discomfort. After a few seconds, it faded to a dull ache. "No, not really. My leg just hurts a little."

"Once you are finished, I will treat you again. Then you will feel better."

"Treat me?"

Moye grinned. "I thought you needed to relieve your bladder?"

"Right. Lead on."

Moye took Jenna's arm. She tensed, but then realized he was merely providing support. Jenna felt embarrassed by her reaction. Considering she was on an alien world, facing any number of untold threats, her behavior was understandable, but that was still no excuse. This all seemed so surreal. She thought back to all those Sunday morning science fiction shows depicting alien beings and planets and realized not even they could have prepared her for the reality she currently faced.

"I'm sorry," she said, leaning on him a little more as a sharp pain ripped through her leg. "I'm a little rattled, what with finding myself on a strange planet and everything."

"You are a *hoo*-man, yes?"

"Human. And yes, I am."

Moye patted her hand gently. "Humans always believe they are the only intelligent beings. That doesn't make it so. Here, do what you need and I will answer some of your questions when you return."

He'd led her to a small, rickety door that looked ready to fall off its hinges. After it swung shut, she looked around and was a little appalled at what passed for a latrine. A single hole in the floor was situated near the back corner, but at least this room had another sink.

Jenna quickly relieved herself, but didn't find anything that resembled toilet paper, not that she really expected to find any. After that, she spent a minute figuring out how to turn the water on in the sink and happily rinsed her face with the ice blue water. She couldn't resist cupping handfuls and gulping the water down. Finally, she forced herself to shut the tap off, but discovered another problem. No towels, perfect.

Okay, drip dry. She could do that.

Jenna wiped her face off on her sleeve and limped out of the bathroom, upset to realize that her leg was hurting more than before. Moye stood ready to assist her back over to the bed where he urged her to sit down.

"Raise your feet and I'll give you another treatment. Your leg will be fully operational after that."

"You make me sound like a robot." She teased him to hide her own discomfort.

Moye bent over and trained a strange-looking device over her leg, just above the knee. It resembled an awl but was two inches in circumference and the tip of it glowed yellow. Just before he touched her skin, Jenna leaned forward and almost stopped him.

"It is all right," he said, looking deeply into her eyes. "It will not hurt."

Jenna was relieved to feel a slight tingling sensation, but no real pain. When she started to relax, her host began to speak.

"You have come to Eris through a rift?"

She nodded. Although she didn't understand the reference to Eris, she could follow his logic. "I followed a couple of guys here. They took my friend and handed her off to someone named Garran."

Moye didn't look up from his ministrations, but Jenna sensed renewed interest by how his shoulders tensed. "It is very far from a portal to here and I sense you are very strong, but you must be careful. Garran and his kind will not hesitate to kill you if they consider you a threat."

"What are you talking about? They don't even know I'm here."

"You were careless. Only luck saved you from being taken." Anger flashed in his eyes, before he resumed healing her. His jaw clenched and for a moment, he was quiet. Then he said calmly, "You were walking through mid-tween, when the moons ride high. The chariots are out at that time and any of them could have seen you."

"You mean the flying ships?" Moye nodded. "What's it called when the moons set and the sun is up?"

"Dark."

Jenna froze and then laughed aloud. Moye smiled.

"You were severely injured when Soto found you. The great bone in your thigh protruded above your knee and your hand was infected. A rock perforated your chest, but fortunately didn't damage your heart. A great fever raged in your body, but you are better now." Moye stood and put his instrument away. "There, try it now."

Jenna stood and didn't feel the slightest twinge. "Hey, that's pretty good. Where'd you get such a device anyway? No offense, but it doesn't exactly fit in here technologically speaking." She glanced down at the hand still holding the healing stick. "Neither does that ring for that matter."

"Sit. I will tell you some of what I know but then you must rest. When the moons rise again, you must leave. It is dangerous for you to remain here. Dangerous for Soto and myself."

After weighing his words, Jenna reluctantly conceded. "All right, you can tell me about this planet and then I want to know about Garran."

"This is Eris and Garran is an Erisian. I have heard that humans call them vampires."

That explained the girl's behavior when she saw Emily. She was probably ready for lunch. Jenna blanched at the thought, but didn't interrupt.

"The technology is taken from them. Occasionally one of them will fall down the Crystal Mountain, just as you did. I obtained the ring in this way. They can fly, but the young ones haven't always mastered their abilities. That is the purpose of the great hunt. This ring allows interspecies communication. The healing device is something their scientists have created. Don't ask me how it works. I don't know."

"What about you and Soto? They just let you stay out here and don't bother you? I can't imagine they're very benevolent."

"Our blood is different. Soto and I are Regalians. Usually the Erisians use our kind as slaves in the mines, but sometimes the princess has mercy. My wife was pregnant so Princess Adrasta ordered our release. She is the only one among them that has any kindness and the others would not dare go against her wishes."

Jenna wanted to ask more questions about the vampire princess as well as Moye's wife, but she was starting to feel a little drained. "I guess that makes you very lucky. Are there a lot of people like you, that don't meet the Erisians' dietary requirements?"

"Oh, yes." Moye answered quickly. "But those living freely who are not Erisian are few in number. All others serve the vampire society as slaves."

Jenna felt anger stir for the first time in what felt like days. "And you just let the murdering vampires get away with using other life forms for food? Why don't you rise up against them, do something?"

"Why?" He looked honestly confused. "They do not harm us and we do not interfere with them. Besides, there are so few of us that any such attack would be little more than a nuisance."

"So you just let them kill people? I can't believe I'm hearing this." Jenna's hands had balled into fists, her heart pounding in outrage.

"Do you not keep livestock on your world for consumption? The Erisians are the dominant species of this world and to fight against them would be lunacy."

"People are *not* cattle. We're sentient."

Moye merely shrugged his shoulders and took a step back. He held a hand out and Soto rushed to his side. "We have done all we can. Rest now and when you rise, it will be time to leave."

"Wait, I have one more question. How did you obtain the rest of your advanced technology? I can't imagine the Erisians just giving it to you."

"My wife worked in the palace before the princess released her. We took what we needed to ensure our survival here in the wilderness."

He and Soto walked out of the room, considerately ensuring that the fabric had dropped over the doorway. Jenna could understand their reasoning for taking the equipment and even the seemingly cavalier attitude about not standing up against the vampires. These people had nothing, most notably a lack of defenses. Interference would only ensure their demise. Jenna took a breath and scooted to the edge of the mattress. As much as she might need it, she didn't intend to rest any more. She had to find her things and get to Saqqara. Emily and the others were in trouble and she'd rested enough.

Jenna found her clothes on a peg in the corner, but much of it wasn't salvageable. One of her boots had the heel ripped off and the right leg of her trousers was missing. Her pistol was gone from the holster, but most of her other equipment was there.

"Not to mention all the blood," she muttered.

Soto surprised her by rushing past the curtain and into the room. He carried a bundle of clothing and a long pair of brown boots. Without a word, he dropped the pile on top of the bed and then scooted back out. Curious, Jenna walked over and picked up a long shirt. He apparently figured out that she wasn't staying until the deadline given by his father.

Jenna dressed in the shirt, a pair of soft trousers that were too long, but when tucked into the boots were fine. The boots were a little snug, but not bad. Jenna kept her gun belt with the accessories that had survived the fall. A heavy, dark brown cloak completed the outfit, though she kept her warm jacket underneath, deciding that the layers would help ward off the cold if she had to trudge through the lower temperatures of the day. The indigenous clothing would help her blend in and the boots were much more comfortable than her old pair.

Jenna ducked under the partition and caught her first sight of the main living area. Twice the size of the bedroom, she spotted another bunk tucked in the far corner, a couple of chairs with a rough, braided rug along one side and a small kitchen area with a tiny circular table and two chairs. It wasn't much, but it had the look of a happy and well-loved home.

Soto sat at the table and looked up with a welcoming smile. Moye sat beside him, carving a piece of wood with a small knife. They looked like the perfect small family. Jenna thought the setting seemed like something out of a Norman Rockwall painting.

She swallowed her apprehension at leaving the relative safety of their abode and tried to project an aura of determination. "Thank you for everything you've done for me, Moye. I understand that your priority is keeping your family safe, so I think I should leave you now."

"You should stay and rest. It is many days to Saqqara and walking at this time of the day is most perilous."

"Like you said, I'm placing you both in danger by just being here. I have to help my friend and I'm eager to continue my journey."

He looked sad, but nodded in understanding. "You must be careful. Watch the skies."

"I will."

Jenna looked at Soto, who stood up and waited to see what she would do next. She wanted to give something back to them for their assistance, but needed everything she had on her. Finally, she removed her watch and handed it to the boy. It was useless to her, but he smiled as if he'd received a grand gift and ran to show it to his father.

She turned to leave.

"Wait," Moye said, slipping the translator ring off his finger. "You will need this to communicate with anyone you encounter. About forty paces from the door, you will encounter a dry riverbed. Keep the moons to your left and it will lead you to Saqqara. If the great moons aren't visible, walk toward the sun. Also, do not let the river deceive you. It will not always be dry."

Moye turned to his son and spoke before translating for Jenna. "Soto will fetch a canteen. It has isokenetic properties capable of filtering out bacteria and filth from any water you encounter."

Jenna accepted the canteen and a small bag of food from the boy. Unaccountably, she felt moved to tears, but resolutely pushed them away. She had a job to do and there wasn't time to get maudlin.

"Thanks again." Jenna walked out feeling stronger than she had in days and set off toward the path.

Chapter Ten

EMILY DASHED TOWARD the forest. She didn't know how much of a head start the Erisians would allow, but guessed it wouldn't be much and she didn't intend to waste any time. She entered the woods along with a small group of prisoners and considered what a tactical error it was just as Fallon spoke.

"We're too easy a target like this. We should break apart."

Emily was astounded. "You speak my language?"

"My people speak many languages. The Erisians, however, utilize a ring to facilitate communication. Nevertheless, I suggest we concentrate on our situation."

She was right, Emily realized. She had to focus.

Their small troop consisted of Emily, Fallon, Charles and three others. Way too many people to avoid detection.

"Charles, can you get a couple of them to safety? At least find a place to hide out?"

"I can try. Nick, Laurel, follow me."

Emily watched the three people take off at a right angle from the rest of them. That left only herself, Fallon and an older man. The stranger headed into the woods on his own without a word.

"Guess that leaves you and me."

"This way," the alien woman called over her shoulder.

Fallon ducked into the brush and tore off down a narrow game trail. The path would be easy for the vampires to follow, but it was the best way to put as much distance as possible between them and their pursuers. Hopefully, they'd be able to dispense with the path later and evade the Erisians or at least get out of their reach. Shadows pressed in from every side, but Emily kept Fallon directly in her sights.

"When's the sun going to come up? I can hardly see anything."

"The sun isn't going to help you. Eris gets its illumination from the moons."

Emily blinked quickly, trying to digest the information. "Are you telling me this is daytime?"

"It is here."

"Perfect. So what do we do now?"

"My ship crashed a few miles from here. If we can get to it, I might be able to make repairs and fly us away from this planet."

Emily tripped over something in the darkness and stumbled for a few paces. She eventually caught her balance and kept moving. "And then what? We just leave all these others to fend for themselves?"

"Yes."

Emily frowned and considered the response. The two of them

against an entire society of vampires sounded like a losing battle, but her conscience had a hard time with that scenario. She wanted to question Fallon further, to insist they do something to rescue the remaining victims, but now wasn't the time so she concentrated and moved deeper into the alien forest.

"Split up!" Fallon hissed. "I hear someone coming."

Acting on pure instinct and adrenaline, Emily bolted left and headed for a thick tree with a low-hanging branch. She hauled herself up and began to climb as quickly as she could, hoping the limbs and foliage would conceal her. Cold wind buffeted her, trying to dislodge her from her perch. Deep in the overhead canopy, she crouched and peered onto the trail below. Fallon had disappeared, but she spotted someone else. The darkness made it hard to be sure, but the figure seemed thin and wraith-like. The individual turned and moonlight illuminated the human female, Laurel.

How'd she get out here by herself?

Emily hadn't any time to wonder. Sudden movement on her right, just at the outside of her peripheral vision made her freeze. An Erisian moved directly toward Laurel, but the vampire was flying. Without any visible means of external propulsion, the Erisian drifted past the tree and honed in on Laurel. Emily knew it was a vampire because of the blood red fire illuminating the teenage girl's eyes.

They could fly? How could a humanoid creature fly without wings? It was against the laws of physics. Stunned, Emily wondered what else they could do.

Physics didn't seem to matter to the girl. With a victorious shout, the nascent vampire dropped out of the air and right on top of Laurel. Emily watched the young human go down with a scream and outrage flooded her system. Emily started to leave her concealment and rush to Laurel's aid when another Erisian, this time a boy, joined his counterpart.

Emily was stunned and shaken by how quickly the vampires dispatched Laurel. She was grateful for the darkness that kept her from seeing the finer details. They tore Laurel apart, fighting over their garish feast. The wet sounds, crunching and grunts were nauseating. Emily gagged quietly and dropped to her knees on the giant limb. Tears of fury and horror flooded her eyes and she wept silently for the girl she couldn't save. To try would accomplish nothing but her own death.

In moments, it was over. The Erisians sprang back into the air, heading off in pursuit of other prey and leaving Laurel's remains as if she was nothing but discarded garbage. They didn't even bother to collect the bracelet Emily heard Erisians used to keep the prisoners in line. She could see it glinting in the moonlight.

Emily waited until she saw Fallon step out onto the path. Senses on high alert, Emily joined her. She didn't look toward the spot where Laurel's body lay. There wasn't any point since they couldn't do anything for her and they needed to worry about their own survival.

"How far to your ship?"

Fallon looked at a device on her wrist that resembled a watch. It was solid silver and an LED interface on the top blinked green. "Two miles, that way."

When she pointed, Emily set off before Fallon could say anything else. They hurried through the woods quietly for a few minutes, each lost in their own thoughts.

Emily's grief over Laurel transformed into worry about a particular sheriff, hopefully safe at home. She wondered where Jenna was. Had Jenna even considered what happened to her? Did she care or was their brief time together so easily forgotten? Was she too busy trying to end a rash of kidnappings that she couldn't be bothered to think of Emily?

She was surprised to find the idea didn't sit well with her. Emily realized she had a reputation for sleeping around. It wasn't a big secret. The staggering part was that she didn't want Jenna to see her as a one-night stand and she wanted her to miss her, to wonder what had become of her. It didn't really matter, Emily supposed, but it felt like forever since she'd seen Jenna, rather than just a few days. Frustrated, she questioned why she still thought about Jenna with all that was going on. Surely, surviving the Ti-gon should be all that was important.

"You're from Earth," Fallon said.

"You've heard of it?"

"It is difficult not to. The planet is so primitive that the Erisians find the population an easy target."

"Hey," Emily complained, "I'd appreciate a little respect since I happen to be one of those Neanderthals."

"My apologies, I meant no insult. I'm just accustomed to species that are more advanced, in a technological sense. If we should have to confront an Erisian, I need to understand your capabilities."

"Trust me; I've had lots of training. My capabilities are just fine."

"Not if you don't understand your target."

"You mean the vampires? You're right about that. I thought vampires were just a product of someone's overworked imagination. Now I find that I've stepped through the mirror of insanity where there are all types of monsters and aliens. I think I need my head examined."

Fallon stopped abruptly and listened for a few seconds before she started walking again. "You're not imagining this and I don't have time to coddle you."

"I'm not asking for special treatment. Just give me the facts."

"The reason your kind doesn't know about this world is that only a few of you are taken at different locations around your globe. Since you don't have the ability to travel between stars during your lifetimes, you aren't exposed to other cultures. Eris is given a wide berth by anyone advanced enough to know about them."

Emily huffed. "So what's your excuse?"

"I told you, my ship crashed. I'm a captain in the Levothos Consortium. The Levothan are at war with Eris because of their barbaric practices. One of their fighters got in a lucky shot and there you have it, I crashed into the foot of their Barlinic Mountains."

"But you can get it fixed, right? Your ship, I mean. If you could just take me back to wherever it is that I arrived here, I'd really appreciate it."

Fallon turned on the footpath and shot Emily a curious glance. "How could I possibly know how you got here?"

"You said my people are brought here all the time."

"Yes, from all over your planet, but there are many portals. I have no idea where you'd return to if I took you to a random doorway."

That explained Nick's accent. People arrived here by way of inter-dimensional rifts, not just space ships. With one careless step, Emily could end up in Siberia. Still, she couldn't be any worse off than she was now.

"I'll take my chances."

Fallon's wrist device beeped once, a low tone that Emily wouldn't have noticed from a distance. The alien captain stepped off the trail and into a thicket where she crouched into the shadows. Emily didn't know what had startled Fallon, but she wasn't going to wait around to find out. Instead, she ducked down and rushed over to squat next to Fallon.

"What is it?" she whispered.

"Four vampires. Two directly along the trail and two others flanking our position."

They were surrounded. Emily looked down at the bracelet encircling her wrist. Either the Erisian youngsters were very good hunters, or there was a locator built into the jewelry just as Charles had said. It was time to switch to combat tactics. Just because the enemy knew they were here, didn't mean they knew what Emily would do.

"How far away."

"Sixty feet and closing in slowly. They're trying to flush us out."

Emily reached down and picked up a short, thick stick. She stuck the point into the dirt as deeply as she could and pulled the monofilament roll from her belt.

"What are you doing?" Fallon questioned quietly.

"Move back the way we came. Hide behind that big boulder we passed a few minutes ago."

Fallon nodded and left, evidently trusting Emily to know what she was doing. Emily quickly strung the wire across the trail and dropped the end on the ground. She cursed the fact that she was about to use the only true armament that she could utilize from a distance, but didn't hesitate to pull the grenade from the pouch. Emily jammed the explosive under a heavy stone and tied the free end of the string to the pull ring. Then she shuffled backward in the weeds toward where Fallon waited.

She found Fallon tucked down behind the boulder and crammed in beside her. "How far away are they now?"

"From our last position?"

Emily nodded.

"Ten feet...eight...six..."

Emily heard the snick of the pull ring as it was tugged from the grenade and quickly closed her eyes. "You might want to duck."

A large explosion lit the darkness and multiple voices cried out in pain. It lasted only a few seconds, but Emily felt her ears ring from the concussive blast. Dirt and debris rained down over their position and she covered her head with her hands. She felt Fallon jerk in surprise, but the Levothan warrior stayed where she was until it was over. All was silent after the explosion and it took a few seconds to realize the Erisians weren't converging on their location.

Fallon peaked around the side of the boulder and then stood up. "I think you killed them all." She sounded reluctantly impressed.

"Let's make sure."

Emily pulled the knife from the boot sheath and carefully approached the place where she'd set off the grenade. There wasn't much left of the enemy and she felt a strange kind of vindication, equal parts satisfaction and anger.

"It's time to get off this path. Can you find your ship if we go overland?"

"Yes. Good job, by the way."

"Thanks. Sometimes archaic explosives come in handy."

Fallon sighed and shook her head. In that moment, she didn't seem different than any disgruntled human. "We don't have much time. The moons are headed toward the horizon. Once they set, the Ti-gon will be concluded."

"And that's bad?"

"If we haven't reached the ship by then, it will be."

The terrain was much more difficult once they left the game trail, but Emily felt safer. Both were quiet as they walked. In the distance, Emily could see a mountain range and hoped Fallon's ship was on the near side. Some time ago, Fallon had told her it was two miles to her vessel. Emily thought they should be closing in on their destination.

The forest gave way to a natural clearing, though the tall grass provided a modicum of concealment. Emily figured they could hide in it if they had to. She'd just opened her mouth to say as much to Fallon when an Erisian swooped out of the sky and snatched Fallon off her feet. Fallon must have been more solid than she looked since the vampire had difficulty gaining altitude.

Emily shouted and ran after them. She could see Fallon struggling with her captor, but couldn't close the distance. Fallon pulled a weapon of some sort from her uniform and fired a ruby beam up at the vampire, slicing through the creature's forearm. Emily was horrified at the sight of Fallon dropping into a canyon and again wondered why the Erisians had left everyone with their weapons.

She lost sight of Fallon as she plummeted over the edge, but rejoiced as the Erisian crashed headfirst into the ground. A sickening crunch told her the vampire wouldn't be moving again.

Emily rushed to the side of the precipice and peered over the edge. Fallon wasn't anywhere in sight. She'd lost her only advantage and now Emily didn't know what to do. She couldn't find the alien vessel without Fallon and she had no idea how to find a portal. Yet she still had to survive. With all these aliens running around the planet, someone had to know the way out.

The moons were beginning to set and the shadows were lengthening. With full darkness setting in, Emily wouldn't be able to spot the bloodsuckers as easily. They were accustomed to this lighting and she wasn't. Now it was about cover and concealment. Emily crouched down and used everything she could find to hide behind while she made her way in the direction she and Fallon had traveled. Even if she couldn't find the ship, she had to focus on putting as much distance between herself and the Erisians and this was as good a direction as any. She prayed that the wristbands had a limited range and she'd eventually exceed whatever it was.

Emily walked for another hour before she had to concede she'd never find Fallon's vessel. When she suddenly stepped into running water, she dropped to her knees and greedily scooped the muddy liquid into her mouth, praying she wouldn't get sick from ingesting a bunch of alien parasites. After a few minutes, she progressed to digging handfuls of mud from the creek bottom and pasting it onto her skin. The mud would mask her body odor and assist with camouflage. Emily realized she expected the vampires to be able to smell her and that the supposition came from watching too much television. Still, she wasn't going to take the chance that they couldn't.

Once her task was complete, Emily scooted into the scrub to find a place to rest. She'd been on her feet for a very long time. The moons were almost down now and she hoped that meant she'd successfully evaded the vampires. She had to consider her options.

Clearly, the Erisians were the dominant species on the planet, but other life forms might be willing to conspire against them. Maybe some already did. That didn't mean they'd be prepared to help her. Tired, frightened, and battered, Emily was reaching the limits of her endurance. She could see the sun rising in the distance, but the small pinprick of light imparted no warmth. Dispirited, Emily forced herself to move on. It took some time to realize that her left wrist had started to tingle. She reached up to scratch, but discovered her wrist wasn't the problem. The bracelet had started vibrating.

"Oh crap," she whispered to herself.

Emily reached for her knife, prepared to saw through her own arm if it was required to get the damned wristband off. She'd barely slipped the tip under the edge when an electrical surge sent her to her knees. Emily struggled against the sensation, fighting to get back to the water in the off chance that the current would carry her away before the Erisians arrived. The shock stopped for a moment and she thought she might make it. Just as she reached the stream, another current ripped through her body and Emily dropped onto her side. Panting and scared, she waited to see if she would be torn apart like Laurel.

Seconds later, a vampire girl landed a few feet from her. Murderous fire burned in the Erisian's eyes and white teeth stood out against the shadows. The girl grinned and dropped a heavy burden onto the ground before she moved slowly toward Emily. From how she took her time approaching her prey, it was clear the girl was savoring the victory she was about to enjoy. The teenager was almost on her when Emily saw a hand grasp her shoulder and fling the youngster away.

"No, Chala," Ilana commanded, angrily. "You must learn control."

The young vampire simpered and looked away from her elder. "But I'm hungry."

"You have already fed on two of the prisoners. The hunger will consume you if you let it. Take this one back to the holding rooms and get her cleaned up. If I find that you have damaged her, the punishment will be great."

Emily had difficulty holding onto consciousness, but she saw Chala approach and she heard Ilana's words.

"We'll keep you in the Ti-gon, I think. Our young can learn much from you."

At the last moment curiosity won out and Emily turned her head to see what Chala had dropped beside her. She found herself looking into Nick's lifeless eyes.

Chapter Eleven

EMILY AWAKENED SLOWLY. Her first conscious thought was that she was tired of waking up with a migraine. Then all of the events of the preceding day flooded her mind, assaulting her with questions. What had happened to Fallon when she dropped over the precipice? Had Charles escaped the vampires or was he similarly back in a cell? Most importantly, would she ever have the chance to let Nick's family know what happened to him, along with all the other victims' families? Regret and hatred suffused her heart.

She'd been an FBI agent for the last ten years and seen many cruelties perpetrated by one human being upon another, but this was different. These aliens lacked any sense of humanity. They preyed gleefully upon the weak and defenseless. Moreover, the Erisians rejoiced in murdering the innocent merely to assuage their hunger and desire for cruelty. The depravity sickened her and she wanted nothing more than to avenge the young man's death by repaying every Erisian she found with the fate he'd endured.

"You're finally awake."

The familiarity of the mocking voice made Emily leap to her feet and rush toward the barred opening of her prison. Her intention was to grab Ilana by the throat and squeeze the life out of her, but the vampire stood too far away to let that happen. With her head tilted back and her hands on her hips, Ilana was the picture of arrogant supremacy.

"Murderer!" Emily railed. "How can you stand there looking so high-and-mighty when you're nothing more than a butcher?"

Her words didn't seem to affect the regent. Ilana raised an eyebrow and a small smile tugged the corners of her lips. That she was amused by the tirade only made Emily that much angrier.

"You think that's funny? Let me out of this cage and I'll show you just how amusing I can be. Come on," Emily goaded, "just you and me. No gadgets or shocking me unconscious. Let's see how tough you really are."

"I have no intention of doing any such thing." Ilana sounded like she was disappointed in an unruly child. "You are much too entertaining right where you are...in the hunt. Speaking of which, you have slept much of the night and the moons will soon rise. Eat your food. You must regain your strength."

The regent glanced down at a corner of the cell and Emily realized a tray sat on the ground. She didn't know how long the food had been there and she certainly didn't feel like she'd slept. Not that it mattered to the Erisians. The vampires would drain her dry eventually. If not tonight then on some other night, depending on how long she survived the pitfalls of the Ti-gon.

"Forget it. I'm not playing your twisted little game anymore. If you're going to kill me then do it and get it over with."

Emily sat down and leaned against the gelatin-like wall. She was tired, hungry, and angry. If her tantrum made Ilana let down her guard long enough to allow Emily the opportunity, she'd take full advantage of it by killing her. Pretending to be beaten, Emily rested her arms on bent knees and lowered her head.

"I didn't realize humans gave up so easily," Ilana taunted. "What will become of your fellow captives without you to lead them to freedom?"

"Nice try, but I'm not responsible for them being here. You have that honor."

For a few seconds, there was nothing but silence. Then the lights brightened around the cages and Ilana said, "Get up." Ilana sounded angry, but Emily deliberately ignored her, keeping her eyes pinned to the floor.

The vampire stepped closer to the cell. "I said get on your feet. The Ti-gon will begin in a few minutes and you will participate."

"That's where you're wrong, Chuckles. You can drag me out of this cell, but I won't be a party to any more of this insanity."

"Would you prefer that I let Chala have you? I could have let her kill you last night."

Emily finally looked up, allowing all of the fury she felt to show in her eyes. "So what, I'm supposed to be grateful? At least if she drains me it'll be over."

A group of Erisians entered the chamber and stopped a few feet away from the regent. Emily recognized many of the vampires from the night before, including Chala. The youngster had a perpetually starved look about her and her glassy eyes wandered all over the room. Emily had used the word insanity to needle Ilana but in this case, it seemed to be the truth. Chala wasn't playing with a full deck. As she remembered Ilana's threat to let the girl have her Emily shuddered, but did her best not to let the sudden fear show.

"Last chance," the regent teased in a mocking voice.

Her gaze held triumph, as if she knew that Emily wouldn't resist when directly faced with the out-of-control juvenile. The taunting was enough to get her dander up and Emily stood defiantly.

"No. If you're going to let her kill me, at least I'll die knowing I didn't bend to your will."

Ilana's eyes narrowed and a worm of apprehension crawled up Emily's spine. She had the impression that she should have gone along with her, but it was too late now.

"You haven't earned a quick death," the regent declared angrily. "Since you refuse to cooperate, let's see how well you do in the selenium mines. I've heard the properties of the mineral are quite toxic for your species."

The word sounded familiar, but Emily wasn't exactly sure what it was. From Ilana's implications, she certainly didn't want to find out. Unfortunately, the alternative was the Ti-gon.

That wasn't true, Emily realized. Ilana had mentioned the nutrition tanks before...the *baribas*. They'd probably need to induce a coma for that so the mines were probably her best bet, whatever the dangers. At least she'd be awake and able to look for a way out.

"Will you at least take the bracelet off?" Emily asked, displaying the offending trinket. "I think it's rubbing a blister."

The last bit of sarcasm was apparently too much for the hunt mistress. "Garran, take her to the mines and introduce her to Sodesh. I'm sure they'll get along quite well."

Judging from the grin on the vampire's face, Emily thought she might be lying. Regardless, that didn't mean she was going to let them see her sweat. "Is that supposed to scare me? I beat you at the Ti-gon and you know it. The only reason I'm still here is because you have no honor. You had to electrocute me to make that happen."

Emily made the comment with as much disgust as she could muster in her tone. The goading worked and Ilana stepped toward the cell just as Garran disabled the bars. Emily launched her body at the regent, her hands outstretched and ready to strangle Ilana. Ilana's eyes widened in surprise and she reeled backward, but her reaction was an instant too late. Strong hands closed over her throat and Emily squeezed for all she was worth. She didn't expect to actually kill Ilana, only frighten her and make the Erisian see that she wasn't invulnerable.

She felt the satisfying sensation of skin and bones compress under her grip, heard the strangled gasp the vampire regent emitted. It lasted just a few seconds, but long enough to see fear in the pale blue eyes.

Garran finally gathered his scattered senses and grabbed Emily by the collar. He tried to tug her from his superior. Instead, he sent both of the women flying. Ilana landed atop Emily as they hit the floor. Emily felt a knee forcefully smashed against her groin. That brief distraction proved to be all that Ilana needed. She easily tore Emily's hands from her throat and quickly gained the upper hand by putting Emily into a headlock.

Hauled to her feet by the arms around her neck, Emily could only pant and struggle futilely against the iron-like grasp. She could hear the fury in Ilana's voice.

"Do you think you can manage to control one small female long enough to deliver her to Sodesh?"

Emily tried to tilt her head back, but her face pressed up against the side of Ilana's breast. As a fan of the female form, Emily reacted without thought, inhaling the other woman's scent. To her surprise, Ilana smelled sweet and clean. Her body was soft and warm and for one smoldering moment, Emily forgot exactly where she was.

Until Garran grasped the back of her shirt and hauled her from

Ilana's grasp. His face was a decided shade of pink and Emily was surprised Erisians could react to embarrassment in such a human fashion.

"My deepest apologies, Regent. She will not elude me again."

"See that she doesn't."

Ilana shot Emily a look that was difficult to interpret, but she could have sworn that she saw equal parts confusion and desire. Remembering her own response such a short time ago, Emily shuddered in revulsion.

Ugh, no way. Emily thought she was losing it.

Garran pulled Emily across the floor toward the exit. She was aware of all the amused Erisians watching the show, but didn't have much chance to look around. They were moving quickly across the room and Garran had her hauled up on the tip of her toes.

"Slow down, will you? I can hardly keep my balance."

"Then I shall drag you," he promised without sparing her a glance.

Emily worried that she'd gone too far needling the vampires, but then again, attitude was one of her better qualities. She didn't resist Garran and was actually looking forward to transferring her incarceration to the mine supervisor. Maybe this toxic mineral Ilana spoke of could help disable the tracking device she wore around her wrist.

Outside the barracks, Emily got her first true look at the area. Before, the prisoners had run straight into the woods, forced to engage in the hunt. Now, she faced Saqqara and blinked in astonishment at the magnificence she found. Slender, column-like buildings reached far into the sky, the dual moons of Eris a breathtaking backdrop for the scene. She didn't know if the structures served for housing, or offices, or even a combination of the two, but each of them appeared constructed of pure crystal. In addition, flying discs zipped around the city at different elevations, although Emily could swear she saw a definite pattern.

Air corridors or something like it?

To top it all off, a huge castle lay to one side, far enough away from the main city to stand out in all its glory. Pennants of green and red flew from the two turrets at each end. To her disappointment, Garran wasn't leading her toward the castle, or even one of the lovely skyscrapers. He was heading toward a dirt lane that circumnavigated the edge of the city and led directly into the opening of a dark, dank mine.

Emily briefly considered asking to become a slave inside the castle, but something told her the palace was more heavily guarded than anywhere else on the planet. She kept her mouth shut until the meager light of the Erisian day disappeared from view. Faced with dark, earthen tunnels illuminated by artificial torches on either side, she found herself truly speechless.

Garran finally stopped in a large, circular chamber, for which Emily was deeply grateful. She'd just caught her breath when she realized they weren't alone. Slowly, she looked toward a darkened dais near the rear of the chamber. It was backlit by a bright orange glow cast from a deep pit. Whether of fire or some other source, the light gave the occupant a sinister shadow that dwarfed the two of them combined. Fear trailed an icy finger down her spine and she struggled to swallow against a desert-dry throat.

"I see you've brought me new meat, Garran. Details?"

The voice throbbed low with menace and as she watched, an extremely tall Erisian stepped into the low lighting where Emily could see his features. Approximately seven-plus feet, the vampire resembled his species only in that he was a bloodsucker. He was the first she'd seen with flame-red hair and brown eyes. Conversely, the Erisian was heavily muscled where the others tended toward lean. His scowl rested on them both and Emily was surprised to feel Garran tremble. The menacing gaze shifted to rest entirely on her while Garran began to explain.

"A lowly human, Lord Sodesh. She is belligerent and uncooperative with the Ti-gon."

Sodesh stared at Emily for a moment before a malicious grin crossed his face. For a second she thought he would actually laugh. "And who could blame her?"

Garran started and flashed an annoyed look at the mine master, regardless of his fear for the man.

"That's right," Sodesh grated. "I have no reverence for the grand hunt. It pales in comparison to the importance in the search for selenium. You know how vital it is in stabilizing our technologies, yet you bring me new workers only rarely."

"With respect," Garran whined, "if the slaves weren't slain so often, there would be sufficient workers."

This time Sodesh did laugh. Emily jumped at the sound because it held no amusement.

"Your attitude will not be tolerated here," Sodesh informed her, ignoring Garran at this point. "If you refuse to work or even slow down for a moment without permission, you will be beaten. The guards are not prone to mercy and they have my authorization to deal with the slaves as they see fit. I suggest you cooperate."

Emily thought Sodesh was full of hot air and overdoing things in an effort to intimidate. Her amused grin drove his fury up another notch.

"Matok!" he bellowed.

She still had a slight smile on her face when a softly muffled noise sounded from one of the tunnels. It faded when she saw the creature that entered the chamber. Although not as tall as the mine slaver, Matok was still tall by Earth standards, and lean. He wore little clothing. A simple pair of trousers hugged his form and showed the muscles beneath. At first, Emily thought he might be blind because his eyes were solid spheres of white. The color made her think of thick cataracts. It would be a snap to get away from these guards if they all had the same condition.

"Do you still believe the guards to be humorous?"

"Not so much," Emily muttered, not realizing she had smiled until Sodesh asked the question.

"Take her to the mines," Sodesh ordered his guard.

Matok crossed over the room, seeming to glide over the uneven cave floor. Before he could lay a large, milky hand on her Emily spoke. "Just tell me where to go. I'll do what you say."

For now.

Emily tried her best not to recoil as Matok reached out toward her. Even in the shadows, she could see the grime covering his skin, the filth under his short nails. He never actually made contact. Only a few inches away, he stopped and grinned, but there was no humor in his expression. She realized she hadn't concealed her discomfort as well as she thought.

Matok glanced toward the tunnel he'd just traversed and then turned back toward her. His tongue slid out of his mouth and Emily could have sworn he hissed. She caught on to the implied command fast enough. Silently, she headed down the tunnel with all of her senses on high alert.

EMILY'S STOMACH COMPLAINED loudly, but she tried to ignore the gnawing sensation. Sweat poured from her brow, stinging her eyes. She quickly thumbed it from her vision and returned to digging after she cast a furtive glance around the darkened mine shaft. So far, there hadn't been the slightest chance to scout the area and that wasn't her intention now. Instead, Emily wanted to ensure none of the guards caught her slight transgression.

She, and all of the other slaves, had to work ceaselessly. She didn't know how many hours she'd shoveled, only that the blisters on her hands had burst long ago. Yet she didn't stop, couldn't stop. Shortly after her arrival, Emily watched one of the ruthless guards beat a man to death because he stopped long enough to cough the dust from his lungs. She had discovered that the appearance of the guards' eyes were deceiving. They could see easily into the darkest corners and she had revised her opinion. Emily thought it much more likely that the guards rarely went to the surface and their eyes had adapted to the subterranean darkness.

Someone slid up beside her and Emily heard the squeak of the cart. Without really thinking about it, she sat the laser-tipped tool on the rough ground and leaned the handle against the wall. She bent over and started picking up lumps of the selenium mineral that was so important to the Erisians.

"Your hands are too damaged to work."

The fact that someone spoke at all was a surprise, though the woman kept her voice low. Emily looked up with widened eyes before she shot a worried glance to the closest guard. The creature watched them, but his energy whip remained attached to his waist. After a moment, he turned away and drifted down a darkened tunnel, leaving them unattended for the first time.

When she didn't respond, the stranger gently took one of her hands and inspected the palm. On the surface, the woman seemed like any other worker. Her clothing was torn and dirty, her face smudged and hands work hardened, but there was something in her eyes that pegged her as different. Emily noticed the ring worn around the stranger's middle finger.

"You're Erisian."

The shorter woman smiled slightly and looked up, her blue eyes catching the crimson glow of the low artificial lights. Her gaze darted around quickly before returning and Emily thought the stranger was concerned the other prisoners would overhear their conversation.

"Most of the slaves think I'm human. My name is Vaden, Vaden Dumal."

Vaden reached into her front trouser pocket and removed a small device that she kept carefully obscured in the shadows. She squeezed a tiny button and a faint yellow glow burned at the tip. Vaden ran the instrument back and forth over Emily's hand and Emily watched the blisters begin to close.

"Better?"

"Yes, thank you." Emily allowed Vaden to attend her wounds but after a second she said, "It's true you don't look like one of them. For one thing, you're the first brunette I've seen and all of the other vamp...uh, Erisians...have long hair. Also you're a little small."

"Small? Oh, you mean my height. Well, in a way I suppose you're right. My mother was human."

Emily decided vampire genealogy wasn't really a pressing matter. "And the reason the guards haven't killed us for slacking off?" Vaden's eyes narrowed and Emily felt afraid of this woman for the first time.

"I'm still Erisian, even if my philosophy doesn't match that of most of my people. I have all of their strengths and the guards fear me. As long as they don't make trouble for me, I pretend to be another broken slave. They stay on Sodesh's good side and I have the latitude to do what I want."

Emily gaped at her in surprise. "Then why don't you leave?"

"Because it suits my own purposes to be here."

She was tired of the cryptic answers. Couldn't anyone on this planet come out and say what they meant? "Are you going to explain that or should I just stand here and tremble in awe?"

Vaden smiled and put her tool away. "Neither. Time to get back to work. I'll explain more when we stop to eat."

"All right, for now." Emily picked up a chunk of selenium and dropped it into the cart, relieved when her hands didn't hurt. "At least now I know they'll actually feed us."

Vaden helped load the cart, then she touched the controls on the handle that activated the anti-gravity feature. The transporter rose from the ground and she directed it away. Emily felt no curiosity for the technology that allowed the cart to hover over the ground. Instead, she wanted to sit down, put her head back, and sleep for a week. In deference to her exhaustion, she briefly closed her eyes. She quickly opened them again when she remembered the look Ilana had cast in her direction before Garran escorted her to the mines.

"I don't want to go there," she whispered under her breath.

Soon the guard slithered back into the chamber. She didn't know if he was the same one from earlier because they all looked alike in the darkness, but she chose not to take the chance. Emily grasped the handle of her laser shovel and got back to work. After a while, new blisters had formed, but hadn't popped when she heard a shrill whine that reverberated at such a pitch that it set her teeth on edge.

As one unit, all the other slaves stopped working and murmured in low voices. Emily gratefully put down her tool and took a second to stretch her back. She followed the others with nothing on her mind except her aching muscles. It took several seconds for her to realize the floor had a definite upward angle. Headed toward the surface, Emily was suddenly much more interested in her surroundings. This might be the only chance she had to scout the area for any possible escape routes.

Emily blinked as Erisian moonlight struck her eyes. Before, she thought the illumination to be equal to dusk on Earth but after working in the mines, it seemed much brighter. She could actually make out details she might not have noticed earlier.

The guards herded the slaves out of the tunnels and around to the side where some food pots were set up. The vampires that escorted them to the surface stopped several feet from the entrance and another contingent took over. Emily was surprised to see two separate feeding stations. Vaden and a few others headed toward the smallest area while everyone else walked toward the largest. It didn't take a genius to figure out which line she should join. She needed to be near the vampire to gather intel and discover if there was an easy way out.

She wondered why they'd enslave their own kind. Emily remembered how Chala mercilessly slaughtered the others during the Ti-gon and found it odd the Erisians would take exception to anything their own species did.

Emily slowly made her way through the line and eventually retrieved a bowl of foul-smelling gruel. Her lip curled in disgust and she longed for the tasteless white cubes she'd been fed earlier. She frowned and walked over to where Vaden sat. The vampire leaned against a wooden, shed-like structure talking quietly with two others. As Emily approached, the man and woman quieted. All three of them held a small silver cup with the remains of what she assumed was their meal. Emily tried to ignore the red smears on the container edges.

"Uh, you said we should talk while we ate," Emily reminded her.

For a moment, Vaden just stared at her. Then she glanced at her companions and indicated with a nod that they should leave.

"Sit down. You never told me your name."

More concerned with other matters, Emily stared at the goo in her bowl and considered how to consume her dinner. She'd been in Japan before and the people there simply drank their soup from a bowl without using a utensil. This stuff was technically too thick to be thought soup, but she was willing to apply the same principles. Tilting the edge of the bowl into her mouth, she experienced her first mouthful of gruel.

"Oh my God," she mumbled and then clamped her mouth shut so she wouldn't spit it out. She managed to swallow and then shuddered at the aftertaste. That was when she noticed the grin on Vaden's face and remembered she'd said something.

"Emily. My name is Emily Bannon."

Vaden's eyes narrowed thoughtfully. "Is it? Somehow I don't think that's quite right."

"What do you mean?"

"Emily, you humans have some strange ideas about my people. Garlic, for example. Contrary to your legends, it won't kill us. In fact, I love garlic. But one thing you did get right, or at least partially, is our telepathic abilities. Empathic is probably a better word." Vaden leaned toward her and whispered, "That's not your name. I sense that you're using a false identity because it's somehow tied in with your duties. I also sense that there's no further need for continuing the deceit so I'll ask again. What is your name?"

Emily briefly thought about maintaining her secret, but as she looked into Vaden's eyes, she suddenly realized there was no point. She could continue the charade and possibly offend Vaden, or she could admit the truth. Vaden was clearly more than she pretended to be, this vampire with the freedom to do what she wanted even if she was supposed to be a slave. There was definitely more going on here than Emily knew and she had a feeling Vaden was the key to her freedom.

"My name is Helene Baptiste. I've been going by the Americanized version of my middle name, Emilia. On my world, I'm an undercover law enforcement agent. I was assigned to find out why people in a small Kentucky area were suddenly going missing."

Vaden surprised her by asking, "Which agency?"

"Does it matter?" Emily asked in a bitter tone. "I let the bad guys get the drop on me and now I'm here. Jenna doesn't know." She hadn't intended to mention Jenna and tried to cover her slip by continuing quickly. "No one knows where I am and now more people are in danger because of my stupidity."

"Your anger can be a powerful tool if you use it properly, Helene, but don't let it control your actions."

Emily resisted the urge to roll her eyes and sampled another mouthful of her disgusting meal. It hadn't improved since the last try. "Please, call me Emily. I'm used to it by this point. So why are you in the mines? I can't imagine Erisians punishing their own kind for anything."

"I told you. I disagree with their philosophy."

"On what, exactly?"

"Life."

Emily snorted. "Look, can we cut the crap? If you don't want to answer, just tell me so."

"I want to answer you. I'm just not sure I can. I don't know you, Emily."

Emily found it difficult to argue the point.

A small group of Erisians rounded the mine entrance and approached the area where the slaves sat eating. Emily immediately recognized Ilana at the head of the procession, along with a rather striking woman dressed in expensive-looking silks and a long, flowing gown. The stranger talked quietly with Ilana and from how the regent responded, Emily guessed the other woman was someone of importance.

Four Erisian guards carrying heavy rifles of some sort flanked the pair. Emily noticed that one of the guards was a short, muscled female. The guards had helmets to help obscure their features and all wore a dark blue one-piece uniform. Only the guard's curves and what little Emily could see of her face gave her gender away. All of them carried swords. Like most of the other vampires Emily had seen, the guards also wore cloaks fastened at their throats by a gold clasp. The clasp held an intricate design but Emily wasn't close enough to make out any details. Of all the individuals she'd encountered in this crazy, mixed-up place, only the vampires carried the gold. Emily thought it might symbolize their nature.

In addition to the armed guards, two huge skinks that she guessed were at least three feet in length paced the group.

"Who's that with Ilana...and why the lizards?"

"That is Princess Adrasta, and the lizards are called naga. They're like the dogs on your own world."

Suddenly Ilana made eye contact with Emily and the blue orbs took on a crimson glow. She'd seen this before when one of the vampires grew angry, but she didn't think that was the case here. When the regent stopped walking, so did the rest of her group. Princess Adrasta raised an eyebrow in amusement and watched to see what Ilana might do next.

"Interesting."

"Huh?" Captivated by Ilana's strange behavior, Emily almost missed the comment.

"Emily, look at me."

It was difficult to tear her gaze from the vampire, but when she did, Emily felt like she'd just surfaced from beneath the ocean. She took a deep breath and focused on Vaden. The Erisian seemed excited for the first time since Emily met her.

"Tell me right now, is there something going on between you and Ilana?"

"What? No, of course not! How can you even ask me that?"

Vaden's face darkened slightly and Emily didn't know if it was from anger or embarrassment. "I realize you're disgusted by my race, but the two of you seem to have a connection. I need to know if you've acted on that impulse."

"No, I told you."

"But you don't deny that there's an attraction?"

"I don't know what you're fishing for, but on my world a physical attraction doesn't have to mean anything. I may be a slave here, but I could never be with anyone like her. She's a monster and I like... Never mind."

Emily glanced over toward Ilana again and saw that the regent was in a heated discussion with the princess. There seemed to be some sort of disagreement.

"You need to play on her interests."

"What are you talking about?"

Vaden took her hand and Emily was so startled by the action that she gave the Erisian her complete attention.

"Ilana is not a monster. She's an Erisian who happens to take her duty very seriously. She is never interested in a member of a lesser species. Never."

"What happened to not agreeing with their philosophy? You sound like you admire her."

"I do. I don't agree with killing others for our continued survival. We have the technology to synthesize everything we need from natural sources. Unfortunately, just like any other species, change comes slowly. That doesn't mean I want to see my people annihilated."

"So what do you want me to do?"

"Take advantage of her interest. Ilana could be your way out of the mines. If you were to become her lover, eventually she might trust you enough to let her guard down."

Emily carefully appraised Vaden's avid expression. "One, I will never be her lover. Yuck. And two, you're up to something. What?"

A commotion in the courtyard caught their attention. Ilana looked furious. Her jaw worked back and forth but she was obviously fighting to remain silent. Her gaze stayed pinned to the ground, but the princess had turned to look at Emily. The same scarlet fire Emily witnessed in Ilana's expression had taken up residence on Adrasta's face.

"This is bad."

"I can't argue with that," Vaden remarked. "I believe Ilana just lost her petition. She brought Adrasta here to approve of her removing a worker from the mines to become her personal body slave."

"And?" That thought was scary enough, and Emily didn't know if she wanted to hear the rest.

"I think Adrasta has decided to take you for herself."

Emily quickly looked at Vaden, her eyes wide and frightened. "You mean she's going to force me to have sex with her?" The entourage headed in their direction and she gulped.

"No," Vaden whispered. "No Erisian has ever used force, at least not for sex. She will try to coerce you, use any other means at her disposal to arouse you, but the act must be consensual. Remember that."

"On your feet, slave," Princess Adrasta ordered arrogantly.

Emily didn't like her tone, but refrained from a sarcastic remark. Instead, she set the food bowl on the ground and slowly stood up. While Adrasta inspected her, Emily returned the compliment. Boldly, she stared into the monarch's eyes before slowly sliding her gaze downward. She meant her look to be insulting, but she was really studying her adversary. Adrasta seemed soft compared to the other vampires, as if she did little work and spent her days eating or lying about.

"Regent Ilana has brought you to my attention. Can you believe she actually asked that I give you to her?" Adrasta chuckled and cast a disparaging look toward Ilana. The regent's face darkened angrily, but Ilana remained silent. "I thank her for her diligence, but I believe you'd enjoy spending your days with me instead. What do you think, slave?"

This game had an old feel to it. Vaden said that Ilana never showed interest in anyone outside her species, but evidently, Adrasta was very different. Emily disliked her immediately and she hated the term slave.

"Truthfully, I think I'd rather go with Ilana."

Adrasta's head went back as if she'd been slapped. Emily calmly shifted her gaze to Ilana and forced herself to smile. Her smile grew when Ilana's eyes widened and she was shocked to see a small blush cover Ilana's cheeks.

The princess recovered quickly. She laughed and slapped Ilana on the shoulder. "You were right. She is unpredictable. I like that. Have her cleaned up and taken to my quarters."

Adrasta took a few steps away to speak to her guards and Ilana took advantage of the opportunity to speak. No one else ventured near them.

"My apologies," Ilana muttered, her gaze still pinned to Emily's. "I'd hoped the princess would approve my petition and I would be able to convince you to stay with me. I did not anticipate...so many things." Ilana sighed and turned away slightly.

Emily didn't expect this. Maybe Ilana had some redeeming qualities after all. Regardless, it couldn't hurt to have her on Emily's side. Any enemy in a foreign port was a welcome boon.

Against her better judgment, Emily raised a trembling hand and touched Ilana's shoulder. She felt warm, strong flesh and caught a whiff of Ilana's unique scent. The attraction she felt earlier struck again, but this time Emily wasn't as unprepared. It was just a chemical response induced by pheromones and a hundred other things she couldn't explain, but there was only one woman she truly desired. And Jenna wasn't here. Emily had to use whatever resources she could to escape and return home, even if that meant taking advantage of someone else's feelings.

"You didn't expect me to be interested in you."

"Are you?" Ilana studied her expression carefully.

Emily remembered what Vaden had said about their empathic abilities and decided on the truth. "Yes, I felt the attraction, too. Unfortunately, your princess seems to have other plans for me."

"She is royalty. It is her right to take any slave she wishes for her own."

"You don't look very happy about that." Emily ensured her tone was compassionate, regretful.

Rather than respond to her comment, Ilana advised her, "If you don't submit to her advances, the princess will eventually release you back to the Ti-gon or the mines. She might even approve my petition at that time."

Emily didn't quite know how to react. None of those possibilities sounded the slightest bit appealing. "Why don't we see how things go?"

Ilana nodded, but Emily could have sworn she saw sadness in the blue eyes. She didn't speak again as the vampire princess approached.

"Come," Adrasta ordered and stalked away toward the castle.

Guards immediately flanked Emily, giving her no choice but to follow and no opportunity to resist.

Chapter Twelve

JENNA STOOD HIGH on the mountaintop overlooking a lush forest. Strange-looking birds boasting small horns reminiscent of a rhino called to each other as they flew around. Their bright colors made them clearly visible against the greenest vegetation she'd ever seen.

She inhaled the crisp air deeply, pleased that her vision was adjusting to the diminished lighting of the beautiful alien world. Five days ago, everything appeared shrouded in shadows regardless of the time of day. Now, with the moons starting their downhill descent, Jenna felt like she could see for miles. Looking out at the rocks, birds, and the river far below, it would be so easy to believe nothing evil could happen here.

Jenna sighed and started down the slope, moving in the same direction as she had for countless hours. Far in the distance, Jenna saw the odd glint of moonlight off metal or glass. She wasn't exactly sure what the causative material was, only that it possessed reflective properties. Yet for all her uncertainties about the future, Jenna knew she wouldn't like what she found.

Upon reaching flat ground, she walked over and squatted by the river's edge. Hair flopped into her eyes as she knelt but she focused on the task at hand. The trek over the ridge had been strenuous and she'd used up most of her water. Fortunately, the canteen Moye gave her seemed to have unlimited isokenetic properties. No matter how many times she used it, the canteen filtered out the thickest sludge, bacteria, or slime and presented her with fresh water. He'd been very generous in offering her the canteen and translator ring. Part of Jenna remained suspicious about his philanthropic behavior. In her experience, no one gave away expensive or hard-to-come-by items without an agenda. Yet she remained grateful for the tools, regardless of his motives.

During most of her journey, the riverbed had remained as dry as it was after leaving Moye's home. Water trickled through the stream here. It wasn't deep but it was enough to refill the water skin. After sipping from the canteen, she looked in her satchel and selected one of her last pieces of bread. Before she could taste her food, a low buzzing sound caught her attention. Jenna scrambled toward the trees for cover, instinctively clutching her meager supplies.

"Not another one," she mumbled, hugging a thick trunk.

In the last six hours, she'd counted nine air cars flying around and the sightings were growing in frequency. Each time one of them zipped into her proximity, Jenna had to hide. It made progress slow, but it was a good sign she was getting closer to a heavily populated area. Jenna only hoped wherever she was headed, it was the same place she'd find Emily.

And the others, she added silently. She meant Emily and the others.

The vessel passed out of range. Jenna waited a few minutes just to be sure and then slowly walked out into the open. Though alone for the moment, she hesitated to resume her journey, and it wasn't just because the moons were about to set. If her sense of distance was still on track, which was a toss-up on a planet where basic physical laws didn't always apply, she should reach the city sometime tomorrow. It would probably be wise to wait until fully rested.

Jenna looked around carefully, noting the deep chasm about a hundred yards on the opposite side of the riverbed. At least there wasn't any need to be wandering around near the deadly drop off in the middle of the night, or what passed for night on this planet, but it was good to know where it was.

She walked into the forest, happy not to have to sleep on the hard ground for the first time in days. It surprised her how quickly the thick overgrowth choked out any signs of rock or dirt. Now she felt encompassed by dense foliage, scrub, trees, and insects. She walked for a short distance from the mountain range until she discovered a tree whose branches made it possible to climb. One particularly heavy limb looked wide enough to lie down on without fear of falling off.

Jenna stood under the tree and finished her bread, sipped some water, and decided to tackle her hair before settling down for the night. At home, she'd go see a hairdresser and get it cut, but she didn't have that option on Eris. Normally, overly long hair would be only an inconvenience. The same didn't hold true on this hostile world. Having her bangs obscure her vision during a crucial moment could spell her demise.

She pulled the knife out of her boot and checked the edge. It was extremely sharp. Despite the keen edge, the weapon wasn't intended for this and Jenna had to hold her bangs with one hand while she sawed through. Once finished, Jenna tried to check her appearance in the river's reflection but the attempt proved futile. There were too many shadows. She headed back to the tree and climbed onto the branch she'd chosen for the night.

The cloak Moye gave her was thick and warm. With it, she had managed to stay as warm and comfortable as was possible without a soft, cushy mattress. Jenna sighed and rubbed the achy spot on her chest where she'd injured herself falling down the mountainside. A scar remained there even after Moye healed the wound, but she expected the throbbing to ease over time.

At least the night in the forest here sounded close enough to home that Jenna started nodding off in minutes. As her muscles relaxed, her mind began to drift to thoughts of Emily. A smile crossed her face and she focused on the remembered sound of her voice, her laugh. Natural progression led to the taste of Emily's kisses.

She moaned and shifted in her sleep, but her dreams were

interrupted by a high-pitched scream. Jenna scrambled into a low crouch and huddled against the massive trunk. For a long while, all she could hear was the pounding of her own heart. Gradually, the quiet of a suddenly hushed forest gave way to normality. The animals returned and Jenna allowed herself to think the cry was that of a strange Erisian beast. Slowly, she relaxed her guard and sat down on the limb, leaning against the great tree.

She felt silly. She was acting like a kid who was still afraid of the dark. This was a forest. Of course there were going to be noises. Jenna closed her eyes and rested her forehead upon her knees. She didn't expect to sleep again for quite some time. Her fears might be irrational, but realizing that wouldn't make the aftermath of her adrenaline rush dissipate any faster.

She concentrated on the sounds of her breathing and the way the leaves rustled in the breeze, trying to relax enough for a few more hours of slumber. She'd seen the lights from a village and hoped to reach the small burg tomorrow. She needed to be ready to face anything.

The snap of dry twigs breaking forced her to instant wakefulness. Someone was walking through the woods below. From the little noise they made, Jenna guessed they were trying for stealth. Had her own senses not been on high alert, she might have missed them altogether. A small snort and a short, brusque curse signaled the newcomer's direction of approach, but why were they sneaking around this jungle in the dark?

Jenna heard a whimper and realized that whoever this stranger was, they were either afraid or injured. Perhaps they'd encountered the creature she heard earlier. On the other hand, maybe this person once had a companion. Possibly, it was that unknown individual she heard scream. Jenna realized it was all speculation.

She didn't know what was happening nor could she afford to become involved. She had enough problems. Jenna held her position and tried to remain as still as possible. Although the sun was high overhead, it gave less light than Earth's moon. She hoped the shadows would obscure her presence and the stranger would pass her hiding place without noticing her. The noise below ceased altogether and Jenna held her breath. When she finally had to release the air, she did so as quietly as she could. The silence stretched on until she became convinced that the stranger had passed. The sensation of eyes upon her caused Jenna to suddenly tense.

She knew that she was no longer alone. The hair seemed to stand on the nape of Jenna's neck. She swallowed quietly and turned her head. Twin orbs the color of flame gazed upon her reclining figure. Jenna lunged to her feet just as the monster flew toward her. The impact of a heavy body knocked her off the massive limb. Jenna felt hot breath near the tender flesh of her neck and tried to push away from her attacker as they fell. The short drop to the forest floor was enough to drive the air from her lungs when the creature landed on top of her.

Training and instinct made Jenna strike forward with the heel of her hand. The blow landed on the vampire's chin and forced his head to snap backward. Jenna took advantage of the move to shove him off her as she lunged to her feet. It was dark beneath the tree, too dark to fight effectively. Jenna turned and ran, intent on clearing the shadows so that she could see what she was up against. She had just cleared the limbs when the thing grabbed her by the back of her cloak and tossed her another ten feet. This time Jenna landed on her elbows. She felt the skin part, but turned quickly to face her adversary.

The vampire was definitely hurt. For all his strength, one arm dangled at his side. The limb appeared twisted at an odd angle and blood streaked the left side of his face. When he stepped toward her, he boasted a heavy limp. Jenna had never considered herself a fan of vampire movies but she thought she remembered something about the creatures needing to feed from humans in order to recover after a serious injury. Whether that was true or not, she didn't intend to give this one that opportunity.

Jenna reached down into her boot and withdrew her knife, keeping her eyes on her adversary the whole time. The blade gleamed wickedly in the scant light available, but at least now she could actually see her assailant. She only wished she'd managed to retain possession of her gun. It might not kill him, but a bullet hole had to hurt no matter who or what you were.

"It will do you no good. I will drain you and leave your body to wither in the wilderness."

His words sounded harsh and slurred. Jenna wondered if vampire fangs got in the way of enunciating correctly. She didn't have time to ask as the creature rushed toward her. He was still fast despite the leg injury and Jenna barely had time to duck to the side. She knew she would never stand if he hit her with his full weight again.

As the vampire rushed by, Jenna leaned sideways but held her right leg out stiffly. At the same time, she swiped upward with her knife. She experienced the satisfaction of feeling the blade slice through tender flesh. The vampire screamed in rage at the same time that he tripped over her extended leg. He was up again in a flash and on her before Jenna could blink.

Strong hands wrapped around her throat intent on choking the life from her. Jenna pushed back against the vampire's chest. He felt made of solid stone. Inch by inch, he moved closer to her neck. Jenna felt dizzy from lack of oxygen. Saliva dripped onto her skin and she shuddered in revulsion. When the tips of sharp fangs finally touched her, Jenna remembered the knife. She squeezed her right hand around the hilt. Unable to see and quickly losing consciousness, she attempted to angle the blade upward.

Pinpricks of pain pierced her skin, but the vampire didn't bite down. Jenna felt him stiffen. His grip eased and Jenna took a deep, rattling breath that helped clear her head. She pushed upward with the knife and felt it sink to the hilt. His body went limp and collapsed. Jenna struggled to free herself of the offending weight and finally managed to climb out from under the dead vampire. He'd fallen with his head turned to the side and the way he stared out into the night assured her he was no longer a threat.

Jenna quickly reached for her neck to assess the damage. Her heart began to settle when she discovered he'd done little more than scratch the skin. The injury stung but at least it wasn't life threatening. Jenna squatted down on one knee to rest. She didn't take her eyes off the vampire while she got her breathing under control. When the shaking finally stopped, Jenna started looking around and saw that her equipment had scattered over the small area.

She retrieved the canteen and food bag, strapping them carefully back to her waist. She cleaned blood off the knife in the high grass and then slid the weapon back into her boot. The clearing was too occupied now for her to consider trying to sleep anymore. One dead vampire was one too many. Jenna pulled the cloak around her body and discovered it had ripped during the fight. One whole side had torn from hem to shoulder.

"That's just great," she complained. Jenna kicked the vampire in the ribs for causing her so much trouble. She didn't feel any better after kicking him, but she did have an idea.

Jenna squatted down beside the monster and considered what she was about to do. The vampire had fallen face down, with the mortal wound in his chest. The cloak he wore should be free of any blood caused by their encounter. Jenna pulled her small flashlight off her belt and hesitated before she flicked it on. She didn't like using the tool for fear of burning up the batteries, but she didn't really have a choice. It was just too dark to see how to remove the cloak without utilizing the light. Jenna was also concerned that the sudden illumination would draw other vampires toward her.

She realized that if any others were in the vicinity they would have rushed toward the sound of the altercation. That fact convinced her it was safe enough so she thumbed the on switch. Jenna squinted at the intensity of the light. She'd been on this planet for so long that she had become accustomed to the shadows. It took some time before she could open her eyes without feeling sharp needles of pain. When she could see again, Jenna approached the vampire.

Disgust caused the hair to stand up on her forearms, but she swallowed and reached under the creature's neck in her search for the clasp. She hoped it would fasten the same way as Moye's cloak. She didn't like scavenging from the dead, but she needed the covering and anything else useful she could find on his body. Luck was with her and a few seconds later Jenna held up the cloak to check for any damage.

She could see with the flashlight's beam that the garment was a muddy green color.

Jenna stood and removed the cloak she'd been wearing for days. She folded it up and placed it into the now empty food pouch. If nothing else, she could use the cloth as a crude blanket. Jenna donned the vampire's cloak, struck by how thick and warm it felt. Unlike Moye's, this one boasted a hood and she happily pulled it into place. She knew that a person usually expended about ten percent of their body heat from their heads.

As the garment settled into place, the shadows seemed to vanish. Jenna could see as clearly as she could on a sunny day at home. She blinked and pushed the hood away from her head. The shadows returned and she was shrouded in darkness, made more extreme because of the brightness encountered moments ago.

"No way."

She pulled the hood back into place, almost afraid the experience wouldn't repeat. Jenna almost sobbed in relief when she could see again. The ability to notice tiny details, like the individual blades of grass beneath her feet or the veins in a tree leaf seemed almost overwhelming. To Jenna it was like suddenly coming up for air after a very long time spent underwater. As crazy as it was, Jenna felt stronger than she had in days. She laughed aloud and switched off the flashlight. As long as she had the vampire cloak, she had no need for the tool. Still, she wasn't foolhardy. Jenna slipped the tool into its place on her belt and went back to searching the vampire.

Jenna found another ring similar to the one Moye had given her. She removed it and slipped the ring into a pocket. Jenna discovered a knife even larger than her own in a sheath around the man's waist. She wondered why he hadn't pulled the weapon and then decided he hadn't felt threatened by her.

She shook her head. Underestimating an opponent could get you killed, she thought. In this case, it had.

Jenna didn't find any food or water, but then she hadn't really expected that she would. Vampires drank blood. She sighed and left the clearing, leaving the dead man where he lay. She needed to conserve her strength and burying him would afford the vampire a dignity Jenna didn't feel he deserved. He was a vicious killer. She was curious how he had arrived beneath her tree in such bad condition. Unconcerned with ever finding out the answer to that question, Jenna struck out toward the village. She hoped to find something to eat there and gain some information about how to get Emily and the others back.

While she walked through what turned out to be a truly pleasant meadow, Jenna discovered that the cloak had pockets. She noticed the colors of the trees and could see which ones had thorns similar to the one she'd stabbed her fingers on after first arriving in this place. Colors here were just a little off compared to Earth norms. Instead of the brown to which she was accustomed, the bark on trees here was more of an off-grayish color. Grass was so vibrantly green that it made Earth grass look pale and half dead. Things that were usually bright at home appeared muted here, but others that seemed dull at home stood out brightly in this place. It seemed that the color spectrum was somewhat inverted.

"It's just like the air," she said, speaking aloud. "The air is lighter here. I can walk a lot farther here than I ever could at home."

Happy with her newly acquired knowledge, Jenna smiled and shoved her hands deeper into the pockets. She felt something hard and square in the bottom of the left pocket. Jenna tried to pull the object out to look at it, but then realized it was sewn into the fabric. She stopped and turned out the pocket so she could see the device. Before she obtained the garment, she would never have been able to see the small controls built into the small square. There were three buttons: blue, red and green. Jenna puzzled over their purpose. She supposed she'd better find out their function now when she was alone and relatively safe.

Jenna pressed the blue button, but nothing seemed to happen. She looked up and around to try to determine if the cloak's visual capabilities had altered at all. She didn't think so. Disappointed, Jenna glanced down and realized that the garment had changed. It seemed to blend into the area, not exactly invisible but so much like the surrounding terrain that it was close enough. This was a camouflage function and explained how the vampire had snuck up on her so effectively. Jenna hadn't seen the creature in the tree until he wanted her to. Scary.

Leaving the function in place as a smart idea, Jenna pressed the red switch. A heads-up display popped into her field of vision. An unintelligible list of information filled the left side of the plane, written in a language she couldn't hope to comprehend. Jenna reached up and attempted to touch the readouts. Her fingers passed right through the alien script and Jenna determined it was some type of projection. She'd decided the HUD was useless for a human until her eyes fixed on the village in the distance. When she did, a red circle encompassed the area in question and a number popped up beside the readout. Jenna read 38R. She puzzled over the display.

Was this some kind of distance measurement? If so, what did "R" stand for and was it closer to a mile or a kilometer? Jenna hoped kilometers. Although still a considerable distance, she'd rather walk twenty-four miles than thirty-eight. At least she thought that was right, considering she was converting American units of measure to the metric system on the fly and she'd never been very good at math. Additionally, the letter wasn't really an "R". It was just the closest comparison she could make. Regardless, Jenna saw little use for keeping the HUD in place considering she couldn't read the information. She pressed the red button again, rewarded when the display disappeared. Good, so pressing the button once turned the device on and pressing the switch a second time shut it down.

Jenna didn't hesitate to press the third and final green button. She immediately slapped her free hand over her ear. This switch somehow enhanced the sound within the hood. The swish of tall grass had become a roar. She quickly mashed the green button a second time and breathed a sigh of relief at the blessed silence.

Note to self...do not press the green button unless absolutely necessary. She would have the splitting headache from hell if she had to listen to that for very long.

Jenna realized these vampires didn't have supernatural abilities. They simply possessed advanced technology. She still couldn't explain their flight capabilities but guessed that also had a scientific explanation. Jenna considered all the vampire legends on Earth and wondered if they weren't rooted in something similar. It certainly took the mystery out of things.

She thought again about how the creature had tried to bite her and realized some of those legends were true. Vampires fed on blood and were incredibly strong. That monster had tried to kill her. Even in his less than stellar condition, he'd almost succeeded. If he hadn't practically fallen on her blade, the results would have been disastrous.

Their strength notwithstanding, Jenna thought she could use this new information against Emily's captors. On Earth, technology had become a bit of an Achilles' heel. Few people could function without cell phones, computers or electricity. She was willing to bet things weren't so different here. These Erisians would rely on their technology too. Jenna would have to keep her eyes open for the right opportunity.

Jenna sniffed and recognized the smell of smoke. She checked the area for signs that she was walking into a forest fire. She didn't see any actual flames so kept walking, paying more attention to her surroundings. Before stepping foot in the natural clearing, Jenna could see a twisted hulk of silver metal. The downed craft still smoked, but didn't appear to be burning.

"That answers that," she muttered, coming to a halt and carefully ensuring that she was alone.

Jenna identified the craft as one of the flying cars she'd spotted earlier. The vampire she'd encountered had crash-landed here. At least she knew these beings weren't immune from mechanical failures. Excited at the prospect of finding something useful in the wreckage, Jenna hurried across the clearing. She easily identified the cockpit and reached down to touch the frame. The metal was cool to the touch and she made a mental note to stay away from the smoking rear compartment.

She searched the entire craft, but found nothing. There weren't any stray weapons lying around or any more fancy clothing with hidden uses. Jenna considered trying to fix the machine and fly it to her final destination. Two things kept her from acting on that idea. First, she wasn't a mechanic and hadn't a hope of repairing the vessel. Then there was the fact that she couldn't make heads or tails of the instrument panel. If she started playing around with the controls, she'd probably initiate some kind of self-destruct or fire off a missile.

Frustration made her slam her palm against the edge of the compartment. She couldn't use the craft, but she couldn't hang out here for long either. Jenna didn't know if these vampires had the Earth equivalent of search-and-rescue, but she didn't intend to take the chance. Resolved to traveling to the village the hard way, Jenna pushed away from the ship and started walking again.

Chapter Thirteen

THE SENSATION OF Ilana's eyes boring into Emily's back was like a weight as Adrasta's guards escorted her away. She turned and met the vampire's liquid blue gaze and found regret there. Maybe Ilana wasn't quite the monster she'd initially thought. Emily raced forward and held her head high. Human slaves nearby looked at her and then quickly away. They weren't quite fast enough to hide the pity. Emily frowned. Why did she feel like she'd suddenly gone from the frying pan into the open, blazing pit?

Princess Adrasta led the party as they traveled toward the castle. Emily took the opportunity to get a good look at Saqqara. Other than the mines and the large containment building where the vampires held victims for the hunt, the city was like something out of a futuristic novel. Flying machines filled the airways overhead, following an obscure type of order that prevented mishaps. Structures all around shone like polished crystal and stretched up high overhead, albeit not as high as the air cars. Underfoot, Emily noticed the slate pavement that would require a quarry of epic proportions. Not to mention the technology and precision required to cut each interlocking piece, Emily thought. The stone covered all pathways throughout the city for as far as she could see.

Up ahead, the castle loomed nearer. Emily had never thought she'd see one outside of a movie. Turrets rose proudly from the perimeter of the structure and she wondered if they housed containment cells at the top. Emily spotted a larger, square construct that she thought might be a keep. The edifice even held a drawbridge that was currently down. Although there was no rank and disgusting water, a deep, empty pit circled the castle. Emily recognized the seeming strategic importance of the pit, but decided it was more symbolic than anything considering these creatures could fly.

Speaking of flying, she mused, gazing upward once again. Why did the vampires require air ships if they could fly on their own?

The answer didn't appear to be forthcoming and Emily forgot the issue as they started across the wooden planks of the drawbridge. Adrasta, who had ignored her up to this point, unexpectedly shouted, "Bathe her."

The simple command generated unanticipated activity, and Adrasta continued on her way without pause. Simultaneously, two guards grasped Emily's upper arms, one of them the female she'd noted earlier. Emily noticed the guard kept a free hand on her sword as she walked, probably to keep it from swinging. Emily gulped nervously as they walked under a heavy portcullis into the castle proper. She might have found the inside of the structure just as impressive as the outside if the guards hauling her down a narrow corridor hadn't distracted her. Adrasta continued up a steep staircase to the next level and Emily lost sight of the vampire princess.

"You don't have to keep pulling at me," Emily said angrily. "I'll walk if you just tell me where you want me to go."

The guards did not respond and they did not release her. Instead, they herded her down a long hallway and forced her to descend into an underground caponnière. Emily knew they weren't going to harm her. She'd heard Adrasta give the order to bathe her, but she didn't like being hauled around and didn't relish the idea of two strangers giving her a bath. She had finally had enough. Emily planted her feet.

Apparently, the guards had not anticipated this and one of them lost his grip. That was all the opportunity she needed. Emily drew back and punched the guard who still held her directly in the nose. The female guard's head reeled back, but Emily didn't wait for her to regroup. Emily kicked the second guard as hard as she could between the legs, pleased when he reacted like any human male. He went down with a groan and she turned back to the remaining vampire. Blood streamed from her nose, but she didn't appear daunted. She swatted Emily's incoming fist aside easily and cinched an arm around her neck. Emily pummeled the vampire's side, but she showed no reaction, hauling Emily toward the end of the corridor while her companion lay writhing on the floor. What Emily found creepier than anything was that the pair still hadn't made a sound other than a single groan of pain.

The only thing Emily accomplished was to delay the inevitable. She found herself in an underground bathing chamber surrounded by four scantily dressed women that she assumed were human. The women wore only short, white robes. Their feet were bare. Two blondes, a redhead and a brunette came toward Emily. The guard still held her around the neck and it was difficult to look up.

"You must release her," one of the blonde-haired women told the guard. She seemed amused. "We cannot clean her if you restrain her."

"She'll fight you, Briana," the vampire warned. Her voice was rough as if she didn't speak often.

"I think not," Briana disagreed gently, though Emily noticed that she lowered her eyes in a manner intended to show deference to the guard. "She is merely frightened, as we all were when we arrived."

The vampire grunted, whether in agreement or not, Emily couldn't tell. Then she released Emily and shoved her toward the group of women. "Adrasta will want her in her chambers. Clean the human up and replace the bracelet."

Emily didn't see the vampire leave the chamber. She turned around and the woman was just...gone.

"My name is Briana."

Emily turned toward her. "Briana," she repeated, attempting to roll the "r" sound but failing miserably.

She wondered if this woman was human and glanced at her hand. Briana did not wear a translator ring. Emily realized that was little proof of anything. She only had Fallon's word that all Erisians wore the device. Short of asking Briana to open her mouth to check for fangs, Emily decided she would find out soon enough. If Briana attacked Emily and tried to bite her neck, Emily would take that as a definite sign.

"Close enough. Please come with us."

Briana turned and led the way toward a large pool of water. Set directly into the floor, Emily thought the bathing area could easily hold a dozen people.

"Now see, why didn't they just ask me to follow them down here?" Emily asked. "Would that have been so hard?"

Briana cast a nervous look over her shoulder toward Emily. "If you want to survive here, you must not resist the Erisians. Causing trouble for Castellan Orsk is even more unwise. She would not hesitate to break your neck and then drain you for her troubles."

"What's a castellan? Is that some kind of title?"

"It is her position. A castellan is the royal officer in charge of the castle. She acts with impunity, bending to no one's will save the princess's."

"That's nice." Emily's words oozed sarcasm but she was too tired to really care. A bath, however, sounded like a wonderful idea. It had been days since she'd felt clean and Emily didn't see a little cleanliness interfering with her plans to escape. "Uh, do you think I could have a little privacy?"

Briana smiled and shook her head. "I'm afraid Adrasta would not allow it. We will attend you." She waved a hand to indicate the three waiting women.

"We don't have to tell her."

The smile disappeared. "Adrasta would know."

The fear in Briana's eyes was real and forced Emily to capitulate. She was still a prisoner and would do everything in her power to regain her freedom, but she would not willingly place someone else at risk. Especially over something as trivial as a bath.

"All right, let's get this party started."

Emily grasped the hem of her black shirt cross-handed and lifted the heavily soiled garment over her head. She dropped the ripped cloth to the floor and started across the chamber.

"I understand that Adrasta intends to keep me as a slave." She kept her voice neutral as she sought to gather information. "Does she only like women?"

"Currently, that is her preference."

Emily undressed slowly, prolonging the conversation. "What do you mean by that?"

"The Erisians are a very long-lived species. Princess Adrasta varies in her tastes from time to time."

"How long lived?" Emily bent over to unlace her boots. "Are they immortal or something?"

"Very nearly so, although they were not always. There was a time eons ago when the Erisians had a lifespan comparable to humans."

That was an interesting tidbit. She turned toward Briana in her curiosity. "How did things change?"

"An Erisian scientist discovered a way to cheat death through manipulating their DNA. This modification left their people incredibly strong and virtually immune to any disease. Unfortunately, there was a tradeoff."

Emily's lips twisted in distaste. "Let me guess, the drinking blood thing?"

"Yes, the Erisians were left incapable of consuming nutrition any other way. Hundreds of thousands perished before scientists discovered the truth. Now, Erisians must travel through portals to ensure the survival of their species."

"How...revolting. I think I'd rather die."

The bath was rectangular in shape and steam drifted lazily into the air. Emily didn't see spigots attached and wondered if the water was constantly recycled and heated by an external power source. Then she got closer to the pool and her musings vanished like the steam rising from the heated water. Perfume filled the air, oily but sweet. The scent tantalized her and despite her previous trepidations, she felt her determination to escape ebb.

Fog invaded her mind and Emily shook her head in attempt to force it away. Before she knew it, her clothes were gone and Emily sat on a concealed bench in water up to her neck. The heat massaged away knots in her muscles. The strange women entered the pool beside her, their robes gone. Emily felt so hazy that she didn't even consider trying to peek at the nubile flesh. Instead, she laid her head back against the side and allowed four unknown people to scrub her body clean. The knowledge that they were somehow drugging her wasn't inducement enough for Emily to resist.

She'd been drifting, half-asleep until she heard someone calling her name. The voice seemed to come from a distance. "Jenna?" she asked sleepily and opened her eyes.

Briana's smiling visage swam into view. Emily took a deep breath and sat up straight. She felt surprised to discover she sat on a low couch against the far wall of the stone room. She didn't remember leaving the scented water. More than that, she didn't remember dressing. Emily's tactical gear was gone, replaced by a blood-red robe that fell barely to mid-thigh. The material was thin like silk but almost transparent. Emily could see her own small nipples beneath the folds of cloth. The garment resembled a negligee that she might find in a cheap Hustler magazine.

A single tie looped from the material covering her left breast, around her neck and tethered to just above the right, leaving her shoulders and back bare. Emily thought she probably favored a floozy out looking for a good time. She felt her face burn in embarrassment.

"You can't be serious. I'm not wearing this rag."

"Then you will wear nothing at all," Briana returned with a smirk, raking her eyes down Emily's body suggestively.

Emily felt the heat rise even hotter to her face. She muttered under her breath, "Bitch."

The invective didn't appear to faze her tormenter. Briana smirked and reached for the bracelet on Emily's wrist. A mysterious tool made quick work of the locking mechanism and the jewelry released its tight grip. She didn't have time to take advantage of the unexpected freedom before someone from behind dropped a silver choker over her head and snapped it behind her neck. Emily gasped and jerked away, but it was too late. She reached up and felt a small circlet on either side of the device.

"Take it off," she demanded, lunging to her feet and spinning around to face a thin, dark-haired woman.

Nervous eyes flitted away and rested on Briana, awaiting her commands. Clearly, all decisions rested with the older woman. Feeling she was getting nowhere, Emily was prepared for violence. She turned back to Briana and rushed toward her. Her patience at an end, she planned to knock them unconscious and make a break for the woods. With the bracelet gone, she just might make it all the way back home. Hands centimeters from Briana, Emily's body suddenly stiffened so intensely that she thought her spine had snapped. Electricity coursed through her veins. Emily's jaw clenched tightly and she fell to the floor.

Emily tried to breathe through the familiar sensation as her muscles contracted harshly. She'd experienced a taser hit before during her hand-to-hand training for the FBI and this wasn't much different. Eventually the fire in her blood cooled and she could draw breath again, though her limbs still trembled.

"That was at a moderate setting," Briana warned her.

Her dulcet tones showed no signs of anger. Emily considered that she had expected an attack eventually. Fortunately for Emily, Briana didn't seem interested in killing her. Instead of speaking her thoughts aloud, Emily swallowed and attempted to sit. She managed an upright position though her head spun.

"The choker is capable of decapitating you, unlike the bracelet."

"Why?" Emily questioned shakily.

"Why the change in control devices?" At Emily's nod, Briana clarified. "The bracelet is a mark for slaves used in the Ti-gon and the mines. Even without a hand, a slave can continue in these endeavors. The chokers are for palace slaves only because they are so close to the princess."

"Okay, I'll give you that, but you could have just told me."

"An explanation is not as memorable as a demonstration. Now get up. You must eat something before I take you to Princess Adrasta's chambers and she does not like to be kept waiting."

EMILY'S STOMACH FELT pleasantly full for the first time since Woeful Pines. She owed that reality to eating something besides tofu-like cubes and bitter gruel. The taste of hot, crusty bread, fresh vegetables and sweet fruit still lingering on her tongue, Emily drained her cup. She placed the vessel gently on the low table before looking up at Briana. The servant had waited patiently while Emily ate her fill. Emily was sharp enough to know there was a hidden reason. Every action these people took possessed a hidden agenda.

"Why do I get the feeling this is the last time I'll eat like this?"

"Because you are perceptive," Briana replied without pause. "I will bring you to the princess properly nourished and hydrated."

"Don't forget clean, but is this the extent of your responsibility? Do you just hand me over to the vampire queen now?"

"She is a princess. Adrasta's mother is the queen, but Queen Ventrix resides on the other side of Eris. It is not likely you will encounter her."

"How nice." The sarcasm appeared lost on Briana. Irritated that she couldn't seem to get a rise out of these people no matter how hard she tried, Emily prompted Briana to continue. "What else are you supposed to do?"

"I am to ensure you understand proper behavior within the castle. You must willingly abide by these instructions."

Emily uncrossed her arms and sat forward on the chair. "And if I don't?"

"Then you will receive sufficient care to ensure your continued existence; nothing more."

"That doesn't sound so bad. Look, Briana, I appreciate that you have a job to do but I am not the sort to be kept as a pet. Can't you help me get out of here? You seem to have a lot of latitude."

Briana's head went back as if Emily had slapped her. "I cannot."

"I know you're scared, but we can make it look like I managed it on my own. No one will blame you."

"No, Emily, you do not understand. I will not go against Adrasta to help you."

"What, how can you choose her over me? We're both human and she's a monstrosity."

"She is my beloved princess." Briana shrugged, indicating that her response was sufficient.

Emily considered Briana and her companions, whose duty it was to initiate new slaves. They showed no desire to revolt and reacted to every situation serenely. Drugged? She rejected that notion out of hand. Their expressions were too clear and focused for that.

"How long have you been here?"

"Almost one hundred years. The Erisian bite imparts long life. This gift can be yours too if you willingly give yourself over to the princess."

Emily noticed the scarring on Briana's neck and her lip curled. "Charming."

She felt sure Briana and the others were the victims of Stockholm Syndrome. Of course, immortality was probably a pretty good incentive, too. Unfortunately, she didn't have the qualifications or the inclination to provide the months of therapy these women required. Besides, for therapy to work the client had to be willing, and Emily didn't believe they were.

"Briana, you should know that I will never stop trying to escape. I'll die caged up here like a rat in a trap."

"You will change your mind. Everyone does eventually. It is time. We must go."

Emily decided that she was well and truly on her own. She moved on to other issues. "If you've been here for so long, how is it that you speak perfect English? Rather, how is it that you speak modern English?"

"There have been many people brought here over the years. I suppose one must adapt. Please, follow me."

Emily briefly thought about refusing to cooperate, but decided to play along for the moment. There were too many vampires and slaves around to try anything stupid. Her captors had to let her sleep eventually. When things quieted down, she would make a move. The collar had to have an effective distance. She remembered the micro-bug she'd planted on the Kurth's living room window. Nothing had truly unlimited range. Her plan involved disappearing long enough to surpass that distance before anyone knew.

She followed Briana, surrounded by the three other women, down the corridor toward the main entrance. None of these slaves had spoken other than to issue instructions during her time in the underground chamber. Guards flanked them the moment they left the bathing area. Emily studied every feature, every stone, as the throng escorted her along the caponnière. The smallest detail might make the difference later. It was then that she realized none of the humans wore a collar. They apparently followed Princess Adrasta and her blood-sucking fiends willingly. Was immortality really all that alluring? Personally, Emily had no desire to live forever. She turned away in disgust.

The guards led her up the narrow staircase to a set of closed double doors on the second floor. The entourage stopped on the landing and Emily wondered why everyone was just standing around if they were worried about keeping the vampire waiting. Then she heard Adrasta's command.

"Enter!"

Okay, they hadn't exactly been quiet, stomping boldly through the castle. Adrasta's knowledge of their presence wasn't an indicator of telepathy. Another vampire myth destroyed, Emily decided. That was good to know and confirmed what Vaden had told her.

Briana stepped forward past the guards and threw open the doors. She entered the room and Emily saw her bow low from the waist. She spoke with her eyes pinned to the floor.

"Princess Adrasta, ruler of Southern Eris, sovereign of all you survey..."

Oh brother. Emily rolled her eyes and thought she might be sick. Somewhere among the group of soldiers, she thought she heard someone snicker. The sounds surprised Emily because she'd believed everyone on this planet had unwavering loyalty toward the vampire in charge. Then again, they might be laughing at how completely Briana humbled herself. Either way, someone wasn't very popular.

"I have brought you the new slave, Emily."

"Then bring her in," Adrasta ordered shortly. "Don't dally."

If anything, Briana bent even lower. Then she straightened and turned toward the group, waving Emily forward. When Emily hesitated, someone shoved her hard in the small of her back. Emily stumbled into the room. The chamber proved to be massive, even by castle standards, or so she imagined. She thought the single space likely took up a quarter of the floor. A canopy bed that would have been specially made on Earth took center stage. It easily dwarfed every king-sized bed Emily had ever seen. However, that was not where the vampire princess reclined.

Adrasta rested among hundreds of multi-colored pillows on the floor near a huge window. The light of two full moons streamed in and bathed her in an ethereal glow. Four gorgeous females attended her. They were some of the most breathtaking women Emily had ever seen. Only one of them boasted short, wheat-colored hair, but it framed her face in a way that it set off and complimented the small features. Emily decided the number four must be especially significant on Eris. She tried not to notice the amount of flesh on display. Breasts strained at skimpy fabric, threatening to spill over. One slave was especially exposed, her olive skin covered only by a thin spread. Emily felt positively overdressed in comparison.

Emily fixed her gaze on Adrasta, staring her directly in the eyes. Her intent was to show that she wasn't afraid, that she wouldn't be cowed. She found amusement in the blue eyes.

"You have spirit. I am sure I will enjoy breaking you."

"Don't bet on it," Emily quipped.

A guard struck her in the back of the leg and Emily fell to one knee. "Slaves do not speak unless so directed," a harsh voice informed her. "You will kneel in front of Princess Adrasta."

Emily scowled back over her shoulder at the helmeted zealot. "Why didn't you say so?"

A backhanded slap rewarded her for her insolence. The blow was forceful enough that it sent her careening a few feet away. Emily landed face down, but lunged quickly to her feet. She spun around and fisted her hands. She didn't care that she was barefoot in a roomful of monsters.

"Enough," Adrasta commanded.

Emily remained tense even as the guard backed down.

"You must kneel anytime you are in the presence of Her Majesty," Briana instructed calmly from behind her.

"I thought you were supposed to prepare me." Emily turned around, keeping an eye on the guards until she faced toward Adrasta.

She met the princess's gaze, noting the hardness. It was a standoff Emily was destined to lose. With eight humans and four guards prepared to force her to her knees, Emily chose to comply under her own steam. Chances were that if she didn't, the soldiers would injure her in the process. Emily needed to be healthy to get out of this hellish place. Slowly, eyes never leaving Adrasta's, Emily dropped to her knees and sat back on her heels. She held her body stiffly, projecting defiance. The princess's smile had vanished.

The guard who had slapped her strode forward and attached chains to the circlets Emily had previously noted on the choker. He secured them to ring bolts on the floor that she hadn't seen when she knelt. The chains would ensure that Emily didn't attack Adrasta if she had the opportunity. She wasn't left in place for long as this was merely a demonstration.

"Guards, take the new one to the keep. Briana, you and I will speak later."

That didn't sound good to Emily, but Briana merely nodded once and followed the guards from the room. Emily felt more concerned with how the stone floor felt against her bare knees. Already she could feel the cold seeping into her bones. Perhaps that was the purpose of such a skimpy outfit, not only to humiliate but also to ensure her discomfort. The chains were released and a strong hand jerked Emily to her feet.

The castellan and another soldier escorted her out of the room, down the corridor and up the stone steps. Emily's eyes continued to dart around taking in every detail. Castellan Orsk stopped outside a heavy stone door. She kept one hand on Emily, presumably to keep her from running off, and felt for a key at her waist with the other. As Orsk shoved open the door and hauled Emily inside, she knew at once what she had to do. The chamber was one large circle and hadn't a single amenity except for a pile of dirty hay against the wall with a small, uncovered window. The window was far too small for her to climb through. As soon as Orsk shoved her inside, someone pulled the door closed and Emily was left to herself.

DAYS PASSED INSIDE the small stone chamber. Emily tried to estimate the time by watching the moons through the single window and scratching a mark against the stone wall with a rock she'd found. Twice a day the soldiers provided food and water through a small aperture set approximately waist high in the door. Emily estimated three full days before they came for her. Again, Castellan Orsk and another flanked her as they escorted her back to Adrasta's chambers. The princess did not speak as Emily was forced to her knees and chained in place. Emily noticed the vampire still had her cadre of body slaves in attendance.

"Here, you have no name unless you earn the privilege," Adrasta told her without preamble. "You will be addressed as slave. You will eat bread and water, nothing more until I deem you worthy. You will sleep on the floor in a cold, dank chamber. Once you realize what an honor it is to be my body slave and come to me of your own free will, this is your future." She waved a hand to indicate her attendants.

Emily held her tongue. She wouldn't remain strong indefinitely on such meager nutrition, but the solitude served her purposes. She waited to see what the vampire would do next.

Adrasta lay in a reclined position, her head and shoulders propped up in such a way that she could easily see the doors as well as the room's other occupants. A calculating look settled in her eyes and she glanced at the naked woman lying beside her. "I am ready, Nicole. Go slowly. I wish to savor you."

Emily's body tensed. She felt sure she knew what was about to happen and she did not want to see this. Emily fixed her eyes on the floor, attempting to chart every groove and crack as Nicole rose and moved between Adrasta's thighs.

"You will watch." Adrasta's command brooked no refusal.

"That's okay. I'm really not much of a voyeur."

Emily's body contracted as a mild shock shot through her system. Adrasta didn't inflict as much pain as Briana had, but Emily felt electricity singing in her veins. The tips of her fingers tingled sharply. She gasped and tried to breathe through the sensation. Still, she refused to observe the tableau.

"If you do not watch, I will increase the intensity until your head explodes. The choice is yours."

This was truly cruel and unusual punishment. Emily had never been one to shy away from casual sex, but she preferred her women in a private setting and one-on-one. This was nothing more than a pornographic display meant to shock and make Emily feel vulnerable. She had been forced to do many distasteful things over the years, but this was certainly a first. Emily weighed her options.

She could either observe as slave women pleasured a demented vampire princess or she could have her brains blown all over the chamber. The decision wasn't that hard. Dead, she had no chance of getting out of the castle or freeing the other prisoners. Emily faced Adrasta, her hatred of the vampire clearly displayed on her expression. Her eyes followed as Adrasta placed a small mace beside her. The rod was short and slender. It would be easy to conceal the device on a belt or tucked into a robe. This must be the control for the collar.

Adrasta relaxed as Nicole stroked a lazy finger down her thigh to the hem of the princess's robes. Her hand slid underneath the robes and pushed them up to expose Adrasta's intimate flesh. Emily directed her gaze toward the group so she wouldn't get a more disabling shock, but she fixed her eyes to the left of Adrasta's head. She focused all of her attention there, trying hard not to capture any details. From the sounds Adrasta made, it wasn't hard to decipher what was going on. It didn't take long for the vampire princess to groan her satisfaction.

Only then did Emily refocus on her face, afraid to be caught looking away. Adrasta's features were flushed, a contented smile on her lips. She seemed to have momentarily forgotten about Nicole, her gaze fixed on Emily. She held her eyes as Adrasta rose onto her hands and knees, treating Emily to the sight of full breasts as the robe fell forward. Adrasta moved forward as Nicole shifted and lay on her back. Her demeanor instantly changed to that of a predator and Emily couldn't look away.

"Do it, Robin." Adrasta held Emily's gaze as the short-haired blonde moved onto her knees behind her.

She stripped off the short robe so quickly that Emily couldn't avoid the sight of the dildo attached to her crotch. Emily didn't see any straps or a harness so she had no idea how Robin kept the apparatus in place. Emily cringed at the size. Easily seven inches long, she estimated the dildo's girth at two inches. That had to hurt.

Robin wiggled her hips and eased down between Adrasta's thighs. She folded the princess's robes high over her back so that Emily could see the whole show. With one hand, Robin grasped the dildo and placed the toy against Adrasta's opening. She appeared to be teasing at first, stroking the tip down over Adrasta in a circular motion. Her free hand grasped the princess's thigh.

Adrasta's eyes closed briefly and her breathing hitched. Emily witnessed the unholy red glow appear in their depths when she refocused on her unwilling audience. Adrasta lifted her hips and leaned into Robin. The top of the dildo slipped just inside and all motion ceased for a moment.

Adrasta gasped. "Can you imagine the feel, Emily? The thickness that you know will soon drive into you?"

Robin pushed forward slowly and her head fell back, a look of ecstasy on her face. She groaned as she buried the rod deep inside

Adrasta. The teasing appeared finished as Robin thrust forward and pulled back. Adrasta's mouth fell open and Emily saw her fangs extend several centimeters. Nicole still lay beneath her and Adrasta leaned into her, hips in the air while she lowered her chest.

The intense gaze finally released Emily as Nicole turned her head to the side. Emily thought she heard a whimper of fear, but the slave never resisted when Adrasta slowly bit into her neck. Blood streamed from two puncture wounds and ran down Nicole's shoulder, soaking into the pillows.

Robin slammed into Adrasta as the vampire fed. Emily had forgotten all about the other two slaves until one of them moved. The second woman lay on her back behind Robin and slid forward between the slave's spread legs until she positioned her face directly beneath Adrasta's body. Without pause, this third woman grasped Adrasta's thighs and rose up far enough to take her in her mouth.

Adrasta groaned low and long but didn't pull away from her feeding. Emily could hear her panting through her nose as she approached orgasm. Nicole had started to struggle, her hands against Adrasta's shoulders as she tried to push the vampire away. She failed and Emily tried to lunge to her feet to help her, but the chains held her in place. She braced her feet against the floor and grasped one of the chains, pulling with all her strength.

"You're killing her, stop!"

No one reacted to her shout. The final slave sat watching and stroking Adrasta's body, seeming enraptured by the sight. Robin suddenly cried out and Adrasta released Nicole as she shuddered with pleasure. Nicole didn't move.

Emily sagged to the floor, horrified by the display and sickened that Adrasta could kill without hesitation. If Adrasta intended to entice her with the pornographic display and the death of an innocent, she had accomplished the opposite. Emily wasn't waiting around for the vampires to add her body to the dead and she would make it her mission to take Adrasta out at the same time.

A few moments later, Robin pulled out of Adrasta and sagged down onto her side, but Emily barely noticed. Adrasta allowed the other slave to climb out from under her before she deigned to notice Nicole. Tenderly, almost regretfully, Adrasta touched Nicole's cheek with the back of her hand, stroking the soft skin. The coppery scent of blood filled the chamber.

"Look what you made me do, Robin. She was my new favorite." Adrasta spoke calmly and took a steadying breath. After staring at Nicole for another few seconds, Adrasta sat back, propped up on Robin's body. She didn't look at Nicole again. "Did you like what you saw?"

Chapter Fourteen

EMILY IGNORED THE question. "Is she dead?" She felt she already knew the answer.

"Why are you concerned for her?" Adrasta frowned. "She was a slave. I can replace her."

"You can't replace a life. You're nothing but a monster." Emily wanted to rail at Adrasta but she couldn't. The tears choked her too badly.

Adrasta rolled her eyes. "I tire of this."

She searched for the control rod she'd used to trigger the choker and Emily tensed. Adrasta pressed something on the scepter and a second later the doors to the chamber opened. Emily recognized the same female guard she'd smashed in the nose earlier.

"Castellan, take this slave to the keep. Have someone come and get this one, too." Adrasta indicated the body by placing her foot against Nicole and pushing her thin form off the cushions.

Emily's fists clenched and her eyes narrowed at the heartless display. She wanted to kill Adrasta, drive a stake through her heart and cut off her head. That's how you killed a vampire, right? Something touched her shoulder. Emily remained immobile while the Castellan detached the bindings from the collar. Using Adrasta's scheming against them seemed like a good idea and Emily feigned defeat by allowing her shoulders to sag and her head to drop forward. Orsk grasped her under the arm and Emily allowed the guard to lead her from the room.

In the hallway, Emily drew in deep cleansing breaths as she tried to dispel the stench of death. Her body trembled not only from outrage, but also from the cold. The short garment she wore didn't provide any protection from the chill of the stone structure. She wouldn't get far dressed like this. A plan began to formulate as Orsk pushed and shoved her up the stairs into the highest part of the castle. By the time they reached the top of the keep, Emily had scrapes on her feet and shins from the rough stone and Orsk's equally savage treatment. The female guard moved swiftly, forcing Emily to keep up.

Emily could not allow Orsk to lock her in this room again. This was the first time a solitary vampire accompanied Emily anywhere and she intended to take advantage. It might be the only opportunity she had.

Orsk placed a hand on Emily's back and tried to push her farther into the circular chamber. Bringing all her years of training to bear, Emily spun around and drove the heel of her hand into Orsk's nose. She attempted to drive the nasal bones directly into Orsk's brain, but didn't count on the vampire's resiliency. Orsk's head went back and blood streamed from her nostrils, but she merely shook off the blow. Emily didn't wait around for her to recover completely. She followed up the strike with a snap kick to the face. Orsk's helmet fell off and went spinning across the stone floor. She surprised Emily by punching her in the side of the head. The blow was so heavy Emily reeled and almost went down. With her face somewhere around Orsk's waist, Emily spotted the vampire's sword. Emily was fighting for her life and it was only a matter of time before someone drained her. She didn't hesitate to reach for the blade.

Emily was well versed in most modern day weapons, but swords did not fit into that category. The blade felt heavy and awkward so she grabbed the hilt with both hands. Orsk kicked the weapon out of her hands and it went spinning toward the wall. Emily responded by punching Orsk in the nose once again. She hoped that by repeatedly focusing on the same location, she could eventually break the bones. Orsk was off balance and Emily grabbed the top of her cloak near the shoulders. She put her whole body into the maneuver and slammed Orsk face first into the wall. Orsk absorbed the impact with her hands and pushed away, using leverage to launch her body into a back flip. As fast as Orsk moved, it wasn't quick enough. Emily was fueled by indignation, hatred and determination. When fighting in the past, she'd always had to hold herself back a little. However, she'd been fighting humans then. These vampires didn't merit the same restraint.

Everything seemed to move in slow motion. Emily watched the smooth turn in the back flip; saw the moment when Orsk lowered her feet toward the floor. She lashed out, knocking Orsk's feet out from under her with a leg swipe. Unprepared, Orsk slammed into the floor. Emily sprinted for the sword.

Orsk seemed dazed, shaking her head as she pushed upward. Emily put all of her body weight into a swing, intending to decapitate. Instead, the flat of the blade collided with the side of Orsk's head. Orsk fell forward and Emily could hear her panting in exhaustion. Before she could get up, Emily struck her at the base of the skull with the end of the sword's hilt. Castellan Orsk fell unconscious to the floor. Emily resisted killing her at the last moment because she'd thought of something that just might get her safely out of the castle and it wouldn't work with the uniform covered in blood.

Emily dropped the sword and it rang as it bounced off the stone, but she was already in motion. She stripped Orsk's uniform from her body, leaving her dressed only in her underwear. They were roughly the same size and Emily had a better chance dressed in the vampire's attire rather than the skimpy red robe. Emily tore the negligee from her body, surprised by how easily it ripped.

"They just don't make clothes like they used to. Clearly not a union job."

Emily tied Orsk up with strips from the garment, doubling the material just to make sure. She bound Orsk's hands and feet and used what little remained of the robe to fashion a gag. The material had ripped easily under her assault, but with her extremities tied so closely together, Orsk wouldn't have the same leverage. Then Emily dressed in the uniform and armor, pleased at the fit and at finally feeling warm. The boots were a bit long in the toes, but worked well enough. Orsk still hadn't regained consciousness when Emily slipped the sword into the scabbard, picked up the helmet and relieved the vampire of her keys. Almost as an afterthought, she took the ring Orsk wore upon her right middle finger and slipped it on. She reached up and wiped blood away from a cut on her cheek. The small wound had already started to close.

She checked Orsk over, noticing that a bruise was forming beneath one eye. Blood streamed from a broken nose and busted lip. Emily felt it was no less than the vampire deserved. She drew her foot back and kicked Orsk in the ribs, disappointed when she didn't get up and fight some more.

"Black and blue are definitely your colors," she muttered.

After jamming the helmet onto her head, Emily headed for the door. A great sensation of satisfaction washed over her as the bolt slammed closed. One down, countless others to go.

No one accosted her as Emily descended the steps to the castle's ground floor. She felt ridiculous dressed in garb suited for Camelot, but it served her purpose. Within minutes, Emily stood across the drawbridge and on the edge of the city. Alone for now, she carefully studied her location. She chose not to go back toward the mines or the holding pens for the Ti-gon. Instead, she noticed air ships ascending from her left. She couldn't see exactly where they took off from because trees obscured her line of sight, but she thought the air cars represented her best chance.

The image of Adrasta killing Nicole flitted through her mind and Emily's jaw tightened. If she could, she would release all of the prisoners from their cells and destroy the castle from the air. From everything she'd ever heard or read in science fiction, air cars should be equipped with defensive weaponry. She struck off without a second thought, gaze pinned on where she'd seen the last ship ascend. Emily skirted the trees and noticed there were two buildings in the distance near what appeared to be a small airfield. She wasn't sure which one housed what she required, but did see a cluster of guards standing beside one of them. Emily couldn't take the chance that the soldiers would realize she wasn't their commander. She chose to try the second structure away from the small group.

"Just act like you belong here," she muttered, trying to screw up the courage to saunter across the open area.

Her plan seemed simple enough; find a car and figure out how to fly it. How hard could it be? Emily approached the blind side of the structure. As she approached the door, she started to worry it would be locked. Hoping for the best, Emily reached for the handle. Just as she made contact, the door swung open from the inside and smacked into her hand.

Emily tensed, prepared for a fight. A young vampire came to a stunned halt, his eyes widening when he saw her uniform. He jumped aside and clasped an arm across his chest, refusing to look at her directly. Emily decided the arm across the chest was the vampire version of a salute.

"Castellan, I beg your pardon."

Emily didn't really hear what he said. She was too focused on the fact that he hadn't recognized her and that her hand smarted from the door's impact. She growled from the pain as she went past him and that seemed to be the correct response. The door swung closed behind her and the guard did not follow. That was too close.

Remaining hyper-aware of her surroundings, Emily walked down a long hallway toward a chamber she could see in the distance. The building in which she found herself opened into a large central room. At first, Emily didn't comprehend what she saw. Row upon row of individual cylindrical containers hung attached to the ceiling and secured to the floor. Banks of machinery ran down the rows, connected to each of the vessels. She wasn't sure how far the building stretched, but she estimated hundreds if not thousands of containers. Vampires wandered among the vats, holding data pads of some sort and stopping on occasion to enter information.

Horror gripped her soul when Emily recognized a person inside each of the holding tanks. Clear tubes ran to and from the bodies, some carrying what appeared to be nutrients while others ran red. It wasn't difficult for her to identify the red substance as it drained from the body into a large diameter hose and into the floor. There was probably a holding tank under her feet. This was the *bariba,* or nutrition tanks, she'd heard about. Footsteps approached, but Emily was shocked into immobility.

"Castellan, forgive me. I did not know you would be inspecting today."

"Are they alive?" Emily's emotions caused the words to sound like a harsh whisper.

"No, Castellan, at least not technically. I have personally ensured that all higher brain activity was terminated. However, the bodies receive sustenance continually through the feeding tubes and the food production levels are optimal."

Emily almost gagged at the description. Sickened, she was unable to respond.

"Castellan Orsk, I mean no disrespect, but does the princess doubt our efficiency? It is just that you've never inspected before. The regent usually oversees our production."

She barely heard him, unconcerned with the discovery of her

identity for the first time since leaving the castle's keep. Emily wanted to save these people, but she was obviously too late. They were already dead and yet the Erisians continued to violate their bodies. With no brain activity, there was only one thing she could do. Emily would ensure the destruction of this structure and give the victims back their dignity. If she died in the attempt, it was the least she could do.

Emily turned away without responding to the vampire. Her intent was to travel back the way she'd come and try the other structure for an air car. Before leaving this planet, she would blast this place apart. She noticed a shadowy figure near the hallway she'd previously explored, but remained confident that her armor would prevent recognition. As she drew closer, that certainty faded. The vampire regent, Ilana, stood leaning against the entrance to the corridor. Her arms were crossed and a half grin twisted her lips. Ilana's eyes rested on Emily and the ember-red glow in their depths caused a tendril of dread to trickle up Emily's spine.

Emily attempted to act naturally, grasping the sword with her left hand to keep it from swinging. She refrained from glancing at Ilana as she passed and entered the hallway. To her dismay, Ilana fell into step behind her. The vampire followed Emily as she exited through the side door and out into Eris's version of daylight. There wasn't much of it left, the moons headed toward the horizon. Already she could see the smaller sun beginning to rise.

"Where are you going, Castellan?" Ilana drawled in such a way that told Emily she knew something.

Emily stopped and turned her head so that she could watch Ilana over her shoulder. She didn't speak as she waited to see what would happen next. Ilana approached, halting inches away. Emily actually heard her inhale deeply, scenting her. A trickle of nervous sweat tracked down the side of her face.

"Odd, you don't smell like Orsk. Now where did you get that armor, I wonder, and what do you hope to accomplish, Emily?"

Emily was so frightened she thought her heart had actually stopped beating. Ilana would not make Orsk's mistake of underestimating her prey. She could kill Emily in a flash. As the seconds ticked by, Emily began to wonder why she didn't. Ilana hadn't threatened her in any way and had not sounded an alarm. If anything, she seemed to be toying with her. Emily frowned and studied Ilana's eyes. She found humor there.

"You're brave for a human. I'll give you that."

"Is that so unusual?"

"More than you might think. Come with me."

Ilana took a few steps toward the Ti-gon holding area and stopped when she realized that Emily hadn't followed. "It's all right. I will not take you back to the castle."

Convinced that she didn't really have a choice, Emily fell into step beside Ilana. They walked across a large, stone courtyard and down a street. Emily recognized the route from earlier in the day. Soldiers passed and each clasped an arm across the chest, striking their fists into their armor. None stopped to confront her.

"Where are we going?"

"Quiet, Castellan," Ilana hissed. "Erisians have tremendous hearing."

Emily's heart took a frightened leap and then settled. Ilana was actually helping her. This was unexpected, but a great relief. Since arriving on this planet, only two vampires seemed trustworthy and Emily wasn't really convinced that would last. In fact, she felt sure they had their own agendas and that she was merely a pawn. Nevertheless, she didn't have any other options because there was no way she was going back to Adrasta.

Ilana did lead her back into the Ti-gon warehouse, but they entered through a back door. Ilana tapped a sequence of characters into a high-tech cipher-lock, apparently unconcerned by an observer. Emily was relieved that Ilana didn't force her to observe the victims of the hunt in their cells. Ilana opened a door and Emily found herself in a well-appointed office. A holographic computer interface projected from a desk surface and a large monitor took up most of one wall. Ilana ignored the computer as she opened a drawer and removed an object the size of a garage door remote.

"You're fortunate that no one really studied your appearance. The containment collar shows above the neck of your uniform. Come here."

Emily obeyed and flinched as Ilana raised a hand. She steadied when Ilana merely pressed a button and the collar dropped away to the floor.

"Why are you helping me?" It was the only question Emily could think of and it was the most important.

"Because Adrasta is a monster. I will not see you returned to her and it is impossible to keep you with me, as much as I would enjoy that. She would have us both killed."

Unaccountably, Emily felt tears spring to her eyes. "I watched her murder someone, a young woman named Nicole."

Ilana nodded. "One of her body servants."

The distaste in the comment was clear. "How can you disapprove?" Emily asked, suddenly angry. "You run the damned hunt, don't you? How are you any better? You say Adrasta is a monster, but what does that make you or the rest of the Erisians?"

"Lower your voice. I follow my orders so that I can continue to help where I may. If I am dead, someone else will take my place that will follow Adrasta without question."

Emily reeled at the wealth of information contained in a few simple sentences. "You're part of some sort of resistance?"

"I wouldn't go that far." The amused expression was back. "I believe in my people, and we have the same right to survive as you do. However, Adrasta is bloodthirsty. There are better ways for our people to thrive without abusing others. I will see her overthrown and another, more benevolent ruler in her place."

"That doesn't explain why you're helping me. You must have seen countless others murdered by her. I just saw the *bariba* and all those helpless people."

Ilana's amusement faded and her jaw clenched. "It is unconscionable, but there are too few of us to stop it. That is part of the reason I assisted you. I have seen many humans as well as other species brought to Eris against their will, but you are the first to display such spirit. I believe you can help make a difference here."

"How?"

Ilana handed Emily the remote she'd used to release the collar. "Take this. There are three buttons. One releases the collars and bracelets, one causes the shocking pain you have personally experienced and the final control activates the portals."

"I heard someone else mention the portals." Emily thought of Charles. "Is that how I got here?"

"Yes, the portals lead into your world in many locations. Once you cross back into your plane of existence, turn this dial at the bottom to the extreme end of the field," Ilana demonstrated as she spoke. "Then press and hold this indicator for ten seconds. The intensity of the field combined with the duration of activation will trigger an overload. Make sure you are clear of the blast radius before you do this."

"How far is the blast radius?"

"Not far, five meters should prove sufficient."

Emily took the device and thumbed the intensity of the dial back to the original starting point. She didn't have any pockets so she reached down and tucked the remote into her boot.

"Is that a one-time deal or can the remote destroy other portals, too?"

Ilana shrugged negligently. "The device will not be damaged, only the targeted portal. Essentially, you may utilize the control as many times as you require."

A plan began to percolate, but Emily focused on more immediate concerns. "Now I just need to get out of here. Is there any way you can get me to one of those air cars?"

Ilana shook her head. "I'm sorry, but the vehicles are keyed to respond only to Erisian DNA. Even if you could decipher the controls, they would not respond to you."

"I guess I'll have to do it the hard way then. Ilana, I really appreciate this but I'm not leaving here without destroying the *bariba*."

Ilana rested a hand on Emily's face. She leaned close and Emily could feel the attraction vibrate between them once again. "I was hoping you would say that. I've done as much as I dare, but I will take you to someone that can help."

Chapter Fifteen

SLOWLY, BIT BY bit, signs of civilization began to manifest. Jenna noticed a ramshackle barn and a wooden, split-rail fence. She didn't see any other people so she kept moving. Eventually she happened upon a dirt track. It would be nothing but mud during a storm, but at the moment it remained dry and hard underfoot. The village proper finally came into view and reminded Jenna of something out of an old west film. She expected to see a bar with swinging doors and saloon girls dressed in short skirts. Instead, she saw people dressed in dirty rags. From a distance, they seemed downtrodden, defeated.

An older woman surprised Jenna by suddenly exiting from a nearby clapboard house. Upon sighting Jenna, the woman cried out and ran back into her home. The door slammed closed behind her. Jenna couldn't figure out what inspired the reaction until she glanced down and remembered the brown vampire cloak. With the hood in place, she resembled one of the Erisians. The woman probably thought she was about to become a meal.

Jenna's stomach rumbled at the thought of food. She placed a hand over her belly and looked around for any hint of a grocery, bakery or butcher. Interesting scents drifted toward her from the far end of the village and she started in that direction. Jenna hadn't taken more than a half dozen steps when she found herself surrounded by a small throng of villagers. Four men and two women stood facing her. They must have dropped almost everything and rushed outside when they heard the stranger's squeal of fright because one of the women held a little girl. The child appeared no older than four.

"How may we be of assistance, Mistress?"

Jenna detected both the attempt at respect and deliberately hidden terror. She considered revealing her humanity, but then quickly decided against it. Right now, the villagers feared her but would likely supply what she needed. If they learned she was just another human, they might hurt or kill her. She had no way of knowing how they might react and wasn't willing to take the risk.

"I mean you no harm. I merely require sustenance."

Her words generated a flurry of activity. The villagers huddled together and spoke so quietly among themselves that Jenna couldn't hear. She thought about activating the cloak's listening field but the memory of the blinding headache she'd suffered before from amplified sound changed her mind. Eavesdropping wouldn't alter the outcome of their decision. Voices rose as an argument broke out and a man stepped toward her, his expression resigned.

"I will volunteer." Voice low and trembling with fear, the stranger kept his eyes on the thick dirt beneath their feet.

Jenna cringed inside once she understood his meaning. "No." She growled her response, disgusted by the thought.

He met her eyes briefly, a look of relief ghosting across his face before hardening into grim resolve. Jenna thought she saw a flash of anger before it disappeared into a façade of neutrality. He turned back toward the small group and reached for the child. The woman holding the girl pulled away, attempting to protect her. A short argument broke out and Jenna heard someone comment on sacrificing in order to protect the village. The man pulled the child away, the woman unable to resist because the others held her back.

"No!"

The man passed the girl toward her and Jenna instinctively took the child into her arms. Jenna vaguely noticed the woman collapse to the ground sobbing. Two others knelt with her, offering comfort. Jenna's mind refused to accept the truth at first. She closed her eyes, dealing with the consequences of her deception. After a moment, she smiled at the girl.

"Hi, little one. My name is Jenna and it is a pleasure to meet you, but I think you should stay with them." She stepped toward the man and handed him the child. "As I said, I mean you no harm. I require real food. Meat, cheese, vegetables..."

Tears flooded the man's eyes and he started nodding his head. "Of course, Mistress, I'll see to it immediately." He kept nodding even as he handed off the little girl to her relieved mother.

Child safely back in her arms, the woman turned to Jenna. "Thank you, Mistress." She whispered the words quickly and then hurried away before Jenna could change her mind about her choice of nutrition. Jenna noticed that none of them had directly met her gaze for any amount of time.

"I am Kwame. Please, come."

He turned away from Jenna, making a sharp, chopping motion that sent the others scurrying away. Jenna thought it odd that they'd all approached her anyway. She couldn't think of any purpose for deliberately approaching a vampire, especially with a small child in tow. Perhaps it was a deliberate move to sacrifice themselves for the welfare of the village. Whatever their reasoning, Jenna felt her stomach rumble in anticipation.

She followed Kwame down a wide dirt street. Windows and doors slammed closed in their wake. Jenna spotted a small furry creature with a twitching nose. If not for the tiny horns sprouting between the ears and the slightly green hue, it could have been an ordinary rabbit. It stood beside a split-rail large animal pen, its nose twitching at their approach. A few feet separated them when the creature suddenly pounded a hind foot into the turf and then high-tailed it for safer parts.

Jenna concealed her smile beneath the cloak. It was amazing how tiny details remained the same regardless of location. That included the frightened reaction of simple villagers to a stranger's presence.

Kwame led her onto a wooden porch and inside a cramped building. She'd never have thought it possible, but shadows were even heavier inside. Little light filtered in through the two windows, but was supplemented by the huge fire roaring in the hearth. One long table took up the majority of the room, surrounded by chairs. A few small, round tables strategically occupied places around the outside edges. Jenna reached into the pocket and pressed the center button on the control. Immediately, she was able to see detail. She had switched it off earlier out of concern for depleting some sort of power cell. She watched Kwame head across the room and speak to a serving woman. Rapidly growing accustomed to the terrified looks, Jenna sought an unoccupied table in the back. Two groups of villagers quickly left the structure, leaving behind only the woman, Kwame and Jenna.

After a heated discussion between Kwame and the unknown woman, he brought a cup of liquid to Jenna's table and placed it in front of her. A quick look assured her it was water. Jenna grabbed the container and raised it toward her mouth, stopping at the last moment.

"I can't pay you."

Kwame shook his head vigorously. "I understand, Mistress. It is not expected."

In other words, Jenna thought, they would give her anything she asked for to avoid having their throats ripped out. She felt bad about the deception, but didn't think there was much choice. She needed food and water. Jenna considered offering some type of labor in exchange for the meal, but had a pressing need to move on toward Saqqara as soon as she could. Given the distinct lack of options, Jenna merely nodded her acceptance.

"Do you work here?"

After momentary confusion, Kwame responded so quickly that the words tumbled over each other. "No, Mistress. I am one of the village leaders. It is my personal honor to serve you."

Uh-huh.

"Kwame, I suspect it's your personal honor because you're protecting your people from my bloodthirsty ways. Isn't that the truth?"

He looked down and shuffled his feet on the dirt floor. The resemblance to a chastened schoolboy was uncanny. Kwame seemed careful to weigh his reply. "They mean no disrespect, I assure you."

Jenna's heart went out to these simple villagers. From all she'd seen, they lived in relative squalor and daily terror. The Erisians possessed technology the likes of which Jenna had never imagined. They flew around in futuristic flying cars and had all the best this world had to offer. In sharp contrast, the human villagers had nothing but rattletrap wooden houses with dirt floors. Jenna hadn't noticed a single electric bulb, in either Moye's home or here.

"It's fine, Kwame. All I ask is a meal and then I'll be on my way."

Kwame turned back toward the serving woman. He didn't say anything else but the relief on his face was unmistakable. He spoke with the woman in the back in low tones. She still refused to cross the room's centerline, but she did prepare a meal. After she placed a bowl of something and a plate of bread on a tray, Kwame brought Jenna's food.

Jenna's mouth watered as the steam from the freshly baked bread and stew hit her nostrils. Although clearly unleavened, and something to which she wasn't accustomed, Jenna pulled off a chunk of bread and shoved it into her mouth. Face hidden beneath the hood, she closed her eyes in relief as the food hit her stomach. Once she'd swallowed, Jenna noticed Kwame still standing beside the table.

"May I bring you something else, Mistress?"

"Jenna," she corrected. "My name is Jenna."

"Yes, Mistress Jenna." Kwame bowed slightly from the waist and Jenna gave up trying to get him to see her as a friend.

She picked up a wooden spoon and started to ignore Kwame while she finished her meal, but then thought better of it. This was a rare opportunity and Jenna would consider herself foolish if she didn't take advantage. "Please, sit down. I have some questions."

Reluctantly, Kwame reached to pull out a chair. Jenna noticed his hand trembling, but ignored it while he settled next to her. He folded his hands together on the tabletop. Again, he failed to meet her eyes. Jenna was getting tired of the subservient attitude. Didn't these people have any backbone?

"Why do you live this way? Doesn't it bother any of you that the Erisians...uh, we...have everything while you're barely scraping by?"

"We are grateful for what we have."

Jenna thought that sounded like a rote answer, intended to deflect. She finally lost all patience. "Cut the crap. I've already said I'm not going to hurt you. Please answer me."

She ate a spoonful of the thick stew, chewing happily on thick meat and vegetables in a tasty broth. It was by far the best tasting thing she'd eaten since coming through the portal. Kwame took his time answering, but Jenna didn't push. She needed answers and scaring him away wouldn't serve her purpose.

"In truth, some of the younger people grow tired of these conditions. Those of us more experienced with the harshness of life truly are grateful for what we have. Our situation could be much worse."

Jenna acknowledged the truth of that. Things could always get worse. She did notice that as Kwame spoke, he seemed to relax more around her. That was good.

"I understand why you're afraid of me, dressed the way I am and coming unannounced into your village. However, I get the feeling there's more to it than that. Have you had trouble with Erisians visiting for the sole purpose of hurting you?"

Kwame nodded slowly. "We are very close to the capital, Saqqara. When an Erisian enters the village, we are required to make a sacrifice."

"Like you did with me," Jenna observed. "Barbaric."

Kwame frowned. "You are not like the others."

"I should hope to hell not. Listen, I'm looking for information about Saqqara. I need to know the best way to get into the city unseen."

"Why? You are free to come and go as you desire," Kwame pointed out helpfully.

Jenna squeezed the spoon in frustration. "That's true, but I'm looking for a friend. She's a human who was taken by someone called Garran. I'd like to get her out of the city without drawing unwanted attention."

"I'm sorry, Mistress Jenna, but I have never been to the city. Princess Adrasta allows humans to survive in the villages because they supply food for the palace slaves as well as hard labor."

Jenna thought of Moye and that he'd considered Princess Adrasta a benevolent ruler. She thought his opinion must be similar to Kwame's, based on the assumption that survival was enough and that they hadn't the right to ask for more. She shook her head slightly.

At this point, seeking information about troop movements and likely holding cells was pointless. By his own admission, Kwame had never visited Saqqara. He couldn't help her. When Kwame asked to leave the table, Jenna nodded. She finished her meal in solitude, surrounded by quiet but aware of the cook's eyes watching carefully.

Jenna had just sat back from her empty tray, pleasantly stuffed, when a ruckus erupted outside. Whatever was happening occurred near the building. Kwame sent Jenna a startled look before rushing out of the door. Jenna turned in her chair and pulled aside a piece of cloth that covered the small window.

Kwame hustled across the dirt toward a newcomer. Jenna identified the visitor as Erisian from the brown cloak. She could tell the vampire had a short stature and lean frame, but with the hood in place and back turned, Jenna couldn't make out any further details. The same group of people who'd greeted Jenna surrounded the Erisian. Jenna was glad to see the woman had left the little girl inside this time.

The vampire turned toward Kwame as he approached and Jenna's blood ran cold. She recognized the murderous glare in the girl's eyes, the hungry mewling sound issuing from between the full lips. It felt like a lifetime ago, but Jenna remembered the clearing in the woods when she'd first arrived on Eris. This was the same monster who'd wanted to feed off of Emily. Only Garran's intervention had prevented her demise.

"Bring me a child, no older than five seasons," Chala ordered. With the hood still adjusted to enhance her vision, Jenna saw the spittle fly as she spoke.

"Please, Mistress," Kwame begged, "take me instead. I am old and my life has been full."

"No, the blood of a child is sweet. I shall have one or I will kill everyone within this filthy haven."

There was no way Chala would change her mind. Jenna couldn't stand by and witness a slaughter without attempting to intervene. Worried about the village inhabitants, Jenna hurried after Kwame. Chala noticed her as soon as Jenna exited the structure. Bewilderment and shock showed on Chala's countenance before disappearing.

"Who are you?" Chala demanded.

Jenna ignored the question. "State your business with these people."

"The same as yours, I'd imagine." A devilish smile caused a dimple to crease in Chala's cheek.

If she weren't so evil, Jenna thought the teenager might actually be cute. Unfortunately, the bloodlust and hatred Chala sported so openly did nothing but turn Jenna's stomach. Drawing on her limited experience with the vampires, Jenna attempted to adopt their manner of speaking. "You will leave this village immediately."

"Who are you to tell me what to do? I've never even seen you before." Chala made a show of studying the gold clasp at Jenna's neck. "You wear the insignia of a prey seeker, but I've never seen you before and I've been with Garran when he brings back new blood."

Jenna didn't know what Chala meant, but she did understand that Chala posed a threat to her cover story. She reached down and removed the hunting knife from her boot, holding it so that what little light that existed would reflect off the blade. "I will not debate the issue. Leave."

The villagers began to back away, sensing that something monumental was about to happen. Their movement was the catalyst that sent Chala flying toward Jenna. The teen rushed forward at an almost unbelievable speed. Her shriek of anger caused a shiver to travel up Jenna's spine and she barely had enough time to raise the knife into a defensive position. Somehow, incredibly, she missed her target. Chala's fists struck Jenna in the chest and she careened backward into the animal pen. Her back hit the top rail of the corral and knocked the breath from her lungs.

Jenna went down on one knee and struggled to draw in a full breath. With difficulty, she kept her eyes on her opponent. Apparently, she considered the altercation with Jenna at an end and she turned back to the helpless inhabitants. Jenna thought such territorial fighting between Erisians might be commonplace. Once one had established dominance, the other would slink away. Whatever the reason, Chala's smug satisfaction and perceived victory lowered her defenses enough to turn her back on Jenna.

"Where is my prey?"

Jenna finally took a lungful of air and shot to her feet. Silently, she ran toward Chala. The vampire turned at the last second, her eyes wide in disbelief as Jenna buried the knife in her neck. Jenna felt a strong sense of déjà vu, remembering the vampire who had attacked in the forest. Just like that monster, Chala sank to the ground with barely a whimper. This time, however, Jenna felt righteous indignation for killing any creature that would actively seek to harm a child. She yanked the hunting knife from Chala's throat and threw her entire body weight into a sideways slice. The blade transected Chala's neck, cutting deeply into muscle, sinew and bone.

A look of confusion ghosted across Chala's face. She attempted to speak but the only sound, a low gurgling noise, issued from her throat as blood streamed down her chest. Chala's head fell back and the wound in her neck gaped open. Jenna had all but decapitated the vampire. She felt vindicated as Chala dropped dead onto the dirt.

An unexpected phrase went through Jenna's head, accompanied by the sound of bagpipes. There can be only one. Furtively, she looked around waiting for the quickening. When nothing happened, Jenna shook her head, chasing away thoughts of the movie *Highlander*. Sometimes she had the strangest ideas at the oddest moments.

Villagers forgotten, Jenna dropped onto her knees beside the fallen vampire. The first rule of survival was to waste nothing. That included anything an enemy might possess. She felt sickened by the necessity. Laying the bloody knife on the ground, Jenna patted down Chala's body. She had no desire to take the vampire's cloak because it was covered in gore. She removed the translation ring from Chala's left hand and shoved it into the satchel at her waist. Other than the cloak and ring, Chala's garb proved similar to the other Erisian Jenna had killed. She started to stand up when she noticed the belt. The man in the woods hadn't possessed one.

Chala wore a silver belt. At first, the belt seemed merely ornamental. Then Jenna noticed the heavy gauge wire soldered at different points along the circumference as well as a circular dial. Another piece of advanced technology? She couldn't figure out how to unfasten the belt.

A pair of worn, leather boots came into her line of sight and Jenna looked up at Kwame. Ignoring the awe in his expression, Jenna asked, "Do you know how this comes off?"

Wordlessly, Kwame squatted beside her and showed Jenna how to detach the band. Jenna didn't know the belt's purpose, but she wasn't going to leave it here. More than that, she wouldn't experiment with it until she was alone. Although these people had been nothing but helpful, they didn't really know her. Their benevolence could change in an instant under the right circumstances. Instinct told Jenna this belt would prove a useful tool, just like the cloak.

Holding the belt in one hand, she grasped the hilt of her knife in the other and wiped the blade off on Chala's thigh. She tucked it back into her boot and stood up, aware of the villagers' stares.

"I think you should do something with that." She waved to indicate Chala's body. "Burn it or something once I'm gone."

"Are you leaving now?"

Kwame sounded so excited at the prospect that Jenna smiled. "Yes. I thank you for the meal, but I think it's best that I leave before something else happens."

Jenna hadn't anticipated a tearful goodbye, but was surprised when Kwame reached out and touched her forearm. He nodded toward Chala. "This one has come many times and taken our children. You have made a friend here today. If you ever require assistance, I will help."

"Thanks, I may take you up on that." Jenna glanced overhead and noticed that the sun was high. The moons had disappeared below the horizon. "Can you tell me of somewhere to sleep for the night? I don't want to bother you more than I already have, but I require a few hours of rest."

Kwame pointed toward Saqqara. "Follow this road. You will discover an old barn before the sun reaches its zenith. You can rest there without fear of disturbance."

"That sounds perfect." Jenna glanced around the clearing but no one else spoke. She turned away and headed down the dirt lane.

Jenna felt strange leaving the villagers behind. A nagging sensation caused her to keep rehashing her time spent there. Eventually, she realized it was the silence she found so unnerving. No one had spoken to her once except for Kwame. She knew the villagers could speak; she'd heard the woman cry out when she thought Jenna would take her child. Shrugging it off as one more mystery she'd probably never solve, Jenna kept walking.

In less than an hour, she spotted the barn Kwame had mentioned. Boards had fallen off in places and the roof didn't look secure, but it was a place to get out of sight. Here there was actual prairie grass. Although it retained Eris's customary yellowish tinge, it still looked and smelled like grass. Jenna closed her eyes, indulging in the familiar scent that reminded her of Earth. Until this moment, she hadn't realized how very much she missed the Kentucky hills and her home in Woeful Pines. The ache in her chest reminded her of how the beauty and serenity of the region had drawn her. Another vision came to mind and Jenna opened her eyes, surprised to find her sight blurred by tears. As much as she missed home, she didn't regret following Emily.

The attraction between them had been instantaneous and powerful. She didn't know if it would still be there when next she saw Emily, but regardless of her feelings, Jenna would have come through the portal anyway. Just knowing that the Kurth brothers had brought people here against their will was enough. She couldn't have lived with herself if she'd known their fate and failed to act.

Jenna had to fight to open the huge door. One hinge had rusted through and snapped so that the door sagged. Finally, she managed a wide enough crack to slip through and crossed over into heavier shadows. Her nose felt assaulted by the ancient odors of moldy hay, animal dung and sour oats. With the hood's sight capability still enhanced, she quickly determined she was alone. Jenna found a spot in the back under a fallen beam that promised concealment from unexpected company. After gathering a pile of straw to protect her from the hard floor, Jenna climbed on top and allowed her muscles to relax. Once she'd become somewhat accustomed to the creaks and groans of the old wood, she shut off the visual enhancement. She welcomed the darkness for the time being and allowed sleep to claim her for a few hours.

AFTER AWAKENING GRADUALLY, Jenna surveyed her surroundings. Nothing had changed inside the barn. She wondered how many years had passed since the building was last used. She felt groggy from a full, restful sleep. After a slow stretch, she emerged from under the fallen beam. It seemed lighter inside the barn and she guessed that the moons had risen. Jenna left the visual display off; worried the small control housed some type of battery that would run down from overuse. She'd traveled all this way without the tool, acquiring the cloak only a few days ago, and Jenna didn't want to become complacent. If she lost the garment or it stopped working, she'd need the natural ability to compensate.

Breakfast was nothing more than a long drink from her water skin and Jenna wished she'd thought to ask the villagers for a few supplies. With no choice but to ignore her rumbling stomach, Jenna inspected the belt taken from Chala the previous day. Again, she noticed the circuitry and a rocker switch near the clasp. Two small gems, possibly diamonds, adorned each side of the belt. Jenna thumbed the switch, caught off guard when the belt suddenly flew toward the ceiling. Instinctively, her grip tightened on the belt and she felt her feet lifted from the floor.

"What the hell?"

Not a big fan of heights, Jenna pulled on the belt. Instead of sinking toward her, Jenna rose toward the device. It continued to climb toward the ceiling, towing her along for the ride. Jenna finally reached up with her other hand and closed the switch. She expected to go crashing back to the ground and braced herself for the fall, but that didn't happen. Jenna drifted safely back to the floor and stood looking at the belt in absolute confusion.

It was then she noticed the hairs standing up on her arms from static electricity. The belt had generated some type of anti-gravity field. The Erisians didn't have the ability to fly at all. Just as she'd suspected after discovering the cloak, that particular skill was technologically related. Jenna tried to cinch the belt around her waist but found it was too small for her. After a bit of fumbling, she figured out how to adjust the length since it was similar to a dog's collar.

Jenna played with the controls for some time, figuring out that the dial near the activation switch controlled the rate of ascent. She still wasn't sure how to propel herself in different directions, and there wasn't a convenient control for that function. She felt sure she would figure it out later and headed for the door.

With the belt snuggled around her middle, Jenna left the relative safety of the barn and started down the dirt track. From where she stood, the road seemed to lead directly to the capital city. Jenna had to dodge a few flying cars, seeking shelter in the high grass, but she steadily closed the distance. A few rolling hills blocked her sight of Saqqara.

Eventually, the sound of rushing water came to her ears. Jenna frowned and kept following the road. It rounded one of the hills and she found herself standing at the bank of a rushing torrent. Jenna remembered Moye cautioning her that the riverbed did not always run dry. That was an understatement. A storm must have occurred somewhere upstream, dumping a deluge into the river. The flood was powerful enough to destroy the bridge that once spanned the banks.

Jenna wasn't about to attempt to swim the whitewater and all of the airships flying overhead made using the belt a serious risk. First, she hadn't practiced using the device and didn't know how to control it. Second, flying would place her closer to the passing Erisians and she risked exposure. With the distinct lack of cover, she needed to get off the road now anyway so she decided to look for an alternate crossing point.

Heading to her left, Jenna planned to circle around behind Saqqara in the hopes that any patrols would be fewer and farther between. Her route took her into the trees and up one of the steeper slopes. Getting under the treetops made Jenna feel more secure. In places, the hill seemed especially steep and she took pleasure in the sensation of feeling her thigh muscles flex. There was no denying that Jenna felt stronger on Eris. That her strength stemmed from a planet with lighter gravity compared to Earth was beside the point as far as she was concerned. The reduced gravity also partially explained how the Erisian technology allowed flight. Everyone knew gravity was really a weak phenomenon, which was why a magnet could attract metals in spite of it. Having a more reduced pull on this planet made all the difference.

Jenna's musings ceased abruptly as she came to the rim of a steep canyon. She looked over the embankment and realized the crater was nothing compared to the Grand Canyon on Earth but it remained daunting. Jenna searched the distance, looking for a way around. She estimated it would take at least two more days to circumnavigate the gorge. Given her distinct lack of food supplies, she didn't think that would be feasible. Going down and across at the narrowest point was also out. Jenna remembered the last time she'd tried to descend a steep decline. The scar on her previously broken leg throbbed as a reminder. It appeared she'd have to try to figure out the anti-gravity belt.

Prudence dictated that she move away from the edge of the precipice. Jenna didn't fancy accidentally flying over the rim and then falling to her death. She deliberately walked under a thick tree with high-reaching branches. If she did lose control and go soaring into the air, she could grab hold of something. She turned the dial to the lowest setting and then pressed the rocker switch to activate the belt. Her feet rose a few inches from the ground, but she didn't go any higher. She continued to turn the dial until she cleared the shrub beneath the tree. Just as she'd suspected, Jenna rose straight up. Her body didn't travel forward, backward or to either side. Up was good, but wouldn't get her anywhere near her goal.

Jenna tried throwing herself forward, but it didn't work. She only wobbled slightly. She tried to ignore the press of stiff material under her ribcage as the belt held her aloft and studied the belt's configuration again. She still didn't see anything obvious that would induce movement. Jenna began pressing every centimeter all along the circumference. Nothing worked. She felt like her lungs were in her throat. Desperate to relieve the pain in her chest, Jenna finally mashed down on one of the diamonds and sailed backward into the tree trunk. For the second time in as many days, all of the air whooshed out of her lungs.

Gasping and choking, Jenna deactivated the belt. She had no recourse but to trust the device to lower her safely to the ground. She immediately dropped to her knees and gagged, thankful for having nothing in her stomach. When she could breathe again, Jenna climbed shakily to her feet. She didn't relish a repeat, and considered ways to lower the pressure on her internal organs. Maybe leaning into the direction of travel would minimize the strain. She mentally braced herself and pressed the diamond on the opposite side, reasoning that if one sent her backward the other would send her forward. The belt did indeed pull her face first, but she'd forgotten to push the rocker switch that activated the anti-gravity field. She had to jog to keep up until she pushed the control again.

"Stupid, stupid, stupid," she muttered, walking back under the tree.

This time Jenna remembered to activate all sequences before choosing a direction of travel. She set the dial to a minimal setting, engaged the anti-grav and then pressed the diamond. Jenna rose smoothly into the air, her feet clearing the underbrush as she flew slowly toward the canyon rim. She leaned forward and pushed the belt back down over her hips. It took some getting used to, but she actually felt comfortable now. She quickly reengaged the cloak's visual aid property and sighed with relief when she could see again without the shadows. Trying out some new piece of tech seemed easier when she could actually see the obstacles in her path.

Jenna's stomach lurched as her feet cleared the edge of the crater, but her altitude lowered with the terrain. She held steady at the same height as she had on the forest floor. Even if the belt did cease to function, she'd only fall from a distance of about four feet. Depending upon the steepness of the slope if such a thing did happen, Jenna doubted she'd incur any serious injury.

Content with the current settings that kept her well below any passing airships, Jenna attempted to remain aware of her surroundings as she drifted. Nothing passed overhead and she figured the Erisians kept to a predetermined set of air lanes. It made sense. Just like any traffic, the goal was to avoid accidents and stay along prearranged routes. Although there seemed a fraction of vampire vehicles compared to Earth vehicles, the logic still held.

As time passed, Jenna became more relaxed. Eventually, she reached the valley floor and started across the gorge. In less than two hours, Jenna reached the opposite slope and began her ascent. She became more vigilant here. The size of the boulders increased until she flew over some the size of a bus and others as wide as a building. Erisians could be hiding anywhere, though she seriously doubted it. They didn't exactly know she was here.

Several hundred feet from the top, Jenna noticed a flash of color off to the side. She held her breath, expecting an attack that never came. The color blue stood out especially because of the dusty surroundings. She thought that she might find something useful there and even if she didn't, it was worth the time it would take to find out. Jenna shut off the forward controls and lowered herself to the ground. The terrain here was steeper than she expected and Jenna slipped back a few inches before she caught her balance.

Jenna stopped abruptly when she realized the swatch of color encased someone's knee. Whoever it was lay concealed behind one of the smaller boulders. She stood there for several long, tense minutes, but the individual never moved. Carefully, Jenna took a step forward. When no one reacted, she gained the confidence to take another. Soon, she neared the stone and reached out to touch the hard stone surface. Jenna hesitated, but still nothing happened. She withdrew her knife from the boot.

Inch by inch, Jenna leaned around the rock barrier and came face to face with the end of a futuristic looking pistol. The wielder of the weapon possessed long, flowing purple-brown hair and blue upon blue eyes. Dressed in a navy uniform with silver accoutrements, she didn't resemble any Erisian Jenna had seen to date.

"I won't hurt you."

"Funny thing for an Erisian to say," the stranger responded.

Jenna felt confused for a moment, but then remembered her cloak was still in place. She pushed the hood back, unable to see as the shadows returned. As her eyes adjusted, she spoke to reassure the other woman.

"My name is Jenna. I'm from Earth."

"Earth? Were you kidnapped and brought through a portal?"

"Actually, no. I followed a friend who was though. What about you? You're not one of them."

The stranger lowered her weapon and lay back on her elbows. "I am Fallon. I am from the planet Levothos. The Erisians took me for their cursed hunt when my vessel crashed here. I escaped when I fell over the edge of the canyon, but I broke my leg in the fall."

"How long have you been here?"

Jenna glanced at Fallon's legs, noticing that the left was crudely splinted with sticks and strips torn from Fallon's sleeves. At least it didn't appear to be a compound fracture.

"Several days. I attempted to climb out but I could not negotiate the slope with my injury. My supplies are very nearly exhausted."

The information didn't make a lot of sense. "Let me get this straight. The Erisians captured you for some kind of hunt, but you escaped and have been in this gorge ever since?"

Fallon nodded.

"And what? They just let you keep any supplies you happen to have on you, including a sophisticated handgun, out of the kindness of their hearts?"

"Kindness does not enter into the equation," Fallon snapped, blue eyes flashing. "The Erisians allow their victims to keep any armaments or supplies because they believe it enhances the Ti-gon and is more of a challenge."

Jenna didn't really understand most of this, nor did she particularly care. She was more concerned about something else Fallon had said. "You have a ship? Can it fly a handful of us out of this hellhole?"

"I don't know. I was captured before I could assess the damage." Fallon sounded suspicious.

"Look, you help me and I'll help you. I came here to rescue someone. If I get you out of the canyon and back to your vessel, will you help me get my friend and get out of here?"

"How can you assist me in leaving the canyon? I do not believe you are strong enough to carry me up the embankment."

"You did see how I got here, didn't you?"

Fallon ignored the question. "If I make it back to my ship," she stated sharply, "I shall fly back to the Coalition and transmit coordinates to destroy Adrasta's castle."

"Fine, have it your way." Jenna stood up. "Stay here and rot."

"I have no reason to trust you. You are wearing Erisian attire and possess a repulsor cinch. Although you may be human, it is more likely that you are a collaborator rather than someone searching for a lost friend."

Jenna thought about trying to explain all she'd gone through to arrive at this point, but realized she'd be wasting her time. "Fallon, I'm leaving. With or without you, I will get Emily back and we will get home. You can lie here if you want."

"You are Emily's friend?" Fallon's hostility evaporated.

Jenna dropped back to her knees. "You've seen her? Is she all right?"

Fallon shrugged. "I last saw her the day I fell into the canyon. She was alive then and it's likely that the Erisians recaptured her. The bracelets we wear contain a locator beacon so that they may find us anywhere." She held up her arm to show Jenna the device.

"Then why didn't they find you?"

"I believe there is a limit to the beacon's range and I passed beyond that distance when I fell."

"Lucky for me," Jenna observed. "How much farther is it to Saqqara?"

"Less than two Earth hours in the direction you were traveling."

"What about your ship? Do you know how to get to it? I have a feeling we'll need some firepower."

Fallon sat up and tucked her pistol into the holster. "I have studied the Erisian terrain extensively so yes, I can locate the *Firestorm*, but it is merely a scout vessel. It does not contain many weapons."

"But it does have some," Jenna said, latching onto Fallon's description. "I can't force you to help me, but I am begging you. For Emily's sake and for all the other victims these vampires have kidnapped, please."

Sighing dramatically, Fallon finally nodded. "Very well, I know someone who may be able to assist in this foolish quest of yours. Take me to the *Firestorm* and if we can get her repaired, I will do what I can."

Far from reassured, Jenna had to settle for the vague promise. She had the feeling it was the most she would get. "Thank you."

"How do you intend to assist me out of this coulee?"

Jenna smiled. That question she could answer with full confidence. "You do remember that I have a repulsor cinch, right? But what about your leg? You can hardly help me in your current condition."

"I can repair the injury as soon as I reach my vessel. *Firestorm* is equipped with emergency first aid gear."

Chapter Sixteen

EMILY FOLLOWED ILANA toward the selenium mines. She wasn't sure this was such a great idea, but didn't really have much choice. It was getting late, by Erisian time, and the moons were beginning to dip below the horizon. She'd been here long enough to understand that the vampires rested while the sun was high and moved about during moon-time. Their active period meant that there were few Erisians around, for which Emily felt duly grateful. Still, she didn't think it would be a great idea to push her luck.

Ilana started for the mine entrance, but Emily held back. "No offense, but I'm not going in there." After all that she'd experienced, Emily thought the shadowed aperture resembled the gaping maw of death.

Regent Ilana turned back to her with a look of confusion. They were still quite a distance from the mine entrance, close to where Emily was the day Adrasta took a liking to her. Emily noticed that it all looked the same. Rails lined the opening to the mineshaft and she could smell the bitter scent of the mineral the Erisians so coveted. The odor alone brought back unpleasant memories.

"The assistance you seek can only be found inside."

"Don't be so mysterious," Emily responded crankily. "Listen, I appreciate that you're helping me, but I might be recognized if I go in there. It's only been a few days since I was gang-pressed into working the mines, remember? Sodesh doesn't strike me as the understanding type."

"That is true," Ilana conceded. "Although you wear Castellan Orsk's uniform, you do not move as she does. Sodesh tends to notice even the smallest details."

Emily nodded. "That settles it then. I'll wait out here. Out of curiosity, why are we here anyway?"

"There is one inside that has many resources. I will retrieve her."

Ilana made the comment as if it was just that simple, but Emily had seen the conditions the slaves were forced to endure. She couldn't imagine the guards would just let one of them leave without a damn good explanation. Suddenly, she had a sneaking suspicion whom Ilana intended to approach. However, even Vaden had to keep up appearances, or so she had led Emily to believe.

"You mean the slaves actually get a rest period?"

"The guards can hardly force them to work all hours of the day and night."

Emily remembered how Garran had commented on the high casualty rate inside the mines and she wasn't so sure Ilana was right.

What about the guard who beat a man for ceasing to work for only a moment? Somehow, Emily didn't believe the Erisians cared at all about the slaves wellbeing.

"If you say so. I'll be over here." Emily pointed toward the area where she'd eaten on the only day she worked the mines.

Without another word, Ilana turned and headed into the subterranean darkness. Emily wandered over toward the corner of the slave's eating area near a livestock-holding pen. She was concerned with sticking out like a sore thumb, but she was alone. Not a soul moved in the shadows, yet the tension remained. Her shoulders felt so tight, Emily thought something would snap. The helmet didn't help matters since the nose guard felt more like blinders, messing with her vision and making her see movement where there was none.

Here in the night, with the soft sounds of animal life and the absence of voices, Emily realized how beautiful Eris could be. She thought of the story Briana told her, how the Erisians had sought to defeat death. In the end, they had only cursed themselves. It was sad, really. With their technological advances, Eris could have been so much more. Instead, their daily grind was centered around how to lure, capture and victimize others for their life force.

Part of her truly sympathized with the Erisians, but the larger part felt only revulsion. Vaden had mentioned that the Erisians possessed the ability to synthesize what they needed. Instead, they deliberately chose the more brutal and cannibalistic option. How many thousands did the Erisians kidnap and murder without remorse for their own selfish purposes? As she thought again of the *baribas*, any half-baked sympathy Emily felt vanished completely. She couldn't see anything redeeming about the Erisians. If she had the tools, Emily would see them destroyed, along with their *baribas* and the portals that allowed the vampires to capture their victims.

A small sound near the mine entrance drew Emily's attention. Concern made her heart rate increase. Ilana had been gone a long time and Emily considered leaving without her. Eventually, someone would come along and question why the castellan wasn't at her post. After weighing her options, Emily decided to retrace the route taken when the vampires had released her for the hunt. The Ti-gon confinement building stood very close to the forest. Of course, Emily had no way to know which direction to take to find home. She was unconscious when the Erisians brought her here. Still, Vaden said there were many portals on Eris. All Emily needed to do was find one that led back to Earth. She'd worry about how to activate it when she got there. One step at a time, she thought.

Emily headed away from the mines and back in the general direction of the castle. The Ti-gon housing area wasn't far away and she could be there in just a few minutes.

"Where are you going?" Ilana hissed.

When she turned around, Emily spotted the regent. Vaden stood alongside her looking amused. "You were gone so long I thought you got caught."

"It's not like I can just walk out," Vaden remarked. "We had to wait until the guard finished his rounds. It's good to see you alive, Emily. You look good in Orsk's uniform."

"Thanks. Can we go now?"

Vaden grinned and Ilana frowned, illustrating the difference in their personalities.

"That's a good idea," Vaden answered. "I received word from one of my contacts. I need to meet with a friend in the high desert. It's only a few hours from here, but it will get you out of the city. We should move before someone finds the castellan. What did you do with her, anyway?"

"She's locked in the keep with a broken nose and a black eye. I don't think she'll be unconscious for much longer and she's going to be pissed when she wakes up." Thinking about the scene Orsk would probably make imbued Emily with a renewed sense of urgency. "The sooner we get out of here the better."

Ilana nodded. "I concur. Take my pacer. It is parked behind the repository. I'll requisition another."

"You're not coming with us?" Emily asked, suddenly concerned for the vampire's welfare. Ilana had put herself in danger by helping Emily, one of the few on this godforsaken world.

"I can't, I have a youngster missing."

"Who?" Vaden asked curiously.

Ilana's face hardened. "Chala. She did not return from the last hunt."

Vaden released a sigh before advising softly, "You need to be careful with that one, Ilana. There is something wrong with her mind."

Emily thought that was putting it mildly. She remembered the teenager with the wild eyes and stringy blonde hair.

"It's the hunger." Ilana looked at Emily, attempting to explain. "On rare occasions, Erisians are consumed with blood hunger upon reaching puberty. Our scientists believe it is some sort of genetic mutation."

Emily didn't really know how to respond. The Erisians had brought all of this upon themselves by tampering with their DNA. "You just be careful. With Chala missing and now the two of us taking off, things are going to get complicated."

Ilana reached out and touched her cheek. "I get the feeling that your interest in me has waned, but I appreciate that your concern has not."

"That whole empathy thing, huh?" Emily felt a little guilty that she didn't feel attracted to Ilana anymore. Seeing Adrasta with her slaves had curbed any intimate impulses, although she had to admit that her feelings for Ilana were just a passing fancy to begin with. There was only one woman Emily couldn't shake from her heart or mind.

Ilana only smiled at the comment and lowered her hand. "You should go."

A touch on her forearm made Emily glance at Vaden. She didn't know what else to say to Ilana. Anything she could think of sounded trite. She nodded and followed Vaden toward the Ti-gon building, what Ilana had termed "the repository." Emily already knew that Vaden stayed in the mines as a way of gathering intel to start a reform movement against the Erisians. Now she realized that Ilana was a collaborator. She didn't have a clue how many other rebels were strategically placed around Saqqara. That they existed at all gave her hope that things would change here in the future, become less brutal.

Emily followed Vaden behind the building and found herself staring at something straight out of Star Wars. The machine resembled a motorcycle, complete with handlebars and a low seat. That's where the similarity ended. This device hadn't a single wheel. Emily quickly surmised that the vehicle utilized the same flight capability as the air cars.

"Does that thing have any weapons?"

"Yes, it has a few. Why?" Vaden turned her back toward Emily as she checked the machine over and picked up a helmet. She jammed it down over her short, dark hair.

"Before we leave I'd like for you to destroy the *bariba*."

Surprise caused Vaden to spin around to face her. "Are you out of your mind?"

"Lower your voice," Emily hissed, looking out for anyone who might overhear. "Are you trying to get us caught?"

"No, but apparently you are."

"I'm not leaving here until those things are blasted into a million pieces," Emily said stubbornly.

"Then you'll be here by yourself. Look, we don't have time to argue. Any minute now, Orsk will regain consciousness and sound the alarm. We will be overrun by soldiers. Assuming we did have time to blow up the tanks, we would not make it out of the city, not on the pacer. Unlike an airship, these vehicles travel close to the ground using repulsion-lift technology. Do you always react so rashly?"

Emily turned her head away to hide the tears. "All those people; I can't stand to know they're being used like that."

"It is disturbing, even to me. The *baribas* are what convinced me to take action against my own people. One day I will tell you how I ended up in the mines, but for now we must concentrate on staying alive."

After wiping the moisture from her cheeks, Emily said, "Right, let's go then."

She didn't feel any better for leaving victims behind, but it wouldn't do them any good if she got herself killed. Because they were already dead, her actions would serve only to free their bodies of further indignity. However, she made a promise to herself that if the slightest opportunity arose to destroy the *baribas* before she left Eris, Emily would make it happen.

Emily climbed onto the pacer behind Vaden and slipped her arms around the tight, muscular waist. She expected the vehicle to accelerate forward, like an Earth vessel. Instead, the pacer hummed beneath her butt and lifted steadily into the air. After stabilizing a good two feet from the ground, the bike eased forward. The pacer's speed steadily increased until Emily had to conceal her face behind Vaden's back because of the wind pressure against her eyes. Vaden didn't seem to mind the velocity as they zipped off into the night. No matter what type of terrain they encountered, the pacer kept the same distance from the ground. Gradually, Emily became accustomed to the feel of the machine. With every mile put between them and Saqqara, she felt the tension in her shoulders ease. Regardless what the future held, at least she was away from Adrasta and her depravity.

After two hours on the pacer, Emily's relief at leaving Saqqara had faded somewhat. Though the ride was smooth, her legs felt cramped and her back ached from staying in the same position for such an extended period. Vaden must have sensed her unease.

"It isn't much farther; just over the next ridge."

Ten minutes later, Vaden slowed the machine. The decline in speed was just as measured as the initial acceleration. When they finally stopped, Emily noticed two people standing off in the distance. Long purple-brown hair caught her eye and Emily smiled as she recognized Fallon. She had thought Fallon died when she fell over the rim of a canyon. Having identified Fallon, Emily realized the hulking machine they stood adjacent to must be her spaceship. The only reservation Emily had involved the other person. Judging by the clothing, the stranger was Erisian. With the hood in place, Emily couldn't identify their gender. Having Vaden here was one thing. As much as she disliked the Erisians, Emily trusted her. She wasn't quite as comfortable with another vampire thrown into the mix.

Vaden lowered the pacer to the ground and Emily climbed off. Vaden remained astride the bike. They were still a considerable distance away. Emily wondered why Vaden hadn't driven right up to the others.

"I thought you said you were meeting a friend. You didn't say anything about there being two people."

"Stay here." Vaden sounded unsure. "I'll find out what's happening."

Emily watched her ride away. She was happy to stand alone, waiting to see how the stranger would react. Prudence forced her to entertain the idea that this was a trap. The Erisians could have captured Fallon and forced her to work with them. Vaden put the pacer down a few feet from the two. Fallon greeted her with a brief hug before motioning toward her companion. The cloaked figure held out a hand toward Vaden in a gesture reminiscent of shaking hands, a decidedly human act.

After a brief discussion, Emily noticed Vaden's trademark grin. She thought Vaden had probably picked up the habit from her human mother. Considering Vaden's mother made Emily wonder if she still lived. Humans didn't tend to fare well around the Erisians. She dropped the line of speculation when Vaden waved her forward.

Emily crossed over the desert sand, deeply aware of the armor's weight and how her boots sank up to the ankles. Taking the uniform to escape the castle was a great idea, but it didn't work so well out here. She hoped Fallon could offer her a change of clothes. By the time she reached the trio, Emily was out of breath. She didn't bother to speak as Vaden made introductions.

"This is my great friend, Fallon. She is a member of the Levothos Coalition and a great supporter of our cause."

"Vaden speaks well of you," Fallon said. "I understand the uniform you wear is not your own?"

Emily removed the helmet, ignoring the sweat that dripped down her temples. "It's me, Fallon. I'm glad to see you alive."

Fallon's look of surprise was priceless. Emily would have laughed if Fallon hadn't wrapped her up in a bear hug. Though they had worked together to escape the Ti-gon, they weren't exactly close. Emily hadn't expected such a reaction. Emily smiled and pulled away after returning the hug.

The cloaked Erisian had stood silently throughout the exchange. Suddenly, the vampire rushed forward and grabbed hold of Emily's armored shoulders. Emily thought she was being attacked and froze in shock when the stranger embraced her. Strong arms held her close against a feminine form. Emily started to push the stranger back when a familiar scent hit her nostrils. She knew of only one person with that particular chemistry. Jenna.

Emily pulled back slightly and pushed the hood from the woman's head. She gasped when she saw Jenna's dark eyes. An aching smile curved the lips Emily had kissed so long ago.

"You."

Emotion choked her. Emily threw herself back into Jenna's arms, relief and confusion warring within her. She smashed her lips against Jenna's, cupping the back of her head. She didn't know what could have brought Jenna Yang to such a horrible place, but she couldn't remember ever being happier to see another human being. Her heart thundered against her ribs and she could only cling to Jenna.

Jenna finally leaned back though she didn't release her hold. "Miss Bannon, I do find you in the most unusual places."

Emily didn't realize she was crying until Jenna wiped the tears away with her thumb. "Did the Kurths capture you, too?"

"No." Jenna shook her head. "I saw them take you through the portal and I followed them. I've been looking for you ever since."

"You came through of your own free will? For me?"

Emily barely heard the wonder in her own voice, too concerned with Jenna's response. Would she say it was her duty, that Jenna had only pursued out of some sense of responsibility? Only then did she realize her true feelings for the feisty sheriff.

"You didn't think I'd let you out of our date that easily, did you?"

Emily felt like she could fall into Jenna's satin brown gaze. Warmth and caring in the dark eyes embraced her like a caress. Despite the obvious weight loss, strange clothing and roughly shorn hair, Emily sensed the same strength in Jenna she'd encountered the first time they met.

"I see you are already acquainted," Fallon observed needlessly.

Emily didn't bother to respond. She staggered forward against Jenna when Vaden slapped her on the back.

"Fallon, do you have anything to eat?" Vaden asked.

"Yes, follow me into the *Firestorm*. Now that you have arrived, I should reset the concealment shield."

Vaden and Fallon led the way into the vessel. Emily followed, happily aware of the arm Jenna kept around her waist. Considering the turn of events, Emily didn't care if they ate bitter gruel or white tofu-like cubes.

"EMILY, I'M SORRY. Destroying the *baribas* is not a wise idea."

Fallon spoke slowly as though explaining something to a small child, which only irked Emily more. She'd been arguing her point for what seemed like an hour. Fallon, Vaden and even Jenna remained resolute.

"Why, because it will set the hounds after us? The Erisians will chase after us anyway. As soon as we free the prisoners from the Ti-gon, someone will sound an alarm. Also, why hasn't anyone mentioned the mine slaves or the people in the castle? If we're going to move against the Erisians, we should try to rescue everyone."

Emily's voice rose as she spoke, her passion for freeing the slaves overriding her common sense. Tactically, she realized that what she proposed would cause all of their deaths but she was no coward. Death was a small price to pay if it meant crippling the Erisian way of doing things.

Jenna stopped her tirade by gently touching her hand. Presently, they all sat inside Fallon's vessel and in her private quarters. Occupying a small table with Jenna beside her and their knees brushing, Emily experienced a sense of guilt for escaping Saqqara's harsh environment.

"You have to pick your battles, Emily. I know that you know that. We can't do everything with only four people."

"Five," Emily corrected. "You're forgetting about Ilana." She'd explained the vampire regent to Jenna while they were catching up on events.

Jenna nodded in acceptance. "Okay, five people. We're still vastly outnumbered. We have a broken spaceship and a land pacer. Think about it."

"So what do you suggest?" Emily asked obstinately. She sat back in the chair and folded her arms across her chest.

"If I may," Vaden said. "I will return to the city for the part Fallon requires to fix the ship and to retrieve supplies for your journey home. I will ask Ilana to access the control room for the *baribas*."

"What's that going to accomplish?" Emily asked.

Fallon answered the question, a small smile curling her lips. "She will set the controls to overload, right?"

"Exactly. However, we must decide which course of action we will take now because once she eliminates the *baribas*, there will be no getting back inside the city. Our timing must be precise."

Emily thought this was finally beginning to sound like a plan. She realized Jenna had a point and they couldn't stop everything the Erisians had in place, but the *baribas* were especially horrifying. There were far fewer slaves in the mines and while Emily wanted to free them as well, they just didn't have the equipment for such an assault. If they could blow the nutrition tanks and free the prisoners from the repository, she would be content.

"Fallon, how long would you need to complete repairs once Vaden returns?"

"If all goes well, approximately four hours. After that, I suggest we sleep for a while before we move."

Thinking quickly, Emily figured the sun and moons cycles. The planet's dim sun currently headed for the horizon and the moons would rise shortly. "Figuring it will take Vaden four hours for a round trip, plus the time she needs to set everything in motion, you probably won't have the part for at least another eight to ten hours."

"If we implement our plan at this same time tomorrow," Jenna continued, "that gives us about fourteen hours to rest and move into place for our attack."

Emily started to argue with Jenna's timetable until she remembered that Eris had a slightly longer day than Earth. "It sounds good to me. What about it, is everyone onboard with this?"

Jenna and Vaden nodded immediately. Fallon, seeming more reserved, briefly considered their options. Emily held her breath waiting to see what she would decide. Without her ship, none of their planning mattered.

"On one condition," Fallon finally said. "I will fly *Firestorm* in concealment mode. You three will free the prisoners from the repository while I hold station keeping. We will load the victims onto the ship and then I will shut down the vessel's cloak. I cannot fire my weapons with the cloak in place. At the instant that *Firestorm* becomes visible, Ilana must act. Once I fire upon the repository, she will not have much time."

Emily could picture the scene in her head. The three women on the ground would have to take out any vampire soldiers before they could raise an alarm. With the Erisians stronger and faster, it would not be an easy task but it was doable.

"So what's your condition?"

"You and Jenna will escort your people back to your home world on your own."

"Are you serious?" Jenna asked. "I barely made it here and I wasn't dragging a pack of people around with me. We'll never make it."

"Agreed." Emily interrupted Jenna as she addressed Fallon. She ignored Jenna's evil eye.

"Emily, it'll never work."

"No!" She stopped Jenna from trying to reason with her. As much as she cared for Jenna, this was too important. "All of you pointed out that we can't accomplish everything with such a small group. Fine. We take out the *baribas* and the repository, and to do that we need Fallon. If she can't do anything more than get us away from the Erisians then that's the way it has to be."

Silence reigned for a few moments until Fallon said, "I would do more if I could, but I have been out of contact with the Coalition for too long."

"You all realize," Jenna said softly, "that once we destroy their food source, the Erisians will be desperate. That act could cause even more abductions while they try to replenish their supply."

"Not if you disable the portals to your world," Vaden pointed out. "I do not have a portal control because the others do not trust me, but I'm sure I can obtain one once I return to the city."

"I have one," Emily said. "Ilana gave it to me so I could get home, but it wouldn't hurt to have another. I do have one final question though. What about Ilana? Won't the vampires be after her once she causes the tanks to explode?"

"Not if she is careful," Fallon answered. "She must not be seen setting the feedback."

Vaden nodded. "Ilana is in place to gather information. Besides, with the young vampire missing, she will be required at her post. If she leaves, the others may become suspicious."

"What young vampire?" Jenna seemed oddly tense.

"A nut ball," Emily responded without remorse. She looked at Fallon. "That same crazy girl that slaughtered Nick and Laurel. I think her name was Chala. Why?"

Jenna chuckled but there was little humor in it. "She's dead. I killed her in a small village before I came across Fallon. She wanted them to supply a small child for her to...eat. I couldn't let that happen."

Jenna's words carried conviction and Emily briefly grasped and squeezed her hand before releasing it. "Good, I'm glad you did. She was scary, even for an Erisian."

"Regardless," Vaden interrupted, standing from the table. "I suggest we begin."

Fallon also rose. "I will continue working while you retrieve what we need. Jenna, I may require assistance."

"Okay. I'm not sure what I can do, but I'm willing to help out."

Fallon nodded and she left the ship with Vaden in tow. Emily and Jenna were alone for the first time since leaving Earth. The silence stretched and became uncomfortable. Emily wanted to say something, anything that would bring them closer together. Surprisingly, she still felt the same desperate attraction for Jenna, but she couldn't get the picture of Adrasta and her dead slave out of her head. Other than the spontaneous reaction when she'd first seen Jenna, all Emily wanted to do was withdraw behind a personal shield. She didn't know how to reach out.

"Emily, are you all right? You look so tense."

Jenna touched her on the arm again, but this time Emily withdrew. Unlike the previous occasions, this gesture was more intimate. She saw the hurt look on Jenna's face, but couldn't bring herself to apologize.

"I guess I've been through a lot. It feels like I've been here forever. The things I've seen, Jenna." Emily shuddered. "I just need some time."

Jenna nodded and attempted a smile. The gesture was meant to reassure, but Emily thought it seemed forced. "Sure, okay. I'll be outside if you need anything."

Chapter Seventeen

EMILY EXITED THE *Firestorm* when it began to feel like the walls were closing in on her. So close to Jenna inside the small space, Emily wanted to touch her. It was as though the tactile contact would reassure her of Jenna's presence. Emily resisted for two reasons. The first involved her recent experience with Adrasta. She realized that equating the vampire's activities with her slaves to true intimacy wasn't logical, but she couldn't get Nicole's death out of her mind. Whenever Jenna, or anyone else for that matter, got too close, Emily automatically stepped away. She desperately hoped that with time and distance from the Erisians that impulse would fade. Emily could see the quickly concealed hurt Jenna hid and felt like an ass for causing so much pain. Emily wanted to be close to her, to hold on and never let go again. The attraction she had for Jenna was just as strong now as it was the first moment they met.

Then there was the lie that hung between them. Emily had arrived in Woeful Pines under the guise of a travel writer. Although under orders to maintain her cover, Emily had willingly gone along with the FBI's directive. Circumstances had altered considerably since then. There was no longer a valid reason to keep her identity secret. Yet Emily didn't know how to tell Jenna the truth and the guilt of her deception weighed heavily. She had to come clean about her reasons for being in the Kentucky backcountry.

She leaned one hand against the nose of the spacecraft and gazed out over the arid landscape. Desert scrub and cactus littered the terrain along with scattered rocks from the nearby mountain range. Not too far away, Emily could see the smattered beginnings of a forest. For all the similarities to Earth, Eris had many subtle differences. It wasn't just that the light spectrum seemed slightly off, with organic things that should be green leaning more toward the yellow side. There were larger differences as well. Though not exactly an expert, Emily didn't believe that mountain, forest and desert environments should exist so closely together.

"Are you well?"

Emily turned toward Fallon's voice, noticing her concern. "I'm fine. Did you need help with something?"

Fallon wiped her hands on a greasy rag. She checked the position of the sun tracking across the sky for a moment. "Jenna and I are almost finished. There is little more we can do until Vaden returns. Would you mind creating a fire?"

"Sure, I can do that but would you mind telling me why? Won't we be warm enough inside the *Firestorm*?"

"Indeed, but I could use some time outside the ship."

"Of course," Emily replied, feeling like an idiot. She'd come outside a short time ago for the very same reason. With the forest so close, gathering kindling and logs should prove an easy task. "I'll see to it. Do you have something I can use to ignite the fire? I don't have any matches."

Fallon didn't ask what matches were. She reached into a pocket and handed Emily a device that resembled a miniature laser pistol. "This is a fire starter. Aim the tip toward the material and depress this trigger."

She showed Emily how to work the tool and then headed back inside. Emily let her go, preferring her own company for now. Emily gathered the makings for a fire, creating a ring from some of the larger scattered rocks to contain the blaze. She piled small sticks and dry leaves in the bottom before placing heavier branches across the top. Relieved that she'd found what she required without the need of an axe, Emily spent a moment checking the fire starter. When she felt confident she wouldn't set herself ablaze, Emily pressed the trigger and watched a ruby beam of light shoot from the tip. The fine stream of light impacted with the base of the fire and flames leapt upward. In seconds, a bright campfire chased the shadows from her immediate surroundings.

"That's nifty."

Emily watched the flames dance for a moment before she tried to stuff the device into a trouser pocket. Her actions dictated by habit, she stopped abruptly when she realized she didn't have any pockets in the Erisian armor. She shook her head and tucked it into her boot before searching for a larger rock upon which to sit. Once settled, Emily rested her elbows on her knees and lowered her head. The heat warmed her scalp and her eyes drifted closed. For long moments, she relaxed and drew in the comforting scent of wood smoke.

A while later, Emily heard someone walking around in the sand but didn't bother to open her eyes. She assumed it was Fallon until someone sat beside her on the ground and she caught Jenna's unique aroma. She remained unmoving, hyper-aware of Jenna shifting around.

"What I wouldn't give for a shower."

The comment made her smile and look up. Jenna held her hands out toward the fire. A dark smudge on her chin seemed so adorable that Emily felt her stomach tingle. "How long's it been?"

"What day is it?" Jenna teased. Then she answered her own question. "My last shower was the morning we stepped onto this alien soil. I've tried to wash up in the river any time I can but I must reek."

Emily disagreed. "You smell wonderful. You smell like you, only more so."

Jenna flushed slightly. "Thanks, I guess."

"You look good in that brown cloak too. How'd you come by it exactly?"

"I took it from a vampire who didn't need it anymore."

There was a wealth of information contained in that statement. It took Emily a moment to sift through the implications. "Wow, that's pretty amazing. These guys are tough."

"Emily," Jenna began hesitantly, "what happened to you? I saw Mike and Joey unroll you from a carpet after they carried you here, but how did all of that come about?"

"A carpet, are you kidding me? What a cliché." Emily shook her head. She wasn't really dwelling on how she got to Eris, more aware that this was the opening she'd sought to tell Jenna everything. Emily considered how to broach the topic and then remembered how she'd been dressed that fateful night. "So I guess that means you saw how I was dressed."

"I did," Jenna confirmed, her voice curiously neutral.

Emily gazed back into the fire, unable to look at Jenna. "My name isn't Emily Bannon."

"I knew it!"

The excitement in Jenna's voice startled her and Emily jumped slightly, finally able to meet Jenna's eyes. "You did? How?"

"You weren't quite as stealthy as you thought. I saw how you watched Mike Kurth when we met him at the gas station. Then there was the way you threw police jargon around so casually. I doubt anyone else would have noticed, but I was a homicide investigator for a long time and I tend to notice inconsistencies. I figured Louisville had sent you down from the Major Crimes Division so I ran a background check on you from my office."

"And?"

Jenna shrugged. "Whoever fabricated your history wasn't very good at math. The numbers didn't add up."

"Great, that means I'm losing it as an undercover agent and that the FBI had their B-team working when they created my cover."

It was Jenna's turn to be startled. "FBI? I didn't see that one coming. As I said, I suspected the Major Crimes unit out of Louisville."

"You weren't supposed to see anything at all. My orders were not to involve local law enforcement. I guess I blew that one too." Emily couldn't help but think about that first night and almost becoming intimate with a virtual stranger.

"Did the FBI send you there to investigate the kidnappings?"

Emily nodded.

"Well don't feel so bad. You figured out the Kurths were involved in all that within just a few days. I've been around those guys for years and never saw it."

"Sometimes we're too close to something and it takes a fresh set of eyes."

"Thanks for letting me off the hook," Jenna said a bit derisively.

"Thanks for not holding my secret against me."

"Never happen," Jenna assured her. "I do understand duty. I'm just glad you told me now."

"Things are different than they were. I had to tell you. Remind me to fill you in later on everything that's happened. Right now, I'm more interested in hearing about your exploits. I appreciate that you came after me, but how did you get this?" Emily reached up and touched the still slightly pink scar on Jenna's cheek.

Jenna explained falling down the mountain and meeting the unusual man and his son. She told Emily about their kindness and how she'd crossed inhospitable terrain to be here. When she came to the story of acquiring the cloak, Jenna's voice faltered but Emily remained quiet and allowed her to find the words. Emily saw the anger on her face when Jenna recounted her experience with Chala in the village.

When she finally finished bringing Emily up to speed, Jenna said, "These people live in squalor but they all seem to be content to let things go on like they are. I don't know how they can live like this."

"It's the whole ostrich routine. They bury their heads in the sand, hoping not to be noticed."

"Funny how that never really works," Jenna observed. "You know ostriches don't really bury their heads in the sand, right?"

Emily felt relieved that Jenna could still joke after all she'd experienced. "I can't imagine the species would survive for long if they did."

"Neither will these people if they don't wake up. They're signing their own death warrants with this complacency."

Jenna sounded so upset that Emily reached out to touch her hand. Her passion touched a chord in Emily. It was this same fire that had attracted Emily from the start, and her feelings hadn't changed despite the time and distance. Here, in this strange and wild land, Jenna looked the part of a fierce warrior. Dressed as she was, coupled with Emily's knowledge of what she'd sacrificed to find her, the image was complete. Emily felt her heart stutter. She longed to soothe the anguish in Jenna's sable gaze.

"You can't force them into action, Jenna. But I promise you that in a few hours, we will strike a blow against the Erisians. Maybe it'll be the catalyst these people need to make them stand up for themselves."

Jenna smiled, but her expression seemed a little sad. "You're always optimistic, aren't you?"

"Always."

Fallon interrupted the moment by stepping up to the fire. "It will be hours before Vaden returns. I suggest you try to sleep."

"What about the fire?" Emily asked. "I didn't think about it before, but what if the Erisians see it?"

Fallon shook her head. "They will not patrol the desert region. Their prey tends to stay toward terrain that is more hospitable. As for the fire spreading, do not concern yourself. I will put the fire out before I go inside."

"Don't you need some sleep too?"

"Yes, but I require less rest than humans. I shall be fine."

Satisfied, Emily and Jenna headed back inside while Fallon took up Emily's previous position on the rock. Inside the cramped sleeping quarters, Emily felt curiously shy. She couldn't sleep in the armor but felt uncomfortable stripping down in front of Jenna. Emily had changed in the castle's keep after tearing the flimsy red negligee from her body and she was naked beneath the castellan's uniform. Fortunately, Jenna didn't look toward her. She merely removed the cloak and hooked it over the end of the bed frame.

Within such a confined area, the crew sleeping area consisted of four sets of bunk beds. Jenna wordlessly climbed to the top of one set while Emily started removing the armor. She placed each piece upon the mattress. When she was finished, Emily slid onto the covers and moved the armor back against the wall. It would be a little close with the armor on the bed with her, but Emily wanted it near in case she had to dress in a hurry.

Emily sighed in relief when her head hit the pillow. It had been so long since she rested upon something soft and the sheets covering her body felt like heaven. Without the hardness of stone under her hips, sleep embraced her and she welcomed a deep, dreamless sleep.

AWAKENED WITH SOMEONE'S hand upon her shoulder, Emily groggily opened her eyes. The *Firestorm's* interior lights illuminated Jenna kneeling beside her.

"Sorry to wake you, but Vaden's back."

Emily cleared her throat against the dryness and rose up onto one elbow. She rubbed her eyes with her free hand, attempting to brush away the fuzziness. The covers slipped down her bare shoulders. Emily reached for them at the same time she noticed the heat in Jenna's gaze.

"I'm up," she muttered. "Give me a minute to get dressed."

Jenna stared a second longer before reaching for the dusty brown cloak. After she left, Emily tossed back the cover and dressed. She slipped on her first boot and stepped down on something hard. She reached inside and withdrew Fallon's fire starter. Emily placed it beside her on the mattress, pulled on her other boot and headed out of the crew quarters with the fire starter clutched in her hand.

The first thing she noticed when she exited the ship was a silver air car. The vessel sat on the far side of the campfire ring. She glanced around and saw the three other women standing at the *Firestorm's* rear. Fallon threw open the cargo hatch as she approached.

"Why the change in vehicle? Aren't you worried someone will notice it sitting out here if they fly overhead?"

"No more so than a strange alien spacecraft," Vaden returned lightly. "However, you do have a point. This is why I shall not be here long. I needed the airship because Ilana informed me that there are eight prisoners she can release from the repository, plus an additional three from the mines. You will need substantial provisions and I could not carry them all upon the pacer."

"She needs us to help unload the supplies so she can fly the ship back and return on the bike," Jenna continued.

Emily blew out her breath, disconcerted by the logistical news. "Counting me and Jenna that makes thirteen. I guess that's my lucky number."

"You're not upset by that?" Jenna asked.

"No, why should I be?"

"Because that's a lot of people to get back to Earth. I thought you'd ask Fallon to carry us back."

Emily shrugged. "She already said no."

Vaden quickly interrupted. "Actually, the humans number only five. The others are of this realm."

Fallon's expression darkened. "I informed you all that I cannot carry refugees. I must get what intel I've gathered back to Coalition Headquarters."

Emily felt relieved not to escort such a large troop of people over the Erisian countryside. However, she was worried Fallon would leave the others stranded. Emily and Fallon couldn't take aliens back through a rift to Earth. If anyone saw them, the resulting panic would make the looting during Hurricane Katrina look like a day at the park.

"They cannot go to Earth," Vaden pointed out, reading Emily's mind. "They also cannot remain here, so I believe that you have little choice. Your destination is Levothos, correct? Levothos has a spaceport. Once we arrive, your passengers can arrange transportation."

"We?" Fallon prompted.

"I'm going with you." Vaden sounded positively excited and Emily quickly smothered a smile behind her hand.

"Who says?"

Vaden snorted, but didn't answer Fallon's question. She started toward the air car, speaking over a shoulder. "Help me unload these supplies. I need to return the vehicle before the moons rise."

The equipment Vaden brought consisted of dry food rations, shelters and fire starters as well as flint. In addition, Emily noticed water skins and brown cloaks like the ones Jenna possessed. There were only a few cloaks, not enough for Emily and the remaining five humans. They'd loaded up the *Firestorm* within twenty minutes and Emily was ready for breakfast, hopefully something besides tofu-like rations. She'd seen the rations with the other supplies and was already tired of them.

"Emily, one moment."

Vaden pulled a black satchel from the cockpit of the airship and held it out toward her. "Ilana said you might be able to use this."

"What is it?"

"I don't know. I didn't look."

Emily couldn't imagine what Ilana would have sent her. Her attention on the heavy satchel, she barely noticed when Vaden lifted off and turned the vehicle back toward Saqqara. She reached down inside and removed her black tactical vest.

"Your clothes?"

Emily nodded at Jenna, not bothering to conceal her grin. "Now I can get out of this damned armor."

"Do you think she put the rest of your equipment in there?"

Emily's eyes narrowed. "What do you know about my equipment?"

"I was following you, remember? I'm not sure what all you had on you, but I suspect you at least had a handgun."

"I did." Emily sat the bag on the ground, aware that the pistol would probably fall to the bottom. She dug around for a moment and then her finger caught on a metal loop. She withdrew the .32. She thumbed open the barrel and ensured a round still resided in the chamber. Additionally, the magazine was still in place.

Jenna looked relieved. "That's great. We can use all the firepower we can find against these guys. Now come on, let's get some breakfast."

"You go ahead. I think I'll feel better once I'm wearing my own clothes."

Emily returned to the crew quarters and happily shucked the Erisian armor. After the hard, weighty uniform, her clothes felt light, airy and thin. Ilana had returned all of Emily's equipment, including the throwing knife and night vision goggles. The only thing missing was her black rain slicker. Emily didn't remember waking inside the repository cell with it so she must have lost the raincoat some time before. It hadn't rained the whole time she'd been on Eris. Emily found it hard to believe she'd been here for less than a week. It felt like a lifetime.

Once in her own garments, Emily felt her nerves wake up. The time for attacking the repository and *baribas* was fast approaching. She entered the ship's operational area and picked up a bowl from the small, round table. It contained a hot cereal closely resembling oatmeal and Emily enjoyed the slightly sweet taste.

Jenna and Fallon had already eaten, but still sat nearby. No one spoke, seemingly lost in private fears and worries. They had gone over the plan a dozen times and all seemed keyed up. Emily wondered how long it would take before Vaden returned. Figuring that the airship would travel much like a plane, she thought Vaden should already be back at Saqqara. A quick exchange of vehicles, two hours of travel time on the bike and they'd be ready to go.

"Are you ready for this?"

Emily started at the sound of Jenna's voice. "I'm ready to get it over with and go home." She placed the empty bowl on the table.

"Me too, I can't wait to sleep in my own bed."

Fallon suddenly stood and tapped her earpiece. After a brief acknowledgment, she said, "Vaden reports that Ilana is in place."

They spent the next two hours re-checking the ship's systems and ensuring that all loose cargo was stowed. Vaden returned and stored the pacer in the cargo compartment. She appeared exhausted to Emily, not surprising with all the traveling back and forth to the city, but Vaden declined food or rest.

"I want this over," Vaden asserted grimly, settling into the co-pilot's seat next to Fallon.

Emily and Jenna stood behind the seats, a hand on the bulkhead for support. The *Firestorm* lifted smoothly from the sandy ground before spinning around. Emily felt the low throb of silent engines vibrate under her feet.

"Engaging concealment shield," Fallon reported.

Emily swallowed hard, feeling excitement thrum through her veins as it always did right before an op. "How long until we get there?"

"Not long, stand ready near the hatch. Vaden, will you join them? I believe they will need your unique talents."

Emily thought that was a strange way to phrase a request, but she wasn't about to argue. As an Erisian, Vaden would have more information on the Erisian Ti-gon including the repository's layout. Ilana had already moved the three humans from the mine into the holding area.

"I'm lowering the *Firestorm* into position. Standby."

Easy for her to say, Emily thought. Her finger rested over the control that would open the hatch. Jenna had pulled her cloak into place, so she could see in the shadows from what she'd said. Vaden wore her usual Erisian cloak, soft trousers and boots as well as her usual cocky grin. As for Emily, she felt more comfortable wearing her black combat wear. It was the perfect camouflage for such a dark planet. She settled the night vision goggles into place and closed her eyes briefly, centering her mind for what came next.

Emily's feet vibrated as the spacecraft settled with a slight bump. She immediately pressed down on the hatch release. Fallon had set down between two large storage buildings, providing them cover. Casting a quick glance around, Emily jogged from the ship toward the repository. She heard swift, furtive footsteps behind her. Jenna and Vaden followed her to the edge of the nearest warehouse where Emily stopped to assess their situation.

No one moved about the courtyard. The sun headed toward the horizon and she could already see the moons beginning to rise. They wouldn't have much time. Meeting her companions' eyes, they both nodded in readiness. Emily remembered her handgun. She reached down and removed it from the ankle holster before returning their nods.

As she headed around the repository, Emily led the others to the same entrance where Ilana had taken her before. She held her breath and punched in the same sequence she'd seen the regent enter. The metal door popped open with hardly a sound and they were inside. All seemed quiet. Emily didn't see any guards and heard only the occasional sleepy grunt from the holding cells.

"I'll release the bars," Vaden whispered before heading into the darkness.

Emily and Jenna helped the captives from their cages, reassuring the victims quietly and hustling them back the way they had come. Having envisioned an orderly retreat, Emily remained aware that things rarely went as planned. Of the eleven, there were three human males and two women. One of the men was Charles Freeman. The balance of individuals were alien, some ascribing to that description more than others. Emily ignored the mix of horns, scales and extra appendages, her attention garnered by a frail, older man. Emily couldn't see how he would provide the Erisians much entertainment in the Ti-gon. He must be one of the people from the mine.

Regardless, he hunched and could hardly shuffle along. Running was out of the question. Emily allowed Jenna to lead the group out of the building while she ran back to help the stranger. Although faded with dust or time and even in the green glow of her night goggles, Emily noticed the purplish hair. She discerned he might be of Fallon's race.

Placing an arm around his shoulders, Emily attempted to hurry the man along. She sensed time running out, but couldn't force him to move any faster. Suddenly Vaden was there.

"I have him."

Vaden slung the old man across her shoulders and they all raced out the back of the repository. An alarm began screaming so loudly Emily thought her eardrums would burst. Erisian guards burst from a barracks behind them and she felt the whoosh as laser blasts barely missed hitting her. Something sharp seared the edge of her shoulder and Emily went down on one knee.

"Emily!" Jenna screamed.

Emily pushed to her feet. "Keep going."

It was weird to see Jenna and the refugees vanish from view as they leapt aboard the spacecraft. When she got closer, Emily could see the inside of the *Firestorm* and headed toward the opening. An Erisian leapt from the second floor of the warehouse and landed on his feet right in front of her. Emily brought her pistol to bear, already squeezing the trigger. The guard fired his laser weapon first. The ruby beam cut across her .32 and Emily felt the metal heat up. She tried to fire but the weapon had already melted in half and she had to let go before it scorched her hand. The pistol dropped uselessly to the ground and the Erisian launched himself toward her, fangs bared and eyes shining like an inferno.

Before he could rip her throat out, Emily saw Vaden grab the soldier around the neck. She put him into a headlock and Emily heard his neck snap. As the guard slumped to the ground, Vaden clenched Emily's forearm and helped her toward the ship. She was in time to witness Charles carrying the older man aboard.

Vaden was last onto the *Firestorm*. Emily hit the hatch lock as soon as the Erisian hybrid boarded. She could hear blasts striking the outside of the hull.

Vaden pressed her earpiece and shouted, "Ilana, now!"

At the same time, Fallon fired up the engines. This ascent wasn't nearly as gentle and Emily lost her balance, stumbling into the bulkhead before falling to her knees. The others didn't fare any better, all of them tossed about the compartment as Fallon maneuvered. Emily struggled to her feet and lurched into the cockpit just in time to see a massive fireball go up from the *baribas*. Fallon fired her weapons on the repository a split-second later and Emily was thrown to the ground again from the resulting explosion. The wound in her arm burned when she hit the deck and Emily cradled the appendage with her other hand. She gritted her teeth to keep from crying out and the pain slowly faded to a sharp throbbing.

When she could stand up again, Fallon had turned them toward the desert. With the concealment shield in place, they were virtually invisible and Emily didn't see any signs of pursuit. She looked around the hold, seeing a few bumps and bruises but no apparent serious injuries. As the others picked themselves up, Emily saw Jenna throw back her hood, her gaze fixed on a young human male. Charles sat against the bulkhead, his eyes wide in excitement and fear. Jenna squatted down beside him and held out her hand.

"Charles Freeman? I'm Sheriff Jenna Yang and it is very good to finally meet you. Your aunt is very worried about you."

"You know my aunt?"

Jenna smiled. "We need to talk."

Those were the last words Emily heard before the world started closing in around her. Something warm and wet slipped down her arm. Her vision clouded and Emily stumbled to one knee. She thought Fallon must have thrown the ship into another turn, but then realized that wasn't it. Emily lost the struggle to keep her eyes open. When she fell flat on her face, she thought she heard Jenna scream her name. As the adrenaline faded from her system, exhaustion took hold. All Emily wanted was to sleep. She'd done as much as she could for the refugees. It now fell to Fallon to fly them beyond Erisian forces.

Chapter Eighteen

"HOW IS SHE?"

"I think she's coming around. Emily, can you hear me?"

Jenna watched Emily's eyes flutter open, uncomfortable with how closely Charles hovered over her shoulder. She'd been so frightened when Emily collapsed onto *Firestorm's* deck. Blood had pooled under her and Jenna had rushed to assist. When she placed a hand on Emily's arm, it had come away covered in red. Jenna hadn't taken an easy breath since.

"What happened?" Emily asked in confusion. She tried to sit up but Jenna held her down.

"Not so fast, just lay still. You took a hit to your arm and lost some blood. Vaden patched you up, but wasn't able to completely heal your wound."

Emily frowned. "Why not? I thought you said they could instantly heal injuries here."

At least she was thinking clearly, Jenna thought. That was a good sign. "Unfortunately, Fallon's first aid kit was also damaged in the crash. Things just aren't working like they should."

"Yeah," Charles interjected. "Jenna had to put in some stitches. It was really gross."

"Thank you for that assessment," Emily mumbled. She rubbed a hand over her face.

Jenna sat up as much as she could without hitting her head on the top bunk. When Emily had collapsed, she and Vaden had carried her into the crew quarters and placed her on the lower bunk. With Jenna's height, it was difficult to straighten up fully.

"Charles, maybe you could give her some space."

"Huh? Oh, yeah sure."

As soon as they were alone Jenna said, "He was really worried about you."

"He's a sweet guy."

"How do you know that? We just rescued them."

Emily shook her head. "No, I met him before. When they made me go through the Ti-gon, Charles was there. You have no idea how relieved I was to see him when we let them out of those cells."

"I wish we could have done more. Don't get me wrong, I'm glad he's okay, too. I just keep seeing all those photos Frank put up on the wall of her diner, yet we're only bringing back a fraction of those people."

Jenna blamed herself for not seeing what was happening. That the Kurths and her own deputy acted together to terrorize innocent people right under her nose was almost more than she could bear. Jenna knew she would carry that burden of guilt for a very long time. She thought of how Cheryl had acted so friendly to her face, discussing her son's propensity for illness as if that was the most exciting thing in her life. All along, she'd been in on it with the others. How could she have missed it?

"Don't beat yourself up, Jenna. The fact is that we couldn't save all of them, but we are bringing some home. Not only that, now we know who was behind it and we will stop those bastards."

Jenna forced a smile. Wallowing in remorse wouldn't help them get home. "You're right. How are you feeling, anyway?"

"A little tired and I have a bit of a headache, but I'm okay. How long was I out?"

"About two hours. You had me pretty scared."

"Sorry about that. Two hours, huh? I can't believe Fallon didn't dump us off as soon as we cleared Saqqara."

There wasn't any animosity in Emily's tone. She was merely making an observation. Jenna cleared her throat to keep from speaking out. Personally, she didn't see why Fallon couldn't take them all the way back to the rift. Fallon kept speaking about duty and the need to report in to her superiors, but Jenna didn't see how a few hours would make a difference.

"At least we're still in the air," she finally said. "I described the terrain I've crossed since arriving on Eris and Fallon has been flying steadily in that direction since we left the city. I guess every minute we're in the air means fewer miles to walk, right?"

Emily must have heard the bitterness Jenna tried to conceal because she took her hand. "I'm sure she's taking us as far as she can. Jenna, above all people, you understand duty. Fallon is no less committed than we are. She's trying to save her people and she's been away from home a long time. I know I can sympathize with that."

"You're right. I shouldn't be so pissed about her leaving us stranded on this world. I guess I'm just worried that we'll lose people along the way."

Emily started to speak, but a shadow fell across them from the doorway. Vaden stood in the arch with her trademark grin firmly in place. She crossed her arms as she looked down at Emily.

"Fallon's setting us down near the Dark Forest in a few minutes. Are you feeling better?"

Emily sat up and Jenna moved out of the way. Jenna thought she should continue to rest, but that was no longer an option. Reality being what it was, Jenna held out a hand to assist Emily to her feet. Ignoring the offer, Emily stood.

"I'm fine. How far do you think it is from here to our gate?"

"I'm not sure where your rift is," Vaden admitted. "However, the nearest portal is within a few days' walk. You'll have to ask Fallon if it's the one you're looking for since Jenna described where you came through."

"It doesn't matter," Jenna said. "I don't care where we come out as long as it's on Earth."

Jenna felt the *Firestorm* settle with a slight bump. She instinctively flexed her knees to absorb the impact. Emily nodded, a look of determination on her face, and scooted past Vaden into the main cabin. The stark white of the bandage around her upper arm stood out against Emily's dark clothing. Jenna noticed the red stain that had bloomed in the center of the compress and made a note to keep an eye on things. Hopefully, Emily wouldn't do anything to pop her stitches.

Fallon had already powered down the vessel by the time they reached the hatch. She stepped out of the cockpit, her eyes quickly sliding over Emily. Jenna assumed she was assessing Emily's condition. Unaccountably, Jenna felt proud of Emily's inner strength though she certainly had nothing to do with it.

"Where are we?" Jenna demanded.

Fallon quirked an eyebrow. "Surely Vaden has already told you?"

"Near the Dark Forest, but that doesn't really tell us anything."

"Come outside and I will show you."

Jenna did as requested, aware of Emily and the others following. Once outside the ship, Fallon pointed directly toward the tree line. Jenna noticed the moons were going down on the opposite side of the sky. Since Jenna had traveled toward Saqqara by following the moons and the sun, this was promising. After taking another look, Jenna thought she recognized the area.

"I've been here before."

Fallon nodded. "From what you told me, you came this way on your journey to the city. It's only two days' walk from here to the portal, perhaps more depending upon injuries."

"That doesn't mean we can find it," Jenna pointed out, feeling a momentary bit of panic. "From this distance, we could miss the rift by miles."

"Don't be concerned. I have something for you that will help."

Fallon led them toward the rear cargo hatch. The covering slid upward, revealing the packed hold and Fallon reached for a dark brown carryall. She squatted down and loosened the cord that tied it closed. Fallon dug around for a moment and then withdrew a fist-sized circular object. When she held it out, Jenna expected some kind of advanced technology. Instead, she discovered an ordinary compass. The needle bobbled around as Fallon handed it over.

"I believe you are familiar with this device?"

"It's the first thing I've seen here that I am familiar with." Jenna took the compass and checked the dial. The directions were marked the same as any ordinary compass. She wondered how Fallon had come by it.

"Don't be fooled. It may look like the object with which you are accustomed, but it has an additional property."

"Oh, what's that?"

Fallon touched the face of the dial, indicating a small bulb. "This will begin to glow when you are within a few runths of the gate, what you call miles. At first, the light will be yellow. It will grow red as you get closer. Should the light disappear, you will know you are going the wrong direction."

"Hot and cold," Jenna quipped. "I like it. That still doesn't explain how we actually get through the gate."

Fallon sighed somewhat dramatically. "Must I do everything for you?" She reached back into the bag and retrieved a thin, silver transmitter. The object resembled an ink pen, but it was only a couple of inches long. Fallon handed the device to Emily. Emily turned it over and over, looking thoughtful.

"Press this switch and it will activate the rift." Fallon demonstrated. "Once you are all through the gate, this control will close the portal. Should you wish to destabilize the gate, press and hold both controls simultaneously. A charge will build to the point of explosion. Ensure you are well clear of the blast."

"No kidding," Emily said. "It's a gate control, but it doesn't look like the one Ilana gave me. I guess it doesn't hurt to have a spare."

Jenna started to smile, but then thought of something. "Can these devices be used more than once? After we blow up the gate that is?"

"I asked Ilana the same question," Emily volunteered. "She says they can. The controller she gave me is different though. It has two more buttons for containment bracelets and collars."

Fallon picked up the thread of the discussion. "The instrument I gave you was devised by Coalition scientists. Our priorities focus more on the portals themselves than releasing individuals already under Erisian control. The compass will locate any rift you are near and you can use the transmitter repeatedly."

"That's great," Emily said, "I understand the portal controls well enough but how would you know where to start to look for one, even with the compass? The Earth is a big damn place."

"True, but we can start with the places our survivors come from." Jenna had yet to speak with any of the refugees. They'd been somewhat busy after escaping from Saqqara, especially with Emily passing out. However, they would have plenty of time to get to know each other during the rest of their journey.

Fallon nodded and turned back to the hold. She began passing equipment back to the others. Emily pocketed the gate control and took a rucksack from her. Jenna followed her example and they finished distributing the supplies. The refugees carried their loads around the side of the ship, forming a loose group as they chatted together. Vaden had joined them and was speaking with Charles. Only Fallon, Jenna and

Emily remained at the rear of the *Firestorm*.

Jenna realized that Fallon was about to leave and held out her hand. Fallon took it slowly. "Thank you," Jenna said sincerely. "We wouldn't have made it this far without your help."

"I am only sorry I cannot do more. After we destroyed the repository, I had decided to take you all the way to your destination."

"You did? What changed your mind?"

"The old man," Emily said suddenly. "How is he?"

"Gravely ill, I must see to it that he reaches adequate medical care soon."

"We won't hold you up any longer then." Jenna released Fallon's hand. "Thanks again."

Fallon turned to Emily. "I wish you to know that your courage and determination have changed my mind about humans. Your world may be young, but there is hope for you."

"Thanks."

Jenna grinned at the somewhat derisive tone. Fallon sealed the hatch and they walked back around *Firestorm's* side. Fallon motioned for Vaden. After offering Fallon one final nod, Jenna and Emily watched the two women enter the ship. A few moments later, the vessel lifted off. Jenna's hair blew back from her forehead and she lifted a hand to keep debris from flying into her eyes.

She met Emily's eyes for a moment and then they turned toward the survivors. Of the five other humans, Charles looked to be the only one in good health. The remaining men and women looked half-starved and beyond exhaustion.

"Something tells me this isn't going to be easy."

Emily nodded. "Something tells me you're right."

Jenna hung her head. She wanted to get moving as quickly as they could, but these people weren't in any condition. The survivors needed food, water and rest. Without it, they would never make the two-day trip back to Earth. The only thing in their favor was that Fallon had carried them so far from Saqqara.

"Head into the trees. We'll make camp here for the night."

EMILY SAT ON the bank of a small lagoon, losing herself in the sounds from a crashing waterfall. She had discovered the spectacle quite by accident. Emily had awakened beside a cold and burned out campfire, only the residual scent of smoke lingering in the air. Her stitches hurt from lying on them and she groaned as she rolled over. A quick glance told her that the size of the brownish red stain on her bandage hadn't grown during the night.

No one else had stirred so Emily climbed out of her bedroll and left the clearing. She couldn't sleep anymore and didn't want to wake the others. Emily needed some time alone and the peacefulness of these woods was a balm to her wounded soul. Stumbling upon the single, narrow waterfall as it crashed into its basin was a welcome respite.

An FBI agent saw the inhumane acts people heaped on others, but Eris was different. The casual victimization of using people for hunting alone illustrated how the vampires equated them to animals. Compounding that, Nicole's death under Adrasta's cruel fangs, fueled the slow, constant burn of fury in Emily's gut. Her fists clenched in her lap.

"You shouldn't go so far away from camp alone."

Emily barely heard Jenna's voice above the roaring water. When she didn't respond, Jenna approached slowly. Emily watched her from the corner of her eye until the booted feet stopped beside her. Jenna dropped to her knees, clearly planning to stay for a while.

"I needed to think."

Jenna pushed the hood back from her face. Emily understood the garment gave the wearer the ability to see clearly in the darkest shadows. In a way, she envied that. Emily wondered if she would ever see anything as she had before. She could remember the brightness of Earth's sky on a summer day and practically smell growing things. Yet, somehow, it seemed like a distant dream. They'd been in shadow for so long on this planet that the darkness had grown familiar.

"Do you want to talk about it?"

Emily didn't know if she could. Tied up and confused with all the rage for the vampires were her feelings for Jenna. Regardless what she had experienced at Erisian hands, Emily had always carried concern for Jenna's safety. She felt the pull of attraction even now, different from what she'd experienced for Ilana. With the vampire, Emily felt a powerful physical pull but no emotional resonance. The passion she carried for Jenna easily eclipsed that magnetism. Jenna was the whole package: beautiful, intelligent, brave, loyal, and incredibly sexy.

"Would you prefer to be alone?"

The pain in Jenna's carefully worded question caught Emily's attention. Suddenly, she knew without question that if she allowed Jenna to leave, things would change irrevocably between them...and not in a good way.

"Do you remember the first time we met? I couldn't keep my hands off you."

Jenna studied Emily's face, a soft smile playing at the corners of her lips. "How could I forget?"

Emily gently stroked Jenna's cheek. "We didn't know each other long before all of this started, but I really think we could have had something."

Jenna's eyes became serious. "And now?"

Silent for a moment, Emily realized this was it. Either she let Jenna go for good, hoping she would eventually find happiness, or she took the plunge. Although Emily didn't have the best track record with women, there was no way she could just walk away. So there it was, time for the truth.

"Do you believe in love at first sight?"

Emily could see the pulse at Jenna's throat, beating a frightened staccato cadence. Her voice trembled slightly. "If you had asked me that a month ago, I'd have said no. Things are different now."

Teasing lightly to reduce some of Jenna's tension, Emily asked, "It's Fallon, right?"

Jenna started and then chuckled, relaxing finally. "What gave me away?"

Emily rose onto her knees, moving slowly into Jenna's space. She raised both hands, cupping the sides of Jenna's face and stroking gently with her thumbs. Inches away, she whispered, "Your eyes. I can always tell how you're feeling by looking into your gorgeous eyes."

Emily kissed Jenna then, brushing their lips together before pressing down. She didn't go beyond that caress, attempting to show with tenderness all that she felt in her heart. They had kissed before, back when they first met. In that first blush of passion's heat, those kisses had been all fire and hunger. Emily had freely taken what Jenna offered. She had crushed Jenna to her, desperate for joining, but it hadn't meant anything.

The soft embrace she offered now held everything–Emily's heart and soul. Jenna accepted with strong arms that held her close, hands splayed across Emily's back. Jenna opened her mouth and Emily dipped briefly inside, tasting and remembering, allowing the pain of so many days apart to heal. When the kiss ended, Jenna pulled Emily's head against her breast, cradling her. For a long while, they simply held each other and listened to the sound of falling water. Jenna eventually, reluctantly, broke the moment.

Emily sat back on her heels, looking deeply into sable brown eyes. "There's something you need to know. My real name is Helene Baptiste."

"Well it makes sense that you'd use a fake name. You were undercover. FBI, right?"

"Yes and although you already know most of this, I want to tell you everything. I don't want any more secrets between us."

Jenna was quiet for several moments. "I understand you were sent there to investigate the disappearances. I even understand why you couldn't tell me. I just can't help but wonder why they didn't send a full taskforce?"

"Normally, they would have. To be honest, it's a miracle the Bureau even found out because all of the missing persons reports were filed in different states. It was only when the computer flagged the origin of the disappearances that we got involved. By then, my superiors decided that an undercover investigation would be better."

"I see. You went in without backup? How does that make sense? Or were you supposed to call in the locals if you got into trouble?"

Emily smiled. "Actually, no. In fact, I was specifically ordered not to involve you. My boss didn't trust you because he couldn't figure out why a prominent homicide detective would give up everything to head out to the sticks. Director Latimer thought you would crack under pressure if things got out of hand."

Jenna was quiet for so long that Emily began to worry. Emily had concealed the truth from Jenna, even if she had already figured out most of it on her own. When Jenna did begin to speak, her voice was so low Emily had to lean closer to hear.

"I assume you read my file so you know about Mandy."

"I do and I also understand. Staying in Boston would have been too painful."

"So why did you tell me now?"

"Because things have happened in a way that you already knew most of it anyway. Also, I love you," Emily stated calmly. "I couldn't go on keeping the smaller details from you, not if we have a hope of any kind of future together."

Jenna kissed Emily's knuckles. "A future, huh? Sounds like you see this relationship going somewhere."

Relief flooded through her at the gentle teasing. She leaned forward and kissed the corner of Jenna's mouth. "Maybe. That depends on how good you are in bed. You know I've been waiting a long time to find out."

"Well, in that case I see things lasting for at least ten minutes."

Emily laughed, looping her arms around Jenna's neck. "Thank you for not holding my assignment against me."

"How can I? I'd have done the same thing. We should head back. The others should be up and ready to move by now."

Emily nodded and stood, offering a hand to Jenna. They held hands as they slowly moved back toward the camp. Now that she had revealed the depth of her emotions and the truth of her identity, Emily could concentrate on more immediate issues.

"How long did Fallon say, two days?"

"Uh-huh. I'd like to try and cut that time down," Jenna admitted. "Every second we stay here we're in danger. We could be attacked at any second."

"I figured as much. I guess it's too much to hope that Adrasta and her ilk would just let us go without a fight."

"Hardly," Jenna admitted. "If nothing else, they'll hunt us down as an example for others. The Erisians aside, I want to get home as fast as we can and destroy that damned rift before the Kurths bring someone else through."

The nefarious brothers had been on Emily's mind as well. "Speaking of the Kurths, I know they weren't acting alone. What are we going to do about the people who caused all this suffering?"

"I'd like to strand every damned one of them here like they did their victims, the Kurths, Deputy Brown and Cheryl Brenner too. It's no less than they deserve."

Emily understood Jenna's anger, but felt guilty for entertaining the idea of turning the tables no matter how just the punishment. No one deserved the Erisians, regardless of their crimes. Unfortunately, that seemed to be the only real answer. She just couldn't figure out if that would be justice or revenge.

"It's not like they'll be punished on Earth," Jenna continued.

"You're right. No one would believe our story for a moment. We'd be lumped into the same category as people claiming alien abduction."

"Maybe we don't have to say anything about the portal," Jenna offered.

"What do you have in mind?"

"I just mean that even the Kurths and Deputy Brown aren't stupid enough to mention Eris. Cheryl has a couple of kids so she'd probably agree to whatever terms we lay out for her if it doesn't involve exile here."

Emily caught on to Jenna's idea. "You think they'll cop to the kidnappings if we promise not to land their butts on Eris?"

"They will if they know what's good for them."

"I'm sure that if we threaten to turn them over to Garran, they'll see things our way."

"That's one of the things I love about you." Jenna squeezed her hand. "Your devious mind."

Emily released Jenna's hand as they walked into camp, not because she was embarrassed at their newfound closeness but because there was work to do. As much as she wanted to concentrate on Jenna, now wasn't the time. The refugees were sitting around the dead campfire, eating. Charles saw them approach and stood up with a welcoming smile. He handed them wooden bowls containing the white, tasteless cubes that made up their food rations.

"Perfect," Emily quipped. "That's just what I wanted for breakfast."

Jenna didn't look any happier with their meal. "Look at it this way, in two days we'll be eating at Frank's and we can stuff ourselves to the gills."

"I'll hold you to that." Emily smiled her thanks and they settled on the leaf-strewn ground.

Charles squatted down and started updating them on the situation. "We're all packed up and ready to go. I don't think anyone is seriously injured so that's a plus. Maybe we can make some good time."

Emily nodded as she bit off a corner of one of her cubes. Apparently, Jenna's decision to rest for the night had been a good call. She was a natural leader. Emily recalled how her boss, Assistant Director Latimer, had told her not to involve local law enforcement.

Ironic, considering the circumstances.

"I didn't want to relight the fire since I didn't figure we'd be here for long."

"Thanks, Charles. That was a good idea."

Jenna nodded her agreement. "Especially if the Erisians are out looking for us. The moons are up and the smoke would have given away our location."

"You think we should walk during sunup instead?" Charles asked.

"No," Emily responded. "I can't see any sense in waiting all day here just for the moons to go down. Let's make tracks while we can."

Agreement sounded all around. Emily finished her meal and scrubbed the bowl out with a handful of leaves. It wasn't exactly sanitary, but she didn't intend to waste their limited water. Jenna followed her example and the group prepared to leave camp. They spread out the supplies, with Emily and Jenna carrying a heavy load. Emily had suggested giving a smaller woman and an overweight man a lighter burden.

"Wait a second," Jenna said as they prepared to move out. "I forgot about the cloaks."

Emily had too. She retrieved the garments and discovered there were only a few. Since she had her night vision goggles, Emily chose to pass them out to the refugees.

"There are three cloaks," she said to the group. "How do you guys want to split them up?"

Jenna had to explain the importance of the garments before the others understood why the distribution mattered. After that, a small but heated discussion broke out as they worked out the details. In the end, Charles and a woman named Yvie both declined. Emily wanted to try and convince Yvie to reconsider. Since she was small and thin, Emily thought she could do with an advantage. One look into Yvie's determined gaze told Emily she would be wasting her time.

They distributed the cloaks and Jenna spent a few minutes showing the survivors how to use them. Emily took the opportunity to learn their names while they were figuring things out. They were going to spend the next two days together and she could hardly go around calling them "hey you."

In addition to Charles and Yvie, Emily met Rebecca, Sean and Kilian. Emily learned that Kilian was Swedish. He'd been passing through Woeful Pines, headed for Nashville on vacation when he stopped at Frank's for lunch. When he came out of the diner, his rental wouldn't start. Emily figured the Kurths had disabled the vehicle so he would have no choice but to call them.

Rebecca, Sean, Yvie and Charles seemed like they were in good shape, especially Rebecca. She had enough muscles to be a bodybuilder. The determined look in her eyes told Emily that she would be an asset. Kilian, however, concerned her. He appeared to be in his forties and was substantially overweight. Emily was relieved that he had one of the cloaks. Should the Erisians come after them, Kilian could use the camouflage properties. It might mean the difference between life and death.

"All right," Jenna said. "I think we're ready to go now."

Emily hefted her rucksack and took up the rear as they headed into the woods. Jenna took the lead since she held the compass and Emily could only see glimpses of her as they walked. The pace wasn't fast, but it was steady. For the first two hours, everything was fine. However, Emily discovered that wouldn't last.

Yvie dropped back beside her, panting slightly. Sweat tracked down her temple though Emily thought the air slightly cool.

"Are we going to stop anytime soon? My feet hurt."

Yvie wore a pair of white tennis shoes that looked fairly new. They were a good brand and unless they were the wrong size, Emily thought they should provide good support.

"Not for a while. We have a long walk ahead of us and we have to schedule our breaks."

"Oh, okay." Yvie's short red hair bobbed as she nodded. "I guess I knew that."

She fell silent and Emily breathed a quiet sigh of relief. Weaving through the trees and underbrush, Yvie stayed close by. Alternately, she began mumbling under her breath and sucking on her teeth. Emily wished Yvie would walk a little faster and put some distance between them, but she seemed determined to stay by Emily's side.

"Say," Yvie said brightly, startling Emily. "Do we have any more of those belts like Jenna is wearing? We could just all fly along and we wouldn't have to wear ourselves out with walking."

"Sorry, Jenna has the only one."

That bit of information seemed enough to quiet Yvie again. For another three hours, the group walked along with little conversation. The moons were high overhead when Jenna finally called a halt. The clearing she found was small, barely large enough for them to sit comfortably. Everyone was tired, but Emily felt they'd made good progress. After a quick meal, more ration cubes and water, Emily stood up.

"Is it time?" Kilian asked. His balding head glistened with sweat but he seemed cheerful and ready to move.

"Afraid so."

"But we've only been resting for about fifteen minutes," Yvie complained. "Can't we wait a little longer? My shoulders are hurting from the pack."

Emily ground her teeth together. She had deliberately ensured Yvie and Kilian received the lightest loads. She didn't have a lot of patience for the complaining. Before she could give Yvie a piece of her mind, Charles intervened.

"I'll carry your pack for a while. I don't mind."

Yvie grinned and started to pass her load to Charles, but Emily intervened. "No. That's awfully nice of you, Charles, but everyone has to do their part."

Charles offered Yvie an apologetic look and headed over to walk with Jenna. Emily ignored the scathing look Yvie cast her way and resumed her position in the rear. When Yvie tossed her head and put distance between them, Emily felt nothing but grateful.

A few hours later, the moons were almost down. Jenna stopped and glanced back. Emily nodded that it was time to stop for the night, or what served as night for Eris. Yvie shot Emily another nasty look, but didn't comment as they started to set up camp. Good. Emily wasn't in the mood for any more carping. Hopefully, they'd be home in one more day and she wouldn't have to worry about keeping these people safe.

"You okay?" Jenna asked, resting a hand on her arm.

Emily noticed she was looking at the bandage. Her wound ached, but there wasn't any aspirin so it wasn't worth mentioning. "Just tired. I'll get a fire going if you want to get our happy campers settled."

"Right." Jenna's amused glance flitted to Yvie and back again. "Happy campers, indeed."

Emily took Charles and Sean with her to gather wood for the fire while the others set about laying out bedrolls and food. Yvie chose to sit down and upend her canteen. Emily noticed Rebecca shaking her head at the other woman before she moved to assist Jenna.

"She'll probably drink all her water and then want ours," Rebecca said loudly, clearly intending for Yvie to overhear.

They hadn't even finished a full day and were already sniping at each other, Emily thought. Thankfully, no one responded to the remark. Even Yvie remained quiet though she did watch Rebecca balefully. Soon, Emily had the fire going and she settled onto her bedroll. The others were already eating, but Emily shook her head at the bowl Jenna held out toward her.

"You really should eat something, to keep your strength up."

"I will in a minute. I just need to rest first."

By unspoken agreement, Emily and Jenna sat slightly apart from the others with their bedrolls close together. Emily sipped from her canteen, quietly assessing their small band of survivors. Kilian's face was still flushed from exertion, but he seemed fine. Sean remained quiet and brooding and Emily realized she hadn't heard him speak since rescuing him from the repository. Yvie sat farthest away, leaning back against a tree. She watched the others suspiciously.

"She's going to be a problem, isn't she?" Jenna spoke quietly so that only Emily could hear.

"I'm surprised she hasn't asked you for your belt so she could fly while everyone else walks."

Jenna chuckled. "Good luck with that."

"It's all right," Emily said, trying to be positive. "One more day and she'll be someone else's problem. How are you holding up?"

"I'm great. After all I've been through since landing on this planet, this is like a summer stroll."

Emily noticed that Jenna seemed alert and cheerful. It was the most relaxed she'd seen her in a while. Heat crawled up Emily's throat and she experienced the sudden desire to kiss Jenna. She wanted to push Jenna back and lay on top of her, explore her body slowly and deeply.

"If you keep looking at me that way, I'm going to spontaneously combust."

Emily averted her gaze and took a larger-than-intended swig from her canteen. "Sorry," she muttered after she managed to swallow.

Jenna squeezed her knee, ratcheting the desire up another notch. "Don't be sorry. I like it. Just hold onto that feeling for a few more days."

Trying desperately to think of an incendiary remark to keep the flirtation going, Emily leaned toward Jenna. Close enough to feel Jenna's breath on her face, Emily started to speak when the clearing erupted in pandemonium. Adrasta, Garran, and Ilana burst out of the trees, followed closely by two more vampires. Caught entirely off guard, the humans jumped to their feet. Reaching for branches and stones as makeshift weapons, they had no time before the Erisians were upon them.

Chapter Nineteen

EMILY SAW AN Erisian with burning red eyes and bared white fangs lunge for Yvie. She had risen to one knee when Emily saw the creature reach for Yvie. She yanked the throwing knife from the belt at the small of her back and hurled it at the creature. The blade embedded itself in the center of his back, right up to the hilt. Things seemed to happen in slow motion for Emily after that.

Yvie shrieked as the vampire fell on top of her, but Emily had already started to turn away. When Jenna and Kilian both winked out of sight, Emily thought someone had struck her upon the head until she realized they had engaged the camouflage settings on the cloaks they wore. With two of their number concealed and another covered by a dead man, the Erisians focused on the remaining four.

Vampires seemed to be everywhere at once. Emily hurried to pull the dead one off Yvie. Before she could assist, Rebecca stepped to Yvie and the downed vampire. She wrapped her arms around the creature's neck. One hand went under the creature's jaw and she gave a vicious jerk. Emily heard his neck snap like dry kindling. If Emily's knife hadn't killed him, Rebecca had just finished the job. Rebecca moved on to continue the fight without helping Yvie regain her freedom from the heavy body.

"Emily!"

She turned at the shout, surprised when she heard Ilana's voice. Adrasta had moved up behind her without Emily hearing. Adrasta carried a long hunting knife with a serrated upper edge. She was so close that she was already on the downward swing with the blade, intent on burying it in Emily's chest. Emily had almost no time to react.

Ilana moved before Adrasta could complete the arc. With one powerful arm thrown around the vampire princess's neck, Ilana hauled Adrasta backward. The tip of the knife caught the front of Emily's shirt, tearing a bit of flesh away with the cloth. Ilana used Adrasta's bodyweight against her, swinging her around and hurling Adrasta against a tree. Adrasta's body impaled itself on a jutting branch, the stump bursting through her chest. Blood and gore sprayed outward, dusting Ilana's face and clothing. Emily saw the surprise caused by Ilana's betrayal on Adrasta's face, but only briefly. She was dead before her eyes slipped closed.

The fight for survival didn't allow Emily time to thank Ilana for saving her life. Worried that another Erisian would attack, Emily turned away. She crouched as she readied herself for another battle.

"Traitor!" Garran roared at Ilana.

Garran rushed Emily, apparently intent on completing what

Adrasta had started. Emily saw the hatred in his eyes. Garran's feet never touched the ground, illustrating how he used the antigravity belt to propel him forward. To the untrained eye, it would seem that he could actually fly. Emily waited until the last second before dodging aside. His outstretched fingers caught the white bandage wrapped around her upper arm, tearing it free. The cloth had stuck to Emily's wound with dried blood and she felt the sting of ripped stitches as it tore away.

Doing her best to ignore the pain, Emily spun as he passed and grabbed at the pistol strapped to his side. All she got for her trouble was being dragged across the campsite, but she refused to let go. Apparently, Garran didn't appreciate a hitchhiker. He swung a fist that connected with Emily's jaw. The blow sent her reeling. She hit the ground hard and rolled to her knees, amazed when she came up with the weapon in her hands. Emily blinked at the pistol in surprise before she suddenly realized Garran was coming back toward her. He had bared his fangs. They appeared to have grown longer by several centimeters. The sight of his elongated teeth was enough to make Emily raise the pistol and fire.

Garran twisted out of the direct beam and the laser blast caught a glancing blow on his temple. He howled in rage and pain and something strange suddenly happened. Garran's body seemed yanked sideways. Emily knew it wasn't something he did on purpose because of his shocked expression. Out of control, Garran crashed headfirst into a thick tree. When he went down, Garran didn't move again. Jenna blinked back into sight and winked at Emily.

Emily spun around to see where Ilana had gone. She found Rebecca, Charles and Sean preparing to move in on Ilana with their makeshift weapons. Yvie and Kilian were nowhere in sight. Emily stepped in front of the vampire regent with her hands up.

"Stop, she isn't one of them."

"The hell she isn't," Charles shouted. "Have you forgotten she's the one who made you take part in the Ti-gon?"

"You don't understand."

Rebecca took over for Charles. "I don't need to understand anything except that she is a bloodsucking vampire."

Jenna stepped around the three and took up position next to Emily. "Ilana is working against the Erisians. She helped us get you out of the city."

That information made Charles and Rebecca hesitate. Sean still hadn't spoken, but he didn't seem inclined to back down. Emily took the opportunity to explain that Ilana's position gave her the chance to work against the vampires from the inside. It took some doing, but finally she was convinced no one would gut Ilana as soon as she let down her guard. That didn't mean they were happy having Ilana around. The three put distance between themselves and Ilana, casting suspicious glances her way.

Kilian blinked back into view, having remained concealed during the battle. He also studied Ilana warily, but finally said, "She could come in useful if we run into any more Erisians."

"Can someone please get this thing off me?"

The question came from the far side of the campfire. Emily suddenly remembered the vampire who had fallen dead atop Yvie.

"You go ahead," Jenna said. "I won't let anyone harm her."

Emily nodded and walked away. She ignored Ilana's remark that the humans weren't strong enough to do her harm. Instead, Emily knelt beside the dead Erisian and pulled her knife from his back. She wiped the blade on his cloak before she pushed him off Yvie.

"Good news, you get an antigravity belt of your very own."

Emily's remark cut off the scathing retort Yvie had prepared to make. "Really? I don't have to walk anymore?"

Figures, Emily thought. Yvie didn't care that she almost died, that they all could have died. As long as she didn't have to put out any effort, she was happy.

"None of us do. With all the Erisians, there are plenty to go around."

Emily ignored the tension caused by Ilana's presence and set about removing weapons and antigravity belts from the Erisians. Adrasta's equipment was covered in blood, but Emily didn't intend to leave the device here for someone else to use against them. She took the belt and shoved it into a sack with the others. She moved to Garran last, discovering that he was only unconscious. Emily considered killing him where he lay. He certainly wouldn't have hesitated to finish one of them off under similar circumstances. Emily reached for her knife and then stopped. Killing another in the heat of battle was one thing, but murdering someone who couldn't defend himself was entirely different. Unconscious, Garran wasn't a threat.

Emily removed his belt and weapons but left him unharmed as she hurried back to the others. "I suggest we get out of here before we have more unexpected company."

"Is Garran dead?" Charles asked.

Meeting his eyes, Emily considered lying. She was afraid one of them would want to kill him before they left the clearing. "No, and I don't want to be here when he wakes up."

"That's it then," Jenna said. "Ilana is coming with us."

"What? You can't be serious." Yvie seemed furious about the decision.

Emily turned to Yvie. "She just saved my life; killed Adrasta to do it. There's no way she can go back to Saqqara. Ilana's coming with us and if you don't like it, you can stay here with Garran."

"It's a trick." Rebecca's scathing tone told Emily exactly what she thought of Ilana's veracity. Emily couldn't really blame them for their distrust.

"Look, I know that none of you like this, but Garran knows what Ilana did for us. We're not leaving her here."

"Do we get a vote in this?" Sean asked, speaking for the first time. From the flinty hard expression in his eyes, Emily could figure out which way he would go.

"No, not really. This isn't a democracy, it's an escape and we're running out of time in this debate. If you're coming with me and Jenna, I suggest you grab your things."

Emily stalked across the clearing and grabbed her pack, grateful they hadn't had time to set up camp before the attack. It would save time now. Jenna and Ilana met her near the tree line and they turned back toward the others. Charles, Rebecca, Yvie, Sean and Kilian stood eyeing each other, clearly waiting for someone to make the first move.

"Well, I'm not staying here with a bunch of vampires out running around. Besides, Jenna has the compass and unless one of you is part bloodhound," Yvie continued, "I think we stand a better chance with her."

"What about the vampire?" Charles asked.

Yvie shrugged. "Better the devil you know."

Emily didn't believe for a second that Yvie wanted Ilana along for the ride. Yvie was a survivor, first and foremost. Regardless of her motivation, it proved enough to silence the others and induce them to follow. After a few minutes, Emily dropped back into her usual position in the rear. Ilana joined her a short time later.

"What's the matter? You don't like walking with the others?"

"They don't like me."

Emily nodded. "That's true, but can you blame them?"

"I suppose not. The Erisians have put them through much."

"That's an understatement."

Emily appreciated all that Ilana had done for her, but she wasn't inclined to let her off the hook. Although a member of a rebellion still in its infancy, Ilana had perpetrated as many atrocities as any other Erisian. Yet, at the same time, Ilana had attempted to make up for a lifetime of depravity. Trying to think about it from Ilana's perspective, Emily attempted to put herself in Erisian shoes. If she'd been born into this world, a vampire with certain biological drives, would she have acted any differently? More than that, would she have had the strength to turn her back on that existence?

Then there was the physical attraction. It was still there, though greatly diminished now that Emily had admitted to her feelings for Jenna.

"Do you know where you are going?"

"I'm following Jenna."

Ilana lifted an eyebrow. "To where are you following her?"

"We're going home, to Earth. We should be there sometime tomorrow."

Yvie apparently overheard the remark and dropped back, carefully keeping Emily between her and Ilana. "I thought we were going to use the belts."

"Yes, and we will. I just want to put some distance between us and Garran first."

"Why? We can move faster if we use the belts."

Emily finally lost patience with Yvie. She spoke to her slowly, explaining the situation to Yvie as she would to a small child. "You're right we could fly like the wind if we used the belts. You just let me know, Yvie, if you would like us to stop now and have a class on how to use them. Of course, Garran could sneak up on us while we're doing that and rip someone's throat out but that's not important if it means you wouldn't have to walk anymore!"

She regretted the childish outburst as soon as she finished speaking. Emily was tired and her arm ached where Garran had torn one of the stitches open. All of that wasn't really a good excuse and Yvie proved it.

"You don't have to be so nasty, Emily. I know you helped save us, but that doesn't give you the right to talk to me that way."

Emily thought she saw tears swimming in Yvie's eyes as she stalked away. Ilana remained silent throughout the exchange and they continued walking. Emily distracted herself from the encounter by concentrating on the sounds of the forest around them. She focused on any sounds that didn't belong, vigilant for anything that might indicate more Erisians on their trail.

After a couple of hours, Jenna called another halt. It was early, but they hadn't had a proper rest before the attack. Emily took the opportunity to distribute anti-gravity belts to the others, giving the first one to Yvie. It wasn't much, but Yvie smiled at her and the tension between them dissipated slightly. Adrasta's belt remained in the bag. There were plenty to go around and Emily didn't want to handle the bloody metal. Jenna had to demonstrate the device properties since Emily had never used one.

Once everyone demonstrated enough proficiency to travel overland, they settled down to rest. Another meal of tofu wasn't what Emily wanted so she sat with her back against a tree and sipped from her canteen. Jenna settled down beside her. She actually seemed to relish the white squares of food.

"You like that stuff?"

"Yeah, it's pretty good. Tastes kinda like nougat."

Emily shuddered. "Ugh, if you say so."

"Emily, did something happen between you and Ilana?"

"What are you talking about?" She couldn't meet Jenna's eyes. Her gaze rested on the ground between her booted feet.

"It's just that there seems to be something in the way she looks at you."

Emily leaned her head back against the tree and considered what to tell Jenna. She decided on the truth. "Nothing ever happened between us. Yes, there was an attraction but that's all. It's nothing compared to how I feel for you." Emily reached out and took Jenna's hand, pulling it onto her knee. "I owe Ilana my life, but not my heart. That belongs to you."

"Good, I'll hold you to that." Jenna kissed her cheek and then rested her head against Emily's shoulder. It felt good just to relax for a few minutes.

Fifteen minutes later, the break was over. Emily was surprised by how eager the others were to move on and then she remembered the belts. Although only Yvie had actually vocalized any complaints, it seemed everyone was tired of walking. They made good time after that, traveling without the need for a break. Hours passed and Emily realized she'd started to nod off as she followed the group.

Shaking her head, she checked the position of the sun and moons. They had chosen to travel during mid-tween, when the moons were up, and rest when the sun rose. Currently, the sun was a third of the way across the sky. No wonder she was so tired.

"Jenna!" Ahead of the small troop, Jenna turned at Emily's shout. "I think we should stop for a few hours."

Emily pointed toward the sky. Jenna flinched a little when she saw the position of the sun. She nodded and halted her forward progress. As they set down, Emily heard someone question why they were stopping.

"We need some sleep," Emily responded. "I know it's not as tiring since we're using the belts, but we still need rest."

This time, Emily was outnumbered. She had claimed earlier that this wasn't a democracy, but that was while they were in danger. With no immediate threat, the others grouped together and insisted that they push on. To the last member, Ilana and Jenna included, they all voted to eat something and then continue toward home. It didn't take much to convince her. Emily was ready to get back to Earth, too.

By mutual agreement, they spent an hour resting. Then everyone shouldered their packs and it was time to go. Emily didn't know how much time had passed, but many hours later, she began to wish they had stopped after all. Her ribs ached from the belt pressing into them and she had trouble keeping her eyes open. She remembered how annoying she'd found Yvie's constant complaining and gritted her teeth to kept her mouth shut.

The trees grew thicker now, so close together that Emily couldn't see the other seven at one time. They moved in and out through the brush and trees, shadows dominated the scene. Just when she thought this journey would never end, she heard Jenna call out. Emily hurried forward so fast that she scraped her shoulder against a tree trunk.

"Damn it," she muttered, moving past Ilana and Yvie to lower herself beside Jenna. "What is it, what's wrong?"

Jenna's head was down as she studied the compass. In the dimness, Emily could see the bright orange color of the dial. "We're getting close. The portal has to be around here somewhere."

"Okay people," Emily shouted. "We walk from here."

"I know it's dark, but we need to keep an eye out for a cave system," Jenna added. "In this darkness we're going to have to rely on the people with cloaks. Stay close together and holler if you find something."

Jenna raised her head and Emily froze when her eyes fixed on Emily's arm. Blood had saturated the bandage and trickled down her arm from the encounter with Garran. Jenna hissed and grabbed Emily's forearm. "You're hurt. Why didn't you say anything?"

All eyes turned to Emily, making her uncomfortable. Jenna's concern made her feel warm, but it would be better if they were alone. "It's nothing major, just a busted stitch. Let's find that rift and I'll let you sew me up again when we get home."

"Fat chance of that." Jenna looked horrified at the idea. "My days of putting in stitches are over. We're taking you to a real hospital."

The others lost interest in the discussion and dispersed to search for the gate. Emily chose to stay with Jenna. They kept a close watch on the compass as they moved back and forth through the woods. In fits and starts, they closed the distance to the rift. At times the dial faded back toward yellow and they had to readjust their path. Eventually, the compass changed and turned darker orange. Emily was convinced they were within yards of the breach. Sure enough, the compass dial segued to a dull red.

"We're close." Emily's heart pounded with excitement. "I'll get the others."

She turned around and almost ran smack into Ilana. The vampire's arms were crossed and she leaned against a tree. Unlike the refugees, Emily understood that Ilana was ambivalent about heading to Earth. She couldn't return home but on Earth she would be an outcast, hunted down and killed if people discovered her true nature.

"Can you help me round up the group?"

"You can't be serious. If I came upon one of them alone in the darkness, they would die of fright."

"Hmm, you have a point. In that case, stay with Jenna. She'll protect you if someone tries to drive a stake through your heart."

"A what?"

Emily had already walked away, smoothing her smile. It didn't take long to gather everyone together. By mutual agreement, they had stayed close to Jenna and her compass. Minutes later, Charles gave an excited yelp.

"Here, I've found a cave opening. Please tell me it's the right one."

Jenna strode up toward him with Emily right behind her. Emily watched over Jenna's shoulder and saw the dial become a dark, ruby red. Their eyes met and Jenna nodded. Happy cries sounded all around her and Emily suddenly had difficulty seeing through her tears. Unable to speak, she swallowed and reached into her pocket for the portal control.

"Okay, give me a second," Emily muttered after clearing her throat. "I've got to remember how to work this thing."

She fumbled with the dials, getting the sequence wrong the first time. Ilana didn't offer to intervene, remaining silent as Emily worked it out for herself. Emily started over and finally managed to enter the settings just right. A humming sound began, almost past the range of human hearing but Ilana slapped her hands over her ears. Then a faint, green glow slowly illuminated, growing stronger by the second. Before she knew it, Emily was looking at the square outline of an artificial doorway.

No one moved. It seemed everyone was eager to go home, but no one was willing to be the guinea pig and cross the boundary first. Finally, Rebecca stepped up to the portal. She swallowed nervously before turning to check with Ilana.

"Is it safe?"

"The doorway is established."

Emily rolled her eyes. "That's a yes, Rebecca. It's safe. Want to be the first to go home?"

"Hell yeah." Rebecca grinned and stepped through.

Emily thought it was weird how she just seemed to disappear into nothing. As Rebecca's foot vanished, Emily realized that it really was like walking through a door. After that, the others followed without prompting. Charles went next, followed by Yvie, Sean, and Kilian.

"After you," Emily told Jenna.

"Are you sure you don't want to go first?"

Emily shook her head. "No, sweetheart. I won't feel right until I know everyone is home, most especially you."

"Just don't take too long."

Jenna leaned forward and kissed Emily gently on the cheek before giving her a look that would melt steel. Then she was gone through the gateway. Unexpected desire burned a path through Emily's body and she had to take a deep breath. She and Jenna had started something before all this craziness and suddenly Emily couldn't wait to consummate that beginning.

"I suppose Jenna is the reason there was never anything more between us?"

Emily owed Ilana the truth. Regardless of any attraction they might have shared, Ilana needed to know there would never be anything more. "Yes, she's the one."

"Too bad, with me you would have experienced more than you

ever conceived of."

Emily gulped at the erotic images that crowded through her mind. "Actually, I think it's a good thing. I'm not sure my heart could take it."

"I guess we'll never know. You should go. I'm sure the others are wondering if I have made a meal of you after all."

Emily could have taken the comment in more than one way and she felt her face burn. Instead, she chose not to take up the bait. "Are you sure you don't want to go ahead?"

"No, I require a moment alone to say goodbye to my world."

"I understand. Don't take too long," Emily said, unconsciously mirroring Jenna's words.

She turned and hesitated a fraction of a second. The first time she'd come through the portal, Emily had been unconscious. She had no memory of crossing the barrier and she wondered briefly if it would hurt. Thoughts of Jenna worrying about where she was forced Emily to close her eyes and take a huge step forward.

Pins and needles crawled across her skin, covering every inch of her body. They weren't nearly as painful as a limb falling asleep, but Emily felt them all the more keenly due to the novelty. Sparkles made it difficult to see at first. Then the world rushed back and she squinted at the pain of blinding light. Once her vision began to adjust, Emily recognized the rough stone and dirt of the inside of a cave. Before going to Eris, the interior of a subterranean structure would have seemed dark. Now it was like the brightest of day.

Her elation at being back on Earth ended abruptly. Two men stood directly in front of her. The Kurth brothers had twin shotguns leveled directly at her. Deputy Clayton Brown stood off to one side with his police-issue service weapon pointed at Jenna and the others. Emily raised her hands in surrender.

Chapter Twenty

"OVER THERE WITH the others," Mike Kurth ordered.

Jenna watched as Emily did as instructed. She hoped Ilana would walk through the gate and provide a distraction. Deputy Brown stood beside an unconscious woman. Jenna assumed this was their latest offering to the Erisians.

"You all okay?" A few nods answered her.

"Shut up," Mike snarled. He turned to keep everyone in front of him as Emily moved. Now, his back was toward the portal. Joey followed his example. "Someone better answer some questions, starting with you, Sheriff."

"What do you want to know, Mike?"

"Let's begin with how you got on the other side of the portal...and what are you wearing?"

The latter query seemed more of an afterthought, but Jenna answered readily. "I followed you when you kidnapped Agent Bannon last week."

"I told you she was a Fed."

"Quiet, Joey. You must have hit your head, Sheriff Yang."

Jenna's eyes narrowed speculatively. "Are you trying to tell me you didn't kidnap a federal agent as well as these other people?" She waved a hand to indicate the small group.

She was fishing, giving Mike just enough to keep him talking. Jenna had never met a perp who didn't like to exaggerate his own brilliance. Mike Kurth was no exception.

"Nah, I did that, but it wasn't no week ago and you know it. Hell, me and Joey don't have a delivery due to Garran for another few days, but we found this little woman sitting on the side of the road. It was too good to pass up."

Something he said seemed to catch Emily's attention, information Jenna assumed vital to their situation. Jenna's heart leapt when Emily took a step forward. Mike immediately brought his shotgun to bear.

"Hold on, I only have a question. I was out for the count when you took me through." Jenna noticed that Emily didn't mention that Deputy Brown had shot her with a tranquilizer gun. "How long ago was that?"

"About a day and a half, why?"

"Dammit, Joey, I said shut your pie hole."

Mike was furious with his brother and didn't notice the rift's event horizon light up. The Kurths and Deputy Brown had turned away from the portal, but Jenna faced it directly. She held her breath when it lit up, yet no one emerged. She began to wonder if Ilana would ever show.

"It doesn't matter when you went in," Mike said snidely. "You're going right back. I'm not about to have Garran breathing down my neck because you escaped. Clayton, get that broad up. It's time to get this party started."

If he weren't so incredibly dangerous, Jenna would have laughed at the cheesy line. Movement from the edge of her peripheral vision caught her attention. Carefully shifting only her eyes, Jenna watched as footprints appeared in the sandy cave floor. It wasn't magic. She quickly understood that Ilana had come through the gate camouflaged in her cloak. The footprints moved directly behind Mike.

Jenna's body tensed slightly, waiting for a cue to act. Clayton Brown had stepped over to pick up their latest victim. His actions meant there was one less weapon trained upon the returning hostages. Ilana would need to move now while the odds weren't so overwhelming.

She didn't have long to wait. Mike's head suddenly swiveled around on his neck until he was looking directly behind. Jenna cringed internally at the snapping sounds of broken vertebrae even as she lunged forward.

Instinctively, Joey's eyes had turned to his brother. Jenna grabbed the front of Joey's shotgun and knocked the double barrels toward the ceiling. The explosion caused by the rounds going off made her ears ring. Rock and debris rained down from overhead, but she ignored the assault as she ripped the weapon out of Joey's hands. At almost the same moment, Mike's shotgun crashed into the cave wall and disintegrated from the force with which Ilana threw it.

The next thing Jenna knew, Mike's body flew through the portal and disappeared from view. A snap kick delivered by Emily sent Deputy Brown crashing to the ground before he could even stand up properly. He seemed unconscious.

"What the hell?" Joey screamed, looking around with wide eyes.

He attempted to back away, but squealed in fright when he came up against an immovable object. Jenna watched as Ilana tossed him after his brother, arms and legs flailing uselessly. Ilana winked back into view, a smug expression upon her pale face. Unlike the others, she seemed to have no difficulty adjusting to Earth's relative brightness.

"Eww, gross. Did you have to break his neck like that?" Yvie looked a little green around the gills as she asked the question.

"At least I didn't drain him first. Perhaps you would have preferred for him to shoot you...or force you back to Eris?"

Jenna didn't agree with Ilana's methods either, but was more concerned with Joey coming back through the rift. At the moment, he was probably checking on Mike but that wouldn't take long.

"We need to get Deputy Brown through the portal as well." Jenna pointed out.

"Are you sure you want to do that?" Emily asked. "I thought we agreed they would face Earth justice."

"I don't like it either, but I don't know what else to do. That woman isn't going to be unconscious for long and this is going to be hard to explain."

"Let's do it." Rebecca showed no signs of remorse or hesitation. Justifiable anger threaded her words. "Why shouldn't they experience the same hell they've put the rest of us through?"

Rebecca didn't wait for permission, bending down to grab the deputy by the ankles. Sean, quiet but no less determined, took Brown's shoulders. The two carried him across to the gate and tossed him through the event horizon. Jenna didn't attempt to stop them. The shotguns and Deputy Brown's service weapon followed. Once all their belongings had vanished from the cave, Ilana aimed a controller at the portal and the green glow abruptly disappeared.

"Not that I'm complaining," Jenna began, "but why did you come through camouflaged?"

"I was unsure what we would find after stepping through the gate. As a refugee upon your planet, I could not take the chance."

"Lucky for us," Charles said. He stopped short of slapping Ilana on the back, the grin fading as he realized he'd just become chummy with a vampire. "Uh, so what now?"

"Let's head home."

Yvie's suggestion was happily embraced by the others, but Jenna couldn't let them take off just yet. They still had a few details to sort out, not to mention another hostage to revive.

"Unfortunately, I can't let you do that. I need to collect all the technology from Eris first. After that, we'll need to work out our story before I take you all to the station and get your official statements."

"Are you serious?" Kilian asked. "My apologies, but I'm starving for some real food and I wish to return home."

Jenna was afraid she was about to have a mutiny on her hands. She could sympathize. "I'm truly sorry, but if we all just disperse there are going to be some difficult questions to answer. Speaking of questions, I have one for you, Ilana. What did the Kurths mean about only a little over a day passing since we went through the rift?"

"You were on another planet," Ilana responded simply. "Does it not make sense that time would move differently?"

"I guess when you put it that way," Emily responded, rolling her eyes. "Still, this will work in our favor. I expected to come back to State Troopers and FBI everywhere since the local sheriff and an agent went missing. Instead, we have some time. Let's figure out how we're going to handle this, and fast before this woman wakes up."

Eventually, they all agreed that the Kurth brothers, Deputy Brown and Cheryl Brenner had kidnapped them and taken them to the woods. The purpose of the abductions was to stage an elaborate hunt, where they chased down the victims and killed them for fun. Jenna knew of an old farm owned by the Kurth family and described the location to the others until everyone agreed upon the details. When asked, they would say that Emily and Jenna discovered the diabolical game, raided the property and freed the hostages. The Kurth brothers and Deputy Brown had escaped.

"There's only one problem with that story," Emily said. "Why didn't we call in backup?"

"No time," Charles responded, stepping in. "You came upon them when... they were about to kill Yvie."

"Hey, why does it have to be me?"

"Never mind that, it'll work. Let's wake up their latest victim and get out of here. If it's only been a day, my Jeep should be sitting outside. I just wish you two had waited to toss Deputy Brown through the gate so I could retrieve his radio."

Jenna knelt down beside the unconscious woman. She reached out to shake her awake, but Emily stopped her.

"Hold on, we're forgetting something. Mike and Joey had a gate controller, too. We need to destroy that damned portal before we go anywhere. I'm surprised they haven't already come back through."

Emily pulled the device Fallon gave her out of a front pocket. Jenna waited on one knee while Emily manipulated the settings. She finally aimed it at the portal and mashed the switch.

"Hold it!" Jenna shouted, eyes widening as she jumped to her feet. Jenna lunged across the small space and slapped the remote out of Emily's hands.

"Hey, what did you do that for?"

"Don't you remember? Destabilizing the portal will cause an explosion. We need to make sure we we're clear before you do that."

"Oh, crap. I forgot about that." Emily looked a little pale.

"Let's get everyone out of here and try this again from the cave mouth."

Jenna asked Charles to carry the unconscious woman and they all evacuated the area. The brightness of the rising sun hurt. Jenna raised a hand to shield her eyes, squinting as she turned back to Emily while the others moved to a safe distance. Ilana seemed uncomfortable in the bright light, but at least she didn't burst into flame. Well away from the cave mouth, Emily repeated her earlier actions, pointing the device back in the direction of the portal.

"I hope this works," she admitted. "Fallon didn't say anything about effective distance."

"You are well within range," Ilana said, speaking in a bored tone.

She'd barely finished speaking when an orange fireball erupted from the aperture. A rumble shook the mountain and threw everyone to the ground. The ensuing thunderclap made Jenna's ears ring and her head felt like it would split open. When she could hear again, Jenna picked up the sounds of rubble collapsing from inside the cavern.

It took a moment to stand because Jenna's knees were a little wobbly. The others seemed to have the same problem. Only Ilana appeared unaffected, an amused smile on her pale lips. She reached down and took Emily's elbow, helping her to rise. After a few minutes, the group limped back together.

"Now what?" Kilian sounded shaken.

Jenna shook her head, trying to ease the sudden headache. "Like I said, I need the antigravity belts and anything else that's not specifically of Earth origin."

No one seemed big on that idea. A lot of grumbling followed her request, but eventually they handed over the equipment. After each person gave up belt, cloak, canteens and other supplies, they wandered away. Only Ilana remained. She stood regarding Jenna with her hands on her hips.

"I will not surrender my technology. Unlike the others, I am not of your land."

Jenna held up a hand to stop Ilana. She kept her voice low so she wouldn't be overheard. "You need the equipment to help you survive here. I get it. However, I just need you to hand everything over until the others leave the precinct. I'll give it back to you then."

"Ah, you do not wish to appear to offer special treatment. Very well, but I will not allow you to change your mind."

"It's not going to happen. After going through hell on Eris, no one understands better than I do." After appropriating the equipment, Jenna moved over to the others. "Now, about our story."

They finalized the remaining details, concluding with how Jenna and Emily—Agent Baptiste—worked together to solve the mystery and managed to save some of the victims. It was just too bad the Kurth brothers and Deputy Brown escaped.

"As for bodies of the missing," Emily added, "we have no idea where our suspects disposed of them."

Jenna agreed. "There will be a search, but the Kentucky woods are massive."

"All of this fiction took place at an old rundown farm?" Yvie inquired.

Jenna described the property again to make sure the details were firmly in their minds. She'd been out there once as the new Bullitt County Sheriff. Nothing remained except a ramshackle two-story home and a dilapidated barn. The barn was large enough to house abductees.

"There's only one problem, Jenna. How would they restrain so many people? If the FBI and State Police swarm over the property, they'd better find evidence."

Stunned by her own lack of foresight, Jenna could only stare at Emily. She hadn't even considered the evidence necessary for crime scene units to discover. Combined with Emily almost blowing them up minutes ago Jenna thought they were all too exhausted to actually pull this off. Getting everything right would be essential. Looking into Emily's eyes, Jenna knew she had something in mind.

"What are you thinking?"

"I know we all want to go home, but we can't miss anything. We'll need to head out there so everyone can picture this place. We'll leave DNA, sweat, fingerprints, the whole works. Maybe one of the guys can even pee in a corner somewhere."

"Are you kidding me?" Yvie began.

"Stop." Jenna had listened to her snipe at Emily all the way home and she was at her limit. "No one wants to do this, but that's the way it is. Do you really think people are going to believe you were abducted and handed over to vampires through an inter-dimensional portal where you were hunted for sport and food?"

"No, I guess not."

"Then shut up and cooperate. Let's get going. You're not the only one who wants a hot meal and a bath."

Jenna had shoved everything into a satchel. She slung it over her shoulder and searched the immediate area, taking a second to remember where she'd parked the Jeep. She saw the Kurths' tow truck with a blown out windshield from the explosion. Right beside it sat Deputy Clayton Brown's cruiser. Jenna walked by them and around a narrow trail, discovering the Jeep right where she'd left it. The SUV appeared untouched. Jenna shoved the bag into the rear cargo area and people started piling in. The vehicle comfortably seated five, but everyone attempted to cram inside.

"This isn't working," Emily grunted. She slid out of the back seat, standing beside the Jeep. "What about the police car?"

Jenna nodded. "Check and see if Brown left the keys in the ignition."

Emily headed back toward the cave system, disappearing around the trail. A few seconds later she shouted, "Found them."

"Great, who wants to ride with Emily?"

Ilana slid out of the cramped vehicle, followed by Sean. Once they'd all loaded up, Jenna climbed behind the wheel. She watched the rear view mirror until Emily pulled in behind her before setting out. Jenna's eyes shifted to the radio and she steeled herself to make the call. As much as she hated lying, the truth simply wouldn't work. Thankfully, she could put that transmission off for a little while longer.

WHEN THEY FINALLY entered the Sheriff's substation, applause erupted. In the ten minutes since Jenna had radioed the office, the dayshift dispatcher, Janet Wise, had apparently called everyone she knew. Jenna recognized deputies from all shifts, Millie Franklin, Lois Freeman and a few others. Charles's aunt was the only family member in attendance since the others lived out of state, although Jenna learned that deputies had contacted them. Janet had thoughtfully called emergency services personnel to the station to give the victims a quick check-up.

Tears streamed down Mrs. Freeman's cheeks and she rushed to embrace her nephew. Jenna allowed a brief reunion before she set to work. All of the kidnap victims were shown to the front office and offered coffee while sheriff's personnel took individual statements. Jenna trusted her people to take care of the details as she dragged Emily over to EMS.

"This looks pretty nasty," the male technician said after removing the bandage from Emily's left biceps. "When did you say this happened?"

"About two days ago." Jenna waited nervously, painfully aware of the time difference between Earth and Eris.

"You've managed to pop one of your stitches. It must hurt like hell."

"It's not so bad."

"Well, it's clean and I don't see any signs of infection. Still, you should get checked out by your doctor."

Emily nodded. "I'll do that. Thanks."

Someone touched her on the shoulder and Jenna turned, leaving Emily speaking with the tech. Deputy Randall quickly brought her up to speed. "So far, the witness statements all agree. We've issued an alert on the Kurths and Deputy Brown. They aren't at home and no one has seen them."

"I doubt we'll find anything. Have units pick up Cheryl Brenner."

"She was in on this, too?"

"Yes, although I'm not sure to what extent."

Jenna had seen Cheryl at the Kurth home prior to Emily's abduction, but that was circumstantial at best. Cheryl could always claim she hadn't seen or known anything. Considering the severity of the case, Jenna should probably question Cheryl herself. The only reason she didn't was that she was too close to things. She needed distance from any suspects or she'd want to beat them to death for what she'd experienced during the last week.

"I'm on it, Sheriff. Uh, one more thing."

"Yes?"

"What are you wearing?"

Jenna glanced down reflexively. She'd worn the breeches, soft boots and cloak for so long that she'd forgotten. "Uh, well, it was an undercover operation you know. Agent Baptiste and I didn't want to stand out."

"Oh yeah, that makes sense. I'll head over to Frank's. Cheryl should be on shift about now."

"Mark, have another car drop by her house. If she isn't working tonight, I don't want to take the chance that someone will tip her off."

Jenna stayed until all statements were finished. Although she wanted desperately to go home, she wouldn't do so until she'd put this case to bed. Emily stayed nearby, sipping coffee as Yvie, Rebecca and

Sean left the station one by one. Charles took off with his aunt. Of the five, only Kilian stopped to say goodbye.

"Sheriff, Agent, I wished to thank you for getting us back. I called my wife and told her I will be home by tomorrow. I wish it could be faster but Sweden is a very long way from here."

Jenna offered her hand. "It was our pleasure, Kilian. Take care of yourself."

"I will."

Finally, Ilana emerged. She appeared relaxed while Deputy Beck looked tense. Jenna thought Ilana had probably used some of her special vampire mind tricks on him. Trying not to smirk, she asked, "Are you ready to go?" Jenna thought Ilana would stay with her until she determined where to go next.

"Yes, but I will not be going with you, Sheriff Yang. I have made...other arrangements."

That was unexpected.

"You know someone else here?" Emily asked.

"It's better that you do not know of my plans."

Jenna didn't understand what that meant, but it didn't sound good. "Plausible deniability?"

"Perhaps." Ilana bowed slightly from the waist. "My thanks, to you both. I should go."

Ilana departed the station after retrieving her equipment and Jenna wondered if they would ever see her again. Somehow, she hoped not. Jenna didn't have anything against Ilana, except for her obvious attraction to Emily, but trouble seemed to follow the vampire. Jenna had experienced enough drama for the near future.

"Same question, Sheriff Yang." Emily interrupted her thoughts. "Are you ready to go?"

"God, yes."

The substation had slowly emptied of personnel until only the usual shift remained. Janet manned the silent radio and deputies were in the field attempting to corral Cheryl. There was nothing left for Jenna to do. She walked out to the Jeep with Emily at her side.

"I have to go by the cabin," Emily said. "I left my cell phone there when I went to the Kurth house last week and I need to check in with Latimer."

"How do you think he's going to react?"

"Unknown, probably a mixture of relief and anger."

"Why anger?"

"Because I didn't call him and tell him I had a suspect."

"Not to mention the fact that you brought me in on this against specific orders not to?" Jenna slid behind the wheel with Emily next to her. "Where to after you finish explaining yourself? Are you planning to stay at the cabin?"

"If it's all right, I'd rather stay at your place. I don't know why, but

I just really don't want to be alone right now."

Jenna took Emily's hand and placed it on her thigh. "You don't have to explain. I feel exactly the same way. To be honest, I don't trust you not to get kidnapped again if I let you out of my sight."

"Funny."

Chapter Twenty-one

"WHAT DID HE say?"

Emily stopped tapping the phone against her chin. She still had trouble wrapping her mind around the concept that only a few days had passed since traveling to an alien world. Somehow, she had expected Latimer to demand to know why she'd gone off grid for so long. Instead, he'd expressed pleased astonishment that Emily had solved the case so swiftly. He was also cheesed that she'd gone against orders and involved Sheriff Yang.

"Congratulations?"

"That's all?"

"He's not sending in forensic teams and additional field agents if that's what you're worried about. Latimer said that since the case is solved, the locals can tie up any loose ends."

Jenna looked surprised. "I guess I should be pissed that he thinks of the police as nothing more than glorified security guards but this is a good thing. We don't have the FBI's resources so it's unlikely the crime scene unit will figure out we staged the scene."

"That's true and now that we've dotted our *i*'s and crossed our *t*'s, I'm going to get a change of clothes together so we can get out of here."

"What about your personal belongings? I thought you said this was a Bureau-owned property."

Emily answered as she walked down the short hallway to the single bedroom. "It is. I'll come back and collect what I need before I leave."

She grabbed a go-bag, tossing in a change of clothes, her .44 magnum along with a couple of spare clips and a toiletry kit. With her job, Emily was accustomed to moving fast with necessary items only. In less than five minutes, she was ready to leave the secluded cabin.

Emily climbed back into the Jeep and slid all the way across the seat until she was right up against Jenna. An arm went around her as they pulled away from the building. Emily rested her head against Jenna's shoulder and closed her eyes. For the first time in many days, she relaxed completely and gave over all control to someone she trusted. She had already started to fall asleep before reaching Jenna's home.

"You okay?" Jenna asked, switching off the engine.

"Hmm, just tired and hungry. What's for dinner?" She followed Jenna into the kitchen from the garage entry, welcoming the shadows of an interior without burning lights. Emily dropped her bag beside the door. "Do you think we'll ever get used to everything being so bright?"

Jenna opened the refrigerator. "I imagine it'll take some time, but we got used to Eris. How about a salad to start with, followed by ribeyes with microwave baked potatoes, corn on the cob, and macaroni and cheese?"

"Sounds wonderful," Emily admitted, "as long as it doesn't take too long. Do we have dessert?"

Jenna pulled a gallon-sized container out of the freezer with a flourish. "Ben and Jerry's banana split ice cream."

"I think I'm in heaven. Where's your grill. I'll start it up so we can get the steaks going."

"I don't use a grill. Instead, how about I start the fireplace and we cook the meat cowboy style?"

"Over an open fire?" Emily felt delighted by the idea. She'd never had a steak cooked that way. "I'm intrigued."

In the end, there was far too much food. A week of nothing but water, crude bread and square food cubes had resulted in shrunken stomachs. They stored half of their meal and placed it in the fridge, but Emily refused to give up on the ice cream. Emily insisted on rinsing out their bowls while Jenna finished stowing the food. It was all she could do to keep her eyes open as warm water ran over her hand. When arms slipped around her waist, Emily started in surprise.

"Leave that, we can finish up later. How about a shower?"

Emily actually shivered at the thought of being clean again. "Are you trying to get me out of my tactical gear? Women usually swoon at the sight of all this spy stuff." She turned in Jenna's embrace.

"Is that so? Well, as it happens, Agent Baptiste, you reek."

"Do tell." Emily's heart melted at the way Jenna's eyes crinkled when she smiled.

"Yes, and we'll talk later about exactly how many women you're referring to. For now, I want a shower and then I want to feel you between me and the mattress."

"Sweet talker." Emily leaned forward and placed a chaste kiss on Jenna's mouth. "Lead the way."

Emily and Jenna started removing clothing as they left the kitchen. Emily's black shirt was little more than rags at this point and she didn't give it a second thought as she dropped it on the floor. Her throwing knife made it onto the side table she passed in the living room and her final sock came off as they entered the bathroom. Jenna adjusted the water wearing only the trousers Moye had given her. They soon landed on the cold tiles.

Heat and humidity caressed Emily's flesh. Goosebumps erupted over her arms and legs as she climbed into the stall. The shower wasn't large, allowing just enough room for them both. Emily took a bar of soap and slowly ran it over Jenna's body, enjoying her first unimpeded sight of the strong, female form. For so long, she had wanted Jenna.

Emily dropped to her knees, running both hands over Jenna's hips and legs. She leaned forward and pressed a kiss into a powerful thigh, noticing the thinness of Jenna's abdomen. Surviving Eris hadn't been easy and Jenna's body showed the still-healing scars. Emily kissed every scrape and bruise. When she glanced upward, she noticed the heat in Jenna's eyes.

Jenna reached down and pulled Emily up into her arms. She pressed Emily against the shower wall, making her gasp from the sudden cold against her back. Emily welcomed the kiss, winding her arms around Jenna's neck and burying her fingers in the thick, dark hair. Nothing else existed but Jenna's lips and the tongue in her mouth, stroking, consuming.

The kiss ended suddenly and Emily moaned when Jenna's teeth grazed her neck. Given what she'd witnessed between Adrasta and Nichole, Emily should have felt terrified by the contact. Instead, she pressed into Jenna and wound her leg around a muscled thigh. The feel of Jenna sucking at her neck was the most erotic thing Emily had ever experienced.

Only when the water grew cold did they finally separate. Jenna shut off the taps while Emily reached for a couple of towels. Shivering and barely dry, Emily stepped out of the shower. She scrubbed at her hair, attempting to wring as much water from the strands as she could. Jenna didn't seem to feel the same impulse. She dropped her towel onto the trousers and then took Emily's hand.

"Bed?"

"Oh yeah, that." Emily felt a little breathless.

She felt her hands shaking as she climbed under the sheets and slid over beside Jenna. Arms reached out, bodies pressed sweetly together. Emily rested her head briefly on Jenna's chest, enjoying the body heat and the sound of her heartbeat. She barely noticed as Jenna's arms went slack. Emily rose up, intending to claim Jenna's lips in another earth-shattering kiss. The brown eyes had closed, Jenna's face relaxed.

"Jenna?"

A reverberating snore was the only reply.

EMILY WINCED AND flopped onto her back. Her eyes moved rapidly under the lids as she experienced again Adrasta's brutal murder of the sex slave named Nicole. In the dream, she cried out, straining at the limits of her chains to rescue the young woman. Her efforts proved in vain. She saw brilliant white, sharp teeth sink into vulnerable flesh. Emily heard the soft exhalation of Nicole's breath, watched as her hands pushed ineffectively at Adrasta's powerful shoulders. Blood ran in twin streams from the puncture wounds, becoming a flood that filled the entire room. Emily was drowning in it, up to her chin in stinking gore.

"No," she moaned, head thrashing. Sweat ran down her temples and she kicked the confining covers away.

She knew she was dreaming, but couldn't force herself awake. Emily did not want to see this again, to watch the life drain from an innocent while she stood by helpless. As the life faded from Nicole's eyes, Emily shouted once more for Adrasta to stop.

"No!"

Suddenly, hands were upon her shoulders. They held her down, pinning her against the mattress. Emily fought back, sure she was about to become the vampire princess's next victim. She wouldn't go willingly to her doom, not like Nicole. The heel of her hand connected with a jawbone and she heard someone grunt. The voice was familiar.

"Emily, stop it. Wake up. You're having a nightmare."

Jenna's voice cut through the fog and Emily sat abruptly, her eyes snapping open. She panted for breath as Jenna pulled her face against her chest. Emily clasped her arms about Jenna's waist, reassuring herself that the dream was truly over. Her eyes darted around the darkened room, ensuring they were alone and back home on Earth.

"I'm all right," she mumbled. "I'm okay, I just need some water."

Shivering despite the relative heat in the room, Emily slipped on the robe she found lying over the back of a chair. The sweat on her body cooled and dried as she padded into the kitchen to draw a glass of water. She had felt so useless during that episode with Nicole, something that didn't sit well with a person who'd devoted her life to helping others. She knew she'd always carry a bit of guilt with her as a result. It was probably why that scene had come back to haunt her now. Emily had made it safely back to Earth, but how many innocents had she left behind?

The only way to make up for such a travesty was to take action. Sipping quietly, a plan began to formulate. Jenna wouldn't like it, of that she was sure. However, it was the only way for Emily to find any peace. She'd have to work through the details, but already she felt the slight sense of panic begin to recede. Emily poured out the rest of the water and placed the glass on the sideboard before she headed into the bedroom. She tossed the robe back onto the chair and stood beside the bed, looking down at Jenna. The light of a full moon streamed in through the window, showing her that Jenna's eyes were open and watching her. Heat flooded her veins, replacing the chill from such a short time ago. Emily's nipples hardened, her breath hitched.

Jenna flung the covers back, inviting Emily to join her. "What are you waiting for?"

"You," Emily breathed, placing one knee on the mattress. "I've always been waiting for you."

In the past, Emily had gone from woman to woman without regret. She'd experienced passion and the emptiness of lust. Now she knew she'd simply been biding her time until Jenna. The true depth of the love, longing and desire she felt for this woman burst in her soul, catching her unaware with the intensity. All she wanted was to show Jenna how she felt, not with words but with her actions.

Emily moved across the small space, placing her arms on either side of Jenna's head. Slowly, savoring the moment, she lowered herself until their skin barely touched. Jenna's lips parted, but Emily didn't kiss her. Instead, she took an ear lobe into her mouth. Sucking lightly, Emily slid her palm from Jenna's shoulder until she softly cupped a breast in her hand.

Fire beat a steady pulse in Emily's groin and she pressed down on Jenna's thigh to relieve the pressure. She moaned at the sweetness of Jenna's flesh against her own. Taking her time, Emily moved slowly down Jenna's body. She tasted Jenna's breasts, but didn't stop there. Hard abs quivered under her tongue, but still she slid lower until she could slip her arms under Jenna's thighs. Emily embraced Jenna's hips, clasping her stomach softly. The caresses were warm, tender, almost fleeting but felt intensely in Emily's heart.

Jenna surged against her, quivering, hands clutching at Emily's shoulders. Emily drew her tongue through the fine, crisp curls, drawing out the moment until Jenna cried out from desire and impatience. Finally, she reached Jenna's slick heat, tasting her passion for the first time. Jenna was like nectar on her tongue, making Emily stiffen as she fought not to give in to her orgasm yet. She wanted to please Jenna first.

Swiping her tongue once around Jenna's hardened desire, Emily parted the folds and slipped inside. Jenna responded to the gentle invasion by gripping Emily's head. Her shoulders lifted off the mattress and she cried out before dropping back. The scent of Jenna's pleasure was in her head, her mouth...all around her. Emily wrapped her lips around Jenna, sucking gently while simultaneously swirling her tongue over the hardened nerves.

Jenna's orgasm washed over her with such force that Emily felt her shoulders lift once again. Her body tensed as she moaned her release. Emily held on, losing herself in the passion as starbursts went off behind her closed eyes. She groaned her own pleasure into Jenna's intimate flesh, trying not to lose contact but helpless in the moment.

When Jenna finally nudged her away from overly sensitive skin, Emily turned her head to the side and rested against Jenna's leg. It took time to get her breathing under control. After her heartbeat returned to normal, Emily wiped the moisture from her face with the sheet. Then she climbed somewhat lethargically back up to Jenna's side, lovingly embraced with her head pillowed against Jenna's chest. Emily's eyes felt heavy, her limbs fully relaxed as she drifted rapidly toward sleep. Jenna's voice pulled her back to the present.

"So what now?" Jenna sounded unsure, almost afraid. "The case is over. Will you be leaving?"

"I've been thinking about that and I don't think I can go back."

"What do you mean?"

"To the FBI," Emily clarified. "I keep thinking about all the people that go missing in the world every day. Then I remember what Fallon said about how many portals there are on Earth. I can't help but wonder how many of those that suddenly disappear have been taken to Eris for sport, the mines or worse yet, for food."

Jenna went still, her body tense. After a few seconds, she relaxed and her fingers threaded through Emily's hair once more. "Honey, you do know it would be almost impossible to find those other gates? The compass won't locate anything from a distance."

"I know, plus I'd have to leave the Bureau, but there is a starting point. With my connections, it would be easy enough to compile lists of missing persons and look for similarities. Just like Woeful Pines, patterns would stand out."

"How would you live?"

Trust Jenna to focus on the practical. That was exactly why Emily needed her onboard for this, not to mention the fact that she didn't want to be without her. "My parents passed away a few years ago. I inherited the estate but I've never touched it."

"You're rich?"

"Not Stephen King rich, but I do okay. It'll be enough to keep us comfortable."

"Us?" Jenna did not sound surprised, merely amused.

"You don't think I'm doing this alone, do you? That is, if you're willing to stop being sheriff."

Jenna suddenly rolled Emily onto her back, pressing down on her from above. Breasts mashed together as Jenna slipped a thigh between her legs. Emily felt her own moisture paint Jenna's flesh. Lips hovered so close Emily could feel Jenna's breath when she spoke.

"Emily and Jenna the vampire slayers?"

Emily smiled. "Exactly. What do you say, partner?"

"I'm not about to let you out of my sight again. Just try going without me."

"Not a chance."

Coming together again, Emily lost herself in the warm loving embrace. Next time, they would be fully prepared for what they encountered, but that was a concern for another day. For now, Emily reveled in their union. She lost track of everything but the taste, smell and feel of Jenna's passion, and for the first time since her parents' tragic loss, she felt whole.

More S.Y. Thompson titles

Under the Midnight Cloak

Lee Grayson is a nature photographer whose father is a senator in New York. She's never felt close to him and her faith in people as a whole is lacking. She moves to the town of Harmon deep in the Adirondack Mountains after inheriting her great aunt's estate, but the local townspeople seem a little...off. Then she meets Ranger Jamison Kessler and learns there's a killer running rampant around the area. Jamison seems to be hiding things from her and Lee is starting to become suspicious.

Lee discovers that her aunt was a central part of this community and that she possesses the woman's unique abilities. She and Jamison are falling for each other, but things take a turn for the worse when the murderer sets his sights on Lee and a cure for his condition which he believes her to be harboring. Their situation is further complicated by the fact that the killer isn't even human. Neither is Jamison

ISBN: 978-1-61929-094-5
eISBN: 978-1-61929-095-2

Under Devil's Snare

Jamison Kessler and Lee Grayson are back in book two of the "Under" Series. Set one year after *Under the Midnight Cloak*, their adversary is very human. Someone has a fixation on Lee that manifests itself in a series of grisly murders, rapidly approaching serial status, and child abductions. These crimes are merely warnings, but what happens if Lee fails to interpret their meaning?

Jamison, Lee and the Panthera rush to save the lives of the innocent while they struggle to identify the instrument of so much suffering. Strains in relationships cloud their ability to see the whole picture. At the same time, U. S. Park Police Detective Patricia Hex shows up to help out but may soon become a threat to the Panthera community. Jamison's concentration splits between Lee, a mysterious killer and trying to keep Hex out of the Council's crosshairs. Her lack of focus may be all the stalker needs to get to Lee.

ISBN: 978-1-61929-204-8
eISBN: 978-1-61929-203-1

Destination Alara

In the 24th Century technology has evolved but greed and war are constant. A rookie starship captain but a veteran of the recent Gothoan War, Vanessa Swann searches the outer rim of the galaxy for any sign of rebel activity. Her favorite pastimes are kicking enemy butt and making time with the ladies. The last thing Van wants is to team up with the Andromeda System's heir apparent and leader of the Coalition flagship, Princess/Admiral Cade Meryan.

Coal black hair, piercing grey eyes and skin the color of fresh cream threaten Vanessa's professional boundaries, but focus she must when faced with repeated attempts on Cade's life. The fate of millions and the threat of galactic war rest on Van's shoulders. Whatever the outcome, their lives will never be the same.

ISBN: 978-1-61929-166-9
eISBN: 978-1-61929-167-6

Fractured Futures

Detective Ronan Lee has just solved the crime of the century, or has she? The case of the copycat killer plunges her into an ancient mystery, but solving the murders raises questions about the world government's true objectives. An unexpected invention gives her the chance to travel to the past. Her target is the 21st century and her mission is to save the woman at the heart of issue. This same woman, Sidney Weaver, is a warm, personable and accomplished actress that Ronan would give her life to protect.

Unaware of what fate has in store, Sidney's life is boringly predictable until a mysterious stranger comes out of the darkness of night to protect her. She knows there's something unusual about Ronan, but despite her misgivings, she can't deny the mutual attraction. All of this takes a backseat when she's plunged into a harrowing game of cat and mouse that could destroy everything she holds dear.

ISBN: 978-1-61929-122-5
eISBN: 978-1-61929-123-2

Now You See Me

Corporate attorney Erin Donovan has nothing on her mind except representing her clients to the best of her abilities. One fateful day, she shows an irritating new client, Carson Tierney, around the tenth floor space of her own building and her life takes an unforeseen direction.

Carson is an awe-inspiring woman by anyone's standards. Possessing genius-level intelligence that has allowed her to become a self-made millionaire of a computer software company, Carson still has a dark secret that could be her undoing.

When the two are thrust together to escape a deadly killer in a high-rise office building while a blizzard rages outside, they have no one to count on but each other. So begins an unexpected yet tender romance. However, unchecked love and desire isn't in their future. The murderer is still out there and he's coming for them. Will Carson's street-wise skills protect them both as Erin attempts to discover the killer's identity just as relentlessly as he is seeking their demise?

ISBN: 978-1-61929-112-6
eISBN: 978-1-61929-113-3

Other Mystic Books you may enjoy:

Ban Talah

by A.L. Duncan

From the crumbling pages of ancient Celtic scrolls comes a vivid world of mysticism and unflinching valor. Ban Talah is the daughter of Tlachtga, Goddess of the Thunderbolt. Unbound by mortal laws Ban Talah must find strength in her own moral constitutions in all their depths and complexities and not distance herself from the deep undercurrent of her immortality in order to fulfill her Geasa, her duty, as a strength and legend to her people. It is the time of King Henry II, ruler of England, where Celtic-Christianity struggled with Rome's papacy and the legitimacy of paganism within the Church. It is a time that begins the reaping of a terrible sowing.

The insidious heart of a French Cardinal, a man of mysterious dealings, has set the elements of evil astir. In order to save Henry's England Ban Talah must first save the Lady of the Land from the bindings of the Cardinal's sorcerous, wintery enchantment, a spell that is also a wicked inheritance of ills against the healers of her people. This is a tale of how one woman led her people in loyalty to a King and the Church a respect in her people, driving all that she fought for into all that she also fought against. A woman whom all called: Ban Talah

ISBN: 978-1-61929-186-7
eISBN: 978-1-61929-185-0

Shadowstalkers
by Sky Croft

The mission of a shadowstalker is simple: stalk, hunt, and kill creatures of the night, while protecting the innocent, unsuspecting public who have no idea of the horrors that lurk in the darkness.

For the Valentine women, shadowstalking is a way of life. Supernatural threats lie in wait around every corner, and danger is a regular occurrence.

Though the mission is simple, Cassie Valentine finds her life is anything but. Not only is she in love with her best friend, but past mistakes haunt her dreams.

Along with her mother, Eve, and her younger sister, Vicki, Cassie must learn to negotiate the perilous terrain of day-to-day life, while also coming to terms with the past.

Will Cassie be brave enough to overcome her fears and give love a chance? Or will the Valentine family fall when a legendary foe resurfaces?

ISBN: 978-1-61929-116-4
eISBN: 978-1-61929-117-1

Twice Bitten
by R.G. Emanuelle

Fiona lost her mortality unwillingly to a woman she once loved. Now she wanders through the decades, a vampire in search of a soulmate. After 200 years, she thinks she's found her, in an upper-class family in New York City at the turn of the 20th century. Her name is Rose, and if only she will come to her willingly, Fiona will have her eternal companion. But Rose loves another, so Fiona sets in motion a twisted scheme that involves the woman Rose loves and a betrayal that will lead Rose into transformation. Will Rose succumb to Fiona's machinations and forever lose the woman she truly loves? Or will she find a way to foil the vampire's devious plan and save her soul—and her beloved's life? She's running out of options and, worse, out of time.

ISBN: 978-1-61929-088-4
eISBN: 978-1-61929-089-1

OTHER REGAL CREST PUBLICATIONS

Sharon G. Clark	Into the Mist	978-1-935053-34-7
Sky Croft	Shadowstalkers	978-1-61929-116-4
A.L. Duncan	Ban Talah	978-1-61929-186-7
R.G. Emanuelle	Twice Bitten	978-1-61929-088-4
Melissa Good	Partners Book One	978-1-61929-118-8
Melissa Good	Partners Book Two	978-1-61929-190-4
Kate McLachlan	Return of An Impetuous Pilot	978-1-61929-152-2
Kate McLachlan	Rescue At Inspiration Point	978-1-61929-005-1
Kate McLachlan	Rip Van Dyke	978-1-935053-29-3
Paula Offutt	To Sleep	978-1-61929-128-7
S.Y. Thompson	Destination Alara	978-1-61929-166-9
S.Y. Thompson	Fractured Futures	978-1-61929-122-5
S.Y. Thompson	Under the Midnight Cloak	978-1-61929-094-5
S.Y. Thompson	Under Devil's Snare	978-1-61929-203-1
S.Y. Thompson	Woeful Pines	978-1-61929-220-8

About the Author

S. Y. Thompson resides in North Texas with her menagerie of animals. She fills her days with writing and playing with her Yorkie and six cats.

VISIT US ONLINE AT

www.regalcrest.biz

At the Regal Crest Website You'll Find

- The latest news about forthcoming titles and new releases
- Our complete backlist of romance, mystery, thriller and adventure titles
- Information about your favorite authors
- Current bestsellers
- Media tearsheets to print and take with you when you shop
- Which books are also available as eBooks.

Regal Crest print titles are available from all progressive booksellers including numerous sources online. Our distributors are Bella Distribution and Ingram.

CPSIA information can be obtained
at www.ICGtesting.com
Printed in the USA
FFOW03n0247190115
10317FF

9 781619 292208